I0680483

The Dream Master
And Other Stories

Featuring:
'Seven Unforgettable
Tales from My Childhood'

**By
Dave Willert**

**Illustrated by
Doug Kuhl**

The three novellas in this book are works of fiction. Any resemblance to actual events or persons, living or dead, is entirely coincidental. The "Seven Unforgettable Tales from My Childhood" are based on actual events.

"The Dream Master and Other Stories," by Dave Willert. Illustrated by Doug Kuhl. ISBN 978-1-63868-203-5 (softcover).

Published 2025 by Virtualbookworm.com Publishing, P.O. Box 9949, College Station, TX 77842, US. Copyright 2025 Dave Willert. All rights reserved. No part of this publication may be reproduced, stored in a retrieval system, or transmitted in any form or by any means, electronic, mechanical, recording or otherwise, without the prior written permission of Dave Willert.

Acknowledgements

I would like to begin by thanking my good friend, Tim Rattray, for contributing his childhood memories for the non-fiction story, '*The Incredible Tale of Tim, Big David and Devil Ringo.*' I would also like to thank my incredible sister, Cathi Foley, for the insightful memories she shared for the non-fiction stories, '*Mary Poppins and the Record Store,*' and '*My Trombone and Me.*' In addition, let me thank the talented Hayley Mills and Walt Disney for making my childhood so very exciting. Finally, I'd like to thank the wonderful Margaret, Alex, Katie and Doug for their never-ending encouragement and unshakable support for my writing efforts.

Dedication

The Dream Master and Other Stories is dedicated to everyone who, like me, loves to read and write, while *always* using their imaginations and creativity to the *fullest* degree! As writer Mayo Angelo says, "*You can't use up creativity. The more you use, the more you have.*" Some say that creative readers and writers are pretty much a dying breed because people don't read much anymore. But I disagree. I believe that a good story, if it's well told, will *always* attract readers. That's why I also believe that creative readers and writers are a resilient, healthy, happy, and ever-growing silent minority of all ages, races and genders; continuing to read, write and imagine new stories every day, as creative readers and writers have always had the habit of doing throughout the ages. ***Here's to us***!

Introduction

"A labor of love always gets its payoff *first!*" This statement perfectly describes the exhilaration I have always felt writing and publishing books over these past fifteen years. *Long* before one of my books appears for sale on Amazon, I always feel a great sense of accomplishment the moment I finish writing it! And regardless of sales, I always write my books with all of the care and excitement I can muster. First and foremost, I strive to create a book that I can be proud of, because I would hate to ever present anything to my readers that represents *less* than what I am capable of. And there is definitely *no* possibility of that disappointing scenario happening here. *This* book, I'm proud to say, epitomizes one of my *best efforts* yet!

'*The Dream Master and Other Stories*,' is my ninth published book. Before you ask, "*Yes!*" I thoroughly enjoyed writing it over these past two years! The three new fantasy/science fiction novellas (*making-up the first three quarters of this book*), in my opinion, are some of my *best*, both intriguing and fun to read, as are all seven autobiographical short stories that follow! This book is definitely suitable for preteen through adult readers.

People have asked me why I love writing fantasy and science-fiction stories so much more than other genres? The answer is really quite simple. I would not hesitate to write in *any style* that I was drawn to, but the truth of the matter is, fantasy and science fiction meet my imaginative and creative writing style *perfectly*, allowing me to have *unlimited possibilities* in every aspect of both the plot and the characters, unrestricted by '*reality*' and '*impossibility!*' This enables me to write stories that are unique, exciting to read and lots of fun to write! A *win* for everyone!

The first story in this book is the very exciting, 'The Three Challenges of Simon Dent.' To begin, one day a young and very reclusive man named Simon, is warned by a spirit (*that only he can see*) that his very *existence* is in grave danger unless he agrees to do something very *drastic*, which it soon unveils to him. But the problem is that even if he accepts, there are *no* guarantees? He'll still have to conquer *all three challenges* in order to save himself! Although apprehensive, he agrees to face them in an effort to hopefully convince *Life not* to completely erase him from existence, past, present and future! The big question remains. *Will he succeed?*

The second story, 'My Alien Summer,' is a fast and furious fantasy-adventure that begins when an alien from outer-space named *Areyoufeelingluckypunk* arrives in Montana one summer day in 1981. The alien inexplicably 'beams' a young college student named Kip, aboard his spaceship, where he immediately attempts to recruit him to find his lost daughter named *Shakenbutnotstirred?* Too simple of a premise? You're right! There's *more!* With the help of his brainy and beautiful next-door neighbor, Hannah, Kip and Hannah soon discover that what they're involved in is a hell of a lot more frightening than anything they could have ever imagined.

The third story (*cleverly doubling as the title of this book*) is 'The Dream Master.' This is an exciting romantic-fantasy about Willy, a classic underachiever, whose happiest activity is *dreaming* at night. In contrast, while living his real life by day, due to a debilitating fear of failure, he never seems to work quite hard enough to truly excel at anything? Enter, Charley, 'The Dream Master,' who inexplicably tells him from his television screen, "*You will never in your waking life see your dreams come true, unless you go after them with all your heart and completely defeat your fears!*" Willy immediately takes The Dream Master's advice to heart. His dreams are now vividly coming to life on a beautiful tropical island while he sleeps at night, but maddeningly *not* in his real life? Especially his 'love-life' with the girl of his dreams, *Melody?*

And now, what better way to end this book than by presenting this never-before-shared collection of short, autobiographical stories (*with some embellishments added to a couple of them as noted*) taken directly from some of my best remembered childhood memories of the 1960s (*predominantly while I was attending Williams Elementary School in Glendora*) that still have an impact on me today! This eclectic assortment of short stories includes an exciting tale of playing *imagination games* when I was young with my best friend Tim; breathtakingly watching the premiere of Walt Disney's *Mary Poppins* at a local movie theater in 1964; how my brother, a friend and I (*all preteens*) influenced by the popular TV musical group *The Monkees*, created a *pop singing group* of our own completely from scratch; how I saw a ghost late at night as a young child and was *terrified*; the 'oddly humorous' tale of my experience unhappily playing the trombone in the elementary and junior high school bands for five increasingly awful years; looking for her and after a decade, finally finding *my first love*; and discovering that I was the only one in class who had *not been invited* to a Halloween party being hosted by two of my classmates in the fourth grade. I've titled this autobiographic collection, '*Seven Unforgettable Tales from My Childhood.*'

The memories I have from these autobiographical childhood stories highlight a much sweeter and simpler time than today, with no cell phones, laptop computers, electric bicycles, Wi-Fi or hundreds of diverse video games, movies or shows that can be streamed onto our phones, computers or TV screens to dominate our time. Back then, especially after school, on weekends and during vacations, like many kids in Glendora, I was left to my own imagination to fill my free time, and I found that to be incredibly *empowering*! These tales also showcase some great examples of *my* childhood angst, fun, and immature reasoning. With any luck, reading these stories might jumpstart some of *your own memories*? You know, by taking *you* back to some of *your* most unforgettable childhood adventures, which may or may not be that different from my own? That would allow you to have the joy of reliving them, just as I am reliving mine through reading *these* stories at the end of this book. *Food for thought?* I sure hope so!

Table of Contents

The Three Challenges of Simon Dent

The Three Challenges of Simon Dent
The Efficient Man

It was early morning on an unusually nice February day in 2010. The sky was clear, the birds were singing in the trees and the temperature outside felt absolutely perfect! Yet inexplicably, it simply felt like any other day to Simon Dent? Simon often saw things quite differently from other people. And there were even times when he really *didn't* see things at all? Behind his back, he was called a *recluse*, a *narcissist* and a *freak* by some of those people he had come in contact with over the past couple of years. But even if he had been aware of this, I'm quite certain *that fact* would not have bothered him one bit! That was because for reasons unknown to us at this time, he had convinced himself fairly early in life that he intensely loved the thought of living alone, and nothing pleased him more than the thought of *never having to deal with people again*! Besides living like a hermit, Simon was a young man who followed a very strict routine every day of his life. This regiment consisted of constant order, repetitiveness and efficiency. He lived in a moderate-sized single bedroom apartment on a secluded street of a small town in Idaho called Grangeville. Simon was 25 years old, tall and lean in stature, and in the name of efficiency, he *always* wore his thick blonde hair in a simple crewcut, which he proudly cut himself. He wasn't bad looking, but the way he dressed made it obvious to anyone meeting him that he made absolutely *no* effort to impress! In fact, it appeared to be quite the *opposite*? To illustrate my point, every morning he insisted on wearing one of the seven pairs of wrinkled and baggy tan shorts he kept in a large drawer in his dresser, pairing them with a tattered black tee-shirt from a large

1

collection of them he stuffed inside the drawer beside it. Somehow he just *couldn't* bring himself to part with any of those garments, regardless of the fact that he had worn every one of them over and over again for the past two years now, making all of them appear (*to anyone looking*) to be completely stretched-out and ratty!

To give you a little background on Simon, after graduating from prestigious Harvard University in Boston, for some unknown reason he decided to return to the state of Idaho, where he had spent a great deal of his childhood. Once there, he soon discovered that he had an inexplicable affinity for the little town of *Grangeville?* But to live there he knew he'd need money? As luck would have it, being quite smart and graduating from a top university like Harvard enabled him to get an extremely lucrative job right away. You must forgive me here, but I *can't* fully explain the particulars of his job, except to say that it was related to the creation and reading of highly complex computer codes? Fortunately, *this* was an area where Simon's genius really shined, and it was also an area which always seemed to have *positions available*, even in Grangeville! So, he quickly found a perfect single-story, one bedroom apartment there, that was also *furnished!* He knew that it would serve him well, so he signed a lease and immediately moved in. An unusual perk this job provided him was that he *never* had to leave his apartment? Before accepting this job, you see, he had vehemently *insisted* on working from home with no further discussion. You can be sure that if he'd graduated from some small *uncelebrated school*, most employers would have simply laughed at him and revoked their job offers to him on the spot! But, that was certainly *not* the case here. Not wishing to risk losing such a brilliant 'Harvard' mind as his, his employers were soon forced to accept his request. Unsurprisingly, since Simon never left his apartment, he had *no* close friends. In fact, he had *no* friends at all? And he really couldn't remember a time when he *had?* Over the years he had rationalized his lonely existence as being perfect for him because he decided that talking and spending time together with 'friends' was really a great big waste of time! He was completely convinced that socializing of any kind would surely take him away from working on his important projects, which to him, was *truly* what his life was all about!

He made a point of walking *sixteen thousand* steps every morning inside his little apartment to help keep him healthy and in-shape. He selected that number because sixteen had the square root of 4, and 4 had the square root of 2, meaning that *both* the number 16 and *its* square root had *square roots*! He found that simple mathematical fact to be extremely interesting. He unquestionably believed that his apartment was the perfect place to do just about anything. And of course, everything he needed in life that *wasn't* in his apartment already, was soon ordered and delivered there.

He was in the middle of his usual morning routine as he walked past his clothes dryer, when he noticed with glee that the time remaining on the timer was only 22 minutes! He grinned. What luck! He had only put his sheets into the dryer five minutes before and already they were almost dry? Imagine that? Simon's walking pattern in his small apartment each morning involved repeatedly traveling from the front door, down the short hallway to the laundry room at the end, reversing direction and coming up the hallway past his bedroom/bathroom on the right, and then back toward the front door, which had the kitchen/dining area to its left and the front room (*as he called it*) to the right. Just a note, his *front room* was not actually a 'sitting room' where visitors traditionally gathered to make polite conversation as the room title might suggest. In *this* case, because he *had no visitors*, it was nothing more than a sad sliver of extra space without furniture that he *logically* named 'the front room' merely because of its proximity to the front door.

Simon had been walking for some time now since last checking the progress of his dryer. For that reason, when he reached it, he excitedly checked the time left, fully expecting his sheets to be close to finished. Oddly, the dryer was still stubbornly showing *22 minutes?* He was both surprised and disappointed, but rationalized that he must have misread the number the first time he'd checked it? So, he resumed walking up and down his little hallway, eagerly expecting to read a much smaller number the next time he looked. But, when he checked a few minutes later, the dryer was *still* posting

22 minutes? This fact suddenly struck him as being highly unusual? That's when he began to uncharacteristically sweat as his brilliant mind could not immediately come up with a rational reason for this dilemma? So, on a whim, he rushed to the kitchen to see what time the clock showed there, and although it was seven in the morning, the digital clock was blinking 2:22? He checked every other clock in his apartment as well, and inexplicably *they too* were all stuck at 2:22?

Overwhelmed, he forced himself to open his apartment door and go outside to see if everything out there was as it should be, or if perhaps the power in the entire building had gone haywire? He quickly reasoned that if this were the case, he would likely find everyone madly rushing about outside like a frenzied army of worker ants, frantically searching for their queen to tell them what to do next? He was actually *hoping* for this explanation because at least it made sense! But, when he tepidly stepped through the front door to his porch, he was shocked to find that absolutely *no one* was around? And even more disconcerting was the deafening silence that accompanied this very queer situation? There was not a bird singing in a tree, or a car driving on the street? Not even the sound of a neighbor's front door slowly creaking open or hurriedly being slammed shut in any number of adjacent apartments? Perplexed and beginning to grow even more anxious, Simon quickly shut his front door and completely panicked! He ran around the neighborhood looking for answers? Although he probably appeared to be crazed and out-of-his-mind, there was *no one* around to confirm that? He had no idea where to find the answers he sought, of course, but he somehow *knew* that they must be hiding somewhere outside his all too familiar apartment! After a short, but intense time of searching, he found himself drawn to the town's mortuary, where the undertaker worked. The reason being that its painted address numbers (*which were neatly stenciled on the curb in front of the building*) were impossibly *blinking 222*? He knocked on the front door of the establishment and when he received no response, he very *hesitantly* opened it and cautiously stepped inside.

If you have ever been to the workplace of an undertaker, you would have immediately noticed, as Simon did, that the place

4

completely *reeked of death?* I'm *not* saying that it strongly smelled of formaldehyde, a chemical often used in embalming fluid. In fact, it didn't actually smell like *anything* at all? When I say it 'reeked,' I am actually describing the overwhelming *feelings* of loss and finality that one often experiences immediately after a loved one has sadly passed away. Quickly realizing that the undertaker was nowhere to be seen, nor anyone else for that matter, Simon suddenly felt free to wander about. He soon came across an open casket located at the center of the room with a young man lying inside of it? The body's eyes were closed, he was dressed in tan shorts with a ragged black tee shirt, and he sported a very *confused* expression across his face? Because he showed healthy skin color (*which actually gave him the appearance of being alive*), Simon found himself bravely placing his hand in front of the man's mouth to check for breathing? And when he shockingly discovered that he actually *was* breathing, albeit faintly, for all of his remarkable intelligence, Simon was unable to rationalize *why* a living man would be sleeping in a coffin in an undertaker's place of work? Looking at the man very closely now, with a start, he shockingly *knew* who he was? In addition to being dressed like *him*, when looking at his face, it was just like *looking in the mirror?* And then as he horrifically watched, the face of the body began to quickly fade, until it had completely disappeared, leaving *no face at all?* Scared beyond belief, Simon glanced at the digital clock on the wall to see that it too was blinking *2:22!* Completely terrified now, he raced out of the building just as fast as he could! He didn't intend to stop until he finally reached the safe confines of his own apartment, which he *never* intended to leave again! But when he arrived at what should have been his apartment building, inexplicably, the entire structure had disappeared and in its place was a weed-infested field? Immediately, he rationalized that he must be asleep and in the middle of a nightmare, because only in that situation could such a crazy conundrum as this one even be possible? But what if this *wasn't* a dream? Just then he was further dumbfounded to see a large sign suddenly appear in front of the now large barren lot, stating, '*Grangeville Apartments to be started*

5

on February 22nd!' He quickly gasped, instantly realizing that February 22nd was numerically 222?

He was gratefully distracted from this horror upon hearing the sharp cries of a baby? He quickly turned and surprisingly saw an expensive-looking black baby carriage, completely unattended by anyone? Very curious, but overjoyed at the probable discovery of another human being in the desolation of his new reality, he rushed over to the carriage and peered inside. What he found was a now calm baby dressed in a white gown with a beautiful matching bonnet.

"*What's up?*" the baby unexpectedly asked him in a perky little voice, causing Simon to immediately back-off in surprise, and inadvertently respond, "Huh?"

"Haha!" The baby loudly laughed. "I see that you are a man of *few words!*"

"What?" Simon's brilliant mind could not immediately comprehend what was going on here, but his enormous ego forced him to retaliate. "Actually," he began defensively, "I memorized the entire dictionary once, so I am a man who knows *plenty* of words!"

"*Knowing* them is not the same as *using* them, *smarty pants!*" the baby laughed playfully.

"Why are you so rude and argumentative?" Simon demanded, at wit's end.

The baby smiled. "Because, Simon Dent, *you* have often been described as being rude and argumentative!"

"Hey? How do you know my name?" Simon asked, while now experiencing unadulterated confusion.

The baby laughed gleefully. "The answer to that question is surprisingly simple. It is because *I am you* as a baby!"

"What? But how can that be?" Simon cried out.

Passionately shaking his rattle now, the baby laughed and laughed. "Don't ask *me*, I'm just a baby!"

"You're absolutely right!" Simon replied angrily. "What do I think I'm doing trying to have a serious conversation with an *ignorant* baby?"

Looking shocked, as if he had just been horribly offended, the baby exclaimed, "Hey! There's no need to get personal here? Actually, babies are not as ignorant as you might think, and they are also the most *honest* people alive, thank you very much! So, believe me, I *do* understand everything that you're saying, and because I *am* you, you can certainly trust me!" he laughed. Then with a smirk, he added, "And also because I *am* you, you have got to agree that if you're as smart as you think you are, then it only follows that I am *just as smart as you are!*"

Simon was momentarily stunned by the baby's completely *sensible* logic? And he slowly replied, "Okay, what you said, *strangely* makes sense to me? But what exactly are you doing *here*?"

"I was sent to *help you*," the baby explained calmly, firmly meeting Simon's eyes as he spoke.

"But how can *you* help *me*?" Simon asked sarcastically.

"I'm not at all sure?" the baby confessed. "But believe it or not, my job has to do with helping you to save your *very existence!*"

"What are you talking about?" Simon's face suddenly grew pale.

"Now don't sweat it, big bro! I know this probably sounds terrifying... and I suppose it actually *is*," the baby winked at him before growing more serious, "but, you're *not* cooked yet! As I understand it, because you are living every day of your life without including others and without any real redeeming purpose outside of your job, *Life* has felt a need to intercede."

"Does that have anything to do with the fact that every digital clock I'm seeing is flashing the numbers *222*?" Simon asked.

"Exactly!" the unusual baby's expression grew somber. "I'm sure you *don't* know this, Simon, but you were born on *February 22nd*."

"What?" Simon gasped. "I was told that the exact date of my birth was *unknown*? Then what does the *flashing* of the numbers 222 mean?"

The baby grew even more serious as he replied, "It means that *Life* has begun evaluating the entire history of *your* life!"

Simon gasped in shock. "*Evaluating* my life? What for?"

"We'll see," the baby shared cryptically.

"When will *Life* be done with his evaluation?" Simon asked with some urgency.

"In just a few days. On your birthday, actually," the baby very sadly replied. "And if it turns out to be *bad* news? *Some* birthday present, huh?"

Simon's mouth dropped. "No! How can I stop this?" he begged. "There must be a way, right?"

"How should I know? I'm just a dumb baby, remember?" the baby said nonchalantly.

"But what will happen to me?" Simon cried out in fear and desperation, with more passion and humility than he had ever displayed to the baby or *anyone else* in his entire life for that matter!

The baby smiled shrewdly and shared, "Well, it's a longshot, but I do know of one and only one way for you to possibly control your own destiny."

The Plan

"The tricky thing is, you'll have to start thinking of your life as something very special that *used* to be yours, but now due to *unfortunate circumstances* brought on by yourself, you no longer own it," the baby began gently. "But fortunately, you will be allowed to temporarily *borrow* it for a few days to help *Life* determine if you deserve to win it back permanently."

"What do I have to *do* to win it back?" Simon asked anxiously.

With a mysterious air, the baby replied, "Well, to keep your life *indefinitely*, you must stop taking it for granted and *fight* for it harder than you've ever fought for anything during your entire lifetime!"

"What do you mean by '*fight for it?*'" Simon asked in confusion.

The baby smiled at him. "You must face whatever tasks *Life* throws at you with *everything* you've got! Because if you should *fail*, Simon Dent *disappears forever!*"

Simon shuddered.

"You got to take what I'm telling you *very seriously!*" the baby insisted.

Looking suspiciously at him, Simon asked, "Why are *you* so concerned about me winning my life back anyway?"

The baby shook his cute little head and rolled his eyes as he laughed over his underlying anxiety. "Isn't it obvious? As I told you before, *I am you*, so if your existence disappears... so does *mine*!"

A solemn Simon nodded, as he immediately understood. Then, he gently smiled for what seemed like the first time today and asked impishly, "So, I suppose I should call you my *inner child*?"

The baby smiled back a bit more relaxed. "Normally, but for the next few days just think of me as your very close friend, whom you are solely responsible for." And then for good measure the baby added humorously, "And of course, you will be responsible for my *means of transport* as well!"

Simon continued smiling at the witty baby in the carriage, when with a loud gasp, he suddenly watched his apartment building suddenly *reappear*, exactly as it had looked before, on the recently vacant lot in front of him?

"It begins *now*," the baby said knowingly. "Soon you will be presented with *three challenges* that *Life* will unveil to you."

"What if I *should* conquer them? What happens to me then?"

The baby grew thoughtful for a moment before speculating, "In that case, I would guess that you would be allowed to resume your life, while I would return to your memories... where I belong."

"You are certainly smart for being a baby," Simon admitted.

"Why, thank you!" the baby smiled broadly with self-satisfaction. "You realize, of course, that you are actually *complimenting yourself*, don't you!" he laughed.

Simon chuckled. Feeling more relaxed now, he asked, "Hey, do you mind if we go to my apartment for a while? I'm feeling a little hungry."

"No! *Don't* do that! You haven't got any food there for babies like me! You don't even have a *baby bottle*?" the baby insisted. "I think I'd much rather take our chances eating in town at a good café?"

"Does Grangeville *have* a good café?" Simon asked in surprise.

"I don't know?" the baby replied. "But we won't find out unless we look?"

Simon nodded, "Okay, fine. It sounds to me like *you're* hungry too?"

"The baby giggled. "No, I'm not! Spirits don't need physical sustenance! They don't even have stomachs!"

He chuckled. "You're a *spirit?* Can anyone else see or hear you besides me?"

"No," the baby confirmed. "I'm afraid the carriage and I are for *your eyes and ears only!*"

Simon smiled, and although he felt nervous about going anywhere outside the sweet confines of his own apartment, and also realized that he was going to look very odd pushing a carriage that no one else could see, he was determined to override his fears. He put his hands firmly on the handle of the baby carriage and began determinedly rolling it in the direction of downtown Grangeville to *possibly* find a café.

A few minutes later, when they arrived at Grangeville's downtown district, Simon was immediately taken aback as he noticed that it had grown by leaps and bounds since he had last set eyes on it only two years earlier? Although the city hall, library and a few other important buildings were still there, now a brand-new movie theatre, a number of new specialty shops and a *café* had sprung-up as well? The cafe was welcoming and bright to look at, and certainly from the outside anyway, it appeared like it *might* be a pretty good place to eat? Simon found himself smiling at the fact that his little town had grown so impressively? But he also experienced a slight pang of regret as he realized that this had all happened while he had *not* been paying attention? Suddenly, Simon's focus was drawn away from the buildings as he surprisingly watched the baby carriage he had been pushing *completely disappear?* Now, standing there before him was what appeared to be a *clone of himself* at about age ten? He was dressed as he himself had probably dressed at that age, in a pair of blue jeans and a white tee-shirt, sporting a very short crewcut.

"Don't look so surprised!" the young boy laughed. "I have the ability to age-shift *to any age* in your past I want to be, and right now something just told me to be *this* age?"

"*Who* or *what* do you suppose told you that?" Simon asked curiously.

"Heck, I don't know?" the boy replied honestly. "But I'm sure it was the same voice that told me to bring you *here* to the cafe? And anyway, who am I to argue? I have just grown almost *ten years older* in less than a minute!" he exclaimed humorously. "How cool is that?"

Simon laughed. "But *why* is someone or something giving you instructions, I wonder?" he asked the boy more seriously.

"I wonder about that myself," the boy shared thoughtfully. "And I don't know if this will help much, but I think that even though *we don't* know that answer yet, you can be sure that when the time is right, *we will!*"

He nodded in agreement with the boy's assessment, surprised and impressed by his ability to be so logical at age ten? "C'mon, let's go inside and find out how good the food is!" he said invitingly.

The two of them walked through the front door of the brightly lit café and were immediately greeted by a friendly waitress, who wasted little time in politely escorting them to a table where they both immediately sat down. Then, ignoring the boy, she smiled and gave Simon a breakfast menu before walking off.

"She really *can't* see you, can she," Simon whispered to the boy.

"Nope," he replied playfully. "Can't see me, can't hear me, completely ignores me."

"How does that make you feel?" Simon asked curiously.

"Spirits don't *feel* like humans do," the boy laughed. "But if I did, I guess I might feel *sorry* for her"

"Why?" Simon asked the boy in surprise.

"Because she is missing the *stupendous* opportunity of meeting *me!*" the boy smiled impishly.

Simon smiled back. He loved the boy's moxie and sense of humor. But if the boy truly was a younger version of him, he wondered *where* those wonderful traits had gone?

11

Soon the food arrived. After receiving and beginning to eat the very tasty ham and cheese omelet he had ordered, Simon whispered to the boy, "Thanks for suggesting that we eat here." Then with a smile he added, "The food is great!"

"You're welcome! But you *could* have found this place yourself and come to eat here anytime you liked over the past year or two," the boy replied thoughtfully. "Why didn't you?"

Simon took a moment and then whispered honestly, "Because I don't like going out alone."

"Aren't you alone *now?*" the boy asked slyly.

"Of course not," Simon exclaimed softly. "*You're* here with me."

"But I *am* you," the boy explained humorously, "and I'm *invisible* to everyone else."

"Yes, but since I can see you, even though nobody else can, I still somehow don't feel alone," Simon explained. "Does that make any sense?"

"Sure, it does," the boy replied understandingly. "But you'd better be careful," he warned him humorously. "Someone might accuse you of having *invisible friends!*"

"Excuse me?" A waitress whom they had *not* seen before, confidently walked up to their table. She was a young woman of average height and build with long and thick natural blonde hair, probably in her mid-twenties, dressed exactly like the first waitress, in a white dress with a pink apron. "Would either of you fine gentlemen care to order anything else? We have an exemplary cherry pie a' la mode?"

Simon was shocked and tongue-tied! She could inexplicably *see the boy?*

The boy somehow pulled himself together and replied, "Nothing for me, thanks. Simon?"

"Uh, no. I'm good," Simon replied softly.

"I'm so glad!" she smiled. Then grinning, she asked, "Aren't either of you gentlemen going to ask me *why* I am the only person in this café who can see *both* of you seated at this table?"

Although Simon immediately felt a sharp chill running up and down his back, he was also very curious to find out *where* this

12

conversation would ultimately lead? Both he and the boy nodded affirmatively.

"Great!" she responded excitedly. "Why don't you two meet me outside after you are done eating. We can find someplace where we'll be alone and then I'll *tell you!*" she promised.

"Is your shift just about over then?" Simon asked curiously.

She smiled. "What shift? I *don't* work here!" she laughed. Then walking away, she added, "Besides, no one can see or hear me except for the two of you!"

Once she had left the café, the boy said, "Well, *that* was sure strange?"

"What do you mean? Isn't she a spirit like you?" Simon whispered in surprise.

"I *imagine* so?" the boy remarked slowly. "But I really have *no idea* who she is or what she was doing here?"

"Who do you *think* she is then?" Simon asked.

After a slight pause, the boy replied hesitantly, "Don't know?"

"Well then, why do you suppose she's here?" Simon implored.

"*Still* don't know," the boy quickly admitted.

"What *do you* know then?" Simon asked quietly, but impatiently.

"Take it easy, big bro! The only thing I know for sure is that she showed herself to us for a *definite reason,*" the boy shared calmly. "Maybe her unexpectedly showing-up like this has something to do with your *three challenges?*"

Simon nodded, as he considered that. Whoever she was, what the boy had just speculated *definitely* made sense. As soon as he had finished eating his meal, the first waitress smilingly presented Simon with the check. Suddenly remembering that he had left his wallet at home, he frantically checked his shorts for any money he might have inadvertently stashed there and *surprisingly* found just enough in his pocket to cover the cost of the bill and the tip? Needless to say, he was relieved! As he and the boy walked outside to wait for the woman, horrifyingly an older man caught sight of Simon *conversing with the air* and gave him an incredulous look? As a result, he and the boy made a fast getaway!

"Hi, boys!" The mysterious blonde woman from the cafe suddenly appeared on the sidewalk with them. She had placed herself right between them, with her arms casually reaching across their backs as if they were all old friends. "Why don't we head over to the park and sit on a bench for a while? What do you say?"

They both nodded obediently. Before long, they arrived at a little community park, where they found themselves completely alone. Once they had sat down on a bench together, with the woman predictably insisting on sitting between them, she immediately began speaking.

"You're probably wondering *who* I am and *why* I made contact with you?" she began, speaking directly to Simon.

"As a matter of fact, I am?" he confirmed slowly. "Would you at least tell us your name?"

The woman laughed. "I suppose I don't really have a name... *anymore?* But, if you must call me something, I used to be called Doris?"

"Okay, *Doris,*" Simon replied hesitantly. "Now, *why* are you here?"

At this question, Doris smiled broadly and teased, "I'm surprised you haven't figured that one out for yourself, Simon, being that you're such a smart guy and all?"

"How do you know my *name?*" Simon asked in surprise.

Doris laughed. "Oh, I know *lots* of things," she replied cryptically. "Now, why do *you* think I'm here?"

He thought for a moment and replied hesitantly, "Does it have anything to do with my three challenges?"

"*It does!*" she beamed. "I knew you were smart! I am a courier sent to you from *Life* to give you your instructions for the first one."

Simon listened intently.

"And ultimately, after seeing how well you deal with that, I'm obliged to share my thoughts with *Life,* as to whether or not you deserve a chance to move on to the next one."

"Do you mean the *next challenge?*" Simon asked in shock.

"Yes," the woman nodded slowly. "The first challenge will be your *last* if you don't find a way to successfully accomplish it."

Simon looked sick and began to sweat.

"Don't worry, Simon. I have faith in you.," Doris smiled. "Let me explain what I am talking about by sharing a little story with you, okay? When I was a little girl, I remember my father once telling me about an important belief he'd arrived at as a dentist. He told me that when one of his patients would get a cavity in a tooth, if left untreated, it could lead to his actually having to *yank* that tooth right out of their head! To possibly *save* the tooth was sometimes very tricky and even risky, he told me. There was never a guarantee that he could save a damaged tooth, and sometimes even when trying his best, his efforts would still lead to failure! But regardless, he always chose *that* road just the same. You see, he explained, although immediately pulling the tooth out would have been much easier for him, it would have meant that he had *given-up* on the tooth, with every reminder of its existence *instantly erased*! My father ended his lesson by sharing with me that no matter how far gone it was, he always looked at and pondered very carefully every damaged tooth he examined from all angles, and attempted to find enough potential in it to warrant at least a *chance* for it to go on existing. In other words, making the tooth *deserving* of receiving further attempts to save it, but with *no* guarantees. Do you understand now?"

"My life, like a severely damaged tooth, is in danger of being *extracted from existence?*" Simon hesitantly asked.

"Exactly," Doris whispered. "As I said, each challenge I give you *requires you* to immediately achieve it in order to move on to the next one!" She paused a moment and then told him very seriously, "Life wants to give you every possible chance to save yourself, Simon, because sadly, once your life has been removed from you, just like the pulled tooth... there's no way of *ever* getting it back!"

Simon felt terrified!

"I didn't mean to scare you," Doris said empathetically. "But I *do* want you to clearly understand the severity of your situation!"

"I do! So, is *this* a spiritual *intervention* then? Like the one Ebenezer Scrooge had?" Simon managed to ask.

Doris smiled. "Yes. That's a very good comparison. Because just like *that* story, in *this* one, *Life* is convinced that there may be hope for you yet!"

"I am very grateful for that!" Simon shared humbly.

"I know you are," Doris replied with a soft smile.

"What is my first challenge then?" Simon asked impatiently.

"Don't worry about that now. I'll let you know when the time comes," she replied kindly.

"Is there anything else you need to share with me?" Simon asked urgently.

"No, I think I've said it all," she replied warmly. "But I've observed that you seem a bit self-conscious about speaking with *invisible spirits* in public," she smiled impishly. "So, to avoid any possibility of you getting caught *talking to yourself* in the future, I would like to temporarily transform the boy here into a separate *living being* from you. In that way you can feel comfortable talking with him any time you choose, and be assured that other people will see and hear him too. If you have no objections, I think we'll name him 'Scott.'"

"I have no objections," Simon quickly replied. "You know, *Scott's* my middle name?"

"Yes, I know," Doris smiled. Then turning to the boy, she added, "Is that fine with you, *Scott?*"

"Will I be able to eat and drink and do everything else that's *human?*" the boy asked excitedly.

"Of course!" Doris assured him. "And I'd like you to act as Simon's younger brother. Will you do that?"

"You bet I will!" Scott beamed.

"Good! Secondly," she said, turning to Simon. "For the next few days during these challenges, I am going to lock-up your apartment, even from *you*. Any objections to my doing that?"

Simon initially began to grow anxious as he considered having to *leave* his precious apartment for an extended period of time, but he quickly brushed those fearful feelings aside as he considered his dire situation. "None that I can think of," he lied. "Except that I'll need to get my wallet from my bedroom first."

Doris laughed, as she magically plucked his wallet from the air and gently handed it to a very *shocked* Simon.

"Hey? How did you do that?" Simon demanded in shock. "Did you break into my apartment?"

Again, Doris laughed. "There was no need for me to do that, Simon. A smart guy like you *must* have figured out by now that I *don't* play by the rules of the living. Think of me as a 'magician' and then this might all make a little more sense to you." Smiling, she added, "How do you think that money magically appeared in your shorts pocket to pay for your breakfast today, hmm?"

Both Simon and Scott looked at her in amazement!

"Oh! And you are *not* to contact anyone you know during these challenges! That would be a *very serious* offense!" Dora warned.

"But what about my job?" Simon exclaimed nervously. "They're expecting me to check-in every day? If I don't, they might fire me?"

Doris laughed. "Come now, Simon. Do you really think they would fire you over *that*? You are much too important to them."

Simon found himself confused once again.

"Don't worry," Doris added calmly. "I'm sure that everything in your life now will be just fine when, *or if*, you return to it." Immediately plucking two bus tickets out of the air and handing them to him, Doris continued, "You will meet your first challenge in Idaho Falls. It's 8:30 AM right now, and your bus leaves in only an hour. *Don't* miss it!"

"Idaho Falls is a long way away. Wouldn't it be quicker to fly?" Simon asked helpfully.

"Yes, but there are the crowds, the long lines and the plane change at the airports that would make you very anxious. You *don't* need that, Simon! A leisurely bus ride is so much more restful," she told him. And then without another word, she vanished?

After initially finding it awkward, but ultimately succeeding in accepting Doris's *impossible* departure, Simon thought of something else, and he instantly grew very anxious.

"I remember Idaho Falls too, Simon," Scott gently shared, sensitive to the way Simon felt. "Not the greatest of memories there."

"Nope," Simon replied automatically.

Breaking the tension, Scott blurted out, "Hey? I am so excited about my new body! I can't wait to try it out!"

Simon laughed. "Can you still age-shift?"

"No," Scott replied, disappointedly. "I guess I'm stuck at this age for a while."

Nodding, Simon said, "You know? It feels *good* having a little brother."

"I'll bet. Especially one who's got so much *in common* with you!" Scott laughed.

Simon smiled broadly, "Let's go to the bus station! I'm anxious to get things rolling!"

"Could we stop at a clothing store first?" Scott begged. "Now that other people can see me, I want to look my best!" Humorously he added, "And the clothes I'm wearing now, look *nothing* like my best!"

Simon chuckled. "Good point! Come to think of it, I'd better get a few things myself!"

The First Challenge

After picking up a few changes of clothes for each of them, as well as two suitcases and a variety of toiletries, Simon and Scott boarded a Greyhound bus for their extremely long ride to Idaho Falls. Because the bus had stopped twice for meals and once for getting a fresh bus driver, the long journey of 481 miles took them nearly *twelve* uneventful hours to complete. In essence, because of the two different drivers, it almost felt like *two* separate but monotonous six-hour bus rides in a row! Scott filled his time by reading and rereading an adolescent joke book he had picked up at the bus terminal. There really wasn't much for Simon to do, however, but think. To begin with, he thought about *why* he had hated his childhood in Idaho Falls so much? But that didn't take him long because he *already knew* the answer! When the bus finally arrived at their destination twelve hours later, about 9:30 at night, both of them were understandably fatigued.

"I didn't know how tired and stiff a real boy *like me* would feel after sitting *forever* on this stupid bus!" Scott quipped with irritation, as they stepped off and retrieved their suitcases from the baggage compartment outside. "Remind me to fly next time! I know it's a hassle standing in lines and changing planes, but I'm *sure* it couldn't be any worse than *this* was!" he complained.

Simon smiled to himself. He could see that Scott was *definitely* a ten-year-old boy now!

As it turned out, they didn't need to walk very far before reaching a quaint and clean little motel called '*Idaho's Best!*' The motel carried a spud theme throughout, with every room key being in the unusual shape of a tiny potato. After checking-in and dropping off their bags in their room, it was already nearly ten o'clock. Since they both felt very hungry, they left to have dinner at a quaint little all-night diner called '*Bite Me*' that sat adjacent to the motel. They had been told when they checked-in that *this* place was perfect for people who were on the go and wanted their food served to them right away! That sentiment was seconded on the wall outside the entrance, where the establishment proudly displayed a plaque with its written guarantee, which read, '*Your meal delivered to you within ten minutes or it's on us!*' After being seated at a table, Simon grew predictably skeptical as to whether ten minutes was truly enough time to prepare and serve a *good* meal? But, he had little time to think any further about it, as almost immediately a very tense-looking young waitress with long brown pig tails, curiously flashing *no* expression at all on her stoic face, hurriedly dropped two menus in front of them and impatiently waited to take their orders. After that had been accomplished, she rushed off to the kitchen.

"What's with *her?*" Scott chuckled. "No time for chitchat with the paying customers?"

"Oh, she's probably just stressed," Simon explained. "I read on a plaque outside that she's got to serve us our meals in ten minutes or they're *free?* And I'll bet the cost of those '*free meals*' is deducted directly out of her paycheck!"

"Oh! That's a *terrible* deal for her!" Scott exclaimed.

"Yes, I suppose," Simon agreed. "But it's a *very good one* for us!" he added playfully.

Scott smiled, and then excused himself to find the restroom. Alone now, Simon again began thinking about Idaho Falls and everything he could remember about it. He truly had a lot of history here, but he soon realized after barely beginning to recall specific details, that he'd feel much better *not* thinking about anything at all from that very difficult time in his life! Soon, Scott returned to the table.

"Did you miss me, Simon?" Scott laughed. Suddenly growing more serious, as if reading his mind, he asked, "Do you remember this city very well?"

Simon was a little surprised by the question, but replied, "I remember *enough*, but I only lived in the orphanage here through sixth grade. Then, for some reason, I was sent away to live at a boarding school in Boston, remember?" Getting more excited, he shared, "I know this city has always been a lot bigger than Grangeville, but even so, it still looks like it's very noticeably *grown* since the last time we saw it, don't you think?"

"Yes," Scott agreed thoughtfully.

"Do you ever miss living here, Scott?" Simon asked.

"In some ways I guess I do," he replied. "I miss the beauty of this place for sure."

And then suddenly Simon spontaneously asked, "What is it really like being my *past incarnate*?"

Scott thought for a long moment and then smiled, "Well, let me put it this way. I hope your past wasn't nearly as good as your *future* turns out to be!"

"Scott! Why do you have to go and bring-up my future?" Simon complained with obvious irritation.

"Oh, come on, big bro! Is there any *better* time to bring it up?" Scott shot back. "You're about to go on your first challenge that will help decide if you even *have a future*?"

Simon, jolted by his blatantly truthful words, quickly agreed, "Sorry, Scott. You're right." Then he smiled and added, "You know what? I hope my future is a *hundred* times better than my past was! How's that?"

"Alright!" Scott shouted encouragingly. "*That's* the spirit!"

About *nine and a half minutes later*, they were served their meatloaf dinners by the now understandably relieved and exuberant waitress, who had rushed through taking their orders earlier. Now, she was very chatty and even expressed her amazement at how much the two of them looked alike (*even after Scott had shared with her that they actually* **were** *brothers*).

As soon as she left, a very energized Scott shared mysteriously, "I've got to say that I'm very happy she beat the clock and got our meals to us in time! Aren't you, Simon?"

Simon smiled, "Yes, I'm happy for her," he begrudgingly agreed. "But it was kind of fun waiting to see if we'd win those free meals? We missed it by thirty measly seconds!"

Scott began laughing. "It's all a *ruse*, bro!"

"What is?" Simon asked in confusion.

"The *ten-minute* deadline!" Scott exclaimed. "I asked our waitress about it on my way to the restroom!" he shared. "The meals are all premade and only have to be *heated up* for a few minutes! They serve them as close to ten minutes as possible to get the tourists, *like us*, really excited!"

"That little jokester!" Simon laughed. "I had no idea?"

"*That's* the general idea!" Scott smiled. "Let's eat!"

Both of them immediately dug into their meals. Their conversation waned a bit as they found their minds now wrapped around the broad array of possibilities for that terribly important first challenge that was looming over Simon! After they'd finished eating, Simon left a *big tip* on the table for the server, thanking her both for her outstanding waitressing and of course, her *brilliant acting*! He found himself chuckling after he'd paid the bill. He then got up and returned with Scott to their room to prepare for bed.

"When do you suppose I'll find out what my first challenge is?" Simon asked impatiently, as he sat on the side of his spud-shaped bed in a pair of red and white striped pajamas. "It's very hard for me to prepare for something when I don't have a clue *what* it is?"

Scott nodded understandingly. "I'll bet!" Then after a short pause, he added, "But to be honest, Simon? I wouldn't worry about it. Doris already told you that she'd tell you when the time was right, and I'm *sure* she will."

He smiled. "You're right, Scott. Thanks!" And then he slowly crawled into bed. Simon was a little jealous of his *younger sibling*, because he always seemed to find a positive spin for every situation? Well, *except* for riding on that bus for twelve 'delightful' hours! he smiled. Then his thoughts quickly moved to tomorrow. Once again he asked himself what challenge *Life* was likely to present him with, and why it was so important for him to be in Idaho Falls for it? Because he couldn't immediately figure it out, he was beginning to think that being smart, even really, really smart like *he* was supposed to be, was overrated! That night, he had a dream. At least he *thought* it was a dream? In this dream, Doris was standing over his bed talking to him?

"Hello, Simon," she said sweetly. "Tomorrow you will begin preparing for your first challenge by walking around town with Scott and observing everything."

"Okay," he replied. "But what's my goal? I mean since this is not my actual challenge?"

"Goal?" she laughed. "Simon, your goal is *always* to win back your life no matter what you are doing." And with that, she disappeared.

Simon was more confused than ever, but fortunately he eventually fell back into a sound sleep.

The next morning, he awoke to find Scott already awake in the bed across the room from him, reading his joke book and chuckling softly. After getting dressed, they headed over to 'Bite Me' for a quick breakfast. They exchanged small talk as they waited to be served in less than ten minutes, which of course, they *were*! But just as soon as their food arrived, Simon excitedly shared his dream with Scott.

"*Wow!* And her instructions were simply to walk around town with me?" Scott reacted incredulously.

"Yep," Simon replied.

"But that's *not* the challenge?" Scott was again mystified.

"Nope," Simon confirmed.

"Well, to be honest, that sounds *pretty dull*. But, we've got to follow her instructions!" Scott gracefully accepted their marching orders. And then growing more excited, he added, "I know! How about if we check-out how much the town has changed since we were last here?"

"Okay," Simon gently nodded in agreement.

"And afterwards, unlike that, we can look for things to do in town that might actually be *fun!*" Scott joked.

Simon smiled.

Before long, they left the diner and began to walk down the city's main street, which coincidentally, was called *Main Street*. Idaho Falls was a beautiful place. Although, just as Simon had thought, it had matured a lot since he had last lived here. But luckily, parts of the downtown still retained that certain small-town charm he had so enjoyed while on outings here with the orphanage years before. Scott and he were so immersed in this lovely atmosphere of bygone days that they *almost* missed seeing what *may have been* the beginning of a robbery taking place at a nearby deli. Simon grew concerned after he watched two men suspiciously lingering outside the door to the deli, intently looking around outside before hurriedly entering it. At first, Simon was very hesitant to act? When he had been younger, he clearly remembered always trying to keep himself safely invisible when things like this happened and *never* getting personally involved! But ultimately he thought better of that *this* time and called 911 on his cell phone. Minutes later, a police car came to a screeching halt in front of the deli as the two would-be robbers had already panicked and run off the moment they'd heard the approaching siren! Simon and Scott never did find out if the place had *actually* been robbed, but from the officers' relaxed reactions, it appeared that a possible robbery had been stymied, and *no one* had been hurt.

"Well done!" Scott said, congratulating Simon.

He acknowledged him with an awkward nod.

Suddenly the sky began to grow dark as if something huge were blocking the sun? An *eclipse* perhaps? Although that seemed to be the most logical scenario, Simon didn't dare look up into the sun to find out! Minutes later, except for the lights in the local buildings, it was *completely* dark where he stood? It felt surreal as Simon recalled this very same event happening during his childhood in Idaho Falls when he had been ten-years-old, and how frightened he had felt? For the next few minutes, it remained dark, and after that, the light began to slowly return. A few minutes later, things appeared to be completely back to normal.

"Wasn't that the strangest thing?" Simon said to Scott, without looking at him. "Scott?" he repeated more urgently as he looked around and grew frightened as he saw *no sign* of him?

"Is there a problem, son?" a tall, thin, young soldier about his own age with short blondish-brown hair, wearing his army dress uniform asked him with concern. "I must say, you look absolutely panicked?"

Simon was shocked, but he immediately replied, "My ten-year-old brother Scott and I just got here yesterday for a little vacation and sometime during that eclipse we seem to have become separated?"

The soldier looked understandingly at Simon, as he shared, "Well, son, maybe it was the eclipse that scared him off? They can be awfully frightening when you're young."

He nodded. "Was that eclipse *expected?*" he asked the man curiously.

The man chuckled. "Why sure! People have been talking about it for weeks! Didn't *you* know about it?" he asked him in disbelief.

"No," Simon replied honestly. "I guess I somehow missed it?"

"Well, don't feel too bad," the soldier chuckled good-naturedly. "Plenty of other folks probably missed it too."

"Why would you say that?" Simon asked.

"I guess it's because there are *lots* of special things missed every day by folks who have simply *not* paid attention to them," the soldier replied. "I suppose sometimes it's probably *easier* for them that way."

Simon *didn't* have a clue why the soldier had shared this odd explanation with him, and he was very *curious* about his intent? But, being in a hurry, he merely nodded in response, and then asked, "Now, about my brother?"

"Oh yes. What does he look like?" the soldier asked.

Simon thought hard, but quickly realized that the answer was simple. "Like a younger version of *me*."

The soldier chuckled. "Alright then! I'll be happy to look for him right now! Could I get your phone number first though so I can call you if I find him?" he added gently.

"Sure," Simon replied. "If you like, I'll just tell you the number and you can add it to your phone contacts?"

The soldier smiled and replied, "I'm afraid I haven't got a cell phone. How about we do this the old-fashioned way?" Handing him a pen and paper he'd pulled from his inner coat pocket, Simon quickly jotted down his cell phone number before politely returning the two items to him.

"Thanks," Simon smiled. "I appreciate your help!"

"Glad to do it," the soldier returned his smile, before turning around and walking off toward the downtown stores.

Simon looked quizzical as the soldier left. There was just something very kind about him helping out like this? And then he realized that he'd been in such a hurry to find Scott that he hadn't even introduced himself or asked the stranger *his* name? He shook his head and chuckled softly to himself as he immediately began his own search. He started by perusing every public building in the downtown area over the next hour, which proved to be very challenging due to the many new structures that had sprung up over the past decade. He *did* receive a very thorough 'self-tour' of the downtown in the process, but he found absolutely *no sign* of Scott whatsoever? Finally, he located him! He was sitting alone in the movie theatre, oblivious to anything *not* on the screen, laughing hard at an old Three Stooges movie?

"Scott! You had me scared to death!" Simon whispered harshly. "Why did you take off like that?"

Scott turned to him with a look of embarrassment. "Sorry, Simon. But, I'm not even *ten* years-old yet!" he pleaded. "We tend to be a little *impulsive* at this age!"

They both laughed, but then Scott grew more serious.

"Doris came by to see me about fifteen minutes ago," he shared. "She said that you are to meet her at a house you'll find at the west end of Main Street just as soon as you leave this theater."

"Did she give you an address for me?" Simon asked logically.

Scott laughed. "No. But she told me you would *ask me that!* She also said to assure you that you will have no trouble finding it!"

"But how did she know that I would be coming *here* in the first place?" Simon asked, baffled.

"Aw c'mon, Simon! *She's Doris!*" Scott reminded him with a chuckle.

Simon briefly smiled, but then sternly insisted, "I don't feel right just leaving you here alone while I'm gone?"

Scott threw his arms up into the air like the irritated child that he was and proclaimed, "Are you kidding me? They're showing a Three Stooges Matinee Marathon that will last for hours! I'll be *fine*, big bro!"

"*The Three Stooges?*" Simon objected. "But they're so silly? I can't remember *ever* liking those guys?"

"Well, you *did!* Maybe you've just *forgotten?*" Scott suggested. "By the way, could I have a little money for refreshments? I spent everything I had getting in here!"

Simon smiled and gave him a ten-dollar bill.

Once outside the theatre, Simon and his great big brain could not figure out *why* Doris had turned her simple instruction of 'getting to their meeting place' into such a complicated ordeal? Honestly, *no specific* directions? Regardless of his minor irritation, he quickly left that question behind as he began briskly walking west down Main Street toward the edge of town. He passed a number of shops and other buildings as well as a park and an older-looking elementary school, and then all at once, just as Doris had said, he *knew* that he'd reached his destination! Without rhyme or reason, there was a single-story wooden house, looking like it had been built many years before, *sitting right in the middle of the street?* It was a good-sized structure that was painted completely white. From the outside, however, although it appeared to be well kept-up, there were absolutely *no signs* that anyone actually lived there? Regardless, he gently knocked on the door. When it quickly opened, he was met by a smiling Doris.

"Come in," she said sweetly. "You're right on time!" Simon was immediately directed to sit down on a lovely green velvet couch from another era in the living room, with Doris soon joining him. "Do you know where we are, Simon?"

Looking confused, he simply replied, "Not really?"

Doris nodded. "We are inside the house that I grew-up in, although in reality, the *actual* house was torn down a long time ago." Then smiling, she added, "But this house was *never* actually here in Idaho Falls. It was in Grangeville." Then she grew playfully serious, "I'm afraid it's location here in *the middle of the street* might cause a few problems for people driving in or out of town, don't you think?"

Simon chuckled. "*Theoretically* yes, but for some reason I'm pretty certain that is *not* true. Why did you put this house in the middle of a street anyway?"

"To make sure that you'd find it, of course!" Doris laughed. "And in answer to your next question, no one else can see it but you and me."

Simon nodded. "In that case, where *exactly* are we?"

Doris grew serious, "We are in another dimension, Simon. One that is connected directly with your past here in Idaho Falls," she replied calmly.

"Then I am guessing that *this* dimension has something to do with my first challenge?" Simon rationalized. "Am I right?"

"*Bingo!*" Doris energetically pointed a finger at him and smiled encouragingly. "I'm sending you back to a specific day when you attended elementary school." Then looking at him inquiringly, she asked, "Did you even realize that the school you passed on your way here was the *same one* you attended all those years ago?"

"No?" Simon replied in shock.

"You will return there as a fourth grader," Doris added.

"But why send me back *there* at all?" Simon asked anxiously. "I only have terrible memories of going to that school?"

Doris smiled encouragingly. "I know you do. I was hoping that perhaps this time things might go a little better for you?"

Simon didn't reply as he fought back the fear inside of him. Years of unhappiness suddenly filled his mind! He tried very hard not to obsess over it though, as he determinedly accepted his fate, and asked, "What is my first challenge then?"

"Your challenge today is simply to *make a friend*," she shared.

Simon grew pale and began sweating as he replied softly, "I... I've *never* been very good at that? Couldn't my first challenge be something else? *Please?*"

Doris smiled warmly in a very comforting sort of way and assured him, "Relax, Simon. Your biggest obstacle in accomplishing this is *you!*"

With that, Simon immediately found himself as a nearly ten-year-old boy at Grover Elementary School in Idaho Falls. He was wearing a pair of hand-me-down blue-jeans and a white tee shirt from the orphanage, exactly like the clothes Scott had been wearing once he'd transformed from a baby to a boy yesterday. Judging by how all of the other children around him were already firmly established in their fun activities across the playground, he knew that he was currently in the middle of morning recess. A rush of troubling memories suddenly hit him hard as he remembered this scene. It was not difficult to recall, because *this* basic situation had been the same for him *every day* at this school for as long as he'd attended it! It had always seemed as though every kid on the playground (*with the exception of him*) was laughing and having fun? He always stood by himself next to an old rusted and ball-less tetherball pole, watching the other kids playing a variety of games together, while he silently counted down the ten minutes until the short recess would mercifully come to an end. He remembered every painful moment of watching those other children smiling and laughing. Actually, Simon had loved the learning part of school that kept him so busy inside the classroom. He didn't *need* any of his classmates then. But aside from his teachers, he had rarely ever spoken to anyone else at the school? And the biggest reason he *loathed* recess so much was because *that* was when it became embarrassingly clear to everyone else that *he had no friends*!

Suddenly, a sharp yell quickly catapulted him out of his mire of self-pity. He instinctively turned to his left where he saw two older boys taunting a younger and much smaller boy, who looked absolutely terrified? Simon clearly remembered this exact event from a moment in his past, although he was ashamed to think about it. Back then, he had been much too afraid to say a word of protest to those bullies or to report it to his teacher. But today, somehow things felt very different to him? He was actually feeling empowered? In fact, he could not subdue the very pointed words that passionately sprang from his lips, as he yelled, "Hey, pick on someone your own size!"

That immediately brought a shocked expression from both of the two fourth-grade bullies, who quickly turned and stared at Simon in shock and disbelief? After a moment, one of the boys shouted in surprise, "You can *talk*, Dent?" Both boys laughed and immediately left the small cowering boy behind, mercifully allowing him to gratefully run away for dear life as they menacingly set their sights on *Simon*!

Simon *didn't* move. He was scared stiff, of course, but he wasn't going to take back his fearless words for anything! He knew that his goal here was to make a friend, but something about bullies in school had ignited a long dormant anger within him. Truth be told, regardless of whatever happened to him next, he already felt vindicated for standing up to them!

When the two bullies reached him, the one who had previously spoken, smiled cruelly while the other one savagely shoved him in the chest with both hands. Simon did not want to fight (*even if he had known how*), so he doubled-down on being defiant instead.

"Do you losers get your jollies out of picking on kids half your size?" Simon demanded. "What a couple of pathetic *cowards*! I'm not afraid of you!"

29

"You're *not?*" the second boy shouted in disbelief. "Well, if you know what's good for you, punk, you'd *better be!* Now, quick! Give us your money and you *might* not get hurt!" the boy snarled at him.

Simon was afraid, but he stood his ground. "No!"

"*No?*" The first boy sarcastically repeated.

"No! You're getting *nothing* from me!" Simon boldly proclaimed.

Both bullies took a long, confused look at each other before the first boy, after hastily looking around to make sure that no teacher was watching them, emphatically grabbed Simon by the collar with both hands and ferociously demanded, "Your money, *now!*"

Fortunately, it was then that the cavalry arrived! The small boy who Simon had initially seen being picked on, returned with two big sixth-grade boys to face the bullies. The aggressors took one look at them and ran off as fast as their cowardly feet could carry them!

"Are you okay?" one of the boys asked Simon with concern.

"I'm fine," Simon replied with a reassuring smile. Then turning to the smaller boy, he gently asked, "How are *you* doing?"

The boy returned his smile, but didn't say a word?

"His name is Jimmy and he's doing fine *now*," the same sixth-grade boy replied gently. "He *doesn't* speak, but I know he appreciates what you did for him today. I'm his brother Ted, and I do too!"

The bell rang, marking the end of recess. Everyone ran to line-up at their class's designated area before walking to their classrooms with their teachers. Simon knew that he had *not* made a friend today, but he was feeling ecstatic anyway about having played a central part in chasing away those bullies. He returned to his classroom and the rest of the day simply flew by. As soon as the bell had rung, announcing the end of the school-day, he picked up his homework and rushed-off toward the bus that would promptly return him home to the Idaho Falls Orphanage. And then out of nowhere, he was suddenly grabbed from behind and spun around? Surprisingly his eyes instantly met those of the two bullies he had faced earlier today? But they somehow seemed *different* to him now?

"Hey, *Simon*," one of the boys, now standing directly in front of him, greeted him with a *much too* friendly grin, while the second boy who now stood at Simon's right, placed an arm across his shoulders? "We're awfully sorry about our little problem today."

"I've gotta catch my bus," Simon insisted quickly, looking uncomfortably from one boy to the other.

"But surely you have time to hear our apology?" the second boy insisted.

"We just wanted to say, *sorry* for hitting you," the first boy added sweetly.

"You *never* hit me?" Simon quickly corrected them.

At that exact moment, the boy at his side punched Simon as hard as he could in his unsuspecting stomach, while the one in front aggressively slapped him across the face. "*Yes, we did!*" the two bullies laughed in unison as they proudly walked off from the ambush they had set and executed *perfectly*.

Simon's face and stomach immediately hurt something awful! He was initially coughing, having trouble catching his breath, while also experiencing far too much humiliation to even try reaching his bus in time. So, he settled for finding a nearby bench and collapsing on it.

"Are you okay?" Mr. Brucks, a concerned teacher quickly ran up to him. "I saw the whole thing from my classroom window! Tony Divas and Brad Sessler will definitely get expelled *this time!*"

Simon was in great pain and all of the happiness he had felt earlier was now *completely gone!* Still, he made a real effort to look up at the teacher with a half-smile and nod his appreciation.

The teacher returned his smile and then helped Simon slowly walk to the nurse's office.

But as they entered it, he was immediately floored by who the nurse was? It was *Doris?*

As Mr. Brucks walked out the door, Doris smiled and said, "Hello, Simon," as she seated him in a chair and proceeded to gently press a damp washcloth to his face.

"Doris? What are *you* doing here?" Simon asked in surprise.

She laughed. "I just wanted to talk with you about your day."

Simon began to grow anxious as he realized that he had *not* conquered or even attempted to complete his first challenge of making a friend, although he was certain he'd made a couple of *lifelong enemies* named Brad Sessler and Tony Divas! He remembered how concisely Doris had presented this first challenge to him, but unfortunately, he was certain that in his passion to right a wrong from his past, he'd gotten *way off track!*

"*Relax*, Simon," Doris assured him, immediately reading the distress that was quickly materializing on his face. "Good friendships are never made in a few hours. But they *can* be started in that time."

"Did I *start* a friendship then?" Simon asked in surprise?

"Only time will tell," she replied mysteriously. Then pausing, she looked intently into his eyes and shared understandingly, "Although you *didn't* choose to complete your challenge as it was presented to you, *Life* has decided to be broad minded about it."

"What does that mean *exactly?*" Simon asked in hopeful confusion.

"It means that you've *passed* your first challenge!" Doris proclaimed encouragingly. "Congratulations, Simon!"

Simon let out a huge sigh of relief, while inadvertently hugging Doris. Luckily, she didn't seem to mind. In the next moment, he found himself back to normal on the street where Doris's house had stood. But it was gone now and so was she. He quickly walked over to the sidewalk and began jogging back toward the movie theatre to share his good news with Scott. When he arrived there, Scott was already waiting for him on a bench outside. Simon excitedly shared his experiences and his relief that he had *passed* his first challenge!

"Way to go, Simon! I never doubted you for a moment!" Scott cheered. "Only *two more* to go, bro!"

Just then, a pretty young woman hurriedly rushed over to them. She was probably in her mid-twenties, about five foot six. She had long, brown hair, hazel eyes and for some reason, shock and excitement was written all over her pretty face.

"Excuse me?" she offered hesitantly. "Are *you* Simon Dent?"

Simon was *floored!* He was certain that the two of them had *never* met, so how she knew him was a complete mystery? Still, he managed to respond to her question with a weak, "Yes?"

Sensing Simon's very obvious confusion, the woman laughed nervously. "I'm sorry. My name is Alice McAllister. We were in the same class at Grover Elementary School with Mrs. Vandersluis in fourth grade? Remember?"

Of course, Simon recalled being in *that* class. He had just *spent the afternoon there*! He thought very hard about a classmate named 'Alice McAllister,' when suddenly his eyes lit-up. He asked her hopefully, "*McAllister*? Did the kids in the class call you *Annie* back then?"

"Yes! That's right!" she smiled. "I asked everyone to call me by my middle name, Alice, just before I started junior high."

"Did you like that name better or something?" Simon asked curiously.

Alice laughed. "No, I had a cousin also named Annie, who came over from England to live with us for a couple of years. I decided to use my middle name, Alice, to avoid confusion when anyone talked to us while we were together." And then she added, "But wouldn't you know it?" she laughed. "After she'd left us, *that* name just sort of stuck?"

Simon smiled as he thrust out his right hand to meet hers. "Nice to see you again, *Alice!*" Looking around for Scott, to introduce into the conversation, he quickly realized that he had once again *disappeared?*

"I apologize for confusing you. I approached you because I heard your young friend call you *Simon*, and since I don't know anyone else with that name, and you have a blonde crewcut like I remembered you having back in elementary school, I was really hoping that it was *you?*" she explained.

"Wow! But how did you even know who I was?" Simon asked incredulously. "I don't remember *ever* talking to you at school?"

"You *didn't*," she smiled. "But you *did* pick-up a dollar bill I had dropped one day and put it in my desk to find," she replied sweetly. "I never forgot how quietly thoughtful you were."

Simon remembered doing that all of those years ago, but he had no idea that anyone had actually witnessed it? "You've got a great memory, Alice," Simon smiled.

She smiled back. "The main reason I was thinking about you, was because many years ago you briefly talked with my older brother Ted, after you somehow got two bullies to leave my younger brother Jimmy alone and terrorize *you* instead," she explained. "Remember?"

Simon was well beyond shocked? What she was describing was something he had done earlier today during his first challenge, which had taken place in *another dimension?* It had *never happened* during his actual childhood? "Excuse me?" he managed to blurt out.

"I heard that story all of those years ago from Ted, about what you had done for Jimmy," she continued, "and how those two bullies had roughed you up after school for doing it?" Looking sad, she added, "For some reason, I never said a word to you about it and I've always regretted that. I suppose I was too shy at the time," she admitted. "And by junior high school, when I finally worked up the nerve to talk to you, you had moved away? Anyway, you can understand my excitement today when I heard your name and discovered that it was actually *you?* I couldn't believe my good luck! For peace of mind, I just have to *thank you,* Simon, for what you did for Jimmy all those years ago!"

"Oh, you're very welcome, Alice," he replied with obvious embarrassment. "If you don't mind me asking, how is Jimmy doing these days?"

"He's doing great!" she declared. "He's in medical school preparing to be a doctor!"

"Really?" Simon exclaimed.

"Yes! Ever since that experience with you, he gradually began talking more and more. Anyone who meets him now, for the first time, would *never* guess that he'd once been a mute."

"You mean he *wasn't* born that way?" Simon asked in surprise.

"Oh no! He was *always* a quiet boy, but he went completely mute once he started school at age five. His doctor told us that in his opinion, it was caused entirely by his terror of facing frightening situations and threatening people in everyday life." Then growing more cheerful, she added, "But after you did what you did, then I think he grew braver and began to realize that there really *wasn't* any

34

reason for him to fear those things anymore! In that moment, outside of the family, you may have become his very first *role model!*"

Simon chuckled nervously. "I don't know what to say?" he admitted uncomfortably.

"There's no need for you to say anything! You have got to be the nicest guy I have ever met!" With that, Alice embraced the completely unsuspecting Simon, and kissed him gently on the cheek.

"So, what are *you* up to these days?" Simon quickly asked, attempting to hide the exhilaration her kiss had brought him.

Alice smiled and replied, "I'm an elementary school teacher in Grangeville, which is also where I live now. I just happened to be here in Idaho Falls for a couple of days visiting my brother Ted and his family."

"I live in Grangeville *too?*" Simon offered excitedly. "Are you *married?*" He suddenly blurted out the question that he was dying to know the answer to.

Alice blushed, and then replied, "No. Not yet."

Quickly glancing at her left hand and noticing that she was *not* wearing an engagement ring, he added, "May I have your phone number to maybe keep in touch?"

Alice smiled. "Of course, Simon," she replied, quickly relaying her phone number to him while he added it to his cell phone contacts.

"I hope we meet again very soon," Simon shared honestly as he met her eyes.

"Me too," she replied with a hopeful smile.

The Second Challenge

Regardless of the fact that he had apparently (*in a roundabout way*) successfully completed his first challenge, Simon anxiously tossed and turned in bed that night, unable to fall asleep? He was simply too worked-up over not knowing what Doris would present to him as his *second* challenge? He *didn't* look forward to returning to his past again, but if she asked him to do that, then he didn't see *any* alternative. Suddenly, in answer to his question, he distinctly heard Doris's gentle voice softly whispering into his ear, "Hello, Simon. For your next challenge, you will walk through three different doors, and afterward you must decide which one of the realities you entered is *best* for your future? In the end, you may choose *only one*! And *not choosing* at all will immediately *terminate* your existence. Do you understand?"

"Yes. But will you at least give me a clue? What *exactly* am I supposed to be looking for?" Simon heard himself plead, though his lips never moved.

"You are searching for the meaning of life," she replied softly. "Specifically, the meaning of *your* life!"

With that, Doris's presence was gone, and Simon immediately began to feel his reality oddly changing? To put it in the simplest of terms, he felt as though he was no longer housed in his body, and his spirit was rapidly traversing through time and space, a journey which took him through a psychedelic smorgasbord of incredible shapes, colors and lights? But, moments later, he found himself back in his body, standing alone in dark *nothingness*, magically suspended in the air? He was experiencing the vastness and utter silence of outer space, but without any planets, stars, lack of oxygen or unimaginable cold? However, as expected, there were three glowing black doors standing in front of him with *no* individual distinguishing features separating them, aside from their proximity to one another? Simon pondered a moment, still unsure of exactly what he was supposed to be looking for, before tepidly walking up to the farthest door to his left. He hesitated a moment and then slowly opening it, he walked through.

He was immediately greeted by a bright and beautiful vision of nature at its most delightful! The sun was shining and the sky was blue, accented by a spattering of fluffy white clouds that were perfectly dispersed above him. The temperature was pleasant and a cool, and a gentle breeze blew playfully over everything. To make things even better, he imagined in his head that a lovely choir, singing beautiful songs, was serenading him off in the distance of this *idyllic*-setting! The mildly hilly ground surrounding him was free of any buildings or signs that anyone planned on building them here anytime soon, and there were tall, healthy pine trees growing everywhere. It was obvious to him that he was *somewhere* in the mountains. A very *stunning* part, in fact! As he walked around admiring his surroundings, he suddenly realized that *this place*, both peaceful and gorgeous, could very well be the perfect setting that he may have always been subconsciously seeking? Why else would he be here?

Just then a large brown grizzly bear suddenly appeared off in the distance which immediately *spoiled* this tranquil moment for him. As the bear began slowly lumbering toward him, Simon imagined that it might be very irritated with him for magically appearing out of nowhere and entering its beautiful habitat? If that *were* the case, knowing full well that he couldn't possibly outrun this powerful creature, he opted to stay exactly where he was, keeping perfectly still, hoping *not* to draw its ire! When the bear finally reached him, Simon grew *terrified*, worrying that his end was near? But, the bear surprised him by *not* standing on its hind legs with its claws outstretched with a ferocious expression, or even growling at him? Without breaking stride, it simply nonchalantly glanced at him, but kept sauntering past in a leisurely, good-natured sort of way. Surprisingly, it *never* paid any attention to him?

Simon let out a muffled and sincere sigh of relief. Once the bear had traveled completely out of sight, against his ever-present fears, he resolved bravely to continue his exploration. Eventually, when he arrived at the outskirts of the forest, he spied a small cabin with gentle white smoke floating from its chimney? He grew both excited and nervous as he considered that the residents of that cabin might be friendly toward him, but then again, they *might not*? What if they were actually *murderous psychos* hiding out from the law in that cabin? Just thinking about that scenario made him grow very fearful? Suddenly, he watched a tall, thin man rush out of the cabin door! He appeared to be middle aged, with a long black beard speckled with gray, wearing faded blue overalls. Simon grew frightened as he couldn't help but notice that the man held a *twelve-gauge shotgun* that he was aiming right at him!

"What do ya want?" the man demanded.

"Nothing," Simon assured him calmly, while trying hard to hide the fact that he was shaking uncontrollably! "I was just looking around. It's very pretty up here, isn't it?"

"Hmm? I guess it is at that," the man admitted as he softened his tone and lowered his shotgun. "You seem like a right friendly young fella! How would you like to visit with me for a little while?" he asked with a smile. "I've got some hot coffee brewin' on the stove?"

"Sure. That's very neighborly of you," Simon replied with relief. "What did you have in mind? Conversation?"

"*Conversation?*" the man hollered humorously. Nah! *That's* for sissies! I thought we'd play with my pet bear, Buster! He must be around here somewhere?"

"Is he tame?" Simon asked.

"Is he *tame?*" the man laughed. "Of course, he is! He's the best and most loyal friend I've ever had in these parts!"

Simon was *very* relieved. "I saw a brown bear walking through the forest a few minutes ago?" he said helpfully. "Could that be him?"

"*Might* be," the man replied cryptically.

"What do you mean by *that?*" Simon asked.

"I mean there are only two bears in this whole gal-durn forest. The other one looks just like Buster, like his *twin* in fact. But that bear's a *mean* one! That's why I always carry my shotgun loaded with rock-salt whenever I go outside! I don't wanna hurt that bear, no matter how ornery it is. But just in case he gets out of control, a blast from my gun is the only way to scare him off!" he decidedly exclaimed.

"What do you mean by '*out of control?*'" Simon asked the man with obvious concern.

"You know. Not abiding by the rules of *forest etiquette*," the man explained with a smile.

Simon found himself confused? "Well, how can you possibly tell those two bears apart?"

"Oh, that's easy!" the man smiled and explained, "I start playin' with whichever one of them two comes by, and if that bear tries to *rip me apart and kill me*, I know it's *not* Buster!"

He'd had enough! Simon suddenly grew terrified, as any semblance of courage in his being immediately disappeared! Completely forgetting the reasons for *why* he had come here or *what* he was supposed to be accomplishing, he left the mountain man still smiling, but now shaking his head, as he raced through the forest like a crazy man until he reached the door. Then with immense relief, he ran back through it! Once again, he found himself suspended in space staring at doors, only this time there were only *two*? He immediately wished he could have a do-over of door number one. This time trying much harder to see the adventure all the way through to the end. Perhaps the mountain man had only been joking about that second bear? After all, he had been *smiling*? Still, he *might* have ended up playing with a *head-removing grizzly bear*!

So, hesitantly turning toward the remaining two doors, this time he chose the one to his right. Searching for the mental fortitude he knew he would need, he slowly walked through it. He immediately found himself on a busy and good-sized subterranean platform, awaiting the arrival of a train. He recalled experiencing this exact situation when he had lived on the east coast. He guessed with confidence that he was in a subway station, perhaps in Boston or New York City? A sign on the wall identified this place as *Grangeville Station*? But Grangeville, Idaho *didn't* have a subway? He decided there must be a street with that same name somewhere in whatever city this was? And then he imagined positively that the city above him was probably exciting and fun to live in! He also imagined that there would probably be plenty for him to see and do here and friendly people all around to help him out if he had any problems? Armed with his positive attitude and enthusiasm, he excitedly followed the crowd as they boarded the next train and prepared to speed off to an exciting destination unknown. The crowded train was hot, uncomfortable and claustrophobic, but fortunately he was quickly able to procure a seat on one side of the subway car, which made things much better. But, moments later, just before the train began moving, he noticed an old man strangely struggling to balance himself as he stood clinging to an overhead leather strap hanging from the ceiling in the middle of the car about two feet in front of him? Feeling strangely empathetic toward him, Simon decided to offer the man his seat. The old man jumped at the chance, nodded gratefully and quickly accepted it, leaving Simon to change places with him on the train. Simon soon found himself standing in the middle of the car, surrounded by strangers who seemed to be eying him suspiciously? He *didn't* like it much, but somehow he was able to hold his emotions in check. That is, until the train actually began moving out of the station. Within minutes, he uncomfortably noticed that the train was steadily picking up speed, traveling faster and faster with *complete abandon?* It was moving so fast now that he felt himself bouncing around in every direction, barely able to keep himself from falling down! And then Simon's great big brain got to work and imagined that the train was surely having trouble *staying attached to the rails?* Looking around him, most of the people in the car took this highly frightening ride in stride, and with the exception of a few angry people who saw fit to inadvertently offer choice curse words or unseemly phrases every time they were thrown one way or the other, no one lost their heads. But to Simon, as terrifying as this ride had already been, even worse was the panic he felt that at any moment now, *this train* was most assuredly going to *derail*, killing everyone aboard, *including himself!* And that's when he happened to look over at the old man sitting in his former seat? Curiously, he sat there very quietly reading a magazine, *completely oblivious* to this horrific journey? Was he perhaps too old to realize that his life (*as well as the lives of all the other unfortunate passengers aboard the train*) was about to come to a *hideous end?* Or did he know something that no one else on the train did, enabling him to keep calm? Maybe he was actually asleep, or even *dead?* Whatever the reason for this absurd contradiction between the man's docile behavior and this horrifying ride, moments later, the train very surprisingly came to a gentle stop and almost everyone aboard calmly disembarked to the awaiting platform.

Wiping his sweating brow and sighing in relief, Simon once again turned toward the old man. Strangely, he was making no effort to leave the train, but remained seated? Curiously though, his eyes met Simon's and then he sadly mouthed the word, *'repeat.'* As Simon exited the train and began climbing the stairs from the subway platform toward the street above, he wondered what the old man had meant? That's when he surprisingly read a sign on the wall that identified this place as still being *Grangeville Station?* Simon was instantly shocked and distressed? Apparently, the train he had just arrived on had taken him on a death-defying journey to *nowhere?* Inexplicably returning to, *or* never actually *leaving* Grangeville Station in the first place? And now the train was probably set to travel that same pointless trip once again? But *why?* Quickly turning around and racing back toward the platform through the exit, he knew that he had to find out the truth by reboarding the train and asking the old man what was going on? But suddenly he became aware of someone angrily shouting at him from behind?

"Hey! You *can't* go back to the platform through the exit, bub! You'll have to buy another ticket!" an irritated security guard yelled from the top of the stairs.

Yet, Simon kept running, hoping to reach the train and discover what this *insanity* was all about?

"Stop!" the security guard harshly yelled, chasing him through the exit.

Simon ran for his life! He frantically tried to reach the train in the station, which was still quite a distance ahead of him, before anyone could stop him! Meanwhile, five angry security guards holding wooden batons high over their heads suddenly descended upon him from nowhere, almost completely surrounding him on all sides! But unexpectedly someone firmly grabbed his hand and quickly pulled him away from the train station and the security guards. They ran down a meandering path which eventually led them to the safety of a poorly lit room, hidden behind some sort of ancient storage area. Simon could not make-out the face of his rescuer, but the hand was soft and the body shape, even in the dim light, was definitely feminine.

41

"Thank you for saving me back there," Simon began sincerely.

"You're welcome," a young woman's voice, which he did not recognize, replied as she gently released his hand and sat on a chair in the room, motioning for him to do the same. "I live down here and just couldn't bear to see you beaten-up, so I brought you to one of my many hiding places from the security folks who work this platform. They'll *never* look for us here!"

Simon was incredulous! "But how can you *live* down here? Where do you sleep?"

"Anywhere and everywhere!" the young woman declared merrily. "Eating, sleeping and washing are no problem for me!"

"Did you *choose* to live down here?" Simon asked her.

"I did," she replied.

"Why?" Simon asked.

"For the same reason *you* chose to lock yourself away in your apartment and *never* socialize with anyone unless it became absolutely necessary," she replied with a glimmer. "Who needs other people, right?"

"How did you know that I felt like that?" Simon asked her suspiciously.

The girl laughed. "Oh, I know a lot of things!"

Her answer *meant* something to him, but Simon did not immediately know what it was, so he asked the girl something he considered to be far more pressing. "Does that train ever stop at any *other* station?"

The young woman giggled. "Of course not!"

"Why?" Simon asked curiously.

"Because *you* won't let it," she answered matter-of-factly.

"What do you mean, *I won't let it*? I'm a complete stranger here! I have *nothing* to do with where the train stops?" Simon exclaimed in shock.

"Don't you?" she replied mysteriously.

"No! Of course not! And even if I did, *why* would I choose to do such a pointless thing?" Simon insisted.

"For the same reason you chose to lock yourself away in your apartment and *never* socialize with anyone unless it became absolutely necessary!" she replied with a glimmer. "Who needs other people, right?"

But before Simon had the chance to ask her *why* she had given him the exact same answer to two very different questions, in that next moment the woman completely disappeared? Then Simon abruptly found himself on the loading platform beside the track at the station, watching the train pull away *without him*? And he couldn't believe his eyes when he saw Alice sitting by a window on it, sadly shaking her head and waving goodbye to him? Seeing *this*, following that very strange escape and conversation with the mysterious underground girl, as well as taking that *train ride from Hell*, proved to be far too much for Simon's brain to process! So, as he already sadly seemed to have the habit of doing, he ran to the door of the portal and quickly jumped through it, instantly returning to the safety of black nothingness.

Alone in the darkness once again, a very frustrated Simon intensely pondered his most recent journey. Due to the fact that what had been behind that second door had left him with more questions than clarity, he was determined now, more than ever, to make his final adventure *end well*! As he hesitantly entered the third and final door, he was initially surprised and yet delighted to find that it led him straight back into his *own apartment* in Grangeville? What a treat! But he soon realized that he was merely an invisible spectator here, watching a much older version of himself plodding through his apartment like a tired and unhappy robot, mundanely gathering his precious sixteen thousand daily steps. As he watched, he suddenly realized that *this* old man looked exactly like the old man who had mouthed the word *'repeat'* to him on the train? So, *both old men* were future versions of *him*? And then he suddenly understood what the man on the train had meant when he'd mouthed the word, *repeat!*' He was undoubtedly sharing that his life was and would *forever* be a daily *repeat* of the day before, with *no meaning* to it whatsoever? As everyone else experienced the ups and downs of life (*riding in the middle of the subway car*) the old man *intentionally* made his life artificially safe and repetitive by purposely sitting it out! At that moment, the older version of Simon in the apartment suddenly collapsed to the floor? His expression was very painful to watch. Was he *crying*? The old man looked both desperate and miserable, as his hands now covered his face! It was as if he recognized for the first time that no matter what he did next, it was *futile*? It was *too late*! He knew that he had already missed his chance to live a happy, full and satisfying life! Simon could not bear to watch the great distress his older self was experiencing any longer, as he quickly ran to the portal door and jumped through it.

As he stood in space, in complete darkness, he heard Doris' gentle voice inside his head asking him, "Well, Simon? Which door led you to your future happiness?"

Simon was anxious and confused? He didn't know what to tell her? Finally, finding his answer, but realizing that it would *not* please her, he decided to tell her the truth anyway. He took a deep breath and replied slowly, "What was behind each of those doors was tempting to me at first, but after staying for a while, I knew that I would *never* be happy with what I found behind *any of them!*" His words sounded even more sad and pathetic as he became aware that there was a sincere *hopelessness* emanating from his voice as he spoke. It was very much like the intense despairing feelings he'd felt when he'd been with the older version of himself behind the third door? That's when he horrifyingly realized for the first time that the hopelessness he heard in his voice must be the sound of his own *death knell!*

Doris did not respond as Simon felt himself growing cold and then suddenly began to disappear from this place, perhaps *never* to exist anywhere else again? He prepared as best he could for the nonexistent emptiness that he believed awaited him as the consequence of his failure.

The Proposition

The next morning, Simon could scarcely believe it, as he actually *woke-up* in his bed at the motel? After going through that huge fiasco with the *three doors* during that stressful night before, he had fully expected this moment and *every* moment afterwards to *never come*? Still, confused as he was, he got dressed as usual and didn't say a word about his disappointing experiences to Scott, until they were comfortably having breakfast at Bite Me, where he quickly brought him up to date.

"Don't worry, Simon," Scott tried very hard to lift his sagging spirits. "Doris *never* told you that you'd failed, right?"

"That's true," Simon replied appreciatively. "But at the end of that challenge, I definitely felt empty, like what I imagined it must feel like to *un-exist*?"

"Ugh! That sounds awful!" Scott sympathized.

"It was!" Simon confirmed with a very passionate expression. "But since I'm still existing now, even after such a wretched performance last night, I'm wondering if *Life* still sees at least a *glimmer* of hope for me?"

Just as soon as Simon had finished speaking, appearing out of nowhere (*as she had the habit of doing*) was Doris, who casually joined them at their table. "Good morning, boys!" she smiled. "How's breakfast?"

"Good!" Scott replied positively. "But Simon and I were just wondering *why* you haven't told him how he did in his second challenge? Is it *bad* news?"

"Not *exactly*," Doris replied, making it very clear that she was holding something back.

"What do you mean by that?" Simon asked anxiously.

"I mean that *Life*, as understanding as he is, *does not* feel that you achieved the second challenge... *completely*, although you do get high marks for trying," she replied.

"It was because I always ran away from what was behind *each* door, wasn't it?" Simon asked hesitantly, already knowing the answer.

"Yes, but before you ran away, you *always* made a real effort to face whatever was scaring you, and that's the *only* reason you still exist now," she explained. "*Life* and I agreed that you performed *just* well enough during that second challenge to warrant one last chance to save yourself."

Simon exhaled deeply. "Thank you, Doris! I am very grateful!"

Doris nodded with no expression on her face as she intently met his eyes, and then she suddenly broke into a gentle smile and said mysteriously, "*Life* has a little proposition for you, Simon."

"A *proposition?*" Simon asked curiously. "Is that different from a challenge?"

"In this case, *yes*," Doris replied. "Since you didn't actually complete your first or second challenges as they were intended, this third and *final* opportunity will have to make up for that. I'm afraid it will be much *more difficult* to complete. The good news is that if you find what it takes to achieve this, regardless of the fact that you faltered on the first two, you will earn your *life back!*"

"Alright!" Simon blurted out with a smile, which quickly turned into a look of confusion, as he asked, "But if I did so poorly on the first two challenges, what makes you think I can succeed with an even tougher one?"

"You *didn't* do poorly, exactly," Doris assured him. "But life was expecting to see something in you that as of yet has not surfaced?"

"And *what* is that?" Simon asked curiously.

Doris smiled mysteriously and ignoring his question, she asked, "Do you consider yourself a gambling man?"

"Not really," Simon replied quickly. "I see myself as more a creature of habit."

Doris sighed. "*Uh oh!* That's exactly what *Life* thought you would say."

"Was that the *wrong* answer then?" Simon asked anxiously.

"Oh no," Doris assured him. "I'm sure that it was an *honest* one."

"Then why do I get the feeling that *Life* is very concerned about it?"

"Let me answer that in this way," Doris began. "A tree is alive and continues growing throughout its entire lifetime, making the world around it a better place in so many ways. But a piece of dead wood, originally derived from a live tree, is incapable of growth and although it can certainly be made into something strong, useful and often beautiful for a time, as well as being used as fuel for burning, it will *never* know the joys of being a tree... or any other living thing... because it's *not alive.*"

46

"Are you comparing Simon to a piece of *dead wood?*" Scott suddenly chimed-in, with a look of shock covering his face.

Doris chuckled, but then immediately grew much more serious as she replied, "Not exactly, Scott. In my metaphor, Simon, you, like the piece of wood, lose the many advantages of living, just as soon as you stop growing. You then sadly become a predictable, unliving, mundane, *creature of habit*, uninterested in ever being anything else."

Simon began to sweat.

Continuing, Doris shared, "But to succeed in your upcoming challenge and win back your life, you *cannot* just run away and give up! You must quickly learn to be brave enough to *change your behavior* whenever it's called for. In other words, you must learn to be *resilient!* That's the change *Life* needs to see from you!"

Simon quickly pulled himself together and realized for the first time, that in her kind and gentle way, Doris actually *was* comparing him to a piece of *dead wood!* But he also clearly understood what he *had* to do. "I accept!" he declared firmly. "What is *Life's* proposition?"

Doris met his eyes very seriously and shared, "*Life* proposes that you return to Grangeville as a stranger named Sheldon, physically disguised, without home, job or close family. You are to be *your brother* if anyone asks."

Simon looked shocked. "So, I'm pretending to be my *imaginary* brother?"

"Exactly," Doris confirmed.

"But what am I supposed to do?" Simon asked in confusion. "What is my challenge?"

"It's a little *different* than your other two," Doris explained. "You must follow this adventure wherever it may take you, without *ever* revealing to anyone who you *really* are until this challenge is completely over. No matter what!"

"*No matter what?*" Simon repeated.

"Yes. No matter how difficult things may become for you. Because if you tell anyone that you are Simon Dent before this challenge is *over*, I'm quite sure you *know* what will happen to you."

47

"What should *I* do in the meantime?" Scott asked Doris with concern. "You know, while Simon is away 'playing Sheldon?'"

Doris smiled. "Knowing how much you 'enjoyed' your recent bus trip with Simon," she began playfully sarcastic. "You're going to be taking *another* bus by yourself back to Grangeville!"

Scott laughed. "That ride wasn't so bad. The problem was that I had finished reading my joke book and had nothing else to read to pass the time?" he explained. "*That's* why I was so cranky!"

Doris laughed as she handed Scott the bus ticket, some money, *five new joke books* and the key to Simon's apartment (*all of which she grabbed from the air*).

"Wow! Thanks for *everything*, but especially the new books!" Scott smiled gratefully, as he accepted all of the items she gave him. "But I was wondering why you don't just send me to Grangeville at the same time you send Simon? That would be easier wouldn't it?"

Doris grew more serious as she told him, "I'm sending you back to Grangeville on the bus so that Simon is left *completely alone* for his final challenge. You should arrive there about the time that it reaches a conclusion. So, no matter what the outcome, the two of you will be together in Grangeville at the end."

"Scott nodded, but he grew noticeably concerned as he wondered what she had meant by, '*together at the end?*'

"Doris?" Simon, began hesitantly.

"Yes, Simon?" she replied.

"There was a classmate of mine in fourth grade, a girl named Alice? She came to see me as a grown-up *after* I'd returned from that first challenge to my *real life*. We talked a lot about elementary school, but she didn't only talk about *real* memories there, she also brought up things that had *just happened* during that challenge in my dimension? I would love to see her again... but that conversation *wasn't* real, right? I mean, how could it have been?" he said disappointedly. "My talk with her was probably just a hallucination."

Doris grinned. "No, Simon. That conversation *was real* all right! But as you know, everything you experienced during that first challenge was only about what *could* have happened if you had done what you did there in real life. None of what you *initiated* in that dimension was real."

"But Alice came back to my *real life* and talked to me about things that had happened *during* that *first challenge?*" Simon repeated passionately. "Isn't that odd?"

"*Very* odd?" Doris replied, squinting her eyes. "Are you quite certain you were back to your real life when this happened?"

"I thought I was?" Simon began to doubt his own memories before he recalled, "I also caught her looking at me from a train window during my second challenge?"

"Hmm?" Doris looked confused, "Well, if you *survive* what you are about to undertake, I'm sure that you can question *Life* about everything you don't understand when you get back."

"But what if I *don't* survive?" Simon asked intently.

"Well, then it *really won't matter anymore*, will it," she said icily. And without another word, she disappeared.

Simon inadvertently shuddered.

"Hey, Simon?" Scott suddenly asked, awakening him from his dire thoughts.

"Yes, Scott?"

"When this challenge is over, and of course, you know that I'll be rooting for you... I'm going to *really miss* being your little brother," he said with a touch of regret.

Smiling warmly, Simon replied, "Don't worry, Scott. We'll be together, for as long as I live, which I hope will be a long time!" he assured him. "Remember? You'll be my inner child again."

"Yeah," Scott replied disappointedly. "That's cool and all, but I'm just going to miss being *real!*"

Momentarily, after leaving Scott, Simon inexplicably found himself on Main Street in Grangeville, sitting on a street curb? There was a large plate glass window in front of the store sitting across the street from him, where he happened to see his reflection. This immediately caused him to *gasp* in shock? *Now* he understood why he was sitting on the curb! Sheldon Dent was a tall and overly lean man of undefinable age, with a facial expression that was a cross between scared and *crazy*! His face was scruffy from many days without shaving, his thick mane of blonde hair was overgrown and greasy, while his face was badly (*and unevenly*) sunburned. He was wearing an old pair of tweed trousers that were being loosely held-up by a lone piece of thick twine tied to belt loops on the left front and right back of his pants and ultimately resting on his right shoulder. He also wore a long-sleeved (*but very dusty*) red and white flannel shirt and a pair of old stained (*formerly white*) tennis shoes without socks or laces. *Everything* he was wearing was much too big for him, as well as being torn and covered with weeks of old dirt and mud. He unhappily imagined that he must look like a tall and lanky pile of rags that had just rolled around in a very sooty fireplace! Needless to say, he was *not* enjoying being this person at all! Suddenly he had a thought. He quickly stood up and excitedly reached down inside his front pockets to see if he had any money to buy some new clothes or rent a room to get cleaned up in? He did find a couple of coins and *half* of a five-dollar bill, but disappointedly, nothing else. Next he checked his back pockets for a wallet, but all he found there was a dirty handkerchief. Now Simon was convinced that Sheldon Dent, his *supposed* brother, was nothing more than a hobo, a tramp, a *bum*! *Life* certainly had a peculiar sense of humor, and at *his* expense! For all of Simon's exceptional mental abilities, he truly *did not* have a clue what to do next? He had absolutely no experience dealing with bizarre situations like *this* one?

Looking around, he recognized a few faces of people he had seen a couple of years ago when he'd first arrived in town, but none of them so much as gave him a second look? He finally caught one older woman staring at him and frowning, but she quickly removed her gaze just as soon as his eyes briefly met hers. As she hurriedly pulled out her cell phone and scurried off, several other folks also looked at him in disgust when they thought he wasn't looking. Finally, he noticed several people watching him as though they felt sorry for him? But they too turned and walked off without a word, the moment he returned their stares. Simon did not like all of this attention. Not only because it was predominantly *negative*, but because he did not feel *invisible* anymore as he had safely felt ever since moving into his apartment in Grangeville? His filthy hobo disguise had now apparently placed him *center stage!* So, not knowing what else to do, he promptly sat back down on the curb with his head in his hands.

A couple of minutes later, a middle-aged policeman drove up next to the curb Simon was sitting on, and stopped his car.

"Hello, sir?" he said politely through his open car window. "Do you live around here?"

About to answer in the affirmative, Simon luckily remembered who he was *supposed* to be and replied instead, "No, sir. I'm just passing through."

"What's your name?"

"Sheldon Dent," Simon replied carefully.

"What is your destination?" the officer asked curiously.

Simon was stumped. "I.. I guess I'm not sure yet?"

The policeman nodded and without expression he immediately got out of his car. As he walked toward Simon, he had a professional and confident look illuminating his face, like he truly knew what he was doing. Simon envied him, because ever since this final challenge had begun, he had never come close to feeling *that?* After politely escorting Simon into his car's backseat, the policeman slid into the front and calmly began driving off.

"Excuse me, sir?" Simon asked with concern.

"Yes?" the policeman replied.

"Are you arresting me?"

The policeman grew serious as he replied, "Not *exactly.* We're simply heading back to the station to sort a few things out."

"What *kind* of things?" Simon asked suspiciously.

"Well, for starters, what you're doing here?" the policeman replied.

"Why does *that* matter?" Simon asked with noticeable irritation.

"Well, the station received a phone call about you from an anonymous caller ten minutes ago. She was very concerned that you might be dangerous. She also reminded them that there is a *law against vagrancy* here in Grangeville, which of course, there is!"

"I'm not *dangerous?*" Simon replied in shock. "And I'm not a vagrant either!"

The officer replied calmly, "That may well be true, but we are still obligated to look into every official complaint." In a friendlier tone, he added, "You know, if you *are* a vagrant, I can point you toward a shelter in town that's surely a lot more comfortable than that curb you were sitting on."

"Oh, I don't live on the streets," Simon assured him.

"No? Then where *do* you live?" the policeman asked him curiously.

Simon didn't immediately have an answer to that question, considering that *Sheldon* was a fictitious character. He knew that if he lied, with a little checking, the policeman could easily find out. So, for lack of a better answer, he replied, "Oh, here and there."

The policeman gently chuckled, thoroughly amused. "Okay, Sheldon. We'll talk more when we get to the station."

When they arrived at the police station, after parking in the back, the officer politely escorted Simon inside the building, past the reception area and into one of several interrogation rooms. After seating themselves on opposite sides of a short table, the interrogation began.

"Please state your name," the officer asked professionally.

"Sheldon Dent," Simon replied dutifully.

"Where do you normally reside?" the officer continued.

"Lately I've been visiting Idaho Falls," Simon tried to skirt the question.

The officer gave him an odd look. "What's in *Idaho Falls?*"

"I grew up there," Simon said, forgetting for a moment that he was supposed to be *Sheldon.*

"In the *orphanage?*" the officer surprisingly asked.

"Why, yes?" Simon felt forced to admit. "But how did you know that?"

"We have another Dent; *Simon* Dent, living in Grangeville. He also spent a good chunk of time in that orphanage. I wonder if you're any relation to him?" the officer asked.

"Why do you ask that?" Simon asked nervously.

The officer hesitated, and then replied seriously, "Because we received a tip from his employer that Simon has *not* contacted them over these past few days and they have grown quite concerned about him, *especially* after they unsuccessfully tried multiple times to contact him on the phone? So, we sent a couple of officers to physically check his apartment for him, but they found *no one* there? His neighbors unanimously told us that he *never leaves* his apartment? So, it appears there may have been *foul play* involved? He is now officially listed as *missing*, and I was hoping *you* might shed some light on that?"

Simon began to regret not calling-in to work, but he *couldn't* tell the officer the truth? He was powerless to help himself right now because of his binding agreement with Doris *not* to tell anyone his real name while on this challenge! He began to sweat profusely. "I truly don't know a thing about his disappearance, but I will admit that Simon Dent is my brother," he lied hesitantly.

"When was the last time you talked to him?" the officer continued.

"I don't remember?" Simon answered.

"Are the two of you very close?" the officer asked.

"Not especially," Simon replied as calmly as he could. "He lives a quiet life here in Grangeville, while I'm more of a... *traveler*."

"*What* are you doing here, Mr. Dent?" the officer's voice suddenly took on a very aggressive tone. "Were you perhaps planning on *seeing* your brother this trip?" The officer asked him very deliberately.

"I was thinking about it?" Simon shared uncomfortably.

The officer smiled knowingly now. Next, he had Simon place his fingertips on the screen of a machine. "If your fingerprints come up on the national data base, we'll immediately find out who you *really* are, Mr. Dent."

"I already told you who I am? I'm Sheldon Dent!" Simon said, growing irritated with the officer. "Why else would I tell you that?"

"That remains to be seen. *Whoever* you are, if you really do know Simon Dent, then I think you already know that he *does not* have a brother or any other known living relatives! Now, tell me what you know about Simon Dent?" the officer demanded.

Moments later, the machine made a dinging sound as a match came up with Simon's fingerprints.

The officer looked stunned as he shook his head. "This machine says that your fingerprints match those of *Simon Dent?* What in the Sam Hill have you done to make *that* happen?!"

"I have no idea why our fingerprints match?" Sheldon passionately insisted. "But as I already told you, we *are* brothers?"

"Did you try to steal his identity by *peeling off his fingertips* and gluing them on to your own fingers?" the officer asked in revulsion.

"No! Of course not! That's *ridiculous!*" Simon exclaimed.

"Then I suppose you have no intention of *stealing* the *fifty thousand dollars* he has sitting in the bank?" the officer had grown angry now.

"No!" Simon pleaded passionately, remembering that he had saved that for a rainy day. Unfortunately, there was *no way* it could help him now no matter *how* rainy it got!

The officer shook his head in frustration and without any further discussion, he promptly ended the interview and escorted Simon down a dark hallway with a number of empty cells lining both sides of it. He stopped and gestured for Simon to enter a dingy little cell located toward the middle of the cellblock. This caused Simon to immediately wonder *why* he'd selected this one for him, since it was by far the smallest cell there? After locking him inside, the officer, anticipating Simon's unhappy expression, very angrily said, "When you're ready to talk and tell me the truth about who you *really* are and *what* you have done with Simon Dent, then maybe I'll consider moving you into a larger, more *luxurious cell,* that might even include a meal!"

The irritated policeman walked away, eventually leaving the cellblock and slamming the door behind him. Simon slowly perused everything around him, but unfortunately, there didn't appear to be anything worth noticing? And with the cellblock *completely empty* except for him, he didn't even have anyone to talk to? So, he sat down on the rock-hard bench that the tiny cell so *generously* provided him, and allowed his head to hopelessly fall into his hands. He quietly bemoaned the nightmarish situation he had been thrust into, and couldn't understand why *Life* had chosen to put him through this? And then unexpectedly, his cell door slowly creaked open? Simon had *no idea* why this had happened, but he was instantly caught between creating two very different scenarios? The first one saw him *staying in his cell* as he was supposed to, while the second, a much riskier one, saw him walking out of the cell and with any luck, *escaping*? Simon vividly remembered how Doris had strongly insinuated earlier that he was like a *dead piece of wood* because he was too much a creature of habit and *afraid* to make spontaneous decisions. 'Learn to be *resilient*,' she had told him? So, after a quick moment of deliberation, he came to the daring conclusion that escape *was called for* right now! He was feeling particularly resilient as he confidently stepped out of his cell and began quietly tiptoeing down the corridor toward the door that would lead out of the cellblock. But all at once, two police officers stormed through that very door with anger and hatred fiercely radiating from their faces! And for no rational reason he could think of, they both had their guns drawn and *pointed directly at him*?

"Okay, *Dent*, or whatever your name is," the tall, younger officer shouted. "Breaking out of jail is an incredibly serious offence, punishable by *immediate death!*"

"What? *No, it's not?*" Simon shouted incredulously. "And anyway, my cell door opened by itself?"

"Of course, it did! *We* opened it electronically, genius!" the younger officer gloated.

"But *you* didn't have to walk out of it, now did you?" the older, much shorter officer smiled. "Doing *that* just told us what kind of dirty scumbag you really are, and gave us a perfect excuse for using our guns! We're going to take great pleasure in shooting the man who killed our good friend Simon Dent!"

"Your *good friend?*" Simon exclaimed in disbelief.

"Yes," the older officer explained. "I played poker with him every Saturday night, and then, of course, we went to church together every Sunday morning and often served as acolytes."

"And he helped me to invest in some really great stocks, as well as adding a second story to my house!" the younger officer exclaimed. "Boy, was Simon good with a hammer and nails!"

"What? No! That's all ridiculous!" Simon yelled, completely beside himself. "In any case, *I didn't kill anyone!*"

"I say *you did!*" the older officer sneered. "And the moment you decided to circumvent the law by escaping from your cell, you made it very clear to us that *you* are nothing more than a *double-dealing degenerate!*"

"Yeah! And you've given us the perfect excuse for closing this investigation early by *shooting you dead* while trying to escape!" the younger officer declared.

"And *getting away with it!*" the older officer quickly added with a devilish grin. "No one will care that we killed a dirtbag like you! In fact, we'll probably be *awarded medals!*"

There was *no* doubt about it. Simon was *terrified!* Unsurprisingly, he didn't choose to converse with these *psycho-officers* for one moment longer! Instead, as he recently had the habit of doing in fearful circumstances, he frantically turned around and *ran for his life!* He heard the officers running after him, but curiously didn't hear the expected sound of their gunshots or feel what he imagined would be the excruciating pain of being riddled with bullets? When he reached the other end of the short cellblock moments later, it led him straight to a *door?* By this time, the two officers were nearly upon him, so not caring where the door ultimately led, Simon hastily opened it and surprisingly found himself *sucked out of the room* and whisked away by a great tornado, spinning him around and round? He had *no* idea where this great wind would take him, but at the moment, he was far too dizzy to even care? All of a sudden and without warning, the tornado gently set him down outside a fence that separated him from a group of young children playing games in the yard on the other side. A weary older woman called to the children from the doorway of a large building not far from them, and they immediately all disappeared inside... all except for *one* single child who remained in the field? It was an eight-year-old blonde boy with a crewcut who was softly crying, and didn't go

56

inside for *fear* of drawing the other children's unwanted ridicule. Simon immediately recognized *himself*! And he knew that he was crying because he had *no friends*. As he watched himself standing alone in the yard weeping, Simon's eyes suddenly focused on a middle-aged man who was also watching the child from behind the fence, several feet away from him? Seeing the man, the boy half-smiled. Simon did too. He remembered seeing this same fellow outside the orphanage fence once in a while? The man had never attempted to jump over the fence or talk to him? He did *not* seem threatening in the least... only *sad*? It had seemed to him back then that this man was actually *more* unhappy than *he* was? He recalled feeling sorry for him every time he saw him?

And then just like that, for no apparent reason (*and with his body still free of bullet holes*), Simon once again found himself locked away in his tiny cell with his head in his hands? It was as if the adventure he *thought* he had just experienced had *never happened*? He expectantly raised his head moments later as he heard the sounds of footsteps walking briskly down the hallway in the direction of his cell?

Momentarily, an old man who looked to be vibrant and sharp regardless of being gray and slightly stooped, was standing outside of his cell gazing at him warmly as the police officer who had escorted him into the cellblock looked away. The old man was well-dressed and carried a legitimate air of importance. After a few moments, he told the officer, "Let me inside, please. I assure you that *this* man is no danger to anyone."

After hesitantly doing as the man had instructed, the officer warned him with obvious concern, "Wouldn't you like me to go inside the cell with you, sir? Just in case?"

The old man chuckled. "It might be a little *crowded* in there for all three of us, don't you think?" Growing more serious, he added, "No, thank you, officer. I'd like to be left alone with this man."

Politely nodding, the officer proceeded to lock the two men inside the cell. He then quickly walked down the hallway, soon disappearing out the door at the end.

"So, how are you, Simon?" the old man asked gently. "I haven't seen you in quite some time?"

Taken off-guard, Simon replied hesitantly, "I'm afraid you're making a mistake, sir. I'm not Simon Dent, I'm his brother Sheldon."

The old man gave Simon a heartfelt smile, and then said, "There's no need to *pretend* anymore, Simon. You have now *successfully completed* your third and final challenge!"

Simon was speechless! He had no idea who this man was or how he should respond to him?

The old man laughed heartily, and then explained, "Trust me. I'm on *your* side."

"Then why don't you believe I'm Sheldon Dent?" Simon asked the man curiously.

"You *can't* be!" the man replied.

"And why is that?" Simon demanded.

"Because I was there when *you* were born," the old man began to tear-up. "And you, Simon, were the *only* baby my beautiful daughter ever gave birth to."

"Your *daughter?*" Simon said in shock.

"Yes," the old man replied, "I am your grandfather, Simon. My name is Sheldon Dory. I worked in town for many years before retiring and then becoming mayor."

"Tell me then," Simon grew excited as he insisted. "What is my mother's name?"

His grandfather smiled and replied, "I'll tell you that in due time, but what I *will* tell you now is that that she was the most wonderful daughter I could have ever imagined!"

"*Was?*" Simon asked sadly.

"I'm sorry," he gently shared. "I'm afraid that she died giving birth to you, just as my wife died giving birth to her."

"That is so sad," Simon expressed softly.

"Yes, it is," his grandfather replied.

"Well, who is my father, then?" Simon blurted out passionately. He had never dared even think about these monumentally important questions before? Instead, he had despairingly accepted very early in life that he was an unloved, irrelevant orphan, destined to make his way through life *alone*! But now? His quest to grasp the answers to the questions of *who* his parents were and *why* they had left him at an orphanage burned hot inside him.

"Your father was a brave soldier that your mother fell in love with," his grandfather explained slowly, trying hard not to relive the sorrow. "He was tragically killed in battle before you were born... and *before* your mother and he had the chance to get *legally* married."

Simon felt stunned. "Then I have no *living* parents? But why didn't *you* take me in and raise me?"

"Well, Simon, I'm ashamed to admit it, but I was confused about what to do at the time, so I made a *terrible* mistake," he continued hesitantly. "You see, those were very challenging times for me back then. I had become consumed with building-up my business because with my wife and daughter both gone, it seemed like that was all I had left?" Bowing his head in shame, he continued, "The way I felt at the time, rational or not, was that in this small town, I just *couldn't* jeopardize my future by allowing the gossip that might well have bankrupted my business had I taken-in my daughter's illegitimate son!"

"Is that *all* I was to you?" Simon screamed in fury, as he found himself filled with rage that had bottled-up inside of him for most of his life suddenly rise to the surface with a vengeance! "Your daughter's *illegitimate son?*"

"Of course *not!* You must believe that I'm racked with guilt and sorry beyond belief about that now! In fact, I was sorry from the moment I made that *abhorrent* decision! But I was too cowardly to do anything about it back then? That's why I'm *here* now, Simon!" his grandfather insisted passionately. "I would give anything to change what I did to you in the past if I could?"

Simon stared at the old man cowering before him and felt terribly conflicted? He knew that the man sounded genuinely sorry for deserting him, but the abandonment still hurt. "Was it you who sent me to the Idaho Falls orphanage?"

His grandfather nodded affirmatively. "I hired a woman to bring you there with a short note I had written. On it, I asked them to name you 'Simon Scott,' as your mother had requested before her death."

"Do you recall if I was brought there in a new black baby carriage, all dressed-up in a white gown?" Simon asked? Remembering how 'baby Scott' had appeared when they'd first met.

"Yes?" his grandfather replied in surprise. "As a matter of fact, you were! But, how could you know that?"

Ignoring his question, Simon asked, "And how did I get this last name?"

His grandfather smiled slightly as he explained, "Honestly, I didn't find out how your last name became *Dent* for the longest time. But while inquiring about your records one day, the woman who had officially admitted you into the orphanage told me that they had gotten that last name from the scrap of paper the note that came with you had been written on."

"But why did you write *that* last name on the paper?" Simon asked curiously.

"I *didn't*," he smiled. "She showed me the original note, and it was written on a piece of my business stationary. The top was, of course, torn off to hide my name, but a few letters of my profession had inadvertently been left on the paper."

At last, Simon's great big brain finally put all of the clues together and *understood*! His eyes grew large as he clearly saw the answers to two *very important questions*, wondering to himself *why* this had taken him so long to unravel? And that's when he remembered the kind soldier's simple words of wisdom to him about the eclipse they had just experienced and *why* he hadn't known about it in advance? *'There are lots of very special things missed every day by folks who have simply not paid attention to them.'* "You were a *dentist*!" Simon proclaimed. "And my mother, your daughter, is named *Doris*!"

"Bravo!" the old man smiled excitedly. "On *both* counts! You are just as smart as your mother told me you were!"

"Was I named after my father?" Simon asked curiously.

"You were indeed," his grandfather replied gently. "It was very important to your mother that your father always be there in spirit through your shared name."

"What was my father's *full* name then?" Simon asked excitedly.

"Simon Scott Kirkpatrick," the old man shared with a small smile.

Simon teared up. "Do you have a picture of my mother and father together?" he asked hopefully.

"Of course," the old man shared kindly, while removing an old dog-eared picture from his wallet and gently handing it to him.

At first glance, Simon immediately recognized his mother, but he shockingly recognized his *father* as well? "I *met* this man!" he shouted excitedly. "He was on the street in Idaho Falls yesterday and was even dressed in his military uniform?" Pausing for a moment, he excitedly remembered something else. "He kept calling me, *son?* I wondered why?" Then Simon's face showed sudden shock and disbelief as he added excitedly, "If he truly *was* my father, knowing that he's been *dead* for the past 25 years, how was it even *possible* for him to talk with me yesterday?"

His grandfather smiled broadly. "I don't claim to know much about life or the afterlife, Simon. But I've recently learned," he winked, "that it's a complete waste of time and a disservice to those spirits who may be trying to help you, to question miracles," he said gently. "It's much better to just gratefully *accept them* and move on."

"Even when they seem impossible?" Simon asked.

"*Especially* then," his grandfather gently replied.

Simon smiled. "Thanks for letting me see this picture," he said as he tried to return it.

His grandfather decidedly waved him off, saying, "No, you keep it. I should have given it to you a long time ago."

"Why did you come to this police station when you did?" Simon asked curiously. "How could you have possibly known that I would be here? And in *disguise?*"

His grandfather grew thoughtful. "You probably won't believe what I am about to tell you?"

Simon smiled. "You'd be *surprised* by what I am capable of believing these days!"

His grandfather returned his smile. "Well, a few nights ago, I was feeling very depressed," he began.

61

"Why?" Simon asked.

"Because my despicable memories of myself deserting you as a baby were hitting me especially hard that night," his grandfather admitted. "I also hated myself because when you moved back to Grangeville two years ago, I *didn't* take that golden opportunity to introduce myself or even send you an anonymous note welcoming you to town? By then, I had grown into such a coward. I honestly didn't feel *worthy* of living anymore?" Growing more nervous, he admitted, "For the first time in my life, I seriously considered ending it all!"

"But you *didn't?*" Simon said curiously. "What changed your mind?"

"This is the really *strange* part," his grandfather admitted. "I know that I wasn't asleep, so I couldn't have been dreaming? But out of nowhere, my daughter Doris, who has also been dead for 25 years, was suddenly alive again, right there beside me, looking very concerned? She was telling me about *you* and how she was worried that you were missing out on so much of life. She asked if I would help her to change your life's trajectory."

"And you agreed?" Simon asked.

"Of course, *I did!*" his grandfather exclaimed. "It was the opportunity I had always hoped for, that would give me the chance to gain a little redemption after my unforgivable behavior towards you! Then, she told me that my code name in this charade was to be..."

"*Life?*" Simon finished his sentence.

His grandfather gently smiled. "Yes. I guess you know *everything.*"

"I'm beginning to," Simon admitted. "So, I was *never* going to have my life canceled?"

His grandfather laughed. "Of course not! Although I know that your mother went to some pretty great lengths to make you *believe* that you were!" Growing more thoughtful, he added, "It was *me*, as you know, who was seriously contemplating canceling myself, not you? So, I believe my daughter concocted that zany plan of hers to save the *both* of us!"

"Did you ever come to see me at the orphanage?" Simon asked slyly, recalling his recent hallucination and distant memories.

"I did," his grandfather admitted with his eyes twinkling. "I kept tabs on you on the last Saturday of every month by flying out of Grangeville on a private plane to Idaho Falls, and arriving at the orphanage before your late afternoon playtime. That's when I watched you come outside with the other children and I made sure that everything seemed okay with you."

"You came all that way every month just to see *me?*" Simon exclaimed.

"Of course! I would have come *any distance* to see you," his grandfather admitted. "I'm only sorry that my professional responsibilities kept me from seeing you more often!"

"How did you know which child was me?" Simon asked curiously. "There were a lot of boys at that orphanage?"

"Honestly? You looked a lot like your mother as a child, and there weren't many other blonde kids there either."

"I wasn't the happiest child then, was I," Simon added.

"No, you weren't. And it almost broke my heart," his grandfather shared. "That's why I set-you-up at a well-respected boarding school in Boston, just as soon as you were old enough to attend."

"So, it was *you* who paid for my boarding school?" Simon asked in shock. "I always wondered about that? What about my college expenses?" Simon suddenly insisted. "I was told that I had received a scholarship to Harvard? Is that *not* true?"

"Oh yes, that's true, alright," his grandfather assured him. "And you *deserved* it! But that only covered part of your expenses. I chipped in for the rest."

Simon gratefully hugged his grandfather.

"Why do you suppose I was *irrationally* drawn to Grangeville two years ago after graduating from Harvard?" Simon asked. "I definitely had *no memory* of ever living here before?"

His grandfather laughed. "I can't say for sure, but that certainly sounds like the work of *your mother!* Even then, she was probably concocting a plan to bring the two of us together!"

Simon smiled and asked, "Did Doris, I mean Mom always enjoy making-up games for other people to play with her, like this one?"

His grandfather laughed. "She certainly did! She *always* had quite the imagination and insisted that whatever she'd concocted, I *had* to play with her! *This time* included!" Pausing a moment and smiling thoughtfully at Simon, he added, "But I believe that what she created here with her heart as well as her imagination, incredibly resulting in finally bringing the two of us back together again, was *by far* her best work!"

The New Normal

Simon was now back in his apartment, sitting around his small oak table with Scott and Doris. Although *Life*, rather his grandpa, had pretty much explained every facet of this fantastic adventure to him, Doris had asked that the three of them meet one last time as soon as Simon had been released (*without being charged*) from the police station. This happily occurred right after he admitted to the police that he was indeed *Simon Dent*. He told them (*through their shocked faces*) that he was only *pretending* to be Sheldon as part of a secret scientific experiment he was conducting about peoples' initial reactions toward vagrants. The mayor, his grandfather, backed him up, and that was that! Once outside the police station when he was alone, Doris had been kind enough to appear and transform Simon back to his normal *non-hobo* appearance, which he greatly appreciated!

"Well, Simon? How do you feel?" Doris asked him gently.

"Shocked, surprised, and *very appreciative*," Simon shared honestly. "You know, even if you hadn't turned out to be my mother, I would still be eternally grateful to you for all you have done for me."

Doris blushed (*if spirits can actually do that*) and returned his smile. "Well, Simon, after that terrifying ordeal I put you through, I'm afraid that I'm leaving you now with your entire future to maneuver by yourself."

"I know," Simon agreed. "But the way I'm feeling right now, I'm sure I can handle *anything* that comes my way!"

Doris smiled. "You can't imagine how happy I am to hear that!" Then she asked thoughtfully, "Do you have any questions for me before I go?"

"I do!" Scott piped-up.

"Okay. What is it, Scott?" Doris asked curiously.

"Well... Did Simon's challenges actually *mean* anything?"

Doris smiled. "Of course, they did! They actually *meant* quite a lot."

"But *nothing* to do with losing my existence, right?" Simon asked playfully.

Doris chuckled. "Not as far as your ability to *keep being* Simon Dent, certainly. Your challenges were there to teach you to be braver and happier by not being afraid." Looking more serious, she added, "I think you learned from that first challenge that even doing what feels like the *right* thing can still sometimes bring *unpleasant consequences*." she explained simply. "And I'm sure you found that *running away* from each difficulty you encountered in your second challenge robbed you of ever discovering the *real* outcome of each of those situations. And unfortunately, *that* in no way brought you growth, satisfaction or wisdom. Remember, Simon. A bad situation always has the potential to surprise you and actually turn out well in the end if you are brave enough to see it through!" She paused for a moment, smiled warmly at Simon and then shared, "But the most important thing I think you learned through these challenges was how to handle the *largely irrational fears* your imagination readily creates for you when you face *any* obstacle. The *fear* of something going wrong has overpoweringly prevented you from moving forward over the past 25 years, wouldn't you agree?"

Simon smiled. "I do! But now I believe I can begin facing each problem I encounter in life *regardless* of my fear and then solve it as best I can!"

"Bravo! No one can be expected to do more than that!" Doris assured him.

Suddenly, Simon had a thought. "Hey, Mom! Were you that weird girl who saved me from getting beaten-up in the subway station? She said, 'Oh, *I know lots of things*,' in answer to one of my questions, which is *exactly* how *you* answered my question a couple of days ago?"

Doris smiled broadly. "It was *that* obvious, huh? Well, I *may* have been that girl. But if I was, saving you was a perfectly normal reaction from a doting mother who couldn't bear to see her son get beaten-up a *second time!*"

Simon chuckled.

"Okay, Simon," Doris announced as she looked lovingly at her son. This is your *last* chance before I send Scott home to your past and return myself to the spirit world. Do you have a *final* question for me?" Doris asked.

Simon paused for a moment and then very simply asked, "Is Scott real?"

"Of course, *I'm real!*" Scott retorted, obviously offended as any ten-year-old boy would be. "What kind of question is that?"

Simon laughed at his reaction. "Sorry, Scott! What I *meant* to ask was, is there any way that Scott can go on living *apart* from me... as his *own* person?"

"Hey! I told you *that* in confidence!" Scott angrily reacted to Simon's apparent betrayal of his trust.

"But isn't that what you really want? You'll probably *never* get another chance to ask for it?" Simon explained calmly.

Scott nervously wrung his hands together before finally admitting, "Well, *yes.*"

Doris looked very apologetic as she explained, "I'm sorry, Scott, but I'm *not* God. I'm only a spirit, and I don't think I have the power to make you a person separate from Simon? The fact is, you *are* Simon! At least a part of him."

A noticeably deflated Scott nodded disappointedly.

And then Simon had an epiphany. "But what if that's *not* entirely true anymore?" he insisted passionately. "I first met Scott when he was a baby, *before* I had my dismal childhood, and although he was pretty *irritating,*" he smiled at him, "he still acted pretty normal. Then you instantly made him ten years old, allowing him to bypass a lot of terrible years for me, and he seemed so different from me at that age? Unlike me, he has a quick wit and sense of humor that joyously *defines him?* Over these past three days I've learned so much about the person I *should have been* by watching how Scott thinks and acts. He's not all screwed-up like I was at that age! I have to say, he *doesn't* seem like a part of me at all? He seems like a completely *different* person, a *better* person, a role model, a wonderful *brother* in fact! Isn't it possible for him to just continue being that? He *deserves* the chance and frankly, I *need* him! He's my best friend! *Please?"*

Doris smiled warmly at Simon. It appeared that she was about to cry, but since she hadn't cried previously in front of Simon, the jury was still out on whether or not that was even possible for a spirit to do? "I'm so proud of you, Simon!"

"For what?" he asked in surprise.

Gently taking his hands in hers, Doris proudly shared, "For learning to be empathetic toward others again. Your unfortunate childhood experiences *ripped* that virtue away from you for many years. But the love of life and caring for others which you so obviously value in Scott so much, has now made its way back to you at last!" She paused and smiled. "Now, the problem of how we can make Scott *real?"* she creased her brow in deep thought. "I am completely convinced that you are *right* about that, Simon!"

Scott looked so hopeful now that his eyes nearly popped out of his head!

Simon suddenly looked inspired! "How did you make him a *temporary* boy in the first place?" he asked Doris.

"I don't really know? I just did it?" she replied with uncertainty. "But I do know that it won't last forever."

"How long then?" Scott asked intently.

"Again, I don't know for sure?" Doris replied truthfully. "*Nobody* does!"

"Will I keep growing older as long as I stay in this body?" Scott asked hopefully.

"Yes," Doris assured him. "You are *mortal* now, and that makes you susceptible to illness and accidents for as long as you live."

"Do you mean to say that I could *die* at any moment?" Scott asked with excitement.

"Under the worst circumstances, *yes*," Doris answered, a bit bewildered by his positive reaction to death? "And you *might* suffer some very difficult physical and emotional experiences throughout your lifetime, as Simon has. Are you certain that you want to be your *own* person? Responsible for making most of your *own* decisions each day, that probably *won't* all turn-out the way you'd like them to?"

"*Yes!*" Scott exclaimed. "For every decision I've already made and every experience I've already had so far, I *felt* and *learned* something! It's simply wonderful!" He paused and then gently added, "And if I sometimes make the wrong decision, that could create a bad experience for me..."

"Like taking that long *bus* ride with only one book to read?" Simon quipped.

"Exactly!" Scott smiled. "I think, what better way is there for me to learn what the *right decision* would have been, than by going through the agony of making the *wrong* one first!"

Doris chuckled. "That's a very healthy attitude, Scott."

"Hey! If I die, Simon won't die too will he?" Scott suddenly asked with great concern.

"No, Scott. I believe, just as Simon has said, that you are *not* him anymore, only *related* to him," Doris explained.

"Then putting aside your *very weird growth spurt* from baby to ten-year-old in a matter of *seconds*... I believe what Doris is saying is that you are *already your own person*, Scott, and have been for a few days." Simon declared.

Doris smiled and added, "Exactly!"

"Hurray! I'm a *real boy!*" Scott cheered. "The first thing I'm going to do is grow out this *stupid crewcut!*"

Simon feigned terrible offense, but then admitted, "You know, Scott? I think I'll do that too!"

Once Scott had completed his celebration, Simon told him sincerely, "I would really like it if you continued living with me for as long as you wanted to. I mean, as my younger brother. What do you say?"

"I *wouldn't* have it any other way!" Scott got up from the table, walked over to a now standing Simon and hugged him.

Doris also got up and moved toward them. "May I have a farewell hug from my two boys?" she asked warmly.

"Of course," Scott smiled.

"Are we going to ever see you again?" Simon asked her hopefully. "You've *saved* my life, Mom, and I can never hope to repay you!"

"Well, there is *one* thing you could do for me," Doris shared mysteriously.

"*Name it!*" Simon proclaimed excitedly.

"I would really like you to consider sometimes *leaving* this apartment, making some friends and perhaps even going into work? Would you at least try to do those things?" Doris pleaded.

"*Done!*" Simon assured her. "As a matter of fact, I already came to those very same conclusions myself."

"Alright! You getting out of this apartment and going to work are both great ways for you to *meet babes*, big bro!" Scott added excitedly.

Both Simon and Doris laughed.

"Well," Doris beamed. "I look forward to coming by from time to time and checking on the progress of my two boys, even if it's only in your dreams. Oh, and thanks, boys, for giving your grandpa a good reason to keep on living! Now I won't worry so much about him." A thought suddenly came to her, as she added, "By the way, Simon. Would you like to take your father's or my last names? Kirkpatrick or Dory? You might prefer one of those over Dent?"

"Thanks Mom, but *Dent* is who I am now and who I always remember being. I believe I'll keep it."

Doris smiled, and said, "I completely understand. Oh, and I almost forgot! Be aware that since we changed your reality by creating Scott, it should come as no surprise to you when you see a *few* other changes in your lives that have been created to compensate, including a second bedroom in this apartment for Scott. But, don't worry. Just a short time after I leave, both of you and everyone else in your lives will all have *different* memories and believe that these changes have always been part of who you are. *Nothing* will feel abnormal to anyone!"

"Is my room there *now?*" Scott asked, filled with excitement.

"Yes, Scott. And as a farewell present from your mother, I have a new bicycle for you sitting outside the front door."

Scott was thrilled! But before he or Simon could ask her any further questions... she was *gone?*

"But I wanted to ask her how all that she had done for me was even possible?" Scott admitted disappointedly.

"Don't give it a second thought," Simon replied kindly. "Our grandfather told me that questioning miracles is a great big waste of time. It's better to just gratefully accept them and move on with your life." Smiling, he added, "I have come to believe that too."

"Then so I do," Scott nodded.

Suddenly Simon's cell phone rang? In surprise, he quickly grabbed it from his pocket and answered. "Hello?"

He grew an uncanny look of combined amazement and happiness on his face as he conversed with the caller. After a short time, he slowly turned off the phone and returned it to his pocket.

"Who was *that?*" Scott asked curiously.

"It was my *father?*" he said, before correcting himself by saying, "I mean *our* father? He wanted to make sure that I'd found you in Idaho Falls after the eclipse?"

Not missing a beat, there was a firm knock at the front door just as soon as Simon had stopped talking? The two brothers looked at each other curiously, before Simon finally went to answer it.

When he opened the door, Alice, dressed in a beautiful black and white dress was there smiling. After gently kissing Simon on the lips, she entered the apartment. "I can't believe that you and Scott aren't dressed yet?" she said in mock-scolding.

"Dressed for what?" Scott asked, completely in the dark?

"For Simon's birthday party at Grandpa's, of course!" she laughingly smiled at Scott.

Simon grew excited as he prepared to be honored with his *first official birthday party ever!* And then he chanced to glance at Alice's left hand, and in pure amazement he noticed that she was wearing

70

an engagement ring? *His engagement ring,* and it was radiantly glowing on her finger? This of course, made absolutely no sense to the great big brain of Simon Dent, but once again remembering what his grandfather had told him about miracles, he smiled. If this was to be the beginning of his new normal, he had absolutely *no complaints*!

My Alien Summer

A full year has passed, so I think it's finally time I talked about a really *mind-blowing* experience I had last summer that I'll bet you'll probably have trouble believing? I know *I would*! And even though it seemed incredibly scary at the time, in the end, I can honestly say that something wonderful came out of it. This adventure took place on the exact day I completed my first year of junior college back in 1981. To introduce myself, my friends call me Kip, but my full name is Kipper Archibald Weiss. I'm ginger haired, freckle-faced, thin and very light complected, standing all of 5 feet 8 inches tall. Disappointingly, I'm 99% sure that I'll *never* be the next Albert Einstein, because as my first year of college so clearly demonstrated to me, the *only* subject I am really good at is creative writing. I lived and attended junior college in Great Falls, Montana, a thriving city of almost 60,000 people. It was on the day, following my last college final of the spring semester, that I was *abducted by an alien*! That's right! I was sucked-up into its shiny silver spaceship while beginning to take a catnap outside my house on our porch-swing?

Once I found myself inside that spaceship and had gotten past the shock and improbability of this ever happening to me in the first place, I felt very surprised to find myself completely alone? To describe my surroundings, the interior of this spaceship probably looked a lot like the inside of a gigantic tin can, creating the largest circular room I had ever been in! It featured a very tall ceiling, but surprisingly, there was absolutely *nothing* in the room? However, in the next moment I was shocked to suddenly discover that for no apparent reason, that vacant room miraculously turned into a completely furnished bedroom. *My bedroom?* It had a bed, a chest of drawers, a large mirror sitting atop it and even a photo album at the foot of the bed; one with actual pictures of my childhood? Next, everything disappeared and the room was magically transformed into my kitchen and dining room? And then all of that disappeared and morphed into my living room? And finally, my bathroom and shower? *What was happening?* And then just like that, it once again returned to looking like the inside of a gigantic empty can of Campbell's soup?

As I stood there in the heart of this strange silver spaceship, pondering my next move, suddenly a small, thin, completely bald-headed green alien with two antennas and a humanish face, dressed in pale purple robes, appeared in front of me from *nowhere?* It was really strange?

"Greetings, Earthling!" the creature proclaimed telepathically in a deep male voice, without moving its lips.

"Greetings," I replied hesitantly, realizing that I had seen this type of alien with a telepathic speaking ability on reruns of old science-fiction television shows from the 1960s. "Am I imagining you?"

"Only my *appearance*," it said telepathically with an equally telepathic smile. "I borrowed this image from your memory, just as I previously borrowed the images of your dwelling."

"Wow!" I found myself yelling in approval, not feeling the least bit frightened. "That certainly is impressive! But *why* did you bring me here?"

Without smiling, the creature telepathed, "I need your help in finding the location of my missing daughter."

"So, you think she's lost somewhere around *here?*" I asked curiously.

At this point the alien with the deep voice became telepathically sad. "Yes," it telepathed slowly. "But more specifically, somewhere *inside your house.*"

The house he was referring to was actually my *parents'* house, which I was currently living in alone. They were off traveling, enjoying the first week of a romantic monthlong vacation in Europe for the very first time in their lives! They had been excitedly talking about it for years! Anyway, this was also the same simple tract home that I had spent the entirety of my life growing up in. The idea of the alien's daughter suddenly becoming lost in *this* humble abode seemed highly unlikely to me? Although I loved my house, I must admit that it looked a lot like something you'd see in a very *B movie*, because the producers couldn't afford to rent a *better one*! But still...

"Why do you believe your daughter is lost somewhere in *my* house?" I asked him frankly.

"Because I can sense her *essence* inside," it telepathed simply.

"Well, what does she look like?" I asked next.

"Unfortunately, I couldn't say?" the alien telepathed. "You see, she has the same ability that I have to change her form at will."

"Hmm? Well, okay," I said. "But if you are so sure that she is inside my house, why don't you just go inside it and take a good look for yourself? I don't mind," I offered logically. "Surely you can do that?"

"I could *try*, but I believe my essence is far too vast to fit inside your tiny, little dwelling," he telepathed without emotion. "My attempt might very well result in *destroying* it!"

"*Her* essence, *your* essence? *What* are you talking about?" I was driven to ask with obvious frustration.

The alien made an odd shrieking sound that under the circumstances, I believed was probably a laugh. "Your essence is simply *everything* that makes you uniquely who you are," he explained telepathically.

"I know *that*," I said, "but are you suggesting that a person's essence is something that can be *seen*?" I asked incredulously.

"The alien shrieked once again. "Well, I *can't* really see it, but I do *sense* the essence of all living creatures," the alien telepathed.

"And you are afraid to enter my house because you have *too much essence*?" I began. "How exactly does that work?"

"My essence is different from yours," the alien telepathed. "Because I can take *any* form while actually possessing *no* permanent body of my own, the experiences that make-up my essence, invisibly grow around me and *can* react negatively to small closed spaces." Pausing, he added, "And I have had so much life experience that I *don't* want to find out how destructive the size of it might be to your teeny-tiny Earth structure!"

"What did you mean by *'reacting negatively to small, closed spaces?'*" I asked curiously.

"Soon after entering your house, it *could* suddenly appear to you and to anyone else watching it, that a powerful *bomb* had suddenly gone off on the lot where your house had *once stood!*" the alien telepathed warningly.

"Yikes!" I reacted. "Does the essence of *all* living creatures grow?"

"Oh yes! With most creatures, although you humans can't sense it, their essence grows a tiny bit larger every day. The more they live their lives and learn, the larger their essence becomes," the alien gently telepathed. "But human essence *doesn't* take on a physical shape as mine does. Yours is completely *mental.*"

"That's so interesting," I said as I took-in his words. It made me think of my Grandpa Roy, who had always been like a best friend to me. Although he seemed to be a small, pleasant and unassuming old man, he had traveled the world *twice*, and every time he came to visit us, our house became *filled* with his vibrant personality and wonderful stories. In short, his *essence!* "But, how do I even begin looking for her when I have absolutely *no idea* what she looks like?" I asked incredulously.

The alien paused a moment and then telepathed, "Do you regularly keep girls in your dwelling?"

"No!" I replied in surprise with a little embarrassment.

"Good! Then my daughter will be the *only girl* you will find there," the alien telepathed.

I gently rolled my eyes, not appreciating how *that* information could be of much help to me? "What I *meant* to ask you was, what's the *best* way for me to start looking for her?"

"You *can't* look for her," the alien telepathed. "*You* won't be able to see her at all unless she *wants* you to. So, first you need to gain her trust. As you roam throughout your little dwelling, speak her name intermittently in a friendly manner and remind her that her loving father misses her greatly." The alien telepathed this message

76

to me so sweetly that it almost brought tears to my eyes. "But if you fail to find her, I will make you wish you had *never been born!*" he shockingly telepathed me in what could only be interpreted as a *very threatening manner!*

"*What?*" I screamed.

Then the alien shrieked once again without changing his lack of expression. "I was only joking," he telepathed calmly. "Will you help me, Kip?"

"How do you know my name?" I asked him very suspiciously.

"I found it inside your mind, of course," the alien telepathed matter-of-factly. "So, will you help me?"

Would I help him? Hmm? "Okay," I replied slowly. "But first I've got to know that your intentions are completely *honorable.*"

At this, the alien suddenly changed his expression by enlarging his eyes and smiling without teeth (*an expression he apparently believed denoted honesty on Earth*) while angling his head first left and then right. "I would greatly appreciate it if the *moment* you found her, you contacted me," he telepathed seriously, handing me a ruby ring. "Now, don't forget to put this ring on your finger the moment you wish to transmit to me."

"Okay. But how will I hear *you?*" I asked.

"Naturally, you will hear my voice inside your head," the alien telepathed, "just as you do now."

I nodded. "But, how should I address you? What is your *name?*" I asked curiously.

"You may call me by my adopted Earth name, 'Areyoufeelingluckypunk,'" he telepathed proudly.

"And your daughter's name?" I asked, holding my breath.

"She has adopted the Earth name, '*Shakenbutnotstirred,*'" he telepathed.

"How did the two of you arrive at such *unusual name choices?*" I asked curiously.

"Both of them came to us through a novel Earth invention you call *television,*" he telepathed.

And with that, the alien attempted to share his honest smile with me one last time, only moments before I was gently returned to the porch-swing just outside of my house.

Now, I don't know about you, but that experience was enough to convince me that *UFOs are real!* That being said, I was very worried about *how* I might logically be able to find the alien's shape-shifting daughter? But, I knew that I mustn't worry about that now. A much more pressing question would be *why* she would allow me to find her? I could already see that my odds of tracking her down were embarrassingly *stacked against me*, and although the alien had said that his threat was a *joke*, I just didn't buy it! My fear of what he might do to me if I *didn't* find his daughter, strongly compelled me to give it a good *junior college try!*

The first thing I did after entering my house was to methodically search every room for any sign of the alien girl in *any* form imaginable or I suppose *unimaginable?* Pleasantly calling out her name, '*Shakenbutnotstirred*,' as her father had suggested, my concentration was on overdrive to be as charming and positive as possible. I fully expected to get some type of a response from her as a result, but once I had completed the search of my entire house, disappointingly, I had *not* received a single sign that she was even here? So, I decided to temporarily push this *failed job* aside for a few minutes while I recharged my battery, so to speak. I looked so forward to relaxing and finally congratulating myself on successfully finishing my second semester of junior college! As I comfortably sat on the couch in the living room with my feet up on the coffee table and my eyes closed, I began to seriously consider that what I had experienced outside *may* have merely been a simple hallucination? A really *good one*, but still about as real as my chances of *ever* being accepted into a top university! I believed that this hallucination theory really held-up too! That was because I had often been told by my teachers during *every grade level* I had attended in school so far, that although I was very creative (*and that was a good thing*), unfortunately it often caused me to daydream and lose my concentration in class, and *that* was a *very bad thing!* Sounds to me like some pretty compelling evidence that I'm not only a hopeless *daydreamer*, but also easily susceptible to *hallucinations*! In addition to that, I also began questioning why super-smart aliens would *name themselves* after old movie characters from 'Dirty Harry' and 'James Bond?' So, there you go! After all of that quasi-intelligent pondering, I suddenly felt tired, and it wasn't long before I drifted off to sleep.

As I came-to, I immediately found myself in the middle of a very *sexy* dream starring an ultra-hot looking babe, *smoking hot* in fact, who was surprisingly right there *in bed with me?* As I looked around, I noticed that we were in a psychedelic-colored room of blacks, reds and purples, complete with flashing strobe lights. Very oddly though, I also noticed that the music blaring through the room to accompany those strobe lights was not the *psychedelic rock music* of the middle to late 1960s or early 1970s that their presence suggested? What I heard instead was a very banal, often out of tune chorus of voices that didn't seem to know the first thing about singing? They were accompanied by some sort of irritatingly shrill instrumentation which I could not come close to recognizing, and together they presented a nonstop medley of *irritating jingles* from a myriad of different television commercials that thanks to the lyrics, I was able to recall hearing over the past ten years or so on TV? Honestly? The *cacophony* of bad singing and even *worse* instrumentation made this so-called 'musical performance,' sound absolutely *dreadful and absurd?* In addition, I knew that this was only a dream because the closest I've ever come to finding myself in bed with a girl in *real life* was when the girl next door (*named Hannah*) and I took a nap side-by-side during our kindergarten 'nap time,' 14 years ago! Getting back to this dream, the hot girl and I were making-out something fierce and it also appeared that for no particular reason... we were both *completely naked?* Suddenly this blonde bombshell, who reminded me of young movie star Hayley Mills (*only older*), who I had adored watching in films from the 1960s, stopped kissing me, and unemotionally said with a smile, "Hi?"

"Hi," I replied awkwardly. And then, suddenly remembering what had happened to me earlier in the day, just in case that alien father *had* been real, I asked politely, "Is your Earth name, *Shakenbutnotstirred?*"

I couldn't immediately tell if her facial expression suddenly flashed terror, anger, irritation or a combination of the three? It all happened so fast? But a moment later, I woke-up fully dressed and *alone?* I quickly got up from the couch, understandably dazed, and walked down the short hallway to my bedroom, where I had a long history of thinking about important questions *without* ever producing one single answer? The difficulty, you see, was that my bed was so darn comfortable, every time I contemplated answers to a question, I always *fell asleep* long before I'd gotten even halfway through the *pondering!*

When I reached my room, I plopped myself down on the bed and laid on my back with my eyes tightly shut. Suddenly I felt another warm body surprisingly snuggling-up very close to me? It wasn't a scary feeling, but as you can probably imagine, it was certainly an *odd one?*

"Keep your eyes closed," a sexy female voice insisted. "Opening them will *break* our connection."

I did as she told me and as I turned to look at her with my eyes fully shut, in my mind's eye I saw that same beautiful blonde girl I had just seen in my dream, except that this time she was dressed in a pair of fashionable blue jeans and a tight tee shirt? *Very tight!* "Are you the one your father calls *Shakenbutnotstirred?*" I asked in a friendly manner, not wishing to scare her off a second time.

"I *am*," she admitted.

"Well, what are you doing here on Earth?" I asked her curiously.

"I thought I had gotten away from my father when I secretly left our planet and came to this one, but he obviously followed me here!" she shared anxiously. "That's why I reacted so strangely to you a few minutes ago. I thought you might be working with him?"

I grew a little nervous because *technically*, she was right! I didn't let on however. "That's understandable," I said. "But why did you have to escape from your father in the first place?"

The girl paused for a moment to pull herself together before replying, "Because he is a very *mean and stubborn man!* When I became an adult some months ago, he still refused to take me along with him on his journeys to explore other planets, as he has a habit of doing by himself every year at this time. So, I decided to take matters into my own hands and do it *myself*!" she shared triumphantly. "I thought I would start with Earth!"

It wasn't the most supportive reaction to her story, I know, but I *laughed*. "How old *are* you?"

"I am equivalent to 18 of your Earth years old," she replied, sounding a bit taken aback. "Why did you laugh at me, Kip?"

"I meant no disrespect, but on Earth, we call your strong feelings of being treated unfairly by a parent, *rebelling against authority*! It's pretty much a rite of passage for every kid on Earth when they reach legal age, believe me!" I explained.

Suddenly her manner abruptly changed. As a result, her voice grew noticeably darker and more ominous. "Perhaps I had better tell you the *real* reason I had to get away from my father?"

"Okay?" I said slowly. "What was that?"

"My father was *forcing* me to marry a male-being against my will!" she began.

"Did you already know this male-being?" I asked her.

"Yes," she replied.

"Did you like him?" I asked.

"Oh yes!" she smiled.

"What is this male-being's name?" I continued.

"He doesn't really have an *Earth* name," she admitted. "But if he did, a good name for him might be *I'mmadashellandI'mnotgoing-totakethisanymore*!"

"Does he have a *bad temper* then?" I asked cautiously.

"Oh yes!" she confirmed passionately. "But that doesn't bother me nearly as much as his complete lack of adventure! I'm afraid that I would grow *so bored* spending my long existence with *him*!" She paused before narrowing her eyes and intensely whispering, "But he is part of a very wealthy family and with my father being so *greedy* and all, he was literally making me marry him for the impressive *dowry* that he was promised, discounting his own daughter's wishes completely!"

"Wow!" I exclaimed. "But isn't it normally the *husband's* family that receives the dowry?"

"Well, yes... but on my planet, I am *quite the catch!*" she explained with a mischievous smile. Then abruptly changing her expression to one of extreme angst, she pleaded, "But I am *not* ready to settle down yet, Kip? As you would say on Earth, I still have many *wild oats* to sow!"

"Now listen, *Shakenbutnotstirred*," I said anxiously. "I *do* feel for you, I really do! But I don't want to get myself caught-up in the middle of some intergalactic family squabble, *especially* when your male-being sounds like he's the *very jealous* type!"

"Oh, he *is!*" she responded cattily. "If he ever got hold of you, especially after I told him how much I liked you, I'm afraid that *Kip Weiss* would find himself completely *disintegrated* into billions of tiny, little specks of dust scattered all over the universe!"

"Okay, *that is not funny!*" I exclaimed, like I was correcting a petulant child. "Now listen, young lady! I *did* speak with your father and he asked me to place this ruby ring on my finger to let him know the moment I found you," I said sternly, as I pulled the ring out of my pocket to show her. "Give me one good reason why I shouldn't do that *right now?*"

"Because putting on that ring will bind you to him *forever!* You will become his eternal slave!" she whispered animatedly. "And you will be forced to leave this planet, *never to return!*"

Shocked by her words, causing me to inadvertently shake in fear, I anxiously asked, "Well, what should I do then?"

"Leave it to me," she proclaimed with a confident smile. "Give me the ring now and I will dispose of it properly. Then, when he beams you up to his spaceship again, you can just tell him that you lost it and have absolutely *not* seen me!"

"Will he accept those answers?" I asked urgently.

"*Of course not!* Do you think he's *stupid?*" Shakenbutnotstirred laughed. "He will go through every inch of your memory and find out right away that you are *lying* to him!" Suddenly looking extremely dire, she whispered fearfully, "He absolutely *hates* liars!"

"Would he *kill* me then?" I fearfully asked her.

"No! He wouldn't *kill* you... exactly," she smiled coyly. "I imagine he would probably punish you in an *Earth television show* sort of way."

"What do you mean by *that?*" I asked urgently.

"I couldn't say for sure what he would do, but I imagine it would be something he has seen on television before, like leaving you alone in a forest full of wild animals who hadn't eaten in days, and then seeing how long it took for them to *devour you!*"

"That's pretty *severe!*" I said with a frown.

"It is?" she acted surprised. "Okay then, perhaps you would prefer a scenario of swimming in a beautiful lake... full of *giant piranhas* and *sharks?*"

I was now *terrified*, and immediately stuffed the ring back inside my pocket.

"I'll see you later!" she laughed playfully, before evaporating into nothingness.

I opened my eyes and immediately sat up on the edge of my bed, shaking uncontrollably. Was she telling me the truth? Although I must admit that the girl's trustworthiness was *greatly in question*, I didn't dare defy her warnings by slipping that ring on my finger or lying to him about losing it, for fear that *Shakenbutnotstirred* had *actually* told me the truth about the terrible consequences that would befall me? Remember all of the trouble Frodo had in 'Lord of the Rings,' once he slipped the ring on his finger? Face it. I was *completely screwed!*

Suddenly, I heard a firm knock at my front door? I involuntarily *gasped*, as it initially caught me off-guard. But quickly recovering, I got up from the bed and rushed off to answer it.

"Hi, Kip!" Hannah, my kindergarten 'nap buddy' from next door announced cheerfully as she gave me a quick hug and then waltzed over to the couch. Hannah was a cute brunette who stood about five foot nine (*an inch taller than I was*) and possessed a pair of very expressive eyes that were a beautiful shade of light blue. Her dark hair hung pleasingly past her shoulders in the back and framed her well-endowed chest in the front. Not that I paid a great deal of attention to that *well-endowed chest*! I always had other things to think about... like her *perfect face*! In addition, she had been anointed the *smartest* student in math and science classes at our high school last year due to her exceptionally high national test-scores! This pretty much *confirmed* just how beautiful and brilliant she really was! I was told by one of my friends that they heard if she didn't become a model first, Hannah planned on becoming a rocket scientist or some other *brainiac* occupation right after she graduated from college! The *only* problem was that her rather large family was always very tight financially, so she had to *earn* the money for almost everything she got, which unfortunately included *college tuition*! But she never complained, and last summer she had surprisingly raised enough money from her tutoring jobs to buy her very first car! Like mine, it was an old one, but she didn't care. It was a dependable Ford truck and it got her around. "How was your last day of finals?" she asked me excitedly.

"Oh, it was a breeze," I assured her, as I plopped down on the couch beside her. "I may not have aced them all, but I'm absolutely sure that I *passed* them. How was *your* last day?"

"Well," she began mysteriously, but then exclaimed, "It was *great* and believe it or not, today was actually my *last day forever* going to Great Falls Junior College!"

"What? Why?" I asked in surprise.

"Because I was accepted with a *full-ride scholarship* to Montana State University in Billings, beginning in the fall term!" she shouted. "I got the letter today and just came over to share the good news with you!"

"Well, congratulations!" I used all of the energy I could muster as we hugged. "I've heard *that* school is pretty hard to get into?"

"Not *that* hard," she replied triumphantly. Then softening her tone, she added with a touch of disappointment, "You'll be going back to junior college next year, right?"

"Right. I like it there. It's so close to home and all," I replied honestly.

"Well, Kip, there are a lot more important things to consider when choosing a college than the fact that it's *close to home*, she offered with what sounded like simple advice cleverly disguising an *important message*? I, of course, couldn't immediately decipher what *that message* was? "Why don't *you* apply to Billings?" she suggested with fervor. "You're a smart kid and a great writer, Kip! I'm sure they'd love to accept you? It would be so much fun going to school there together, don't you think?"

There it was! "I missed the deadline for applying, didn't I?" I asked her matter-of-factly.

"My counselor told me a couple of weeks ago that the school had decided to *increase* their enrollment for next year's allotment of transfer students. She said that they should still be adding them through July?" she replied hopefully. "How about it, Kip?"

"I'll think about it," I smiled, and then I decided for some unknown reason to take Hannah into my confidence. "You know, Hannah? Believe it or not, I've been visited by *aliens* from outer space today!" I whispered intently. "Right after I got home from school!"

"*Aliens?*" she repeated facetiously. "You mean like little *green* men?"

"*Purple!*" I replied. "Although only one of them looked like that. The other one looked more like Hayley Mills! What should I do?"

"*Hayley Mills?*" Hannah repeated in astonishment, while looking at me in sincere confusion? But then her tone quickly changed, as she obviously decided to appear encouraging. "It sounds to me like you've got the beginning of an *excellent* science fiction story there!" she exclaimed. Then with no expression whatsoever, she added, "Just as long as you *lose Hayley Mills!*" And then with a very *sincere* smile, she gently pleaded, "*Don't wait* too long to apply to university though, Kip! Going there together would really mean a lot to me!" With that, she rose from the couch and headed toward the front door.

"Okay! Just let me think about it for a couple days!" I replied as I too got up from the couch, waved goodbye and slowly closed the door behind her. Well, I guess she *hadn't* believed my alien story after all. *That* was disappointing! After returning to the couch and sitting down, a very strange question suddenly popped into my head? Hannah and I had always been good friends and neighbors, but she had never once talked to me about going to university together? *Why now?* Even in kindergarten, I remember having a tiny little crush on her (*which I have admittedly never lost*), yet she had *never* appeared to reciprocate my feelings in any way? She had briefly dated a handful of guys in high school (*none of which was me*), but for some reason, she never really had a steady boyfriend? I also dated a bit in high school, but based on the results, I can assure you that there was *no match* for me in Great Falls, Montana, with the highly improbable, nearly nonexistent possible exception of *Hannah?*

Suddenly remembering my alien dilemma, I slowly reached inside my pants' pocket, hoping beyond hope that I would *not* find that damn ruby ring! I further wished that it was actually just another make-believe part of my dream world? But when I reached the bottom of my pocket, *there it was!* I quickly pulled it out and carefully examined it. It looked to me like any other ruby ring that one might find at the jewelers or even a high-end toy store, except that it was pretty plain? There didn't seem to be anything special about it at all? It was at that very moment that I actually considered putting the ring on my finger just to find out if this part of the alien adventure I had apparently stumbled into was actually real? But somehow I just couldn't take the chance? So, I carefully slid the ring back inside my pocket, closed my eyes and began repeatedly whispering the name of the alien girl, '*Shakenbutnotstirred!*' I was feeling very confident she would show-up, and she *did!*

"Hi!" she playfully announced, as she happily bounced over to the couch and pressed her beautiful body next to mine. Surprisingly, she apparently had no recollection of the intense fear she'd permanently *scarred* me with the last time we'd gotten together? "And *who* was that girl?" her face suddenly darkened as she purposely pulled away from me.

"That *girl's* name is Hannah. We are next-door neighbors," I explained calmly. Then softening my tone, I said, "I called you because I wanted to speak together about something important."

"*Important* huh? Okay," she agreed. And then beginning to grow angry again, she added very cattily, "But, I really *don't* like her!"

"Hannah?" I looked for confirmation.

"Of course, '*Hannah!*' What a *stupid* name!" she sneered.

"You don't even know her!" I laughed. "Anyway, our talk has nothing to do with her."

"*Good!*" the girl declared as she slowly threw back her mane of blonde hair, revealing a most seductive expression on her face, reminiscent of a sexy shampoo commercial I'd recently watched on television? And then she suddenly smiled as she added, "Would you like to go away with me to someplace *fun* for our talk? Just you and me?"

"Like where?" I asked curiously.

"To the *clouds*," she replied with an even bigger smile. And before I had time to even consider her proposal, *there* we were in the clouds, high above the city? To be honest? I wasn't frightened in the least? Far from it! Looking down, the beautiful sight of the distant city below simply blew me away! In addition, I quickly discovered that unbelievably, *I could fly?* As I playfully flew about the clouds, continuing to gaze down at the city of Great Falls, I felt like Wendy, John and Michael must have felt as they looked down on London on their way to Neverland with Peter Pan and Tinker Bell! But in this case, I'm quite sure that I was flying *without* the help of *fairy dust!*

"This is *so much fun!*" I exclaimed from my impossible perch in the clouds. But then I remembered what it was we had come here to do, so I begrudgingly left my playtime behind and growing more serious, I asked her, "Could we talk now?"

"Of course," she agreed from the other side of the cloud. "What is it you want to talk with me about?" she asked, magically creating two chairs that were facing each other on the cloud for us to sit on.

I smiled as we sat. "I want to talk with you *about you*," I shared with a friendly air.

"Me?" she asked in shock. "Why?"

"Because I don't know much of anything at all about you except what little you shared with me earlier?" I explained. "Would you answer a few simple questions for me?"

"Sure," she agreed with a coy smile. "If I must!"

"Oh, you *must!*" I smiled. "But *no lies!* Even if you are just kidding around, okay?" My closed eyes sternly met hers.

The girl sighed. "Alright. What exactly do you want to know?"

"For starters, I understand why you came to Earth, but *why* are you in *my* house?" I asked calmly.

She laughed. "Well, I didn't plan on hiding here, but your house was the first one I saw when I arrived on your planet," she explained calmly.

"When *did* you arrive here?" I asked intently.

"This morning. But I kept to myself until after my father had talked with you," she admitted.

"Why was that?" I asked curiously.

"Because I figured that since he already knew that I was here, I might as well make it as *difficult as possible* for him to find me!" she smiled. "I thought I'd use the extra time getting to know *you* better."

"And that was *because?*" I didn't really understand what she was alluding to.

"Because I have watched *a lot* of your television programs, and that gave me a great idea!" she said cryptically. "I've decided that I want *you* to be my *very first Earth boyfriend!*" she excitedly proclaimed. "We've already been naked together in bed!" she recalled proudly. "That's a good start, right?"

"No, *Shakenbutnotstirred*," I replied calmly. "To me, that was only a *bizarre* dream that I had no part in creating," I explained. "When two people decide to be boyfriend and girlfriend, every romantic decision they make should be *mutual.*"

"Oh," she replied in confusion. "Is that a *rule?*"

I chuckled. "Not *officially*," I admitted. "But I believe a lot of people on Earth with a boyfriend or girlfriend would agree with me."

"Don't you *love me?*" the girl dramatically asked me, with angst dripping from every syllable, like the star of some over-the-top soap-opera.

Considering the *extremely* short time we had known each other, that question seemed incredibly *premature*, but remembering how volatile she had become in past conversations and wisely not wishing to upset her again, I gently replied, "Maybe I *will* love you sometime in the future, but right now I hardly know you?"

"Do you already love that *other girl* though? That *Hannah*?" she asked me pointedly. "Don't lie! I can read your mind!"

"Okay. Well then, I guess *maybe I do*?" I replied honestly. It immediately became strikingly evident to me that I had *not* given the alien girl the answer she had hoped for. She lost little time in revealing an expression of intense horror seasoned with a hefty dose of anger, and just like that, she *disappeared*? After that, I felt myself abruptly leaving my chair in the clouds and opening my eyes to find myself sitting right back on my couch at home?

I shook my head. "*That* went well!" I mumbled to myself sarcastically. After spending way too much time attempting unsuccessfully to reengage *Shakenbutnotstirred*, I finally gave-up and dejectedly remained on the couch, where I proceeded to watch lots of afternoon television shows before finally dozing off.

I awoke with a start? Frighteningly, I found myself in a dreary, dank dungeon made of mortar and stone, seemingly from a dreadful time during the Medieval Inquisitions back in the 12th through 15th centuries. The only light in the dungeon was created by a small number of lit torches on the walls, making it visually dim throughout. But the *worst* part was that the entire dungeon *smelled hideous*, like rancid armpits and stale urine! That odious stench nearly made me gag! Disappointingly I could find *no* openings to the outside where fresh air could have thankfully entered the dungeon and cleansed it of that *awful smell*! Looking around, I saw that I was attached to a brick wall by long chains with thick and rusty manacles firmly locked around my ankles. Mangy rats were chaotically running all over the floor across the dark shadows created by the dim light, which somehow strangely made me fearful? One of the rats, a large brown one with extra-long claws, inexplicably wearing a tiny black derby hat on its head, stopped and took an *intense hungry* look at me before finally scampering off. Now *that* was creepy? Browsing around further, I was shocked to see the skeletal remains of quite a few *former* humans chained to the walls just as I was now? But, as far as I could see, aside from the rats, I was now the only *living* creature in the dungeon.

"So, you've finally decided to wake-up, have you!" the alien calling himself *Areyoufeelingluckypunk*, suddenly appeared and telepathed me without expression. He looked exactly the same as when I'd met him earlier in his spaceship. "Why did you fail to contact me the moment you discovered where my daughter was?" he telepathed threateningly.

"I was going to contact you, I really was, but your daughter talked me out of putting on that ruby ring," I replied confidently. "She thought it might be a very *bad* decision that I would *regret* for the rest of my life!"

The alien did not immediately telepath a response, but I could feel seething and intense anger filling the dungeon around me, which I had absolutely no doubt belonged to *him*!

So, deciding to backtrack a bit on my moxie, I smiled and said, "Since you already know that I've found your daughter, I'll just give this ring back to you now and our little contract will be completed, alright?" Politely, I removed the ring from my pocket and offered it back to him.

"*Put the ring on your finger, Kip!*" The alien telepathed sharply. "If you do not, I will be forced to leave you here to *die!*"

Have you ever in your life faced such a conundrum? I must admit that I had *not!* I certainly *didn't* want to die, but a lifetime of servitude to him? "*Never!*" I replied bravely, while also fearlessly throwing the ring at him. But, as he calmly bent down to pick it up, and then carefully placed it somewhere inside his robes, I suddenly realized something. In this situation, using the word, 'never,' and aggressively throwing the ruby ring at my alien captor, was probably *not* terribly conducive to procuring my freedom!

"*So be it!*" the alien roared telepathically. "Enjoy playing with your *little friends*, Kip!" And with that, he disappeared, leaving me feeling sick and alone, desperately in need of some good news!

Looking around again at my surroundings and searching for anything at all that I might rationalize as being positive, I *still* couldn't find a thing? But, I quickly became aware that aside from the skeletons, this dungeon looked remarkably similar to one I recalled seeing in a scary Edgar Allan Poe movie recently on TV? I wondered if the alien had watched that *same* movie while reading my mind, and then used it as inspiration to create this place? I chuckled *without* joy. The truth was, just as he had inadvertently shared with me when we had first met earlier today, he was capable of seeing the *entire contents* of my mind. So, in that way, I suppose I was indirectly responsible for this whole mess, and it was a fool's errand to believe that there was any possible escape from it! I sighed and closed my eyes because the truth was, no matter how many times I told him, *never*, I was still a *coward* at heart and really *didn't* want to see what terrible and painful things the alien had in store for me next?

Several minutes passed before I somehow managed to open my eyes again. But the moment I did, I really wished I *hadn't*! The rats, which had previously been chaotically scampering about, had now grown eerily still throughout the dungeon? In fact, they were each intensely staring at *me* through the shadowy darkness, licking their rat lips as they did? I couldn't help thinking with dread that *this* had been what *Areyoufeelingluckypunk* had meant when he had said, 'Enjoy *playing* with your *little friends?*' I instantly got an awful pain in the pit of my stomach, as I realized that regardless of what happened next, I was *not* going to like it very much!

The brown rat with the extra-long claws, wearing the derby hat, whom I recognized from earlier, appeared to be the rat leader. It raised its right front paw and suddenly hundreds of rats began to bare their teeth and make *evil rat noises* at me! As the rat leader lowered its paw, the mob of rats slowly and uniformly (*almost as if they were choreographed*) began marching toward me like talented little dancers from a very *obscure* Broadway musical called **RATS**, or perhaps just a well-trained army regiment from *rat hell*! At that moment, I had an epiphany, although it *wasn't* a particularly pleasant one. I imagined that those skeletons on the walls were actually the remains of other human prisoners who had also said the word, 'never," to *Areyoufeelingluckypunk*, and *lived to regret it*! Why hadn't I thought of that sooner?

As I covered my face with my hands in terror and prepared to scream bloody murder the moment those ravenous rats began sinking their tiny but *hideously sharp* teeth into my flesh, I thought I saw my on-again, off-again alien 'friend' called *Shakenbutnotstirred*? But before I had the chance to utter even a single word to her, my focus became completely obliterated by the *sudden* feeling that my entire body was being roughly shaken? Slowly, I opened my eyes to surprisingly see *Hannah* bending over me, her eyes filled with concern? But the moment our eyes met, she sighed with relief?

"H... How did you get into this dungeon?" I asked her in shock.

"We're *not* in a dungeon, Kip! This is your house and you're sitting on the couch. I was able to get inside because as we both know, you *never* lock the front door," she reminded me.

"Right! Well, *why* are you here then?" I asked her very curiously.

"Your *'not so imaginary'* alien friend, who looks like *Hayley Mills*, visited me as I was napping this afternoon," she anxiously told me. "She shared a lot, Kip! Then she insisted that I run right over to your house as fast as I could to *physically* wake you up! She said it was the only escape from the nightmare you were trapped in!" Hannah paused for a moment, and then said very seriously, "She also told me to remind you *not* to ever put that ruby ring on your finger *no matter what!*"

I gasped! "You *know* what's going on?"

Hannah nodded. "Yes! I probably don't know the whole story yet, but I know enough to see that you're in *deep trouble!* I strongly suggest that we leave town as fast as we can!"

"*We?*" I asked her in surprise.

"Someone's got to help you get out of this mess!" Hannah exclaimed. "I've got an aunt who lives in Hardin? I could ask if we could stay with her for a while?"

"But what if *the alien's father* follows us there? He's pretty crafty! *That* could put your aunt in terrible danger?" I said intensely.

"You're right!" Hannah admitted disappointedly. "Okay, then we'll just have to keep ourselves from falling asleep!"

"That doesn't matter," I explained. "Just closing my eyes for a second seems to be enough time for either one of them to slither into my mind."

Hannah looked very worried. "Then what *do* we do, Kip?"

It was absurd hearing the 'always confident Hannah' sounding so unsure of herself that she was actually asking *me* for advice? But because of the specialness of this moment, regardless of my fears, I vowed to come-up with an intelligent plan and *fast*! Although I worried that it might take me a while, the answer actually came to me in a flash. "We need to contact the alien girl," I heard myself suggesting with confidence. "I believe we can trust her."

Hannah immediately glared at me with intense shock and disbelief consuming her eyes and face. "*Are you kidding me?*" she vehemently disagreed. "I know you can't see it now, Kip, but remember all of that stuff we've heard for years about *blood being thicker than water?*"

"Yes. But maybe that's *not* applicable here considering that *she's only a spirit?*" I replied in complete sincerity.

Hannah rolled her eyes at me in disgust. "*Of course, it's applicable!* She and her father are *family!* Surely *that's* more important to her than helping us?"

"But she's the one who sent you to save me in the nick of time before hundreds of rats *ate me alive!*" I insisted very emotionally.

Hannah grew thoughtful and calmly suggested, "I really feel for what you believe you went through, Kip... but in truth, what you *may* have experienced was simply a very intense and believable *bad dream.*"

"Really? You think so?" I asked her in shock. "*How?*"

"Well," she began. "What if the alien girl's father had some way of playing mind games with you?"

"*Mind games?*" I asked her curiously.

"Sure. Like a hypnotist!" Hannah replied.

"Go on," I encouraged her.

"Well, everything you saw might have simply have been part of an elaborate ruse, orchestrated by *him*!" Hannah explained.

Suddenly I had a thought. "Going along with your theory, what if the dungeon I was trapped in was actually an illusion he created for me in a *dimension*? Maybe his spaceship *wasn't* even real? Do you think *that's* possible?" I asked.

"Wow! Do you mean the kind of dimension that *Einstein* suggested?" Hannah asked me with surprise.

"I think so," I replied hesitantly. "More or less."

Following my response, Hannah grew noticeably more serious. "Hmm? *That's* a very interesting thought, Kip? Last week I read an article about the *possibility* of other dimensions in our world," she began. "In the end, the authors were non-committal, but they *did* think the possibility warranted much more study. They further suggested that if we did have access to other dimensions, under the right circumstances, they believed it would be *possible* for a person's essence to travel there while their body stayed exactly where it was, in a natural sleeping state? In *theory* anyway."

"Do you think that's what happened to *me*?" I asked excitedly. "What did your article say were the *right circumstances*?"

"Well, as I recall, the person simply had to be absolutely convinced that what they were experiencing was *real*," Hannah replied. "As *you* were!"

"Hmm," I uttered while thinking. "So, you're saying that the alien may have controlled my mind into believing that a *fictitious* situation in the dungeon was real?" I asked in disbelief.

"No. Not exactly," Hannah said. "If my theory is correct, the alien *didn't* control your mind at all. It only *suggested* through what it made you see, that everything you were experiencing was real. That made *your mind* do the brunt of the work, vividly creating his suggestions, and making *you* believe it! And since you are so very open-minded and creative, his plan would have worked in spades!"

"Wow!" I exclaimed. "That would certainly explain why waking me up made the nightmare completely go away!"

"Exactly," Hannah agreed. "But don't get too excited about it yet, Kip. Remember, everything I've told you is only quick *speculation* about what *may* have happened to you. Just an *unproven* theory. The actual possibilities might be *endless*?"

I nodded. "But *why* would he do that to me?" I asked intently. "That's the part I don't get?"

Hannah shook her head. "Me either?"

"Not to change the subject, Hannah, but we *still* need an escape plan? And after *all* that the alien girl has done for me, won't you at least *try* to *believe* that we can trust her?" I insisted. "She may be our only hope?"

Hannah very unhappily deliberated for a few moments. "I get your point," she begrudgingly admitted. "If the alien girl hadn't contacted me when she did, then as I see it, even if the situation you found yourself in *wasn't* real, because you believed it *was*, it could have ended very *badly* for you." Growing extremely animated, she added, "You could have become so frightened about what you perceived was happening, that fear could have actually caused you to have a heart attack and *die?*"

I shuddered at her last words, and then replied, "*Exactly!* But the alien girl recognized that and *told you* how to save me? That's got to count for something?"

"I still *don't* trust her!" Hannah said firmly. "There's something really phony about her?"

I chuckled. "Girls always say that about *other girls!*"

Hannah cracked a smile. "Okay, Kip. Maybe you're right," she finally gave-in. "Let me get a hold of your *alien* friend. How do I do that?"

"Just close your eyes and call her name, *Shakenbutnotstirred*," I explained simply.

"Excuse me?" Hannah instantly looked at me in disbelief, as if I were joking, "*That's* her name?"

Realizing how difficult it must be for her to believe that, I calmly explained, "Yes. Apparently she was influenced by a James Bond movie she had watched on television."

"This is just getting *weirder and weirder*," Hannah commented, shaking her head. "Do I *dare* ask? What's her father's name?"

"*Areyoufeelingluckypunk.*"

Hannah laughed, "Of course, it is!" Then she quickly grew serious. "Okay," she told me before closing her eyes and preparing herself mentally for the task at hand. Soon she chanted, "*Shakenbutnotstirred*, we want to talk with you! Please come to us!"

"Is anything happening?" I asked Hannah impatiently.

"Not yet?" Hannah replied. And then a sudden spark of excitement crossed her face, which unfortunately, after a few moments turned to disappointment. "She wants to speak with *you*," she said coolly.

"Okay," I agreed, quickly closing my eyes. I immediately saw a smiling alien girl who looked a lot like Hayley Mills, but as soon as I did, *Hannah disappeared?* "Hey? Where has Hannah gone?" I asked her in surprise.

"I don't want to talk with *her*," the alien girl uttered distastefully. "I will *only* talk with you!" she pouted.

"Now listen, *Shakenbutnotstirred*!" I scolded her firmly. "Hannah will be doing whatever *I* am doing! No discussion! She has got to be *included* in this talk!"

"Fine," she relented. And instantly a very shocked Hannah appeared standing there alongside me.

"What is it that you and *she* wish to speak to me about?" the alien girl asked dryly.

"Well, to begin with, thank you for contacting Hannah about my predicament in the dungeon," I said sincerely.

"You're welcome," the alien girl's eyes met mine sincerely.

I was touched by her reaction, and I knew right then that we could trust her. "Is your father after me?" I asked her bluntly.

"Yes!" the alien girl replied intently.

"Why?" I asked.

"I don't know?" she said. "But from what I've observed, he seems to be *obsessed* with you?"

"In a good way?" Hannah asked.

"With my father, it's *never* in a good way!" the alien replied sincerely. "I'm so sorry, Kip."

I shuddered. "I believe we *urgently* need your help escaping from him then! Will you help us, *Shakenbutnotstirred*?"

Shakenbutnotstirred gave Kip a sincere smile and replied, "Of course, I will!"

"Where exactly will you be taking us?" Hannah asked suspiciously.

"A place you probably don't know, where my father would *never* think to look for you," she replied cryptically. "Once you are there, he will become very frustrated after looking for you without success, and I know from experience, he will then angrily return to our planet, making it safe for you two to return to your lives."

"That sounds great!" I exclaimed.

"Of course, there is one very *necessary* thing you must do for me first," she said mysteriously.

"Okay!" I proclaimed a little too anxiously.

"Allow me to temporarily cohabitate in *your* mind with you," the alien girl said directly to Hannah.

"Why do you need to do *that*?" Hannah asked her in shock.

"Because my father and I are only spiritual beings with no bodies of our own like the two of you. As you already know, we are only able to communicate with you while you are either asleep or have your eyes closed," she explained. "So, you see, in order to effectively help you to escape, I must be able to communicate with you *all* the time!"

It sounded logical, but with some misgivings, Hannah asked her, "If I let you do that, what will happen to *me*?"

With a reassuring smile, the alien girl replied gently, "You'll be *fine*. You will still be in control of your mind, completely able to operate your body and communicate through your mouth just as you do now. Except, of course, when you *choose* to let me do it."

"And will you leave my mind the moment we are safe?" Hannah added intently.

"Of course," the alien girl smiled reassuringly.

"Do you *promise*?" Hannah demanded, meeting her eyes intensely.

"Yes. I promise that I will only share your mind with you until the two of you are safely out of danger from my father and *not* a second longer!" *Shakenbutnotstirred* pledged.

"Hey? Why don't you share *my* mind instead?" I objected. "I would really prefer that you left Hannah completely out of this!"

"I *can't* do that, Kip. It has to be Hannah," the alien girl stubbornly insisted.

"Why?" Hannah and I protested together.

Smiling directly at both of us, she proclaimed, "Because in the short time I remain on this planet, I want to experience what it feels like being an Earth girl, and especially one who has *you* Kip, as her *boyfriend!*"

There was no further discussion as the alien girl seemed to have us both over a barrel. In fact, Hannah and I reluctantly agreed to the pact only moments later. Then, after Hannah went home and packed a few extra clothes and other items she thought she might need on our road-trip, while I did the same thing here, we loaded our bags into my VW bus and followed that by meeting in my living room. As we looked at each other, Hannah seemed frightened, so I hugged her tightly. After what seemed like quite a while, she gently pulled away from me and we shared a warm understanding smile. Next, we closed our eyes and called *Shakenbutnotstirred* by name to consummate the deal.

Soon, we found ourselves driving away from Great Falls, Montana, the *only* city that Hannah and I had ever lived in, bound for a safer destination that our alien friend was guiding us toward. It was very interesting driving my bus while sitting next to two very *different* girls housed in the *same* body? Although the alien girl was cohabitating in Hannah's mind, just as she had said, Hannah had no trouble speaking-up whenever she wanted to. She had already argued with her body-mate a couple of times, as people in very close quarters are prone to do. Nothing huge, but reassuringly it demonstrated to me that Hannah was *still* in charge. I had to laugh though. To anyone watching Hannah talking to herself, I wouldn't have been surprised if they had thought she was 100% *certifiable!*

"How much further do we have to go, *Shakenbutnotstirred?*" I asked Hannah's body.

"I would say several hours of your Earth time," the alien girl's voice readily replied through Hannah's mouth.

"Do we have enough gas to get there?" Hannah's voice alertly asked me?

"Probably *not*," I admitted sheepishly. "I don't need much gas just driving to school and back, so I *never* fill the tank."

Hannah chuckled good naturedly. "Then why don't we stop at the first gas station that comes along, okay? There's nothing worse than running out of gas in the middle of a *getaway*!" she smiled impishly at me.

I smiled back, appreciating a little humor right now.

"What is *running-out of gas*?" *Shakenbutnotstirred*'s voice asked curiously.

"Well," I replied as simply as I could. "It's when the fuel that makes a car like this one *go* is all used up, so the car doesn't move anymore."

"Oh," the alien girl said whimsically. "In my world there is *no fuel* for anything? Everything we create just works!"

I laughed. "If only *that* were the case here!"

Ten minutes later, I found and drove my bus into a little do-it-yourself gas station about 20 miles outside of Great Falls. As I opened my door and began to get out to pump the gas, *Shakenbutnotstirred* suddenly stopped me.

"Don't go! Let *me* put the fuel into your car for you," she said calmly. "I really want to learn how?"

"Kip, *don't* let her do it! She doesn't know what she's doing!" Hannah interjected.

"Why don't *you* tell me what to do then?" the alien girl suggested sweetly to Hannah. "I won't do anything without getting your approval first? Okay?"

In the next few minutes, the alien girl, with explicit directions from Hannah, filled my tank and then one of them paid the man twenty dollars to cover the cost of the gas, which they took from the wallet in Hannah's purse. Neither of the girls *asked me* for any money, but I really wasn't surprised. You see, Hannah knew from years of experience that when it came to money, I *usually* came up a little short. In the past, whenever we had gone out together as friends to watch a movie or have lunch, she had always been happy to pay for things if she knew that *I couldn't*, and that was pretty often! Soon, we were driving off once again with at least one of the two girls sitting next to me smiling broadly on Hannah's face!

"I think I am beginning to feel a little *hungry*? Shouldn't we have brought some of that gas along with us for refueling our bodies?" the alien girl asked simply.

"Oh, no!" Hannah's voice replied humorously. "Drinking gasoline is *poisonous* to any living creature. We eat food."

"Oh yes! I have seen examples of this *food* on television, but I don't understand why you spend so much time preparing it instead of eating grass like cows and horses do?" the alien girl asked simply. "Grass requires *no preparation* at all?"

I laughed. "You're right about grass for horses and cows needing no preparation. But, food for humans is usually seasoned with spices and cooked a special way to make it a more *pleasant tasting* fuel to eat than plain grass," I explained gently. "Eating good food that's well prepared keeps human bodies energetic and healthy, while tasting good at the same time."

"Where can we get some of this *good tasting food*?" the alien girl asked excitedly.

Hannah smiled. "How about if we stop at a restaurant the moment we see one?" she suggested helpfully.

"Thank you!" the alien girl grinned. "That would be nice!"

After driving several miles more, just as soon as we approached a steakhouse, *Shakenbutnotstirred* suddenly became very excited on Hannah's face as she exclaimed, "How about *that* one?"

"Maybe we should wait a little while before we stop to eat? You know, get a bigger head-start? I know a *great* steakhouse in the next town?" Hannah suggested.

"No!" *Shakenbutnotstirred* insisted. "I want *this* one!"

"Okay," I smiled good-naturedly, as I pulled my VW bus into the parking lot. But I couldn't help wondering what it was that made *this* restaurant so special to her? I'm sure that Hannah felt the same way?

This particular restaurant was named after an infamous battle, popularly known as '*Custer's Last Stand*,' that had taken place in Montana in 1876, where 200 members of the U.S. 7th Cavalry had been soundly defeated by thousands of Indian warriors. The battle was colorfully depicted outside of the restaurant on a huge billboard that looked out toward the road where drivers couldn't miss it, assuredly making this place a very popular *spontaneous* tourist stop. The restaurant sat in the middle of a small downtown with a handful of shops on either side of it. The sky above it was overcast from smoke blocking the sun, while a dreadful odor filled the air all around us?

"What is that awful smell?" *Shakenbutnotstirred* asked with irritation. "And *where* is it coming from?"

"It's coming from the slaughterhouse over there," Hannah pointed down the street at a very large building just off the main street with a cluster of smoking chimneys sprouting out from the roof.

"What is a *slaughterhouse*?" the alien girl asked curiously.

I hesitated and then explained, "It's a place where they turn live cattle into meat for people to eat. But I understand they kill them very humanely, without any pain."

"Oh," the alien girl replied, surprisingly without *any trace* of emotion? "What does this *meat* taste like?"

"Why don't we go inside and find out?" Hannah excitedly suggested.

The interior of the steakhouse we entered was predictably decorated in brown wood, with rustic brown tables and chairs evenly spaced throughout the floor of the dining area. But it was completely empty right now, so I surmised that tourist season had not begun yet? The ambience in the room was noticeably dark, due to the thick smoke that permeated the air outside as well as the deep brown paneled walls that surrounded us. That's when I spied an older waitress who was dressed in a white frock that doubled as a poster covered with some of the same colorful scenes from 'Custer's Last Stand' as the billboard outside. She was thin, about five foot two with short gray hair. The waitress offered us the tiniest of smiles as she promptly seated us at a square table with four chairs, placed two menus in front of us and walked off. Not the *warmest* of receptions, but I decided to forgive her if the food tasted good.

"So, this is a *restaurant?*" *Shakenbutnotstirred* quietly asked with delight filling her eyes.

"Yes, it is," Hannah replied from the same lips. "*When will you be leaving my mind?*" she asked her impatiently.

"Like I told you before, Hannah. Just as soon as the two of you are safe," the alien girl insisted sweetly.

But Hannah was not altogether placated. "And when will *that* be?" she asked sternly.

Shakenbutnotstirred smiled. "Soon."

As we looked over the menu, beef steak was apparently the *only* meat they served, which came as no surprise to me, due to the restaurant's close proximity to the slaughterhouse.

"I guess I'll have a steak with a baked potato and a garden salad," Hannah smiled.

"Will that taste good in my mouth?" the alien girl excitedly asked.

"Yes! It should taste very good in *my mouth*," Hannah corrected her.

"Of course," the alien girl laughed. "I'm sorry! *That's* what I meant!"

"That's okay," Hannah replied. "I'm sure that the taste of steak, salad and baked potato will please you too! And anyway, there's not much else on this menu we can order?"

I laughed. "True! So, two steaks, two garden salads, two baked potatoes and two cokes?" I asked.

"What's *coke?*" the alien girl asked.

Hannah didn't offer her a response, so I jumped in and explained that it was a dark, sweet, fizzy drink, and she apparently found my minimal explanation satisfactory. A few minutes later, the waitress took our orders and then walked off toward the kitchen. She came back shortly carrying two tall, clear plastic tumblers full of bubbly, dark caramel colored coke, with paper straws already placed inside each one. She gently set them down on the table and after completely ignoring Kip, while giving Hannah a friendly smile, she left.

"I *don't* think our waitress likes you very much," Hannah smiled humorously at me.

"Don't be so quick to judge!" I protested with a smile. "Believe me. I'll *grow* on her once she recognizes my uncanny wit and charm!"

Hannah and I laughed, but the alien girl surprisingly did *not* join in the fun? I suppose she hadn't had much exposure to *our type* of humor during her short time on this planet. In fact, aside from what they had perused on television shows, perhaps *humor* in their culture was mostly an '*alien*' concept? As soon as Hannah had stopped laughing, the alien girl became completely obsessed with the coke that sat on the table in front of her? Finally, unable to resist it, she grabbed the drink and began ferociously sucking it into Hannah's mouth through her straw, until her tumbler was *completely empty*! A huge smile of satisfaction soon crossed Hannah's face.

"Where on Earth did you learn to use a *straw*?" I asked her in surprise.

"I didn't learn to use it on *Earth*," she replied, missing my meaning. "I learned to use it by watching television shows back home on my planet! A straw is such a fun way of bringing fluid into your mouth, don't you think?"

Both Hannah and I smiled at her comment. But shockingly, after taking a good look at Hannah, for the first time since her mind had taken on a '*roommate*,' I frighteningly saw *subtle traces* of the alien girl in her face? Thankfully there were no actual physical changes that I could detect, but regardless, the alien girl's essence was *decidedly* there! For Hannah's sake, I really hoped that just as *Shakenbutnotstirred* had promised earlier, her 'visit' would be a short one!

"You seemed to really enjoy the taste of that coke," Hannah commented politely.

"I guess I did?" the alien girl replied hesitantly. "The problem is, I have nothing to compare it with yet? That was my very *first taste* of anything at all as a human."

"Well, I'm sure that our order will be on the table shortly, and then you can compare all of the great tastes and textures you find in the food on your plate to what you experienced with the coke," I said encouragingly.

"Is it possible for you to cohabitate with any *other* type of living creature on Earth besides humans?" Hannah asked abruptly.

Hannah's face grew thoughtful before the alien girl replied, "I imagine so? My father says that other creatures on Earth should be very easy to dominate because he believes their minds aren't strong enough to even know what's happening to them when that process begins. But he also says that humans appear to be the most challenging creatures on Earth to control."

"When did he tell you *that*?" I asked suspiciously. "You haven't been in contact with him since you arrived on Earth. Right?"

"Right," *Shakenbutnotstirred* smiled a little too much. "I think he told me that sometime in the past."

"And don't you mean 'cohabitate with humans,' *not* 'control them?'" Hannah's face grew skeptical.

"Yes, of course. I meant *cohabitate* with them," the alien girl nodded.

"Is it so difficult for you to cohabitate with humans because you have to *ask* their permission first before you can enter their minds?" Hannah asked, ignoring the subtle fear she was just beginning to sense.

"In your case Hannah, yes, because your mind is very strong and would never allow anyone to cohabitate with you otherwise," the alien girl explained.

"But what about when you visited me while I was napping?" Hannah asked, perplexed.

Hannah's face laughed as the alien girl replied to her as if speaking to a small child. "*Every* Earth creature's guard is down while they're asleep, so when that's the case, I can enter their minds freely *without* permission!"

"So, is my mind strong as well?" I asked hopefully.

Shakenbutnotstirred chuckled. "No. Your mind is much *easier* for me to enter than Hannah's."

"Why?" I asked, a little taken aback.

"Because, being the creative person you are, you are so open-minded and trusting that you will not question, but quickly believe virtually *anything*, especially when it's coming from a charming and pretty girl who looks a lot like *Hayley Mills*," Hannah rolled her eyes and explained before the alien girl had the chance to.

"*Exactly*," the alien girl beamed. "Perfectly said, Hannah!"

That's when I first sensed that the demeanor of the alien girl had dramatically *changed* from what it had been only minutes before? If I was to believe my eyes and ears, she seemed to be acting *less* quirky and immature and decidedly *more arrogant?* "Hey, *Shakenbutnotstirred?* Were you lying to me about that ruby ring?" I pointedly asked her. "If I *had* put it on my finger, would I really have fallen into your father's power?"

The alien girl first met my eyes seriously, and then began laughing uncontrollably. "Well, yes, I *was* lying to you, and no, you would *not* have fallen into my father's power!"

I was suddenly *speechless?*

"You really shouldn't believe everything a stranger tells you, Kip! Especially when that stranger is from another planet!" the alien girl giggled. "I was just helping my father by telling you that lie."

"Helping him *how?*" I demanded.

"Helping to make *you* believe that everything he told you was the truth!" she smiled.

"Why?" I insisted.

"So, out of your own fear, you would feel compelled to trust me. That would allow me to freely lead you somewhere where my father could more easily capture you," she bragged.

"*Capture me?*" I blurted out in shock. "So, you've been working with him all along?"

"Of course, I have," the alien girl laughed once again. "You see, that's what my father does on his hunting trips! He captures odd creatures from other planets and brings them *home!*"

"Where do you plan on taking us next to deliver us to him then?" I asked anxiously.

"You'll find out," she shared guardedly.

"Do you mean to say that this is a *hunting trip* and you have already *captured me?*" Hannah screamed.

"Yes!" the alien girl exclaimed. "You are my *very first catch!* Isn't it wonderful, Hannah?" And then backtracking a bit, she explained, "Well, at least you are *partially* captured. But by tomorrow morning, you will be *completely* in my power!"

"*What?*" I yelled at the alien girl. "You little *cheat!* You promised Hannah that you would leave her mind?" I shouted. "I can't believe that we trusted you? I'll bet you don't even have a boyfriend with a ferocious temper named *I'mmadashellandI'mnotgoingtotakethis-anymore*, do you?"

"No!" the alien girl giggled. "We don't even *have* boyfriends and girlfriends like you humans do!"

"So, you and your father are nothing more than a couple of galactic parasites and liars who hunted us down for *sport?*" Hannah asked in disbelief.

"Basically, although that is a *very crude description* of what we do," the alien girl feigned offense. Then Hannah's face smiled way too widely as the alien girl expounded, "My father travels through space every year. *Lying*, as he has shared with me often, can be a very valuable *tool* in controlling the weaker minds like *yours*, Kip! But I am especially proud of this ridiculous charade we created to catch you! How *predictable* you humans are?" Making an attempt at a *humble* facial expression, she added, "Of course, my father and I can't take all of the credit. Your television programs have really taught us a great deal about how *stupid* and easily *manipulated* the human race is!"

"If we're so stupid, what made you decide to come to Earth in the first place?" Kip demanded, beginning to sweat uncomfortably.

"My father had never been here before because he considered Earth to be very backward, and he was certain that it would be a *wasted* trip! But, he finally agreed to bring me here *this year* as a gift!" she laughed. "And what a *wonderful* gift it has turned out to be!"

"So, at first this was only supposed to be a *sightseeing trip* for the two of you?" Hannah asked incredulously.

"Yes, at *first*," the alien girl replied. "But that changed just as soon as my father discovered something here that he believed could be *very lucrative* for his business?"

"What was *that?*" Hannah asked intently. "And why are you involving *us?*"

Before the alien girl had the chance to answer Hannah's questions, the waitress arrived with two plates of food, which she gently placed in front of Hannah and me. Then she surprisingly smiled at Hannah once again and declared, "Good work, *Shakenbutnotstirred!*"

I jumped in my seat! "You're not *Areyoufeelingluckypunk*, are you?" I asked in shock.

The waitress laughed, smiled broadly, nodding her head affirmatively.

Turning toward Hannah, I exclaimed, "So that's why you insisted on coming to *this restaurant, Shakenbutnotstirred?*"

"Ooh! The redhead's a *winner!*" she replied sarcastically.

"Welcome to our little *trap*, Kip!" the possessed waitress smiled arrogantly. "If you will now allow me to cohabitate with your mind, my plan will be painlessly completed."

"No, Kip! *Run and hide!* Don't let them take you too! They are not planning to *ever* let either one of us go!" Hannah shouted.

I couldn't begin to understand how Hannah could *know that*, but I completely believed her! Suddenly a swarm of frantic thoughts filled my head, not the least of which was the fact that I could *never* leave Hannah behind in the evil clutches of these two alien predators! So, I grabbed her hand and we ran out of the restaurant, toward my VW bus as fast as we could! The waitress tried to stop us, but she wound up sprawled out on the floor after tripping over the chair I had deliberately thrown in her path. Moments later, Hannah and I (*and the monster that resided within her*) found ourselves furiously driving away!

"You are *very strong*, Hannah," the creature we had previously known as *Shakenbutnotstirred*, said angrily. "You fight me at every opportunity. Why don't you just relax and enjoy the ride?"

"Because I've got to stay alert! I'm afraid of what you might do next!" Hannah retorted honestly. "You have clearly demonstrated that you *can't* be trusted!"

The alien girl laughed. "Well, *that's* fine with me! You *can't* stay alert while you're sleeping?"

"I won't let her fall asleep until you are completely gone from her!" I declared.

"Oh, *how sweet!*" the alien girl laughed sarcastically. "*Little Kip* is going to try to save Hannah? What a hoot!"

"What did you mean, Hannah, when you told me at the restaurant that she and her father were *never* going to let us go?" I asked intently.

"Yes," the alien sneeringly encouraged her. "What *did* you mean, Hannah?"

Hannah's face suddenly grew very frustrated as she replied, "Sorry, Kip? I don't know why, but suddenly I can't remember what it was I was going to tell you?"

"Haha!" the alien girl laughed with glee. "You let your guard down, Hannah, and I was there to confuse your mind! Oh, what *fun!*" Then she added sarcastically, "Now I suppose poor little Kip will *never know* what you meant to tell him?"

"*Shut-up, you lying cow!* You bet I'll remember it eventually!" Hannah declared passionately. "And I'll get you out of my head too!" Pausing, she determinedly added, "You just wait! I'll find a way!"

The alien girl was quiet for a moment, perhaps pondering her next verbal barrage when she blurted out, "We're not really after you anyway, Hannah! It's Kip we want!"

"Give it a rest! All of your lying is getting very boring!" I said in annoyance.

"I'm *not* lying!" the alien shot back. "Not this time."

"Okay," I softened my voice and asked slowly. "Why would you want *me?*"

The alien girl hesitated for a moment before replying, "I've said too much already. Believe me, you'll find out soon enough!"

And then the conversation abruptly stopped. I was very curious to find out *why* the two aliens would want *me*, but with such a dismal track record for telling the truth, *Shakenbutnotstirred* was probably just spewing out more random lies just for the fun of it. That's when I noticed a car in my rearview mirror that was driving very fast and getting increasingly closer to us? In fact, it *appeared* to be chasing us? It was a yellow cab, and as it brazenly drove up alongside of us on the *wrong* side of the road, I suddenly shuddered to see the *possessed waitress* from the restaurant smiling wickedly at me right there in the front bench seat of the cab beside the driver? *Damn!* I floored the accelerator, and with knots in my stomach I tried to figure out a way to shake them?

Hannah glanced over at the car, and then *Shakenbutnotstirred* shared joyously, "Hurray! There he is now! When my father gets hold of you two, you won't know what *hit you!*"

"Quick, Kip! Turn left!" Hannah yelled.

"But there's *no road* there, Hannah? That's an open field?" I argued in confusion.

"*Turn left!*" Hannah insisted in no uncertain terms.

So, I *did*! I didn't understand exactly what we were doing, and I worried about the longevity of my tires and shocks in this rough and bumpy terrain, but I bowed to what I knew was Hannah's far superior intellect. Looking back to the highway as we drove through this forgotten field in rural Montana, the yellow cab had abruptly stopped and parked right next to it without actually following us in? The driver must have had second thoughts about continuing to follow us if it meant driving off-road and risk damaging his car, no matter how much money the waitress had promised him! The possessed waitress wore an angry grimace on her face as she watched us driving away. And then, as she and the driver both reentered the cab, presumably to return to the restaurant, something *strange* happened? Suddenly, the very same waitress who had been possessed only minutes before, jumped out of the car and ran *screaming* down the highway in the direction of the restaurant as if the Devil himself were at her heels! Meanwhile, the *newly possessed taxi driver*, like 'The Hound of the Baskervilles,' tenaciously drove

109

his cab into the field pursuing us just as fast as his car would take him! In a couple of minutes, the cab was already no more than ten feet behind us!

"Okay, Hannah! What now?" I yelled as I tried very hard to stay in front of our pursuer.

"Ha!" *Shakenbutnotstirred* laughed! "You're as good as *caught!*"

"Don't worry, Kip!" Hannah shouted encouragingly. "Make a sharp right turn after that long bank of trees!"

This time I didn't say a word, but did *exactly* as she had said!

With alarm, I heard my tires squeal for a long moment as I took the turn very quickly. The ground beneath us was still pretty damp from recent rains and that made it all the more difficult for me to keep control of the car while traveling at such a high speed. But fortunately, I had plenty of practice driving this old bus on just about every off-road surface in Montana, and as an added bonus, I had recently gotten a new set of tires as a birthday present from my folks, which thankfully managed to help me adequately maneuver this terrain without *killing us in the process!* In the meantime, the cab came barreling around the trees at an even *faster* speed than I had and frighteningly nearly caught us! But luckily for us, it hit a mud-slick, the driver lost control and ended up crashing into one of the trees! He angrily got out of his cab and hatefully stared at us, unable to do anything at all about his unfortunate situation, as we quickly drove off!

"Great plan, Hannah!" I exclaimed, as I slowed down and turned my VW bus around to reenter the main highway.

"Thanks," she replied graciously.

"But, how did you know it would work?" I asked her in amazement.

"I *didn't?*" she admitted. "But I knew that the ground around the trees would be wet and muddy and after riding around with you for a few years, I *trusted* your ability to handle it. I also *assumed* that since the possessed cab driver was anxious to catch us, he would drive *too fast* and the rest is physics!"

"*Hmph!* You humans think you are *so smart*, don't you?" *Shakenbutnotstirred* angrily shouted. "But even now, my father and I can sense your impending defeat in the not-too-distant future, so *be ready!*"

"Hey? What's with the threats? This is *not* a war?" I reminded her. "We are just trying to survive!"

"Oh, you'll survive alright, you red-headed, freckle-faced freak!" she taunted me.

"What does *that* mean?" Hannah challenged her.

"That's for *you* and the redhead to find out!" the alien girl seethed nastily.

Ignoring her last remark, after reentering the main road and leaving the muddy field behind us, I decided to continue going in the same direction as we had been traveling before. Fortunately, the *new* destination I had in mind could be reached by using this same road. I only hoped that the alien girl's father would *not* find a way to track us.

After driving without conversation for almost an hour, it was *Shakenbutnotstirred* who first broke the silence. "So, where are we going, Kip?" she asked me very sweetly.

By this time, I had quite understandably grown immune to the alien's fabricated charms, even though when I shut my eyes for a moment, she *still* looked like my first movie crush, Hayley Mills! So, as a reply, I sarcastically paraphrased the line that she had so unkindly delivered to Hannah and me an hour earlier, "That's for *you* to find out!"

Well, the alien girl cohabitating in Hannah's mind was apparently *not* in a joking mood, nor did she evidently believe that turnabout was fair play! She instantly screamed and threw a fit, thrashing and kicking, trying to knock the *bejeegers* out of me, which was making my driving seem even *scarier* than usual! I could tell that Hannah had her hands full trying to restrain her, and I was very thankful that she actually *could!* When the alien girl had finally settled down, she let slip a hateful smile as she said, "Kip is lucky to have such a strong girlfriend to fight his battles for him, don't you agree, Hannah? But like I told you before. Tomorrow morning things will be *very different!*"

111

Hannah did not reply or give the alien girl a response of any kind, but that somehow gave me *hope*? You see, this was the *second* time that I remembered the alien calling Hannah 'my girlfriend,' and in my opinion, Hannah's lack of a response to that statement was almost as good as a confirmation that she *was*, don't you think? I mean it *was* possible?

Soon, we arrived at our destination. It was a small rustic cabin that sat alone in this part of the forest, overlooking a small lake or a *large pond*, depending on the year's rainfall. The cabin had previously belonged to my Grandpa Roy and he had used it for frequent fishing trips throughout his long life. Over the past ten years or so, being retired, he had the time to dramatically improve the livability of the place by adding electricity, running water, a water heater, an indoor bathroom and several modern appliances to it. And then, when he had passed away a few years ago, apparently knowing how much I loved the place, I was informed by my parents that he had actually *left the cabin to me*? What a wonderful surprise *that* had been! But, being the owner of this cabin could have proven very difficult if not *downright impossible* for a perpetually penniless junior college student like me, whose only sources of income came from odd jobs and parental donations! Luckily, my parents were kind enough to step-in and pay for the upkeep and taxes on the cabin until I finished college and got a proper job. I *loved* it here! But surprisingly, it was a place I had *never* shared with a soul before today? I must admit, I really felt happy that I was finally sharing it with Hannah.

Keeping our bags inside the bus, Hannah and I got out and entered the cabin. There were plenty of toiletries stored inside and under the circumstances, we saw *no need* for a change of clothes. The first thing we did was to open the windows to air the place out a bit before we sat down in the front room, which took-up most of the cabin and served as a catchall. To be precise, the front room was comprised of a small kitchen including a refrigerator, stove and sink, a small eating table with four chairs, and a couch where we were both currently sitting. There was no television set here because there was *no* reception. But, after what she had done to us, there was *no way in hell* I would even consider rewarding *Shakenbutnotstirred* with her favorite television shows anyway! The rest of the cabin consisted of two small bedrooms, a combination bathroom and shower tucked between them, and a large walk-in utility closet which my grandfather had used to store his huge collection of fishing gear. That however, had been cleaned out soon after he'd passed away, and the closet now served as a pantry. My dad and I had built shelves for it, last summer. Now sitting on those shelves were a moderate supply of both canned and boxed foods, as well as six cases of bottled drinking water, which I had recently stocked it with.

"What do we do now?" Hannah asked, obviously searching for an idea. "Over the next few hours, I'm sure that *Shakenbutnotstirred* is just waiting for me to fall asleep? How can I possibly stay awake all night?"

"Don't *waste* your time trying!" the alien girl interjected smugly. "Haven't you ever watched 'Invasion of the Body Snatchers' on television? It's one of *my favorites*! No matter how hard you try, Hannah, it's inevitable that I *will* surely possess you in the end! So why not just stop fighting me and make it easy on yourself?"

"But what if your father *doesn't* find us?" I suggested hopefully to the alien girl. "Then what need would you have to possess Hannah? His plan is obviously to possess *both* of us?"

"You're right about that," the alien replied confidently. "But I have little doubt that before this night is over, I will possess Hannah and my father *will* possess you!"

"What makes you so sure that your father will even find us?" I asked her curiously?

Shakenbutnotstirred let out a condescending and sneering laugh before insisting, "You must know by now that my father can be *very tenacious* about getting what he wants, and he *always does*!"

"But how could he possibly find us in such a secluded place as this?" Hannah challenged.

The alien girl haughtily laughed again. "*Silly Hannah*. You and Kip can *never* hide from him as long as I am cohabitating with you, because all my father has to do to find you is search for *my essence*!"

"What do you mean?" Hannah exclaimed.

"I mean the more I experience, the larger and brighter my essence becomes, and the *easier* it is for him to sense it from *any* distance away!"

"Do you mean that you are like some sort of bizarre *tracking device?*" I asked in shock?

"Yes!" *Shakenbutnotstirred* laughed gleefully. "Isn't it wonderful, Kip?"

Hannah and I looked anxiously into each other's eyes, both of us intensely sensing that we were in for a *very long night!*

Shakenbutnotstirred smiled at me and gently said, "I know you understand now that running away from my father is pointless. So, why don't you and Hannah just do the smart thing, starting *right now,* and stop looking for a way out, which quite obviously *does not* exist?"

"Why don't you just shut your 'bitchy pie hole,' you *boy chasing body stealer!*" Hannah suddenly shouted in anger and irritation.

The alien laughed. "I wish I could, Hannah," she said facetiously, "But I'm just having way too much *fun!*"

"Pay no attention to her, Hannah," I said. "She's just trying to sneak deeper inside your mind, and I'm guessing that when you're angry it's probably easier for her to do that."

"Bravo, you cute, little redhead you!" the alien girl exclaimed menacingly. "But no matter. I'll get in soon enough."

"Who *are* you?" I demanded. "You had such a *different* personality when I first met you? You were immature, but you weren't so angry and mean? There was something almost likeable about you then?"

The alien girl laughed arrogantly. "I've learned to always be whoever I *need* to be at the moment," she replied without emotion. "*Whatever* gets me what I want."

"Where did you learn to be like *that?*" Hannah asked quizzically. "Without any sense of right or wrong I mean?"

"From watching many, many shows on television," she replied. "Some of the most dishonest and dispicable characters are the biggest winners!"

"Yes, but surely getting what you want isn't worth ruining the lives of other people, is it?" I suggested.

"Oh, *isn't it?*" she grinned way too big.

Her last words and expression were *chilling*, and neither of us responded. Ignoring her, I got up and grabbed a couple bottles of water and a tin of canned stew from the pantry. Next I got two bowls, two forks and a couple of napkins from the kitchen cupboard and set the table with them. Following that, Hannah sat down at the table, I heated up the stew and soon joined her for dinner. We ate quickly, as I know we were both famished by this time! *Shakenbutnotstirred* did not comment at all while we ate, so we enjoyed our meal that much more. When we had finished, Hannah volunteered to wash our plates and utensils while I took the trash outside to a large county dumpster that was placed on the roadside for use by campers and local residents. When I returned to the cabin ten minutes later, I walked in to hear a *ferocious* verbal battle going on between Hannah and *Shakenbutnotstirred?*

"I don't care if you thought our meal tasted *disgusting*," Hannah said firmly. "Kip and I happen to like stew!"

"I'm sure that the *gasoline* would have tasted a lot better than *that* awful concoction!" the alien girl insisted angrily. "I *hate* stew!"

I temporarily forgot all about our current plight and couldn't help laughing as I walked through the door. "Stew is a nutritious human food, *Shakenbutnotstirred*. Perhaps you don't like being human after all? You know? *This* would be a great time for you to leave Hannah before we eat again?"

Hannah's face suddenly grew very dark and angry as the alien girl whispered harshly, "Just wait until my father gets here!"

I felt a chill running through my body as I processed her words, but I tried very hard to hide my fear as I brazenly replied, "I'm looking forward to it!"

When Hannah returned to her face, she looked at me with a very concerned expression? She never explained what that expression specifically meant, but to be honest, she *didn't* have to! As the sun set and the hours began to pass-by more slowly, Hannah and I decided to stay together on the couch. *That* seemed to be the best way for us to keep each other awake all night.

"I'll bet you're both feeling very tired about now?" the alien girl suddenly shared in a gentle and soothing voice. "Don't you want to lie down on those nice comfy beds? Just for a few hours?"

"What about *you?*" Hannah quickly challenged. "Don't *you* want to rest? How about leaving me and cohabitating with that '*nice comfy bed*' you were just talking about? I promise you that it *won't* fight you the way *I will!*"

Shakenbutnotstirred laughed. "Very funny! You know that I *never* get tired," she bragged. "It's one of the many advantages of not having a body."

"But you *do* have a body now, don't you?" I insisted. "Can't you *feel* what Hannah feels, now that you're cohabitating with her? Oh, I'm *sure* you do! As long as you're together, it only makes sense that if Hannah feels tired, *you feel tired!*"

The alien girl did not respond, and I took that to mean that I may have unexpectedly hit a nerve?

"Yes!" Hannah quickly joined in. "Didn't you tell us that you wanted to cohabitate with me so you could experience what it *felt like* being an Earth girl? Well, getting tired is a *big part of it*, let me tell you!"

The alien girl did not say another word all night, and that made Hannah and me very happy! Soon, I decided to pull-out my grandpa's old chess set because I remembered playing Hannah a lot when we were kids. As luck would have it, she was all for it. So, although neither of us had played for a number of years now, we prepared to pit our wits against each other through exciting battles on the chess board over the many upcoming hours, in *hopes* of keeping each other awake throughout the night!

"What do you think happened to *Shakenbutnotstirred?*" Hannah suddenly asked me as I considered my next move. "It's not like her to leave our conversation and *willingly* miss a chance to be *obnoxiously irritating?*"

I laughed, fully expecting the alien girl to respond, but surprisingly she *didn't?* "She's probably just pouting and giving us the *silent* treatment!" I smiled.

Hannah didn't reciprocate. "To be honest, this is getting a little *spooky?*" she admitted hesitantly. "What do you *really* think she's doing?"

I pondered this for a moment before finally replying, "I really have *no* idea? But I think as long as we're awake, it probably *doesn't* matter."

Hannah nodded. "Okay," she readily agreed. "That makes sense." Then looking at me very curiously, she asked, "This cabin is great and all, but how long do you think we'll need to hide-out here?"

I thought for a short moment and then replied simply, "I guess until one of us comes up with a plan to *permanently* rid ourselves of those two aliens? Although, I do think it might be a little tricky, since they're bodiless spirits? But I'm still *confident* there's a way!"

"Let me think on it for a while. I promise, if there is truly a way, I'll eventually find it!" Hannah replied with her confidence clearly beginning to make a comeback.

"Okay," I agreed encouragingly, and then we resumed playing. I, in *no way* resented staying up all night with Hannah. In fact, it was the most fun I'd had in as far back as I could remember. Maybe since we were kids? But I definitely *regretted* never spending this much time with her lately? Why had I been so blind as to never admit to myself how much I truly liked her? "Hannah?" I asked.

"Yes?" she replied.

"I'm sorry that I got you involved in this mess. Earlier when you came by my house, you sounded so happy about going to university next year. You should be celebrating now instead of being holed up here with me!" I apologized.

Hannah turned to me and smiled. "Don't be such a *downer*, Kip! What could be more fun than having an exciting adventure with my best friend?" she replied sincerely.

I was pleasantly surprised by her response, and immediately smiled back at her. "So, *I'm your best friend?*" I asked.

"There's no one else in the world I'd rather be hanging out with right now," she replied.

"Well, if you put it *that* way, then I guess you're *my best friend* too," I admitted.

"Great! But that doesn't mean you have to keep letting me *win?* she laughed. "As far as chess goes, I could probably beat you and frost a cake on the top of my head at the same time!"

I chuckled at her humorous words, until I stopped to realize that if there was anyone in the world who could make good on that boast, it was *her!* So, I *didn't* let her win for the rest of the night. Even so, she still won more than her share of the many games we played.

The night seemed to pass very quickly after that, and before we knew it, the sun had slowly begun to reveal its magnificent face, announcing the start of the new day! This spontaneously caused us to smile at one another as we basked in the knowledge that we had successfully stayed up all night together, and *loved* every minute of it!

"That night just flew by, didn't it?" I said robustly.

"Yes, it did," Hannah agreed.

"Why do you think that was?" I asked curiously.

"I think you know why," Hannah smiled. "It was because we're so *simpatico*," she smiled warmly.

I didn't respond, but I completely agreed.

Breaking the wonderful mood, suddenly we heard a fierce pounding at the front door, which seemed to rattle the entire cabin! Then a deep man's voice suddenly demanded, "Open the door *now* or I'll knock it down!"

Hannah and I quickly exchanged glances, and this time they were laced with *terror!* We had absolutely *no intention* of opening the door, as I hurriedly took her hand and led her through the cabin to a secret door located at the rear of the left bedroom which led to the outside. It was discretely camouflaged there by a tall wall of Italian cypress that I really hoped our visitor had not yet discovered! "C'mon!" I whispered intently as I passed through the door.

"I'm moving as fast as I can, but it's taking most of my strength to keep my 'lesser half' *quiet!*" Hannah frantically explained as softly as she could.

We ran out of the cabin only seconds before the mystery man effortlessly forced the front door wide open as if the lock had *never* existed! We didn't take time to chat, however, as we jumped into my VW bus and instantly drove off, screeching tires and all! As we left, we saw a *huge* man with bulging muscles (*resembling a professional wrestler*) staring at us in disbelief from the front door? Luckily, Hannah had the foresight to grab a steak-knife from the kitchen as we were leaving and slash the sides of the front and back tires on the right side of his large black truck, which had been conveniently parked right next to my bus. So, for the immediate future anyway, we could count on thankfully *not* being followed!

Shakenbutnotstirred laughed arrogantly, "How do you even *know* that man was my father?"

"*Wasn't he?*" I asked assuredly. "He seemed every bit as rude and arrogant as *you do!*"

"Yeh! And *whoever* he was, he broke into our cabin, threatened us and *deserved* to have his tires slashed!" Hannah declared with a smile, which *Shakenbutnotstirred* did *not* share.

"Okay, he *was* my father," the alien girl finally admitted. "But don't you see now that there's *no escape?* He'll simply possess somebody else and catch you both in no time!"

"Whatever happens, you and your father *won't* succeed!" I announced brazenly. "I *promise* you that!"

"We'll see about that," the alien girl retorted with ominous overtones and an inhuman glare.

"Where to now, Hannah?" I asked excitedly as we approached the highway.

"We go *home!*" she said. "No more running away! We're going to get home and just like Custer, we're going to *have* our last stand!"

I was initially shocked by her words? But somehow, since they came from her and knowing that regardless of where we chose to hide, we'd eventually be caught by *Areyoufeelingluckypunk*, it made perfect sense. After that, our conversation slowly faded and then eventually went completely dead as I continued to feel nervous during the entire drive home. You know? Our odds of surviving this upcoming ordeal were probably *a lot* like Custer's were during *his* last stand! So, I suppose it was wishful thinking, but in the end, I hoped like hell that we fared a lot better than *he did*!

We arrived back at my house a couple of hours later. It was approaching midmorning now and before I parked, I quickly perused the street to make sure that no suspicious-looking cars or people (*aliens*) were hanging around nearby? Feeling satisfied that all was clear, I followed Hannah out of the bus. The 'three' of us had not conversed during the entire second half of the drive home, I suppose mostly due to our fatigue. But with *no one* talking now, I suddenly grew concerned? "Hannah, are you all right?"

"Oh, I'm *peachy-keen!*" Hannah replied in a tone that sounded frighteningly like *Shakenbutnotstirred?*

"*Hannah?*" I exclaimed in horror.

"Relax, *Redhead,*" Hannah's lips said calmly. "Hannah is still with us but she's where she can't answer you right now, okay? I'm afraid you can only talk with *me!*"

"What have you done with her?" I demanded.

The alien girl laughed. "What do you think? I'm *possessing* her, of course."

"How?" I asked in disbelief.

Looking extremely proud of herself, she declared condescendingly, "Well, *you* actually helped me to do it and I thank you for that! When you told me last night that I must be tired if Hannah was tired, as strange as it seems, I realized that *you were right?* So, I had a nice peaceful sleep all night long, while the two of you forced yourselves to stay awake. During the drive here, Hannah was finally overcome with fatigue and couldn't help but drift off to sleep. Then I simply took over her mind, *exactly* as I said I would! It's absolutely wonderful *always* being right!" she bragged arrogantly.

I was shocked and immediately consumed by a hideous wave of nausea, like *nothing* I had ever experienced before? I didn't have a clue what to do next? Everything seemed so surreal? It was as if Hannah's life and mine, as we had known them for all of these years, were suddenly *over*? I tried very hard to pull myself together and quickly come up with a brilliant plan like Hannah would have done, but after thinking very hard about this dire situation, I *couldn't* come up with a single thing? After that, I felt myself quickly slipping into a deep and terrible depression. I feared that because the aliens had already *won* this battle with Hannah and me, in a short time they would silently win their much greater challenge of conquering the *Earth*! Hypothetically, it could not be long before this whole planet would be flooded with their *unhuman kind*, possessing and using us for whatever terrible purposes they wanted! And to make matters worse, I couldn't help but feel that somehow this was *all my fault*? I could barely endure the guilt and hopeless feelings that I felt, but I just couldn't shake them? And then as we slowly walked toward my front door, Hannah's left arm suddenly and *bizarrely* shot out into a nearby hedge that was covered with hundreds of bees collecting nectar and pollen. The bees went *crazy* at this perceived surprise attack, and immediately one of them angrily *stung* her! I quickly pulled her inside the house and slammed the door shut behind us!

"*Why* did you do that?" I exclaimed to Hannah's face, even though I knew I was speaking to *Shakenbutnotstirred*.

"I didn't do *anything*?" the alien girl insisted, completely shocked. "That arm went flying out *by itself*?" And then as confirmation that Hannah had indeed been stung, *Shakenbutnotstirred* suddenly began wailing at the top of her lungs as she suddenly felt the sharp pain of the sting! In addition, the tender inside part of Hannah's left arm, where the bee had stung her, was already turning a terrible bright red and swelling something fierce!

"If *you* didn't do this..." I pondered aloud, and then had an exciting but seemingly impossible thought. "Was it *Hannah*?"

"*Of course not!* How could it have been her?" *Shakenbutnotstirred* wailed. "I am *possessing her now*, remember?"

Suddenly, I surprisingly felt genuinely hopeful as I gently asked, "*Hannah*! Can you hear me?"

"Yes," a small voice replied from Hannah's lips. "I *can* hear you."

Upon hearing those words from Hannah, I suddenly felt delirious with joy! "Do you want me to put something on that sting? Maybe even try to pull out the stinger?" I asked gently.

"*No!* Don't do *anything!*" Hannah commanded in a much stronger voice.

"Awwwwwww!" the alien girl screamed. "What am I feeling?"

"That's called *physical pain, Shakenbutnotstirred,*" I told her with a complete absence of empathy. "When you possess a human's body, prepare to feel everything *they* feel! Sometimes a bee sting gets so painful, you want to die!"

"*Am I going to die?*" the alien girl blurted out in both terror and surprise.

To be honest, I was not even remotely prepared for her to ask me *that* question, but I suddenly saw my advantage and ran with it! "*Probably,*" I solemnly replied, as the words seemed to effortlessly fall from my lips.

"But, I have *no* body! How is *that* even possible?" the alien girl screamed through the pain.

"Because you entered *my* body and now you are *locked* into it as part of me. *That's* why you are feeling my pain!" Hannah explained. "Sadly, for you, I am now in complete control of whether or not you may *ever leave!* In the meantime, If I die, because you are now part of me... *you die too!*" Hannah declared morbidly.

"*No!*" the alien screamed. "Please no!"

"Your chance of staying alive depends entirely upon how well Hannah's body fights-off the bee venom in her bloodstream," I told her very seriously. "Unfortunately, a bee sting is *fatal* more often than not."

"But you don't want to see Hannah die, do you?" the alien girl asked desperately through excruciating pain. "Surely you will do everything you can to save her?"

"Of course, I will!" I declared.

Shakenbutnotstirred immediately sighed with relief.

"But that doesn't mean *you* will survive too," I added nonchalantly.

"*What?*" the alien screamed.

"Even now, Hannah's body is desperately fighting *you*, a dangerous foreign presence in her mind, and it's very possible that you will be completely *eradicated* before Hannah dies! That will allow her mind to stop worrying about you and focus *completely* on fighting the bee venom, hopefully leading to a full recovery for Hannah," I calmly explained. "Unfortunately, if that should happen, *you* won't be around to see it."

"Alright! I give up! I'll leave her body!" the alien girl declared frantically.

"No!" the little voice of Hannah replied sternly. "You *won't!*"

"Please, Hannah? Let me go!" the alien begged. "I want to live!"

"*No!*" Hannah answered both louder and harsher.

"I can't stand this pain much longer!" the alien girl shouted, while battling her self-inflicted hysterics.

Fifteen minutes later, there came an ominous knock at my front door. "This is *Areyoufeelingluckypunk?*," the high voice of a young child declared. "I have grown weary of your childish antics, Kip! Open the door *now!*"

Opening the door, although I was shocked and sad at what I saw, I did not let on as I came face to face with Hannah's eight-year-old brother Teddy, a skinny kid with shaggy brown hair, bright blue eyes like his sister, and a mouth with a couple of front teeth missing from *natural* causes. He had a habit of playing outside by himself a lot and that's probably when the alien had unfortunately caught him! Possessed-Teddy arrogantly walked inside my house and sat down on the couch.

"Where is *Shakenbutnotstirred?*" his bright childish voice demanded. "I do not sense her essence anywhere in this house?"

"That's because she's *not* here!" I replied cryptically. "She's somewhere else... dying!"

"What do you mean *dying?*" the alien possessing Teddy immediately demanded.

"On this planet, many natural things exist that are capable of killing us. At the top of that list are *bees!*" I explained.

123

"Bees?" the alien chuckled in humorous surprise. "You mean those cute little flying insects that buzz around collecting nectar from flowers?"

"*Yes.* You'll be surprised to learn that in addition to being painful beyond belief, their sting can often be *fatal!* Hannah was stung while *Shakenbutnotstirred* was possessing her, and now they are both dangerously close to *death!*"

"Balderdash! You're just making that up! Bring my daughter here *immediately!*" Little Teddy impatiently demanded.

"As you wish," I obediently agreed. A quick phone call to Hannah's house brought her right over with the alien girl still in tow. As I opened the front door, Hannah entered, with the alien girl moaning horribly through her lips, begging, "Father! You *must* save me! Do whatever they ask!"

"Is this some sort of *trickery?*" The alien man demanded through Teddy's voice. "Are you all right, *Shakenbutnotstirred?*"

"*No!*" she screamed. "Can't you see that I'm in *great pain?*"

"Then just *leave* her body!" he answered, trying his best to remain calm.

"I *can't!*" *Shakenbutnotstirred* screamed in irritation.

"Why not?" her father, through Teddy, demanded.

"Because I *won't let her!*" Hannah declared forcefully. "I am back in control of my own mind, and will *not* let her go until both of you agree to leave Earth and *never* come back again!"

Areyoufeelingluckypunk, in the body of young Teddy, instantly grew an expression of disbelief on his face, and then roared, "Enough of this foolishness!" Turning directly toward me, he seethed very tensely, "You and Hannah have done something *quite clever* here in hopes of escaping me, which I must admit, I do not yet fully understand yet, but *I will!* Now, for the last time, will you agree to my possessing you?"

I *glared* at him in contempt, refusing to answer his question! *Areyoufeelingluckypunk* angrily mumbled a few words under his breath and I immediately blacked-out.

I awoke to find myself once again in his spaceship? This time there was no furniture that he had gleaned from my memory in that cylinder-like room. It was completely empty, except for the two of us.

"We have reached the end of the chase, Kip," *Areyoufeelingluckypunk*, in the form of the green alien with purple robes who I had first met yesterday, telepathed calmly. "You *must* surrender to me now or I will be forced to make things *hideously unbearable* for you. Do you understand?"

Although the alien spoke to me calmly, his threat was still very *alarming*! I had already experienced his ability to effectively terrorize me once before, through yesterday's traumatic experience with the rats in the dungeon! What *other* 'unbearable' things could he possibly be dreaming up?

Literally reading my mind, he telepathed understandingly, "If you don't agree to let me possess you now, I will be forced to send you to a truly *monstrous* place that is so terrible, it was cast out of my world many years ago and sent here to reside on Earth! The *being* who is in charge there is far crueler and much more powerful than I could ever be! You will be subjected to him *unless* you agree to surrender right now!" And then with a gentler tone, he added, "I like you, Kip. I really don't want to see you get hurt, but I *will* unleash him on you if I have to! What is your answer?"

Perhaps it was due to my fright or my now intense stubbornness, but I would not, I *could not* surrender to him! So, just like before, I did *not* say a word.

The alien immediately became enraged as he telepathed, "Have it *your* way! Go *rot in Hell!*"

Suddenly, *everything* around me turned pitch black? I honestly couldn't see a thing? Not even a speck of light? But I knew from the sudden chill I felt, that I was *not* in the alien's spaceship anymore! And then I heard a deep and disturbingly sharp voice echoing all around me, laughing menacingly. "Hello, Kip. Welcome to *Hell*! I am *The Influencer*, and you are now in my '*Chamber of Torment!*'" the voice proudly proclaimed. "*Areyoufeelingluckypunk* always sends me the *stupid creatures*, like you, who need to learn some *respect!*" Again, he laughed, completely unhinged. "As I'm certain he has already told you, I am a much more *effective persuader* than he is, and believe me, that is an *understatement!*" Pausing dramatically, he then declared, "I am willing to do *anything to anyone*, no matter how objectionable and painful they may find it! I *thrive* in this world of agonizing pain and hopelessness!" There was an ominous pause before he added happily, "*I love my job!*"

Shaking-off his last comment, I very hesitantly asked him, "Why do you refer to this place as *Hell*?"

The Influencer let out a crazy laugh. "Isn't it obvious, Kip? This place, just like the actual Hell, is designed to keep you in intense fear and pain *forever!* Can't you already feel the *chill* in the air? Over time this place could become *colder* and *colder*, until you could barely stand it! Or I could torture you in any number of other ways! Truly, my arsenal of *methods for torment* is growing larger and more hideous every day!"

I inadvertently shivered! I certainly didn't like what he was telling me, but I still maintained hope (*although I'll admit that the size of it was growing decidedly smaller by the second*) that there *must* be some way out of this other than giving-in, although I frustratingly could not think of one?

Obviously sensing weakness in my thoughts, The Influencer declared, "There is absolutely *no escape* from here, so you may as well stop wasting your time thinking about it! You have *no hope* at all that anyone will suddenly appear here from nowhere to help you either! I'm afraid that *Areyoufeelingluckypunk* has left you alone with me, to *painfully* spend the rest of your pathetic human life!" Then he paused, and softened his voice, "That is, unless you *agree* to let him possess you right now! Well?"

I was more frightened than I'd ever felt before, but I was still not willing to give-up? Not yet! So, in protest to his request, I remained completely silent.

"*You fool!*" The Influencer roared with anger. All at once the darkness around me was completely obliterated by a *blinding*

126

brightness? This was no ordinary brightness emanating from one distinctive source, like the sun. *This* powerful light illogically radiated from every square inch of space around me at an incredibly high intensity? In fact, I didn't dare open my eyes for fear of *blinding myself!* I even felt the heat from the light beginning to *burn my skin* right through my clothes, as I also endured a very unpleasant stinging sensation all over my body! Out of nowhere, in addition to the intense burning light, next I experienced what I could only describe as my *worst nightmare!* Although I couldn't see them, I suddenly felt a horde of bugs begin scampering up and down my legs, over my arms and chest, and even across my face, causing the pain I felt from my burns to become even more extreme with every disgusting step they took! I frantically swatted at them to get them off of me, but it *didn't* help? Inexplicably they seemed to be stubbornly *burrowing* into my body with no hint of ever leaving?

"If you are wondering what sort of *bugs* are running amuck all over your body," the deep voice of The Influencer (*clearly enjoying the fact that I was already scared out of my mind*) excitedly explained. "They are eponymous beetles, also known to the Egyptians as *Scarabs!* When I give them the signal, they will each slowly begin *tearing away at your flesh* while the intense light continues to burn you, until eventually there will be nothing left of Kip Weiss but *brittle bone*, which will in time turn to dust and blow away! A very *slow, hideous and painful* death, if I do say so. It may even take *decades* for you to *completely* die?" His voice paused momentarily, before adding, "Are you finally prepared to give up? This will be your *last chance!*"

I *don't know why*, but out of nowhere a question suddenly forced its way into my conscious mind? "Is this the *same* torture that I faced in a dungeon yesterday with ravenous rats?" I asked suspiciously, suddenly seeing a blatant similarity between *Areyoufeelingluckypunk* and The *Influencer's* ideas of torture?

"Oh no!" The Influencer responded quickly. "I understand that the rats in *that* dungeon were going to eat you alive! The Scarabs here have absolutely no interest in that. They simply intend to cause you as much grueling pain as possible for *much longer* than you can possibly stand it!" he howled morbidly, while his hideous laughter once again echoed endlessly off the walls all around me!

I was finally worn down enough by The Influencer that I'd reached the point where everything that was happening to me or threatened to happen to me in the future was almost *too much* for me to bear! I was *well beyond terrified!* I did not want to give-in, but what choice did I have? I *had* to succumb to The Influencer's wishes or be painfully tortured for *the rest of my life?* And then suddenly, like a bolt of lightning, my mind grew strangely relaxed as it abruptly *refused* to accept this dire prognosis or the frightening situation I had seemingly found myself in? I was initially confused by this, but quickly understood. The reason my mind was *not accepting* what my senses told me was real, stemmed from my earlier suspicion that *this* torture oddly resembled the first torture I had endured at the command of *Areyoufeelingluckypunk?* Hmm? I knew that *both* he and The Influencer could read my mind, and that these two torture scenes had *both* undoubtedly come straight from my memories of watching too many low budget horror films over the years? But the almost identical torture choices, you know, very slowly eating or tearing off my flesh, seemed *way too similar* to be a coincidence, didn't it? To me, it seemed like the type of torture a creature *without a body* might be obsessed with creating... *twice!* And then there was the fact that The Influencer was advertised to be a *lot scarier* than *Areyoufeelingluckypunk*. But since I could never see him, judging only by his voice, that was plainly *not true?* The fact is, although he was way over the top, like Dracula or some other 'scary' monster from an old movie, he was only shockingly scary *initially*, the way an over-the-top character in a carnival funhouse might be. After a while, his forced persona didn't seem to work for him as well? In fact, on the *scary-meter*, he and *Areyoufeelingluckypunk* now came across to me pretty much *the same?* Based on those facts, I was now convinced beyond a doubt that the two aliens had to be *one and the same* entity! But was it really probable, I asked myself, that *Areyoufeelingluckypunk* was simply creating a hallucination of everything that *seemed* to be happening to me in Hell and that The Influencer *did not even exist?* Why would a powerful creature like him choose to do that? And then I vividly recalled Hannah suggesting to me yesterday that she theorized the frightening 'rat-mare' I had experienced yesterday was *not* real at all, and only *seemed real* to me because I was simply *convinced that it was*? I had never actually tested her hypothesis, but I was certain that *now* would be the perfect time to do it! So, I pulled myself together and brazenly shouted, "This is *not* real! *None* of it is!"

"Of course, it's real!" a noticeably shaken Influencer stubbornly insisted. "And if you don't agree to let *Areyoufeelingluckypunk* possess you in five seconds, the Scarabs will slowly and very *painfully* begin tearing off *all* of the live flesh from your bones! One, two, three, four, *five!*"

Ignoring his tired words, I knew what to do. "*Scarabs and intense light disappear!*" And immediately, all of my pain was gone, along with the intense light and the bugs?

"*I made that happen!*" The Influencer frantically declared, trying hard to sound confident. "I'll give you one last cha..."

"*Influencer, disappear!*" Beginning at that moment, I never heard The Influencer's overly dramatic and irritating voice again!

Suddenly I felt as if I was waking up? When I opened my eyes, with relief and joy, I found myself once again back at my house *exactly* where I'd been prior to being whisked away to '*Hell!*' I was once again facing Hannah's little possessed brother Teddy.

Areyoufeelingluckypunk (*aka Teddy*) instantly flew into a tremendous rage and proclaimed, "No more delays! I am going to *possess you*, Kip, whether you like it or not! Any last words?"

Taking a long glance at Hannah, I smiled slightly as I suddenly understood! "*Knock yourself out!*" I said to *Areyoufeelingluckypunk* through Teddy, as I turned back to him with a grin. Immediately, Teddy, the *real Teddy*, was *thankfully* free of the alien parasite, and I sighed with relief. Looking around the room at his screaming sister Hannah, and a facially contorted *me*, as I was in the process of being possessed, Teddy merely smiled at us and waved goodbye. It was as if his visit had now come to an end and *that* was all there was to it?

I have always loved watching the simplicity of a young child's mind at work. Teddy probably had *some* idea what was going on right now as well as what had just happened prior, but he *didn't understand* or question either one as he calmly walked out the door? He may have thought that Hannah and I were simply practicing improvisations for a summer drama class we were taking, like we did last year? That would make sense, right? In any case, it was time for him to go home for a snack, and that's *exactly* what he was doing! At that moment, *I truly envied him!*

"*Awww!* What is this fierce pain I am feeling?" *Areyoufeelingluckypunk* suddenly bellowed. "Make it *stop!*"

"I have a better idea!" I replied defiantly from the same mouth. "Rather than allowing you to possess me, forever taking away my ability to think for myself, *I hope you die!*"

"*Die?*" he repeated fearfully. "I *don't* want to die?"

"Yet, if you continue cohabitating in my mind, *you will!*"

"Then I don't want to cohabitate in your mind anymore!" the alien man exclaimed. "Please set me free, Kip?" he begged, as he suddenly realized that I was holding him prisoner against his will, in the very same way that Hannah was holding *Shakenbutnotstirred?* And after the way he had treated me, he also had to know that I was probably *less than likely* to grant his request for freedom.

"I don't know?" I replied hesitantly, enjoying this moment very much as I suddenly found myself firmly in control of the situation. "You see, *Areyoufeelingluckypunk*, twice before you made me believe that all of the nonsense you created in your spaceship and dungeon was *real*. But *this* time, I discovered that the moment I *disbelieved* in your bloodthirsty Egyptian Scarabs and that *ridiculous Influencer*, your power over me completely vanished? Apparently, *nothing* about you is real, is it." I paused dramatically before continuing. "But, something you *can't* control and I *can*, is happening to you right now! The pain you are feeling is *definitely real* and it will stay with you as long as you cohabitate with me in my mind! Your little tricks can in no way make that pain go away and you can *never escape* from it unless I choose to let you go! I hope in your final few minutes of life you will finally believe in the intelligence and fighting spirit of the human race! You see, two bees stung me a short while ago and their venom is now surging through my veins! One bee's poison can be deadly for any being *not* born and raised on Earth. But the poison of *two bees* will almost certainly kill that being in *30 minutes or less!* Unfortunately, if we *don't* release you soon, that means you will *die!* We will then keep your daughter imprisoned in Hannah's mind in great distress until she either dies or is *driven crazy!*" I declared intensely.

Just then, *Shakenbutnotstirred* began wailing uncontrollably. "Father! Help me! Please! I *don't want to die!*"

"Yes, yes, I will!" the terrified alien father assured his daughter. Then he frantically asked me, "*What is it you want?*"

"Hannah and I want you and your obnoxious daughter to leave our bodies and return to whatever *hell-hole in the dregs of space* you came from, *never* to return to Earth again!" I demanded forcefully.

The alien's expression on my face grew even more desperate as he quickly realized that I held all the aces. "Agreed!" he begrudgingly assured me.

"And if you should *ever* decide to break our agreement by returning to this planet," I warned menacingly, "the *bees*, as well as their much larger cousins the *wasps*, will *kill* you sure as I'm standing here! They will be driven mad by the smell of bee venom in your essence causing them to immediately swarm any creature that you possess and make sure that you both *die* an excruciating death!" I exclaimed. "Here on Earth, we consider bees and wasps to be the sacred guardians of the entire human race!"

"Don't worry! I never want to experience this pain or return to Earth again!" the alien man cried out. "You have my solemn word!"

"No lies?" I double-checked, acting as if the sound of my voice could easily *penetrate* his very soul.

"*No lies*," *Areyoufeelingluckypunk* confirmed. Then softening his voice, he asked, "But don't you even want to know the reason we were hoping to take the two of you back to our planet?"

Before I had the chance to respond, Hannah declared, "I'll tell you why, Kip. It's because they *loved* your red hair and freckles and intended to make you the main attraction in their traveling circus!"

131

"*Traveling circus?* Is this true?" I demanded.

"Yes," *Areyoufeelingluckypunk* replied. "I have never before seen another intelligent *natural red-haired creature* on *any* planet I have ever visited! If my plan had worked, we would have continued hunting down and possessing other redheads on your planet forever! You redheads would have made me *rich*, Kip! I could have traveled to every other planet I know, set-up additional traveling circuses there, and raked it in! But, I severely misjudged you Earthlings! With your mighty bees and your ability to keep us *trapped* indefinitely inside your minds once we enter them, you and Hannah have vanquished our dreams and now I am forced to humbly admit defeat!"

"But *why* did you insist on also taking Hannah?" I demanded. "She's not a redhead?"

"Because the two of you are *simpatico*, just like Hannah told you at the cabin, you idiot!" *Shakenbutnotstirred* bellowed angrily through her ever-increasing pain.

"You belong together," her father insisted honestly. "We thought that taking her along would keep you happy in your new life with us, Kip."

"But we've *never* even gone out on a real date together?" Hannah said in confusion.

"Yes, but that doesn't mean you didn't *want to?*" *Shakenbutnotstirred* insisted arrogantly.

"Release us *now!*" *Areyoufeelingluckypunk* demanded. "I promise you that we will *never again* bother either one of you or return to Earth!"

I nodded firmly at a very stoic Hannah and just like that, without smoke or fanfare, we released *Areyoufeelingluckypunk* and *Shakenbutnotstirred*, finally finding ourselves free of the aliens, never to see, hear or sense their bee infested essence ever again!

Hannah immediately rushed over and grabbed me in the tightest bearhug I had ever experienced, and it felt so good!

"How did you ever get out of *Shakenbutnotstirred's* power once she began possessing you?" I asked earnestly, just as soon as our hug had ended.

Hannah laughed. "I was *never possessed* by that cocky brat! She only thought I was. As a matter of fact, I was able to think just as clearly then as I can now?" Then triumphantly, she added, "Once we had returned to your house, and she claimed to be possessing me, I realized that because I didn't believe any of her silly declarations, I was actually *unaffected* by anything she said or did? But I decided to play along with her so I could make the final ending of this adventure as *exciting* as possible, just in case someday you might get the urge to write about it! After all, it is a pretty *fantastic* story!"

I laughed, and then an important question came to me, "But if *Shakenbutnotstirred couldn't* possess you, how was it that *Areyoufeelingluckypunk* was able to control the minds of that waitress, cab driver, body builder and your brother Teddy?" I asked, perplexed.

Hannah nodded. "Well, *Areyoufeelingluckypunk* undoubtedly had a lot more experience controlling other creatures' minds through instilling *unreasonable fear* into them than his silly *rookie* daughter did! So, when he got into their minds, I'm certain that he must have been *very convincing* and made them each believe that they had no other choice! His method probably works similarly to *brain washing* or like I suggested before, *hypnosis.*" Pausing momentarily, she then added, "Unfortunately, aside from *me,* and later *you,* no one else apparently thought to *challenge* the notion that a strange voice had gained control over their minds simply because it *declared to them it had?*"

I smiled at her in awe. "You know, I was wondering? How did you *know* that a simple bee sting would have such a painful effect on *Shakenbutnotstirred*? I mean, she was a *bodiless* alien from outer space?"

Hannah smiled as she explained, "Elementary, Kip. Like we hypothesized up at the cabin, since she and I were sharing the same body, which led us to believe she would feel tired at the same time I did, it only stood to reason that because the bee sting had a painful effect on *me,* she would definitely experience the *same* agony!"

133

Hannah explained. "And then when she bragged about *sleeping* last night due to feeling fatigued, while the two of us forced ourselves to stay awake, I *knew* I was right! She *had* to play by human rules while she was cohabitating with one! That's when I decided to *get myself stung!*"

"Wow!" I declared. "You know, I watched you concentrating so hard on everything you told her right after you were stung, and I initially wondered why? But then it hit me? *Shakenbutnotstirred* could *not* read your mind when you purposely locked it, so she *never realized* that we were faking her out? The moment I understood that, I just copied your lead. I went outside, got myself stung like you had, and ran with it! That was probably the most important thing I have ever learned *completely* through observation!" I laughed. "Exactly *what* brilliant stroke of genius led you to come up with that?"

"That was *no* brilliant stroke of genius, Kip," Hannah laughed. "That was *experience!* While I was remembering how *Shakenbutnotstirred* always talked about watching television programs, I happened to think about how my family's TV set sometimes scrambled the picture when the signal got disrupted. I simply applied that same concept to *this* by blocking my thoughts from her!" Then she added, "And I soon discovered that besides keeping her out of my thoughts, a terrific perk was that it also *trapped* her inside my mind!"

"Wow!" I exclaimed. "I honestly had *no idea* why that was working for me too, but thank goodness I had the good sense to keep copying you!"

"Yeah. Just like you did on our tests in Freshman Algebra class," she laughed.

I smiled. She *wasn't* wrong.

"Hey? How did you learn to read *Shakenbutnotstirred's* mind anyway?" I asked curiously.

Hannah smiled. "It was as easy as *telling my mind* what to do! After all, the mind is a very powerful thing! Since she was reading my mind, I simply told my mind to read *hers!* And it worked! Tit for tat."

"That's amazing!" I exclaimed. Through this wonderful wave of happiness, I remembered a very uncomfortable thought, which I now felt compelled to share with her. My expression showed obvious remorse, as I hesitantly said, "I'm sorry, Hannah, for *not* believing you in the beginning about *Shakenbutnotstirred* being untrustworthy and in cahoots with her father. It was all because I was taken-in by her lies that you were forced to get involved with this whole mess in the first place."

"Oh, don't feel bad," Hannah shared gently. "There's been no permanent harm done. Besides. They would surely have thought-up some other *boneheaded scheme* to possess us if that first plan hadn't worked." Smiling, she gently added, "And you know what? I was *not* about to make you face all of that terror alone. That's not something a *girlfriend* does!"

Her last sentence sent *happy shivers* up and down my spine, and I couldn't help but smile back at her. My girlfriend?" I asked.

"*Your* girlfriend!" She confirmed with a smile.

This was exactly what I'd hoped for during the entirety of this whole adventure! Once again we embraced. I can't remember *ever* feeling so happy! After a few moments, I asked her, "Why do you suppose they created such an *elaborate plan* to catch us? Surely they could have thought of a much *easier* way to get the job done?"

Hannah laughed. "I'm sure they *could* have, but I'll bet those aliens probably recognized your creative mind right away and decided to have a little *fun with it!*"

"What do you mean by that?" I asked.

"Oh, you know, by convincingly creating things for you in the other dimension in order to keep you believing what they wanted you to believe until they sprang their trap on us at the restaurant. For all of the trouble they caused us, I have to admit that they were *very clever!*" Then with a smile, she added, "You were going to be their *star attraction*, Kip, so they were working overtime to reel you in. You should be *flattered!* You were the target of a well-traveled, fast-talking proprietor of a galactic circus and his *rude, exceptionally spoiled daughter!*" she laughed.

135

I laughed too. "Well, in any case, I'm certainly glad that *our* human minds proved to be more cunning than whatever *they* have for brains!"

"Agreed! And you know what?" Hannah smiled. "I think that by foolishly believing they could outwit *us*, those two arrogant fools obviously suffered from *colossal delusions of grandeur!*"

"Yeah!" I chuckled. "They probably took their *role models* from cheesy aliens they had watched on really bad sci-fi shows on television!"

"Yeh! Maybe even from *cartoons!*" Hannah laughed.

I laughed too! Then, growing thoughtful, I said, "Thanks again, Hannah! Your quick thinking saved thousands of redheads like me, all over the world, from being taken away to an alien planet against our will! And I am so glad the aliens *didn't* decide to land in Ireland or Scotland first! Did you know that those two countries have the *highest percentage* of redheads in the world? Those aliens would have thought they'd died and gone to *redhead heaven!*"

"You're welcome," Hannah said meaningfully.

I accepted her response with a smile. But then I thought of something else and grew uneasy. "You don't think all of that stuff I said to *Areyoufeelingluckypunk* about the strength of the bee venom killing him in thirty minutes, the bees and wasps protecting the Earth and the venom staying in the aliens' essence forever was *too much* do you? I mean, I *may* have gone a bit overboard? It could have *backfired?*"

Hannah laughed. "*Stop* second-guessing yourself, Kip! What you told him and how you delivered it was *perfect!* And *you* should thank your lucky stars that you are so incredibly creative *and* can think on your feet so well!"

"Thank you, Hannah! I really appreciate that!" I replied, turning a little red.

Hannah smiled. "You know, Kip? The way you lied so believably makes me think that you could be an outstanding actor or maybe even a politician if you wanted to be?"

"*No, thanks,*" I laughed. "I think I'll just stick with writing."

"Okay," Hannah nodded. "But I just want you to know that I *couldn't* have defeated the aliens by myself. I *don't* have a creative mind like yours, Kip. Remember when *Shakenbutnotstirred* told us, '*Lying can be a valuable tool in controlling the weaker minds.*' She was right! *You* took a page right out of the aliens' playbook and used it against them! It didn't matter *what* you told them, just as long as *they* believed it! And they *did*!" Hannah smiled. "So really? I think saving the Earth from their future treachery was definitely a *team effort*!"

I beamed at her last comment! "Thank you! I guess turning the tables on them was certainly fair play."

"Who cares about *fair play*? I'm just glad they're *gone*!" Hannah shouted in relief.

"Ditto!" I confirmed, joining her happy mood. And then I did something I had never done before in all of my years of knowing Hannah. *I kissed her*. Not one of those super showy TV kisses... but a gentle and meaningful one.

As soon as we'd finished, there was a slight pause before either one of us spoke. "That was very nice," Hannah said sweetly.

"Yes, it *was*," I confirmed shyly.

"But how do you know it was really *me* who you kissed?" Hannah asked playfully. "I could be *Shakenbutnotstirred* pretending to be me, couldn't I?"

Kip laughed. "You forget that *Shakenbutnotstirred* and I already kissed in a dream and believe me, *our* kiss put that one to shame!"

"Good answer!" Hannah beamed.

"But how do you know it was *me* who kissed you and not *Areyoufeelingluckypunk* pretending to be me?" I challenged her.

Hannah smiled broadly. "Duh!" she exclaimed. "Your kiss was everything I've always dreamed it would be! No stupid alien could fake that!"

I smiled back as I mischievously asked her, "Fess up! How long have you had the *hots* for me, Hannah?"

"Oh, about as long as you've had the *hots for me*," she laughed. "Since 'nap time' in kindergarten!"

I laughed too, and we again embraced warmly.

"Say, have you decided to go to university with me, Kip?" she suddenly asked with some urgency. "Now that we've finally dispatched the aliens and gotten together in the process, I'm afraid that I couldn't bear to be away from you for *even one semester?*"

Hmm? Would I be going with Hannah to university? Well, *if* I was accepted, there could be only one answer. "I have my answer, Hannah," I smiled.

"Well, *don't* keep me in suspense! What is it?" she asked excitedly.

"You must know that after this little adventure, I will *never again* feel safe in this world without *you* to protect me!" I shared with a meaningful chuckle. "So, *duh!*" Growing more serious, I said, "Of course, I have to be accepted to your university first. So, I guess I'd better send in my application right away!"

"Well actually, Kip, I know it was sort of underhanded of me, but with your parents' help, I sent *your* application, along with some samples of your writing to the university at the same time I sent mine. I hope you're not mad at me?"

Although I was genuinely surprised, I replied encouragingly, "Of course not, Hannah! It was very sweet of you to think of me. Is there any timeline for when I might expect to receive their decision?"

Hannah smiled the biggest smile I had ever seen in my entire life. "There is," she calmly said, before pausing, and then exclaiming, "*Congratulations, Kip!* You've been *accepted* into the prestigious *School of Arts and Letters* at The University of Montana at Billings for next year's fall semester! I'm so proud of you!"

I was blown away! *Me* accepted into one of Montana's best universities and attending it with Hannah? Excitement gripped my entire body as a great big smile spontaneously appeared on my face. At that moment, there were absolutely *no words* forming in my mind that could have possibly expressed my great appreciation, admiration and love for Hannah, or my immense joy that we had *finally* found each other! So, I settled for gratefully smiling back at her, just before I wrapped her tightly in my arms while we shared the most passionate kiss I could ever have imagined! And I planned on holding her like this, *just* like this (*metaphorically speaking*) for as long as we lived!

The Dream Master

Have you ever woken-up in a cold sweat, desperately *afraid* of what your future may or may not hold in store for you? Well, *I have*! I really didn't want to be *that* person, but I *was*, just the same. My name is William Karros, but my friends have always called me *Willy*. To look at me, I am darker complected due to my Greek heritage on my mother's side, tall, due to my Scandinavian heritage on my father's side, in reasonably good physical shape because I work-out at the gym twice a week, and I have facial features that I am told make me *not completely hideous* to look at. Not bad, huh? But for some reason I usually appeared to folks who didn't know me very well as being a rather ordinary guy. In fact, even to those folks who *did know me well*, I often came across in that very same disappointing way? I was beginning to think that the way everyone seemed to see me was sadly who I *really was* and I would continue to be *ordinary* for the rest of my life?

Following my unspectacular graduation from high school, I took some classes at city college for a while, but after two years of going to the beach more often than attending my classes, it was clear that I needed to go in a different direction. A *very* different direction! So, with some help from my dad, I was hired by a company owned by a friend of his, and I proceeded to do construction work for five years. The pay was good, so I excitedly moved out of my childhood home into my first studio-apartment! I suppose I didn't mind the work itself too much, it's just that working outside most of the time often brought uncomfortably *extreme* temperatures and conditions which I never really got used to. That's when I logically decided that my next job *had* to be indoors in constant air conditioning! This led to my *not* so 'intense' *three-week training course* to become a bartender!

141

After completing the course, I was immediately hired at the bar of a swanky hotel, not too far from where I lived. Granted, I took a pretty hefty pay-cut compared to my last job, which forced me to move back home with my dad, but aside from that, the transition was relatively painless. I ended up working at a number of different bars and restaurants over the next few years, where I always seemed to develop a very good rapport with the patrons and often got lucrative side jobs working their private parties as a result. In fact, it was at one of those parties that I met my former girlfriend, Bernadette. I'll say more about her later. All of these bartending jobs paid okay and the tips were nice, so I continued doing it for five years. But on my thirtieth birthday, I surprisingly suffered an early *midlife crisis* that hit me especially hard? In fact, I felt very anxious about it! I somehow knew that the only way to feel better about my life was to get a *real job* with better pay and benefits like most of the people I knew seemed to have.

Well, I settled on what some folks would (*I suppose*) call their 'dream job.' Just to *apply* for it, I had to go back to city college and take a number of very challenging business and math classes that took me a full year to complete! I'll admit, there were times I considered giving up, but in the end I successfully passed them all! On top of that, I was then asked to take a comprehensive test on everything I was *supposed* to have learned, which actually scared me to death! But fortunately, I passed that too! It wasn't long before I was hired by a nationally known company, and became a full-time sales rep for them! Okay, basically I *sell insurance*. The jury is still out on just how *dreamy* this job actually is, but for the moment anyway, it pays my bills, adds a little money to my retirement fund each month and keeps my weekends free, so I really *can't* complain. In fact, I can honestly say that I really hope to remain at this job a lot longer than I did at any of my other ones. I hate to admit it, but the reason for that is *not* because I love working here? It's because I have absolutely *no idea* what kind of job I could possibly find next that would be as secure as this one is? And *that* scares me? I am now 33 years old, *never* earned a degree from college and I'm certainly *not* getting any younger! Sadly, if I lost this job today, I just know that people would start seeing me as a *loser*, and unfortunately... *I already do!* The bittersweet good news about my current situation was that although I was still living in my childhood home in Bree, California, now I *owned it*. I inherited it from my dad after he sadly lost a bout with pneumonia last year. I would much rather have my dad back instead of owning this house, but at least it makes my life much easier to have my housing taken care of. I can barely remember my mother, as she died before my third birthday due to complications following an aortic aneurysm. But my father continually shared wonderful stories about her, so I have always felt as if she was somehow watching over me from heaven. Anyway, after my dad passed away, I felt lost in so many ways? To begin with, I had absolutely *no* direction in my life? Every weekday morning, I was often uninspired and even lethargic as I forced myself to get out of bed and go to work. But six months ago, something very unexpected happened to me that changed my life forever! Let me start from the beginning.

It was 1977, and I was hanging-out in my house one night with fellow misguided underachiever Andy Kowalski, a tall, thin, dishwater blonde dude with shaggy hair and a happy disposition that *always* made people smile. I have known Andy since junior high and we shared a lot of great times together in school, although *most* of them fell under the category of *getting in trouble*! Aside from that, I guess in most ways we had predictably been pretty *average* students in school, with *no* teacher ever presenting either one of us with an award for *exceptional achievement*. In addition, although we were never disruptive enough to get suspended, sometimes in the name of fun, we made some pretty *bad* decisions. Like the time we filled-up a couple of whoopee cushions, placed them on our seats at the back of the class and spent most of the period sitting on the edge of our chairs, pretending to be actively listening to the day's lecture. As soon as our English teacher had finished her lecture on poetry, just a few moments before the bell rang, we proudly *sat on our whoopee cushions*, causing an enormous '*passing gas blast*' that delightfully filled the room! Just as we'd expected, the class laughed hysterically and we were so proud of ourselves! However, the teacher (*although,*

I believed we were two of her favorite students) was *not amused!* It was only because of her fondness for us that we got away with only a stern warning that day. Unfortunately, our antics didn't help us later when taking our final test for the semester! The fact is, we couldn't remember *anything* about that poetry lecture that we were supposed to have paid attention to that day, consequently neither one of us had taken a single note to study! We had been way too excited thinking about sitting on our whoopee cushions to pay much attention to *anything* our teacher was sharing with the class. As a result, we failed the test, and our final grades for the semester were lowered from B- to C-, and that C- was *probably a gift!* That's why I very confidently believe that *misguided* and *underachiever* are a couple of more than fair descriptions of both of us. Tonight, we had already shared a sixpack of some very cheap beers (*that tasted more like dirty water*) called *Bitchin' Buzz*, that Andy had bought *on sale* at the grocery store he worked for. We weren't drunk, but we were both feeling pretty relaxed as he surprisingly asked me, "What are we going to do when we finally grow up, Willy?"

"*Finally grow up?*" I repeated slowly. "Well, Andy, I'm afraid I haven't really given that much thought?" I laughed. After releasing a loud belch, I added more seriously, "I guess we'll probably just go our separate ways and like they say, *find ourselves.*"

"Okay. That sounds pretty cool," Andy casually nodded his head. Suddenly growing more passionate, he added, "And I'll bet our '*separate ways*' will lead us to some far-out experiences we've never had before! Right?"

"Sure. Why not," I replied automatically, without really considering the depth of his words at all. But as I suddenly *did* realize what he had meant, I asked him curiously, "Why do you think *that*, Andy?"

Andy smiled, and replied, "Because face it, Willy. You're *too good* for the job you have and I'm the most *senior* 'junior checker' at the supermarket! As *semi-successful* as we both are, I just think that now we're ready to blast-off and like you said, find ourselves!" Then a look of utter terror suddenly crossed his face as he asked, "But how will we know when we've finally gotten there?"

Andy, who I often thought of as a good-natured cross between a hippy and a surfer dude with just a touch of country bumpkin, was a very good friend, a *forever* friend, loyal to the end! But, just like me, his life had been floundering for quite some time, for *years* in fact? And just like me, he still hadn't discovered the way to get his life on track? In this moment of searching, I knew that I had to say something stupendously smart. "Why don't we just meditate about it?"

"Wow! That's a *gnarly* idea!" Andy exclaimed encouragingly, obviously loving the idea, but also applauding the fact that we had come-up so quickly with *any idea at all!*

Soon, each of us went into a deep meditation and searched for the identity of that magical sign that would irrevocably signal us when we had finally found ourselves? Several minutes later, we were done. *We had nuthin'!* So, just like every other time Andy had left my house or apartment over the years, he gave me the peace sign and headed home (*where his parents also lived*) on his vintage Honda 90 motorcycle.

A week later, Andy and I met-up again at a local bar we frequented called *Benny's.* But surprisingly, even before a drop of alcohol had touched his lips, he excitedly declared, "Willy! I think I've finally *found myself!*"

Was I expecting to hear anything even remotely close to that coming from the mouth of my misguided and underachieving chum? Hell, no! "Great!" I put on a happy face to cover my surprise. "What made you come to *that* conclusion?"

Andy beamed. "I've just been promoted to *senior checker* at the store, and the manager told me that with a lot of hard work that showed them what I was *capable* of, I could become an *assistant manager* someday real soon!"

"Well, congratulations, Andy!" I exclaimed with my mug of beer lifted to the sky as I gently clinked his, "I'm so proud of you! You deserve this! What did your folks say about it?"

"Oh, they were really happy for me, man," he exclaimed. "But for some reason, my dad was way more interested in *how soon* I would finally be moving out of *his* house?" he laughed.

I laughed too, but at the same time, I found myself somehow *envying* him? I mean, go figure? I owned my own home and made a pretty good income, yet *he* was the one who got *promoted?* So, I felt more like a *loser* than normal. "Is your work schedule going to change much?" I asked.

"Oh yeah," he replied. "Super drastically! Beginning Wednesday, I'm scheduled to work 40 hours a week instead of 25, and I'll be working five days a week; Wednesday through Sunday!" He paused before excitedly adding, "And guess what? I'm also getting a *frickin' raise!*"

Ignoring the second part of his comment, I asked in shock, "You're working *weekends?*"

"*Have to*, dude. For a while anyway," he explained. "My boss says, agreeing to that schedule and keeping my weekends free to work from noon to ten, will really help the store and my chances of ever being considered for a future promotion!"

Once again we clinked our mugs together, albeit a little less enthusiastically than last time and I continued to smile broadly, although I really wasn't jumping for joy in the inside over his new schedule. But, I genuinely *did* feel happy for Andy, and the fact that he was finally finding himself! His promotion proved to be that magical sign that told him he was on the *right track*, while that great big grin on his face absolutely confirmed it! I felt glad for him, sure. But as a consequence, I felt *lost?* Not only was my best friend leaving me behind with his job promotion, but now he wouldn't even be free to go out drinking with me on weekends? This was *terrible!*

That night, after returning to my dark, empty house, I flopped down on the couch and wallowed in my hopelessness. I had no other great friends like Andy, no family, and as far as finding a woman to share my life with, to this point anyway, it had turned out to be a much more difficult job than I had ever imagined? The truth was, the only women I really saw a lot of these days were the ones I worked with in the insurance office. Unfortunately, up to this point they mostly turned out to be too young, too old, not interested, or happily married with kids! "Face it," I told myself sternly. "You've partied your best years away, you *idiot*, and haven't taken a single thing seriously!" Revving up for my final damning self-criticism, I added, "So, is it really any surprise to you, *Mr. Shit for Brains*, that you're destined to spend the rest of your sad and empty life *alone?*" Mired in self-pity and depression, I slowly flicked on the television set and surfed the channels to waste some time. Suddenly, I stopped on a show that I had never heard of before, that was airing on a channel I had *never known existed?* But I had no desire to question those obviously nonsensical elements, because the name of the show had truly *piqued* my curiosity? It was called, *The Dream Master?* You see, in my mind, I was a 'dreamer extraordinaire.' To expound a bit, understand that I looked forward to dreaming continuously every night! I often dreamed about things I thought I wanted out of life; goals that unfortunately ranged from *unlikely* to '*are you kidding?*' But regardless, those dreams always gave me some tangy food for thought when I woke-up. So, as the TV show had just started, I sat back and listened very intently to a tall, thin man dressed in a white suit, with brown hair. His unbelievably positive facial expression illuminated the entire screen as he calmly began sharing his thoughts.

"Hello, friends. I'm Charley, *The Dream Master*. Welcome to my show! Since you are watching this program, I'll bet you are fascinated by your dreams and want to learn more about them? Am I right? And I'll also bet that you have *one* very special dream that you wish would come true? Well, I hate to be the bearer of bad news, but unfortunately our dreams are not that easy to realize. What we dream about each night is usually a chaotic mixture of truth and fantasy that lacks much organization or coherency." And then he added with a sudden burst of energy, "But, fear not, my friends! Help is on the way! Tonight, I will begin the simple process of teaching you how to *control* the essence of your dreams by preparing your mind for just such a task. First, silently repeat this mantra in your head ten times beginning a half an hour before bedtime, '*My mind is clear to dream and I can't wait!*' And then fifteen minutes

147

before going to bed, set your parameters by focusing on three things you want to experience in your dreams. For example, you may want your dreams to be with a special person, romantic and exciting? Silently repeat these three very important parameters ten times. And as you are lying in bed, just before falling sleep, open your mind and spontaneously think of only happy thoughts. As many as you like! *That's it!* That ought to get you started. Good luck! See you next time!" And then the television screen unexpectedly turned to snow, and he was *gone?*

"Hey? Wait a minute? That wasn't a *real TV show?*" I yelled out loud, shocked and disappointed, feeling as if someone had just played a very cruel trick on me! As a result, I found myself abruptly turning off the television set in anger! I had so wanted to learn about dreams and dreaming, but The Dream Master had left me wanting more? *So much more!* After taking a deep breath, I realized that my disappointment *may* have actually been his intention all along? You know, like the old show biz saying, '*Always leave them wanting more?*' I smiled, and then before going to bed, I carefully followed the three steps he had suggested; mantra, parameters and happy thoughts. As I began to fall asleep, I grew excited as I suddenly felt my mind spiraling through space like a football thrown by an all-star quarterback into the *never-fail* arms of the receiver! I somehow knew that I was in for a *very exciting night!*

Once I had grown coherent, I found myself casually lounging on the beach of a beautiful tropical island? The sky was blue, the water was clear and the beach was covered in sparkly white sand that seemed to go on forever? I knew that I was dreaming, and although my sense of reality seemed to be a bit hazy right now, I *did* remember traveling to the Hawaiian Islands with my dad as a child. But somehow this place seemed even more impressive than *that* had? Oh, the immediately noticeable features of the island were similar enough to the sandy beaches and lovely ocean I had experienced in Hawaii. But this place was even more magical, more vivid and much more *secluded?* In fact, there didn't seem to be *anyone* else around? That was probably a good thing, come to think of it, because I shockingly found myself sitting on the sand of that beautiful beach *stark naked*? But the truth was, I was also feeling extremely relaxed by this time, so a little self-nudity didn't bother me one bit! It wasn't long before I boldly decided to explore the island. As I got up and left the enticing beach behind, heading inland toward the mysterious forest, I saw a vibrant multitude of eye-catching plant life of all shapes, sizes and colors, but disappointingly, *no* living creatures? I then fearlessly explored the entire island, but *still* didn't find anything but plant life? Now, I know that this place was exceptionally beautiful, but without even a pet to share my thoughts and feelings with, it almost felt as if *that didn't matter* at all? I mean, half the joy of being in a wonderful place for the first time is *sharing* it with someone else! Right? That was when I had a very exciting epiphany. Why not distract myself from feeling lonely by actually making myself a skirt out of some wild grass and colorful leaves that I had been seeing around the island? That was something I had absolutely *never* done before! Then, in addition to creating an appropriate 'islander image' for myself, I'd become *too busy* to be depressed! I was *sold*! In addition to making my skirt, over the next few hours I continued to explore the island, as well as beginning to make a small raft using random pieces of wood tied together with strong, wiry vegetation. When it was completed, I planned to explore the entire circumference of the island! And of course, I had prepared a comfortable place to sleep in a tree, as well as discovering a couple of fresh-water lakes. And if *that* wasn't enough, I soon walked into an orchard full of many different types of tropical fruit trees? I immediately surmised that this magical place was capable of supplying me with plenty of bananas, pineapples, mangos and other tropical fruits to sustain me for an indefinite time period! I suddenly felt *productive*, like I hadn't felt in a very long time? My life still didn't feel complete and I was still here *by myself*, but at least I had things to smile about! And then out of nowhere, I suddenly spied a beautiful young woman strolling through the forest, excitedly looking at everything around her? Like me, it seemed as if this was her very first time visiting this beautiful island? If that *were* the case, and she wasn't a native of the island, then *who was she*? As she continued walking closer and closer to me, I instantly forgot about everything else I was doing and *gasped*! Although I could have been mistaken, she looked exactly like a woman at work who I had had a crush on over the past year? Her name was *Melody Wentworth*? Even though this woman, like me, was wearing simple clothing made of leaves and grass, she still looked absolutely *stunning*! And then I woke-up.

As I drove my car to work that morning, I couldn't help thinking about the epic dream I had had last night? But, as wonderful as it had been, it was the approaching of *Melody Wentworth* at the very end that had created the greatest stir in me? But curiously, although I recalled preparing for the dream just as the Dream Master had suggested, I *couldn't* recall Melody Wentworth being even a footnote anywhere during that entire preparation process? Unless, I had spontaneously made her one of my happy thoughts at the end? *Yes!* I think *that* was it! But even if I had, to be perfectly honest, I hardly knew her? She was one of many secretaries in my insurance office, while I was one of many agents there. However, I'll admit that I *had* often wished that fate would intercede in my life and find a way of bringing us together by making her *my* secretary? There was just something very special about her?

When I arrived at the office that morning, I didn't see Melody anywhere around, which truly disappointed me? But, a couple of minutes later, I inadvertently smiled as she happily waltzed through the room. She then gracefully sat down at her desk, located about three feet in front of Mr. Irving Chapman's private office. Mr. Chapman had been an insurance agent in this office, like me, before becoming our new office manager a little more than a year ago. He was a tall, slightly overweight man in his early forties with a healthy crop of graying dark hair on his head and the friendliest persona you could ever imagine. Irving Chapman had been among the top-selling agents in this office since long before I had arrived here, so it came as no shock to anyone in the office when he was ultimately offered and accepted this plum promotion after the previous manager had retired. Melody was his private secretary.

150

"How're those sales coming along, Karros?" Mr. Chapman asked from behind me, where he had suddenly appeared out of nowhere?

After feeling myself jump in surprise, I quickly pulled myself together and replied, "Just *great*! I was about to make a few more phone calls."

"That's the ticket!" Chapman exclaimed. "Keep that nose to the grindstone, Karros! Maybe someday *you'll* be office manager like I am now!" Then he chuckled, "I'm sure that *stranger things* have happened."

For all of the vibrant pleasantness that resided in the tone of his suave voice, Mr. Chapman never missed an opportunity to remind all of us lowly working stiffs in the office that *he* was in charge now, through the use of thinly-veiled and charmingly delivered *condescension*. To tell you the truth, he had been a real jerk as a colleague, but as the boss, he had already moved *lightyears beyond that*! As he walked away, my short conversation with him very clearly reminded me of *why* I had never liked the guy very much!

"Hi, Mr. Karros," a smiling Melody walked over to my desk. Watching her made me happily relive thoughts I'd recently had about she and me being together! There was no denying her natural beauty. In appearance, she was probably in her mid-twenties, of medium height, with warm brown eyes and thick blond hair that she wore long over her shoulders. She also had a kind, but playful smile that she often flashed to those people she spoke with in the office, having the predictable effect of always putting them at ease. But it was her *gentle spirit* that really held me captive.

"Oh, good morning, Melody. You can call me Willy," I said as professionally as I could, considering how excited I actually felt having this conversation with her.

"Okay, *Willy*," she said jovially. "May I borrow a few stamps? Sorry. I just discovered that I'm completely out?"

"Sure," I smiled back. "How many do you need?"

"Oh? About *200*," she replied with a very serious expression.

I was immediately *shocked* and my face unfortunately *couldn't* hide it!

And then a moment later, she broke into infectious laughter and admitted, "*Just kidding!* How about ten?"

I smiled and then chuckled. "No problem! Apparently you are an *actress*, as well as a secretary?"

Melody smiled. "No! I just like to joke around with my friends."

I smiled back at her. "You can ask my secretary Beverly for the stamps. She probably doesn't have 200, but *ten* should be no problem!"

Melody laughed. "Thanks, Willy! I suppose I should have asked Beverly in the first place, huh?"

"Oh no. I'm glad you dropped by," I assured her, "And in the future, I hope you won't be a stranger."

"I won't," she assured me with a sweet smile as she walked off toward Beverly's desk.

That short exchange with Melody, as ordinary as it may have sounded to anyone else, had been by far the most *exciting conversation* I could remember having (*outside of my dreams*) with a woman in a very, very long time! Remember me mentioning my old girlfriend Bernadette earlier? Well, she came close to generating this kind of excitement in our conversations only once or twice during our entire yearlong relationship whenever (*as I shockingly learned later*) she had really *wanted something* from me. As a matter of fact, on the day she had broken-up with me, she blatantly admitted as much, as she condescendingly told me that she was leaving me because I just 'wasn't worth the effort' and in fact, I *never had been!* The last I heard, she had joined an acting troupe in Stockton, California, and was preparing to audition for a job as a '*live entertainer*' on a cruise ship. The thing is, unlike Bernadette, Melody didn't seem to have an ulterior motive, but had radiated warmth and charm *naturally* when she had spoken to me... and I *really* liked that!

The rest of my workday proceeded like it always did. I added a couple of accounts, took care of a few problems, but spent the bulk of my day just gabbing with clients and potential clients on the phone. You know? Maybe Andy was right when he alluded to the fact that I was *good* at my job? Just as I prepared to go home, feeling pretty positive about things, I suddenly became aware that Mr. Chapman was glaring at me from his open office door?

"Mr. Karros? Would you please step inside my office?" he said firmly.

This was certainly curious? In the short time he had served as office manager, Mr. Chapman had rarely ever spoken to me, and had *never* called me into his office before? Something *bad* had to be up? As I walked through his office door, he commanded politely, "Have a seat."

I did as he instructed, and then courageously asked, "Forgive my curiosity, but what is this about?"

Mr. Chapman laughed without humor and replied, "I see that you're a man who likes to get right to the point, Karros. Okay. I was informed that you were disrupting the entire office this morning by loudly laughing and acting rather immaturely toward my secretary Miss Wentworth. I do not wish this office to become embroiled in a lengthy and potentially expensive harassment lawsuit down the road, so I am asking you politely to please treat her more like a colleague and less like a *personal conquest.*"

I was knocked down speechless and made no effort to hide my shock. "The truth is, Mr. Chapman, Miss Wentworth just dropped by my desk to borrow a few stamps," I explained as calmly as I could. "I admit that I was friendly toward her, but I'm sure I didn't say or do anything that could have been misconstrued as *inappropriate?* Where is your information coming from?"

"Now Karros. You must know by now that like any good administrator, I *can't* reveal my sources," Mr. Chapman replied mysteriously. "But just know this. I have eyes and ears in this office *everywhere!* In any case, regardless of your 'innocent intentions,' we must nip the potential seriousness of your behavior in the bud before it turns into trouble."

"Exactly which part of my behavior do you wish me to *nip?*" I asked, irritated and just beginning to grow a little angry.

Mr. Chapman smiled at me like an overbearing father, "*Ignore her,*" he ordered. "This advice may save your career at this company!"

"With all due respect, sir, I *can't* ignore her," I replied. "As you said, we're colleagues?"

"Alright," Mr. Chapman begrudgingly agreed. "But see that you dial it down... *a lot!*"

"Will I need to get a lawyer to fight these allegations?" I suddenly blurted out what I had been thinking for the bulk of this entire conversation.

"No, no!" Mr. Chapman quickly waved off that idea. "God knows we aren't at that point yet, Karros. I'm sure we can avoid that ugliness altogether if you simply follow my instructions."

I nodded and left his office feeling both confused and unhappy. When I arrived home, my television set was already turned on and by some strange coincidence, *The Dream Master* was the program airing? I'll admit that I had been thinking about that show while driving home, just to get my mind off of my disheartening conversation with Mr. Chapman, but this *still* seemed rather weird? As I walked into the living room and headed for the couch, from the television screen, The Dream Master, himself, appeared to be patiently waiting for me to become comfortably seated? But that wasn't possible, was it? Whatever the reason for his pause, it was not until I'd sat down on the couch that he finally began to speak?

"Hello, everyone. Today I'd like to talk to you about 'making your dreams come true?'" he began seriously. "Isn't that the most ridiculous statement you've ever heard? I mean, everybody knows that dreams are *not* real! So, they can't possibly come true... *or can they?*"

He really had my attention now, and I couldn't wait to hear what he had to say next?

"Making a dream come true *begins* with selecting one that is very special to you. One that you're highly unlikely to *ever* quit on regardless of the obstacles, and one that you will *fearlessly* and *aggressively* attempt to move forward on right away!" The Dream Master began excitedly. "To put it another way. You will *never* in your waking life see your dreams come true, unless you go after them with all your heart and completely *defeat* your fears!" he said with heartfelt conviction, like an impassioned football coach at halftime!

Suddenly smiling very charmingly, he added "The way to accomplish this is through dreaming about it at night and making that dream *exactly* the way you want it to be, without any trepidation to derail it. Doing this will give your dream a dry-run, so to speak," he added joyfully, assuming that everyone watching his show was just as obsessed with this as *he* was! "This should help you to decide if *that* dream is worth pursuing? *Some* aren't even worth the time you spend dreaming about them! You'll *know* if your dream turns out to be a *stinker*, even before you finish dreaming about it, believe me! There's just one more thing," he added mysteriously. "*Nothing* in your dream realm can be controlled by your subconscious desires if you don't believe in the *power of dreams* to begin with!"

After a short pause, The Dream Master smiled and said from the television screen, "What do you think, *Willy*? Do you believe in the power of dreams?"

I nearly had a heart attack! "Ar...are you talking to *me*?" I stammered.

"Of course, I am!" he confirmed with a smile.

"Well," I began, completely thrown, but trying very hard to believe that this impossible situation was *actually happening* to me? "I... I think so?"

"Bravo!" The Dream Master exclaimed. "And do you believe in *me*?"

"I'm not sure?" I replied slowly.

"Well, thank you for that!" he graciously shared.

"*Why* are you thanking me?" I asked curiously. "I haven't done *anything*?"

"Oh, but you *have*," The Dream Master politely contradicted me.

"*What* have I done?" I asked in confusion.

"You have given me hope that you may *someday* believe in me!" he explained.

I chuckled. "Why does *that* matter?"

"Why?" he replied in shock. "Why, it matters *greatly*!" The Dream Master declared.

I looked at him in disbelief and said, "But you still haven't told me *why* it's important?"

"Isn't it obvious?" he asked me with more than a hint of irritation.

"No, it's *not!*" I replied defiantly.

The Dream Master smiled. "Alright, I'll tell you. It's because just as your dream itself requires you to firmly believe in it in order to experience it while sleeping, you must also believe in *me* if you are to have any chance at all of watching that dream eventually become reality."

"Why?" I still seemed to be missing his point.

"Because," he continued, "I *can't* help someone unless they believe in my abilities."

"*What* abilities?"

The Dream Master smiled kindly. "Just as a car enables you to reach a distant destination relatively quickly, I can help you to find out if your dream is a good one *long before* you waste a good chunk of your lifetime searching for the answer to that very same question. And if it *is* a worthy dream, then I can help you on its exciting journey toward becoming reality!"

"You can *make my dream come true?*" I exclaimed in disbelief.

"No, Willy. I'm afraid not. But I can help *you to?*" he replied calmly.

"But why are you even talking with me?" I asked him suspiciously. "No offense, but I don't recall ever asking for your help?"

"You're right. *You* didn't," The Dream Master confirmed. "*Your father* did!"

Again, I was stunned? "You spoke with *my father?*" I asked in disbelief. "But he passed away last year?"

"I'm quite aware of that. I spoke with him only last week and since he was no longer in your life, he asked me to offer you some help in reaching your dream," he replied. "No offense, but he seemed to think *you'd need it!*" he added with an impish smile.

I didn't know whether to laugh or be insulted by his last comment? So, I ignored it altogether. I did remember having a number of very emotional conversations in the months before my father had passed away and I may not have appreciated them fully at the time? But considering the screw-up I have always been and how much he cared about me, I don't doubt that my dad *had* been very concerned about my future! Still, I didn't know exactly *what* to say to The Dream Master, so I took the simplest route and asked, "What dream of mine was my father talking about?"

"I'm sure he *didn't* know?" he calmly admitted. "I'm not even sure that *you* know?"

I thought hard, but every dream I had considered achieving recently seemed to be out of focus, mixed-in with all of the others? "You're right. I guess I haven't really concentrated on any *one* dream? To be honest, I've been considering quite a few of them," I finally admitted.

"Of course, you have!" The Dream Master smiled kindly.

"You said earlier that the first step in making a dream come true is to *dream about it*," I said confidently.

"Yes!" he replied sprightly.

"Well, isn't that just a little bit *simplistic*?" I asked in disbelief.

The Dream Master laughed. "Of course, *it is*," he replied with his now patented smile. "Dreaming about your desires is *truth*, and truth is *always simplistic*, Willie. Dreams only appear *complicated* when they become mixed-in with other *unnecessary* elements to confuse you."

"Such as?" I asked him curiously.

"Such as dreaming about a particular new car you want to buy and simultaneously worrying about the payments," he shared. "You must either dream about the car *regardless* of the payments, or become so obsessed with the payments that you *can't* even imagine buying the car, causing you to give up and *not dream* about it at all!"

His simple but clear explanation hit a bullseye in my mind and I suddenly found myself *believing* in him? "Am I *awake*?" I asked him hopefully.

"Of course, you are," The Dream Master assured me.

"Then I *already* fully believe in you!" I was quick to reply. "You're right there talking with me on the television screen. Right?"

157

"Right," he laughed. "And I suppose that situation makes *perfect sense* to you?"

After quickly considering what he had said, I replied, "Well, no. Not really? What's going on here?"

And then The Dream Master smiled widely like the Cheshire Cat in Alice in Wonderland, with his body slowly dissipating before my very eyes, until only his wide smile and eyes remained? And just as soon as they had disappeared as well, I found myself waking-up on the couch? My TV set was turned off and nothing seemed odd, except for the vivid memory I had of my long conversation with someone on the television screen calling himself 'The *Dream Master?*' Was I going *crazy*? I finally decided that today must have been a lot rougher than I had originally thought? So, I opted to just relax. I changed into my pajamas, turned the television back on, plopped myself back down on the couch and began watching and listening to typical television fare for hours. Fortunately, this mundane activity accomplished its goal of making me drowsy. Finally, I turned off the television set and too exhausted to move, I couldn't help but fall asleep right there on the couch for the remainder of the night. But *not* before performing the three preliminary steps I remembered The Dream Master teaching me yesterday; *mantra, parameters* and *happy thoughts*, just in case they could do their magic one more time?

When I became coherent, I gratefully found myself on that same beautiful island as before, only *this* time I was inexplicably sharing a passionate *kiss* with Melody Wentworth? As the unforgettable kiss slowly drew to a satisfying conclusion, I looked around and unlike my prior visit to this island, I saw that we were not merely standing amongst the trees, but outside of a small hut built of wood? We were also surprisingly joined by a group of lively chickens and a very *affectionate* collie?

"Shall we get started?" Melody asked me with an excited smile.

"Get started *doing what?*" I asked her in confusion, remembering that this was only a dream, and dreams are famous for not always *making sense?* However, with Melody here, sense or no sense, I can assure you that I had *no* desire to wake-up any time soon!

"Building the chicken coop, of course," she laughed. "Have you forgotten already?"

"I guess maybe I have?" I replied hesitantly. "Would you mind refreshing my memory?"

 "Alright," she chuckled. "After we were married yesterday by the captain of that passing ship and his sailors constructed this little house for us as a wedding present, he gave us tools, nails, a stack of lumber and these animals to assist us in building a better life for ourselves."

"That was very nice of him," I replied, with absolutely *no* memory at all of him *or* of being married?

"It sure was!" Melody agreed. "What a sweetheart! Remember? I told you last night that a chicken coop should be our very first project to house the chickens he gave us?"

I immediately showed a quizzical expression on my face as all of this information was flying through my brain, but *failing* to find a memory to go with it? But, I nodded anyway.

"Okay then!" she smiled. "Now, in case you've forgotten, the captain felt badly about leaving us without more food, so he told me that building a coop for the chickens was the best way to make sure they didn't wander off," Melody explained.

 "But *why* didn't the captain just take us away with him on his ship?" I insisted. "We *did* ask him, didn't we?"

"Of course, we did!" Melody confirmed. "But unfortunately, his ship was too full of the bananas we gave him to take-on two more passengers. But he promised to tell the authorities exactly where we were, just as soon as his ship reached land again."

"Couldn't he have just radioed the authorities that information?" I asked her in disbelief.

"Oh, Willy," she laughed. "You drank a lot of beer last night and probably don't remember that the captain told us his radio hadn't been working for days."

"Okay," I at last conceded. "But where did the *dog* come from?" I asked, pointing to the collie that was nuzzling me like there was no tomorrow?

Melody smiled. "He belonged to the captain. He told me that he was the most loyal and caring friend he had ever had!"

"Then why did he give him to *us*?" I asked curiously.

"Because he thought we needed him! He wanted to give us a best friend on the island in addition to each other," she explained.

"That was thoughtful," I said curiously. "What's its name?"

"It didn't really have one, so we decided to name it ourselves. I suggested a few ideas, but you insisted from the start that we name it, *Andy*! So, we did!"

I had to *laugh*. There was no use continuing to play devil's advocate or fighting this new reality, so I decided to blindly accept whatever had supposedly happened here yesterday, while my memory had apparently been held captive by a *beer-induced stupor*! I further decided that continuing to insist on making *sense* of everything in this most happy situation would undoubtedly turn this exciting adventure into a major buzzkill, and there'd be *none of that here* if I could help it! So, I smiled at Melody, and armed with a hammer, nails, saw and the pile of boards the captain had left for us, I immediately began building the new home for the ten or so chickens we were now responsible for. This was regardless of the facts that A, I had *never seen* a chickencoop before in my life, much less built one and B, I didn't have any *instructions* at all in regards to how to build one? Although I had worked on large scale construction for five years, I had very little experience working with wood, and absolutely *no* experience dealing with chickens? Still, I seemed to know enough about what I was doing to get started, and as I worked I was even impressed at how well it was coming along? And then within a few hours, I *miraculously* completed what I believed to be a small chicken-coop! Soon, the happy chickens ran inside without urging or complaint!

Melody oohed and awed at the new chicken coop for ten minutes before deciding that we, along with our trusty dog Andy, should leisurely walk to the fruit trees to gather food for our next meal. Once we arrived, she also pointed out particular leaves from specific plants on the island that the captain had assured her yesterday, were nutritious, tasty and safe to eat. So, it was decided that the leaves and fruit would make-up *all* of our meals, unless of course, there was a *grocery store* hidden nearby where I could buy a loaf of bread and jars of peanut-butter and jelly? Smiling, I knew we weren't in Bree anymore, so we would just have to make do with what we already had. Next, we had to decide the fate of our noisy chickens? I had *zero* experience or interest in killing and plucking the feathers off *anything*, and Melody saw the chickens as being our 'untouchable' *pets*, so we quickly agreed to keep them only for their eggs and their friendship. As for what we fed Andy and the chickens? Surprisingly, they were all able to fend for themselves on the island? It beats me how, but they apparently found *plenty* to eat amongst the trees surrounding us.

"How are you feeling today?" I gently asked Melody as I plucked a ripening bunch of bananas from a tree.

"I feel *wonderful!*" she beamed. "I may be lost on a tropical island, but it's with the greatest man I know!"

I smiled, quietly accepting her compliment. "Are we *really* married?" I asked her incredulously. "I can't remember any ceremony, but I must admit that I would *love* for it to be true?"

Melody laughed, and I took-in every wonderful aspect of that beautiful sound. "Of course, we're married, Willy!" she assured me. And then she kissed me.

Suddenly, we both noticed a very ordinary looking little gray and brown sparrow hesitantly standing at the edge of its nest in a neighboring tree? All of a sudden it jumped from it, *unsuccessfully* trying to flap its wings and fly? Fortunately, it fell harmlessly to the ground onto a soft pile of leaves that effectively broke its fall. The little bird seemed frustrated, but not any worse for wear. It didn't make a sound or attempt to get away as I gently picked it up and placed it back inside its nest.

"That was very kind of you," Melody smiled. "I hope that little bird learns to fly *all over this island* to its heart's content!"

I smiled back at her and simply replied, "Me too!"

The wind suddenly began whipping-up, causing every tree around us to bend, acknowledging its *mighty* power! We looked at each other knowingly, and instinctively began running back toward our little hut, carrying the fruit we had taken off the trees. As soon as we reached it, I opened the door for Melody and Andy to rush inside as I followed, and immediately secured the door behind us.

After putting the fruit down on a shelf, which I suppose acted as our makeshift food pantry, we relaxed. This was my first time inside this simple little structure and it looked *exactly* as I had imagined it. The interior wasn't painted or decorated yet, but I knew it would just be a matter of time before Melody and I put our heads together, soon making the place look *perfect* for us! And although I was not known for my artistic prowess, in this case, I was actually formulating a few ideas right now that I somehow knew Melody would like? Our little hut may have been no more than a one room shack built of nails and wood, generously caulked with tree sap, but it quickly proved to be both water and windproof as it easily rebuffed the intense efforts of both forces to get inside. Andy contentedly curled-up in a corner of the room as Melody and I smiled at each other. I honestly don't know which of us had the idea first, but soon we were peacefully cuddling on our leafy bed together, enraptured in love. We didn't even notice the constant pattering of raindrops hitting the roof or the ferocious howling of the wind, as we had much more important things to think about. To be honest, I have never experienced anything more *perfect* than this in my entire life!

When I awoke, I was lying comfortably on my couch, *smiling*! I vividly remembered every last, wonderful detail of that fantastic dream, and wished that I could return to it immediately! But sadly, dreams don't work that way. So, I took a quick shower, got ready for work and left my house within the hour.

When I arrived at the office, everything seemed to be as it always was. I immediately greeted my secretary Beverly, as I always did, and then sat down at my desk. As the morning progressed, *nothing* happened out of the ordinary, which was a grave disappointment to me after having experienced such a wonderful dream last night. I saw Melody at her desk, but she never even attempted to look at or contact me in any way? I was nearly ready to admit that she obviously had *no interest* in me whatsoever, and my only basis for thinking she *had* was last night's dream, when I suddenly noticed an envelope with my name neatly written across it, discreetly tucked under my word processor? I immediately felt excited! Oh, I know. It could be a note from Mr. Chapman or a reminder to pay my five-dollar office party fee, yet I somehow *knew* that it was from Melody?

Nonchalantly looking around to make sure that no one was watching me, I quietly opened the envelope and read the contents of the short note enclosed.

> Dear Willy,
> I don't mean to be too forward, but would you like to share a cup of coffee with me tonight after work? If you do, meet me at Lucinda's Diner on Bree Street at 5:30. There's nothing to get concerned about. I just feel like talking with you.
> Thanks, Melody

At first glance, that note appeared to be pretty innocuous. I really had *no idea* why Melody wanted to meet with me in the first place and why she had chosen *not* to ask me in person? And then it occurred to me that she might be confirming what Mr. Chapman had warned me about yesterday; that I was unintentionally *harassing* her? So, her purpose for this proposed meeting *might* be to give her a private place to politely ask me to stop my inappropriate behavior? If that *were* the case, at least, I reasoned, she *wasn't* complaining to Mr. Chapman a second time? Doing *that* could've surely cost me my job? However, regardless of what the note actually meant, I felt terribly *confused*? It's true that my relationship with Melody had only thrived in my most recent dream, but still, unreasonably or not, I had really expected today to be the start of something *wonderful*?

The rest of the day went by very slowly as I simply could not get the note or the possible reasons behind it out of my mind? I caught a glimpse of Melody a couple of times, and there was even a moment when our eyes met, but there was certainly *no sign*, not even a hint that she liked me coming from those beautiful brown eyes. I guessed that I might be in for a very tough *cup of coffee* tonight, but luckily that was *not* for certain? So, to be fair, I tried very hard not to hang on to any specific expectations, good or bad. Instead, I threw myself into my work, hoping that I wouldn't spend the rest of the day continuing to overthink my upcoming meeting with Melody. Unfortunately, I failed miserably! Finally, five o'clock arrived. As I got up from my desk, prepared to leave, I suddenly spied Melody in Mr. Chapman's office sharing a tight hug with the man? I couldn't see her face, but Mr. Chapman was certainly in a good mood? And then I found that I couldn't watch that scene any longer because for obvious reasons, it made me feel *very sad?*

I hadn't thought about it when I'd first read Melody's note, but regardless of the fact that I lived in Bree, I surprisingly had *no idea* where our meeting place, 'Lucinda's Diner,' was located? In fact, I'd never even heard of the place before? So, after quietly asking around and wandering the downtown area of Bree Street from beginning to end a couple of times, I finally located it. It was a quaint little hole-in-the-wall joint tucked in between two much larger businesses, with a painting of a classic brown teapot gracing its front window. Although it didn't look like any diner I'd ever seen before, the good news was that from the outside anyway, the place looked both charming and mysterious; two attributes that I could not deny would certainly give me a much-needed boost! Within moments, I walked inside. Once there, I immediately spied Melody sitting by herself in the back of the room at a small oak table covered with a petite white lace tablecloth. I took a deep breath and approached her.

"Hi, Willy," she smiled as I sat down at the table, facing her. "You decided to come!"

"Of course!" I smiled back. "This is really a cute place? But I've lived in Bree most of my life? How come I've never seen it here before?"

"I couldn't say? I only found it last week?" she explained. "I liked the look of it, so I popped in and *loved it*! I'll bet you'll love it too!"

"This place is a *diner*? It seems more like a teahouse?" I commented, pointing directly at the painting of the teapot on the window.

Melody smiled. "Well, they serve food here too," she explained, "and they do quite a good business at lunchtime I'm told?"

"Okay," I said, accepting her explanation. "But I think I'll just have some coffee. What would you like?" I asked.

"Coffee sounds great," she agreed. "Lots of cream for me."

A charming waitress soon descended on our table and took our orders. She was only gone a couple of minutes before returning carrying a full tray. She first delivered a small porcelain pot of coffee along with a beautiful cup (*obviously made of fine china*) to each of us. Next, she placed a small pitcher of cream, a similar sized bowl of sugar, and a small plate of what she called (*in her cute British accent*) 'English biscuits,' although here in America, we'd probably call them *sugar cookies*.

"Hey? I didn't order those?" I whispered in surprise, and then smiling I added, "I hope you like *English biscuits* with your coffee?"

Melody laughed. "I certainly do!"

"Why do you suppose they sent those to our table without being ordered?" I asked perplexed.

Melody smiled. "It's no great mystery, really. They served them to me the other time I came here too. I spoke to the waitress about it right after she had brought them to the table and she told me that the owner and his wife, who happen to have just immigrated here from England, believe that English biscuits complement both coffee, tea, and any other hot beverage *perfectly*. So, they always serve them here *free of charge*!"

"Wow," I exclaimed. "*Free cookies*! No wonder you like this place!"

Melody laughed.

"You know, Melody?" I blurted out. "I think this is one of the coolest places I have ever been to!"

Melody laughed. "I knew you'd like it!"

Suddenly remembering tonight's purpose, but hesitating to break the playful mood we had created, I tried and failed to find a smooth transition. So, abandoning that plan altogether, I bluntly asked her, "So, about your note? You wanted to talk with me?"

"Yes," she confirmed in surprise, as if she wasn't quite ready to discuss it either?

"What was it you wanted to talk with me about?" I asked her curiously with just a touch of dread.

"Nothing mind boggling, I promise you," she smiled. "I just wanted to get your advice on something?"

"Sure," I agreed, suddenly feeling a lot more at ease. "I'll be glad to give my opinion on *anything* you like!"

Melody chuckled and also grew more relaxed. Then she looked directly into my eyes and breathed deeply, before asking me, "What do you think is the best way of finding out if someone you know likes you?"

Initially I was surprised by what she had asked me? Her very simple question reminded me of something a kid might ask their friend in *junior high school*, and I almost felt like laughing! But I could tell that she was very serious, so I wisely decided to keep that to myself. "Do you mean the fraternal or romantic kind?" I asked her curiously.

"The *romantic* kind," she replied firmly.

"Hmm? I'm not sure I'm the best person to ask," I replied slowly.

"Really? Why do you say that?" Melody asked.

"Because I've liked *you* ever since I first saw you in the office a year ago, and I don't think you ever knew it?" I explained hesitantly. "Obviously I *suck* at nonverbal communication!" I laughed awkwardly. "Oh well. I guess we would have clicked a long time ago if our feelings for each other had been mutual."

Suddenly, Melody looked both ecstatic and shocked, in the same excited expression. "I... I was hoping you would say something like *that!*" she hesitantly declared.

"*What?*" I gasped.

"What I mean is," she smiled, "over this past year, I sometimes saw signs at work that you *might* be interested in me, but they never

166

seemed... you know... *definite?*" she explained. "Finally, once I'd found this place, I thought it would be fun for us to meet here and find out for sure. So, here we are!"

I smiled at her in disbelief. I could *not believe* what I was hearing? It was wonderful, and it was happening to me in *real life!* "Well, then just know that I like you *for sure*, and I can't wait to get to know you better!" I said excitedly and way too fast, as I rushed to get the words out.

Melody giggled. "Same here!"

"What is your favorite color?" I asked her spontaneously.

"Is that an important question to ask someone on a *first date?*" Melody asked facetiously.

I smiled. "Why not!" I laughed. And then growing more serious, I added, "Anyway, I am a bit curious?"

"Okay," she surrendered with a smile. "But only because you're a *bit curious*," she chuckled. After pondering the question for a few moments, she replied, "How about red and yellow polka dot?"

"*Tricky!*" I laughed. "But why *two* colors?"

"Because I *couldn't decide* between the red and the yellow, so I thought I'd get clever!" she said impishly. "What's *your* favorite color?"

I smiled. "Right now, I'd have to agree with you and choose red and yellow polka dot," I professed calmly.

"Are you *copying* me just to get on my good side?" she asked humorously.

"Well, *yes*," I admitted with a sly smile. "It just seems like the right thing to do under the circumstances."

Melody smiled back and reached her right hand across the table where it immediately intertwined with mine. "I think we may have *more* in common than you think," she said.

"Oh?" I replied curiously.

"Yes. We've proven that we both have that very special ability to take small talk to a *whole new level!*" she chuckled. Then glancing out the window and inexplicably growing concerned, she gently drew her hand away from me and added, "I've really enjoyed spending this time with you tonight, Willie! But I think it's best that we *don't* let anyone at work know that we're dating, okay? At least for a while?"

"Okay," I immediately agreed. "But if we don't let it affect our work, then where's the problem?" Then I paused, and added seriously, "Unless this is about your relationship with Mr. Chapman?"

"*Mr. Chapman?* Heavens no!" she immediately retorted. "I *don't have* a relationship with Mr. Chapman beyond being his secretary!" Then softening her tone with her eyes twinkling, she added, "The real problem is with your secretary Beverly. She read me the riot act after I borrowed those stamps from her yesterday! And then she told me *not* to give you any grief!" she smiled. "If I didn't know better, I would have sworn she was your *mother?*"

I laughed, and then growing more serious, I remarked, "I wonder why she treated you like that? She's the sweetest lady you could ever meet? Like someone's *grandma?*"

"I may have told her that you were *nice*," she admitted.

"What's wrong with that?" I asked in confusion.

"It's not *what* I said but the *way I said it!*" Melody laughed. "I think I must have shocked her with some of my bizarre facial expressions! *Please* apologize for me!"

I laughed. "I will. Hey, would you like to come over to my place to continue this riveting conversation? I don't have any English biscuits, but my coffee is free?"

Melody smiled, but then immediately looked confused. "I'd really like to, Willy, I really would… but I'd better *not*," she confessed uncomfortably.

"*Your* place then?" I quickly searched for an alternative.

"No, I'm sorry Willy," she said apologetically. "I don't think this is the right time."

"Of course," I backtracked. "I apologize if I came on too strong."

"Oh no, you most definitely *did not*," Melody assured me. "It's just that I don't want to take any chances."

"Chances of *what?*" I asked in surprise.

Melody suddenly looked at me intensely, in utter confusion, as if she were about to cry? "Never mind!" she managed to utter before quickly getting up from the table and rushing out the door of the diner, leaving me with a plate full of English biscuits, two ceramic pots and cups of coffee, several unanswered questions, and utter confusion as to *what* had just happened?

That night, as I sat on the couch in my pajamas, I hoped beyond hope that The Dream Master would contact me and explain what had just taken place between Melody and me? I *had* to know! Thankfully, as I switched on my television set, I was gratefully rewarded.

"Greetings!" The Dream Master announced. "I hope that your dreams are going well?" After a short pause, he continued, "I am sensing that some of you may have developed a few questions as a result of them? Let's start with... *Willy*! What are your questions today, my boy?"

This time I was ready for this *highly implausible* conversation with my television set! "My dream last night, in a roundabout way, very closely predicted what eventually happened to me in my real life today?" I shared.

"Yes?" The Dream Master smiled and encouraged me to continue.

"But, by the end of the day, for no apparent reason, it all *changed?*" I explained. "Why?"

"*Why* indeed!" The Dream Master declared. "As I've explained to you before, your dreams are merely representations of how you *want* things to turn out, not what they currently *are*. Real life can change the story you experienced in a dream very quickly."

"But in some ways my dreams and real life were very similar for a while? How can I bring those two realities together *permanently?*" I pleaded. "My dream last night was *perfect!*"

"I'm very glad for you, Willie. Dreams like that are wonderful to experience! But you must remember that it was *still* only a dream," The Dream Master gently explained. "I *can't* just wave a wand around or recite an incantation to make that dream come true, just as your wishing for it and then snapping your fingers most assuredly *won't* make it happen either!" Pausing to think, he added, "A dream

169

becomes real, Willie, because in addition to you passionately desiring it, *everything else* needed to make it happen must somehow fall into place at the same time! And that, my boy, can sometimes be a very tall order!"

"But you are *The Dream Master*! Surely you can help me?" I begged.

"I am sorry, truly," he began apologetically. "But, Willy, I am a creator of illusions. It is *you* and everybody else in this world who must attempt to make their own most precious dreams come true. My illusions are only meant as a way for you to understand more vividly what your dreams are. I play *no* hand in the poker game of reality! Good luck!" And with that, as he disappeared, for good measure, my television set turned off by itself?

But I was *not* done yet! Not by a longshot! Regardless of the fact that The Dream Master had shockingly chosen to *desert* me in my time of need, I was determined to have my questions answered! I quickly got dressed, looked up Melody's address and drove over to her apartment on the other side of town. When I arrived, her lights were on, the drapes were drawn, but she was *not* alone? There was a man there who I immediately recognized as being *Mr. Chapman*? I couldn't hear them talking, but I did watch them embrace, exactly as they had done at the office earlier? And then it dawned on me. What if tonight's meeting for coffee *wasn't* for Melody to find out how I felt about her at all? Perhaps it had simply been a *scheme* of hers? Pretending to like me just to get her secret boyfriend Mr. Chapman *jealous*, so that he would *propose* to her and she'd live happily ever after? Maybe her plan *began* with the stamps? Now that I think of it, that whole conversation had seemed very unusual? I wondered. Was everything that happened that morning with Melody planned out by her in *advance*? Unfortunately, I *had* firsthand experience being used by women in similar ways in the past, yet I was having a great deal of trouble believing that Melody could actually think like that? Like I was merely someone to be *used* by her as part of a larger plan? I suddenly realized that I had far more troubling questions now, than I would have had if I had *simply stayed home tonight*? Why had I insisted on driving out here? *Why*? I was

170

completely crushed as I drove home. When I arrived at my house, I changed back into my pajamas and feeling extremely depressed, I went to bed and very quickly fell asleep.

I became coherent sitting at my desk in what appeared to be just another typical day at the office. But it *wasn't?* For one thing, Melody was *nowhere* to be seen? I strolled through the office under the guise of leisurely walking toward the water cooler for a drink, but still saw no sign of her? I must have checked everywhere and growing disappointed, I'll admit that I was really convinced she was *gone?* When suddenly I heard the voice of Mr. Chapman coming through a very tinny loudspeaker proudly proclaiming, "*Your attention please*! It is my great pleasure to announce that after a very hot and steamy relationship over this past year, Melody Wentworth and I are finally *engaged* to be married!"

Applause erupted with abandon throughout the entire room from agents and secretaries alike, along with dignitaries from town (*including the entire city council*), as well as the President of the United States, who had inexplicably decided to attend this celebration with a handful of secret service agents surrounding him. Soon, Melody walked out of Mr. Chapman's office like a robot, with a sick smile plastered across her face, curiously wearing a *black* wedding dress? Without emotion, she showed everyone in the room her shiny engagement ring with its impressive diamond that appeared to be ten carats or more in size! But curiously, it had a peculiar little sign hanging from it reading, CUBIC ZIRCONIA? Suddenly, Melody shot me a quick and desperate glance with her eyes, seemingly telling me that she was experiencing *extreme terror?* Then, she very clearly mouthed the word, "*Help?*" Unfortunately, Mr. Chapman caught that exchange between us and immediately bundled her back inside his office where he apparently had been holding her captive.

As I returned to my desk, I suddenly heard a soft slithering sound behind me? I quickly turned my head just in time to see a jet-black cobra hissing as it reared its ugly head, "Forget about her, Karros! She's *mine!*" As I looked more closely at the snake, I was somehow *not* surprised to see the head of Mr. Chapman on it? "Just let all of this go!" the snake hissed in the smooth and convincing voice of the man. "I know you cared a lot for Miss Wentworth, but because of your highly inappropriate behavior, I'm afraid you've *lost her forever!*"

After that, I watched the snake arrogantly slither off into Mr. Chapman's office with the door loudly slamming shut behind it. I turned back toward my desk and started my work, which apparently consisted of staring at a picture of Melody at the *exact* moment she had turned to me asking for help only minutes before? I was feeling so *confused?* In spite of the fact that she was apparently engaged to another man, she had very clearly asked for my help? But *what* type of help did she want or need from me? Curiously, the tiny gray and brown sparrow that had appeared in my last dream was suddenly *on my desk?* It was half-heartedly flapping its wings and running around in circles, trying to fly away, but to no avail? Now I felt even *more* confused?

The next morning, I woke-up feeling a bit disoriented? What I knew to be *true* and what I had *dreamt* over these past few nights was beginning to collide in my mind? To make matters worse, since all of my dreams had aspects of reality in them, if I didn't think hard about them first, I *knew* that they could very easily *usurp* the real truth from my memory. But fortunately, I still had a pretty good grasp of what was *actually* going on, whether I liked it or not! I also knew that there were several very big questions I was obsessing over that really needed answering if I was to have any hope at all of unraveling this whole confusing mess currently residing inside my head? The most important question being, how Melody *actually* felt about me?

When I arrived at the office, the first thing I noticed was that just like in my dream, Melody was nowhere to be seen? Also, as in my dream, I searched the office for any trace of her, but to no avail? I returned to my desk and did what I should have done in the first place! I grabbed the staff phone list, and looked for her number! But when I called it, surprisingly, I was immediately told that this number was no longer in service? There were no other phone numbers that I could find listed there for her, so I had now reached the point where the *only* option left to me promised to be highly unpleasant. I had to speak directly to *Mr. Chapman!*

Hesitantly walking up to his office door, I found it surprisingly wide open, with him apparently deep in thought, staring intently down at his desk. I knocked gently on the doorframe, and he slowly brought up his head to meet me. A sly expression slowly crept across his face as he said, "Come in, Karros. I was expecting you. Be sure to close the door behind you."

Uh-oh! In the past, anytime one of my former bosses had told me to '*close the door behind me*,' I always knew that I was either going to be fired or given some confidential information that they didn't want anyone else in the room to hear. I had *no* idea which of the two it was today, as I slowly closed the door and sat down on a chair opposite his desk, but my gut assured me that it was definitely *one of them!*

"What's on your mind, Karros?" Mr. Chapman asked politely.

"What's on *yours?*" I shot back with a little attitude. "You said you were *expecting* me?"

Chapman laughed without smiling as he quickly processed my reply. "So, I did." Meeting my eyes firmly, he began, "I think you came in here to find out why my former secretary Miss Wentworth is not in the office today. Am I right?"

I knew that if I admitted what he had suggested was true, I would be confirming that I had circumvented his direct order to me earlier this week concerning staying away from Melody, but what the hell! "Yes! Did you just say *former* secretary?"

Mr. Chapman didn't immediately respond to my question, instead he grew very serious. "Yes, I did. Do you want to hear the *whole* story, Karros? It involves you too?"

Not having *any* idea what to expect, I hesitantly nodded.

"Okay," he began. "Two days ago, Miss Wentworth secretly came into my office while you were off to lunch, complaining of your *inappropriate* behavior during the stamp incident."

"But I saw you hugging her in your office? What the hell was *that* all about?" I demanded.

"Easy on the jealousy, Karros. You're coming across as a pretty *pathetic* character, don't you think?" Mr. Chapman said condescendingly but controlled, with his eyes still glued to mine. "If you must know, I was merely consoling her. She was very upset."

I nodded.

"To continue," Mr. Chapman said, a little irritated by my interruption, "the next day, Miss Wentworth, as I understand it, invited you to a coffeeshop to politely ask you to stop harassing her..."

"That's *not at all* what happened!" I passionately exclaimed.

Blatantly ignoring me, Mr. Chapman continued, "Then you invited her to go home with you, and she refused. When you persisted, she *ran* out of the coffeeshop! Am I close?"

"Well, yes. Those events *did* happen, but your interpretation of *why* they happened is completely wrong!" I insisted.

"*Are they*, Karros?" Mr. Chapman asked sarcastically. "I don't think Miss Wentworth or the board of directors for this company would agree with you!"

"I also saw you at her house last night hugging her? How do you explain *that*?" I passionately insisted.

Gasping in surprise, Chapman sneered and replied aggressively, "Doing a little *stalking* too, are we? I should really ask what *you* were doing there last night?" Then softening his tone, he replied, "After your coffeehouse fiasco, Miss Wentworth called me and asked if I would come over to talk with her. She was again, *very upset*. So naturally, since we are quite close friends at work, I drove over to her apartment, very concerned about her. When I arrived, I tried my best to console her and eventually she calmed down." And then with an unfriendly glare, he said, "That's what *you* probably observed." Pausing for a moment, he then continued. "Then she began honestly talking to me. The gist of what she told me was that because you obviously had an unhealthy obsession with her, she didn't feel safe around you, and *absolutely refused* to return to work as long as you were there! Although I tried very hard to change her mind, she *resigned* her position right there on the spot!"

"Does she still live in that same apartment?" I pleaded.

"No," Mr. Chapman replied coolly. "I understand she moved out of there, first thing this morning."

"Where can I find her?" I insisted.

"Nowhere that *you* can go without being *arrested*! Miss Wentworth told me last night in *no* uncertain terms that as long as you didn't bother her anymore, she would consider not suing the company or you personally. But if you should find out where she's living and attempt to see her again, then *may God help us all*!" he exclaimed. "The police are already aware of this nasty little situation, and although they can't arrest you without proof, they will certainly keep you under surveillance for the foreseeable future! I advise you to just let all of this go and lay low for a while, Karros. I know that in your own way you cared a lot for Miss Wentworth, but because of your highly inappropriate behavior, which I certainly did warn you about earlier, I'm afraid you've *lost her forever*!"

I *shuddered* at his words, as I realized that I'd heard a very similar sentiment coming from his alter ego, the *snake*, in my dream? "I'll *never* stop looking for her!" I found myself passionately declaring.

Mr. Chapman, completely taken off-guard by my defiant outburst, genuinely looked *shocked*? But after quickly recovering, he shook his head angrily and exclaimed, "You are a *fool*, Karros, and you leave me *no choice*! Clear out your desk! *You're fired*!"

'Well, I guess I found out some confidential information *and* got fired!' I said to myself, looking for a little humor in this situation, but unfortunately *finding none*! After clearing out my desk and leaving work, I spent the remainder of the day feeling very sorry for myself due to my blatant inability to do *anything* right! If Melody truly *did* feel about me the way Mr. Chapman said she did, then I simply *had* to see her again! If for no other reason, to understand *why*? What exactly had I done? And, what exactly had happened at the Diner that night that could have possibly caused her to quit her job and disappear? Honestly? She looked as white as a sheet when she had run out of there? I was so confused? And I knew that trying to find her now could be very dangerous for me after being explicitly warned by Mr. Chapman *not to*! It could even land me in jail? Or get me sued? But I knew that regardless, I would have found the courage to go see her *right now* if it had been possible! My problem was that I didn't know *where* she was or her current *phone number*, meaning of course, that I had *no way* of getting in touch with her? The day and night dragged on, and finally, after finishing a couple of beers, I grew so tired and miserable that I fell asleep lying on my back on the living room floor. I had been trying very hard all evening to find and focus on just *one positive thought*, but to no avail? However, I easily found a bundle of *negative* ones without even trying!

As I grew coherent, I found myself back on my tropical island, only this time everything seemed to have gone completely *berserk*? The little house the sailors had built for Melody and me was in a shambles, as if a huge boulder had somehow fallen on top of it? The chicken-coop I had built with my own two hands had met with a similar fate, with no chickens to be seen anywhere? Checking further, I found that the nearby fresh water in the island lakes had inexplicably turned green and tainted with salt, while the formerly beautiful vegetation that *had* covered the island, including the fruit trees, was rapidly turning limp and black? For some reason I knew that something evil, some *monster*, had mysteriously appeared on this island paradise soon after I had last left it, and was methodically demolishing the place? I had no idea why, but it was apparent that this monster was intent on destroying any life it could find here, until every living thing on the island was completely *obliterated*! And then I suddenly felt sick and terrified as I realized for the first time that Melody and my dog Andy were nowhere to be seen? In fact, there were no signs that they had *ever* existed here before? Oh God!

I had never been so frightened in my life! Not knowing what else to do, I simply ran away in fear as fast as my legs would carry me! But the more I ran, the more I sensed the monster continuing to destroy every living thing on the island! That's when I first frighteningly realized that the monster was also determinedly making its way closer and closer to *finding me*? I didn't really understand *why*, but it scared me to death and I was certainly in no great hurry to find out! Fortunately, I soon discovered a good-sized tunnel at the side of a hill that was large enough for me to crawl through and hopefully hide in. But not having seen the monster yet, I worried that the tunnel was possibly large enough for *it* to follow me in? Maybe this tunnel was actually the gateway to its *lair*? I won't lie! That thought *chilled* me to the bone! But, I really couldn't worry about that right now! As I hurriedly crawled through the tunnel, it surprisingly emptied me into a cave? As I stood there, for the first time since coming back to the island, I *didn't* sense the monster at all, and inadvertently let out a sigh of relief. I could only hope that this meant I had successfully thrown him off my scent, at least temporarily? As I began cautiously exploring the interior of the cave, hopefully discovering quickly if any creature currently lived here, I quickly realized that there was light inside from the tunnel, making it possible for me to at least dimly see around me. What a break! After taking a few steps, I also noticed that this cave was much more spacious than I had originally believed? And then I found some very old remnants of dried fruit on the ground and I smiled. It was clear to me that this place had once been inhabited by fruit eaters, which was something the monster definitely *was not*! To be honest, I was really not sure if the monster ate anything at all? Whatever creature or creatures *had* lived here before, judging from what I had seen so far, had obviously *not* been back here for many years. And then as I walked further away from the tunnel, I noticed that the light in the cave had *not* diminished at all? Perplexed, when I looked up at the ceiling, I saw some very strange ivy-like plants growing there that interestingly *glowed*, giving off enough light to make the *entire* cave visible to me? Looking around as I walked deeper into the cave, I noticed that there were areas on the floor covered in ancient leaf debris that I imagined could possibly be where the cave's inhabitants, human or *otherwise*, may have slept? After journeying a bit further through the cave, I spied a large flat boulder that could have very easily been used as a table for eating or working? But as I reached the end of the cave, I experienced one of those *eureka moments* as I suddenly knew the truth! The apparently *human inhabitants* had scratched simple drawings on the mostly granite walls of the cave at some point during their tenure? These drawings included stick figures of themselves and their simple lives. Besides them, there were drawings of fruit trees and the sandy beaches which I now knew so very well. But further down the wall was a drawing of a *huge beast* with long, sharp fangs and claws! And *that* was the last picture I found? Nearby, I spied a spear which was strangely topped with three different heads, each one made of razor sharp and polished stone. One was colored bloodred, one was white, while the third one was deep black? Perhaps this spear had been created specifically to kill that beast on the wall and the former inhabitants of this cave just never had the chance to use it? In any case, the moment I picked it up, it strangely made me feel *very powerful?*

Time passed, and I thankfully didn't hear anything outside that even remotely sounded like a *great beast.* But, I knew in my heart that hiding from it in this cave would not lead to its destruction or bringing this island back to life? So, with the three-headed spear tightly grasped in my hand, I cautiously crawled out of the cave. When I reached sunlight, I gasped! There was now almost *complete devastation* on the island as far as I could see! Most of the plant life was turning black, dry and crumbling to dust. In fact, there was very little life left to prove that this island had *ever* flourished with life before? That is, with the exceptions of me and that tiny sparrow which sat frightened in a nest, still attached to a disintegrating tree in front of me. And then I froze as I suddenly heard the sound of someone or something fast approaching?

"Hello, Willy!" a familiar tall, thin man dressed all in white, suddenly appeared and greeted me calmly, like an old friend. It was The Dream Master?

"What are *you* doing here? And why is everything on this island dying?" I demanded.

He looked at me in surprise, as he gently replied, "I am here to do *your* bidding, Willy? I am obliterating your dream of living in paradise."

"Wh...What are you doing that for?" I exclaimed. "It was *perfect* here!"

"Yes. It **was** perfect here, but you no longer feel that way do you?"

He was *right*! When I thought of this island now, the excitement I had originally felt for it seemed to have strangely disappeared? It was as if there was no longer any reason for me to exist here? But oddly, I didn't have the faintest idea why? It just felt as if all reasons for staying on the island had deserted me? "*Why* do I feel this way?" I finally asked the man, begging for the answer?

The Dream Master shook his head and said, "How should I know? *You* created this world and now *you* want it completely destroyed with no memory of its existence remaining. I merely read your heart and obey."

I gasped in shock! "Do you mean to say that I *created* the monster that's destroying this island?"

"You *did!*" he confirmed.

"I *didn't mean to!*" I pleaded. "Please take it away? Bring this island back to how it was!"

The Dream Master paused and then explained apologetically, "I'm sorry, Willy. I *can't* stop a dream once it's been started. It must be allowed to playout to the very end."

"And where is my wife Melody and my dog Andy?" I asked anxiously.

"They *don't exist* on this island anymore, Willy. Soon *you* will be the only life left here," he gently explained.

It was then that I looked again at the tiny sparrow, still wanting to fly more than anything, but too paralyzed in fear to even try? "Will that little bird survive?" I asked softly.

"Not as things look right now," The Dream Master admitted sadly. "The monster you created will be here at any moment to kill it, the last bit of innate life left on this island!" Growing more serious, he added, "In fact, as I'm sure you have already considered, the monster will probably not stop until *you* are destroyed as well! It's time for you to wake-up to reality, my friend."

"No! I'm *not* leaving here until that bird flies safely away and the *island is restored!*" I declared passionately. Suddenly a question struck me that I knew The Dream Master could answer. "I found this spear in a cave. Is it important?"

"If you're trying to *kill* the monster, it is!" he replied very seriously.

"But why does this spear have three different colored heads at the end of it?"

"Because there are *three different parts* of the beast you must kill in order to guarantee that it never returns again!" The Dream Master replied. "The black head destroys the evilness it is consumed with, the white cleanses all of its misdeeds, while the red spearhead is the one that kills its body and soul," he added very seriously.

"Is there anything else I should know before I face it?" I asked as bravely as I could.

He fidgeted uncomfortably, and finally said, "If your heart is set on going through with this, Willy, all I can tell you is to stay *very* attached to that spear, up until you finally use it. And when you do, *aim* for the beast's heart."

"Where is the beast's heart located... *exactly?*" I curiously found myself asking.

"I'm very glad you asked me that, Willy," he replied with relief. "Because when you look at the monster, it's heart will *not* be where you probably think it should be! It sits directly in the *front* and *middle* of its stomach area, just above its legs. Here the beast has no protection at all! Strike the beast anywhere else and the spear will simply bounce off!" Growing quieter and more intense, The Dream Master added, "Remember, if you should *miss* your aim the first time, you will more than likely *not* get a second chance!" And then he disappeared.

I felt sharp chills chaotically racing up and down my spine at hearing his warning. I realized now, that as its creator, my upcoming confrontation with the monster was inevitable if I hoped to have any chance at all of returning this island to the lush life it had known before. There was *no* backing down! I kept fighting my all-consuming fear but regardless, I knew this was something I *had* to do! It wasn't long before I saw *death and devastation personified* as the monster finally arrived in all its hideous glory, stomping loudly as it did! It shocked me to realize that I had subconsciously created this *foul thing?* Quickly perusing the creature, I noted that it looked a lot like *Godzilla* with exaggerated fangs and claws, and the added speed of a raptor dinosaur. It stood all of *twenty feet* tall, had thick, dark, scaly green skin covering nearly every inch of it, giving it the ominous appearance of wearing armor! That is *except* for a small area in the front of its body, one foot square, about two feet above its stocky legs, where there was a *small patch* that looked different? Just as the Dream Master had said, that area had '*no protection at all.*'

As I expected, the monster *breathed fire!* It had been busily taking advantage of this ability to burn *almost everything* on the island to ash! I knew that this was only a dream, but I couldn't help feeling nauseous and filled with terror in spite of myself! I even considered running back into the cave? But I knew I had to face this terrible creature eventually, so I stood my ground. It wasn't long before the speedy fire-breather showed me just what it could do! First, it ferociously torched most of the vegetation around it that was not completely dead already. And I might mention that it was a very good thing I had *not* decided to run back inside the cave, because the second thing the monster did was to *obliterate* the entrance to it, causing rocks and boulders to completely fill the crawl space and possibly the cave itself, as it viciously stomped the ground above it! I actually began to seriously reconsider my decision *not* to leave this place? And then I felt sick as I realized for the first time, that since I had created this monster, it would more than likely have the ability to *think* identically to the way I did? So, how on Earth could I ever hope to outwit it?

Next, the monster slowly approached me with its eyes firmly focused on *mine*, like a savvy gunfighter from the old west confidently entering the street for a *one-sided duel* with the scared-to-death sheriff. I held my spear up, and couldn't help noticing that the evil creature slightly flinched, as though it had experienced a traumatic episode with the spear sometime in its past? It quickly regained its composure, however, as it powerfully and emphatically began running toward me with intense hatred in its eyes. Suddenly a burst of fire angrily shot from its mouth, like a flame thrower! I realized then that there was no time for me to escape, so I bravely prepared myself for what would surely be my *hideous demise!* The fire rained fiercely down upon me, but *impossibly* I was not burned nor left feeling any pain? To be sure that I wasn't dead, I looked down at myself and felt my face with my free hand? Everything seemed okay? Then I looked at the spear in my hand in awe? It had to be *magical?* And it became absolutely clear to me at that moment that the *magic spear* was the *only thing* that could defeat this thing!

Furious at discovering that I had somehow survived its first onslaught, the monster immediately prepared to attack me once again. But, suddenly its attention was acutely drawn to the small sparrow, *still* fearfully tied to its nest. I frowned as I understood only too well that the monster aimed to dispose of this tiny bird first, before finishing me off! So, with spear in hand, I rushed at it with every intention of ending this battle here and now! I was more than ready to thrust that spear with all the strength I possessed right through its *black heart!* But, I should have remembered how I'd guessed it could anticipate my actions, because it *did!* As I furiously approached it, the beast astonishingly turned directly to me and savagely ripped the spear out of my hands? As I watched in horror my *magic weapon* quickly fell to the ground, landing directly at its feet! As a result, I was thrown about ten feet away, landing hard on the ground. It was then that I recalled the Dream Master's dire warning! 'If the spear fails to do the job the first time, you will more than likely *not* get a second chance!'

Everything changed now as my situation suddenly felt more desperate than ever! My only hope of killing the monster was the spear that was now securely *trapped* beneath it, where short of a miracle, I couldn't possibly hope to reach it? I knew that I had already lost this confrontation, but surprisingly, what seemed even *more* important to me right now than killing this monster, and I didn't immediately understand why, was *saving the life* of the innocent sparrow at all costs? So, I quickly pulled myself up off the ground and yelled at the monster, trying desperately to draw its attention away from the helpless bird! As I did, the monster once again sent a fiery storm of hatred my way. Fortunately, since I did not have the spear to protect me, I quickly jumped behind a large boulder to avoid the firestorm! Peeking out moments later, looking at the bird in the nest to make sure that it was still safe, I was shocked to see a *different creature?* The sparrow looked to be the same physically, but somehow it didn't seem *scared* or *ordinary* anymore? It had suddenly grown brave and daring as it decidedly flew out of its nest on a beeline for the monster's face! As the monster angrily turned toward the flying bird, I realized that the sparrow had just selflessly gifted me a miraculous *second chance*, so I mustn't waste it! Because the monster was focused entirely on the sparrow, I hastily slid under the horrid creature, picked up the spear from the ground beneath it and desperately propelled it as hard as I could into its heart! I then quickly rolled out of the way, as I watched the creature writhe and scream for a few hideous moments, before ultimately *dropping dead* to the ground!

With the monster was *dead*, I should have felt deliriously happy and celebrated my victory! But strangely, *I didn't?* Instead, I felt sad and empty inside? You see, the monster had determinedly knocked the sparrow out of the air, and it now laid motionless on the ground beside it? I couldn't fathom *why* the sparrow had not simply flown off to safety on another part of the island once it had realized that it could finally fly? And then I suddenly *understood*. The sparrow had only been able to fly once it had been given a *heartfelt purpose* for doing so? By watching me trying to save it from the monster, it had *found that!* It seemed so clear now that unwittingly we had destroyed the monster *together?* And since this was *my* dream, I did *not* want it to see it end this way; with the brave little bird who had saved my life and this island being killed? But I was no Dream Master, and I didn't really know what to do? So, I thought hard about what I had done to originally create my dreams as the Dream Master had taught me, using three components, *mantra*, *parameters* and *happy thoughts?* Would these three things work equally well to bring a dead dream creature back to life? There was no way of finding out until I tried? So, I *did*. My mantra was wishing the bird alive again, my parameters were a happy and successful effort, and for my happy thoughts I recalled its bravery in saving me! But, nothing happened? *Nothing happened?!* This was devastating, to say the least! But then I suddenly thought of a *fourth* component that could very well be required for something as seemingly impossible as this was? I added a deeper *faith and determination* that what I was asking would come true! In fact, my request had now actually become an *order!* But still *nothing* happened? But then very suddenly I saw the bird *twitch* for the first time? I was *overjoyed!* And then the bird began to shake all over? After nearly a minute of this, the convulsions finally stopped, as the sparrow astonishingly came back to life, good as new? It immediately flew over to me and alit on my hand for just a moment. Although, all I had done was will it back to life, the sparrow seemed to be thanking me profusely as if I had done much more? And then I smiled at the sparrow, likewise appreciating the selfless act it had done, enabling me to kill the monster! Surprisingly, the little bird touched its beak to the skin on my inner right arm and quickly but painlessly scratched a line with three attached tangents at the end, which could only represent the spear that had killed the beast! My arm was bleeding a little now, but I didn't care. Although that great moment was already etched in my memory, now it was permanently etched on my arm, as well! Then the little bird, knowing that its work had only just begun, gently left me and confidently flew across the island. As it passed over each stretch of land, all of the black remnants of plant life magically returned to beautiful lush trees and foliage! It also changed the seawater lakes to freshwater again and brought back the fruit trees! In short, the entire island soon *returned to normal!* I quickly ran to find Melody, Andy and my house on another part of the island. When I arrived, I was relieved to see that both structures looked as good as new, and the chicken-coop was now full of happy chickens again! But unfortunately, *not everything* was right? Neither Melody nor Andy had returned?

I was completely *baffled?* The monster was slain, the island was lush, yet I felt *awful?* I couldn't help myself as I desperately fell to my knees and pleaded, "Will somebody please *help* me?"

184

Immediately, out of nowhere, Andy the dog calmly trotted up beside me and said, "Be patient, Willy. Believe me, *you've got this!*"

That's when I woke-up. After quickly remembering that I had been fired from my job yesterday, I didn't feel any particular reason to hurry. So, I leisurely got dressed and had breakfast before deciding to walk around outside and think. I mean, what else was there to do for an out of work *loser* like me? Outside was extremely overcast, as an unexpected fog-bank had arrived to cover the little town of Bree. I welcomed this chance to hide from the world for a while, and although it was a little cold outside, I didn't feel a need for a coat. As I wandered the foggy streets, pondering each piece of my broken life, I even thought about calling Andy (*the human*) about working at his grocery store? After all, regardless of the fact that I had never worked in a store like that before, I was sure that he'd give me a stellar recommendation? But then I remembered that I had invested a great deal of time and effort over the past few years learning to become a competent insurance agent, maybe even a *pretty good one*? And for that reason, I vowed to find another similar position somewhere, starting tomorrow.

"Good morning, Willy," the familiar tall, thin man dressed all in white, said cheerfully, as he appeared out of nowhere and walked up to me.

"Good morning?" I said, completely shocked at who I was seeing. "What are you doing here in my real life? You aren't *real* are you?"

The man known as The Dream Master laughed. "I'm as real as you are, Willie. I think what you meant to say was, 'What am I doing in *your reality?*'"

I looked at him quizzically. "Of course! But *why* exactly are you here?"

"I'm here because *anything* is possible in the dream realm. Even jumping out into the 'real world' for a little jaunt now and then when I find it absolutely necessary," The Dream Master said mysteriously.

"And just why is your coming here *absolutely necessary* now?" I asked, still confused.

"Because it's become very clear to me that you *don't* have the final piece of the puzzle you need in order to find out if you can move your dream into the other realm," he began understandingly. "Especially the part about Melody Wentworth."

"What about *her?*" I demanded suspiciously.

The Dream Master laughed. "Come on, Willy! Let's not feign ignorance here. I know how you feel about her, and I also know that for peace of mind, you *need* to find out how she really feels about you! Right?"

"Right," I nodded sadly. "But from what Mr. Chapman told me, she *never* wants to see me again!"

He smiled, and placed a gentle hand on my shoulder. "Now, Willy. You *mustn't* believe everything you're told. Sometimes, what other people tell you is merely their own desires neatly disguised as facts. And sometimes... they are *downright lying!*"

I looked at him in surprise, and asked, "But how will I *know* when someone is lying to me?"

"That's easy," The Dream Master gently assured me. "You merely listen very hard to your heart, and it will tell you. Hearts *never* lie!"

I was amazed by the simplicity of his answer? But even more importantly, I *knew* that he was right! "Thank you, Charley," I said, remembering The Dream Master's first name. "I may not get the girl of my dreams, but at least what you told me just now makes me think there's a chance she doesn't hate me."

"*What?* You're not even going to *try* to find her?" The Dream Master immediately became loud, defiant, and in total disbelief? He was angrier and more passionate than I had ever seen him before as he lambasted me! "What about that fearless man on the island who killed the monster? *Huh?* Where's your *courage*, man? Where's that *determination?*"

The Dream Master had very surprisingly given me an intense verbal thrashing! But sadly, I *knew* right away that I deserved it! I lowered my head in shame, unable to meet his vibrant eyes. "But

186

everything on that island was just make-believe. A *dream*!" I mumbled. "When it comes to reality, it was all completely pointless."

"Oh? *Was it?*" The Dream Master asked mysteriously. "Look at the inside of your right arm, Willy!"

I brought my right arm up and stared at it in disbelief? *There*, as plain as day, was the now healing scratch of the magic spear that the sparrow had carefully scratched there with its beak? "How is this even possible?" I stammered.

"*Anything* is possible if you truly believe it," The Dream Master said gently.

And at that moment, I realized that I *did* believe in the sparrow and what it had done? And I cared about it so very much! To me, the sparrow was much more than a mere character in a dream? It had *saved my life*! I guessed *that* was why I was able to see the mark it had left on my arm in the dream.

"As I told you before, all meaningful achievements begin with *meaningful* dreams, Willy," The Dream Master explained calmly. "Dreams that we passionately believe in. Don't you *passionately believe* that this girl is at least worth the effort of finding out how she truly feels about you?"

And suddenly I understood! I should have left that island and gone back to reality as the *confident man* that I had become there? *That* was the purpose of the dream! It *wasn't* pointless at all? Now I understood that until I believed the *significance* of what I had accomplished on that island, there was little hope for Melody and me of *ever* getting together in real life. It was as simple as that! "You're *right*!" I exclaimed. "You're *absolutely* right! Melody is worth a thousand attempts to find her and plead my case! I may not know where she's living right now, but I'll *never* stop looking for her!"

The Dream Master smiled gently as he met my eyes and then handed me a folded piece of paper. I opened it to very surprisingly find Melody's name and address neatly written on it, clear as day?

"Where did you *get this*?" I asked him incredulously.

Calmly he replied, "Does it matter? Congratulations, Willy! You don't need me anymore."

Listening to his startling final statement, I suddenly felt like a young child again, having just finished my swim lessons and *now*, whether I felt ready or not, I was about to be *thrown* into the deep end of the pool to either *sink or swim!* "Are you sure?" I asked him with uncertainty.

"Of course, I'm sure!" The Dream Master exclaimed with a warm smile.

"Before you go, can you at least give me a small hint as to whether or not Melody cares for me at all?" I asked.

He shook his head knowingly. "Sorry. I wish I could, but I *never* really get involved with reality much. That's *your* realm, Willy! Only *you* can find the answer to that question."

"But if she *doesn't* care at all for me, then even if I did find her, I'd be wasting her time as well as mine, wouldn't I?" I pleaded.

A thoughtful smile crossed The Dream Master's face as he gently replied, "When your five senses fail to adequately answer an important question like this one for you, you must trust your inner feelings. Now think, Willy. Is there a *real chance* that Melody *might* care for you?" After sharing those simple words, he smiled and then quickly disappeared into the fog.

Once again I felt lost, when suddenly I thought of something very important that The Dream Master had said on his television show. *'You will never in your waking life see your dreams come true, unless you go after them with all your heart and completely defeat your fears!'* Wow! He was so *right!* What did I have to lose by asking Melody one simple question? If she told me that she had no feelings at all for me, then it might hurt at first, but it would still be a lot better than *not* knowing the truth, and wondering about it for the rest of my life! And with that, I looked at the address on the scrap of paper The Dream Master had given me and excitedly realized that it was less than a mile away! I began walking faster than I had walked in years! When I arrived, I found that the house Melody apparently now lived in was part of a middle-class housing tract that had probably been built a decade or so before my own house. As I approached the dwelling, I initially got cold feet, but knowing full well that I wanted to do this more than anything, I left those defeatist feelings far behind me. I'll admit, it was not what I normally would have done in a situation like this one *prior* to my verbal reaming by The Dream Master today. But now, excitedly, I had found the motivation and determination I needed to dump my fears and move forward *whatever* the outcome! In addition? I was really tired of feeling *ordinary*. Now was my chance to feel exceptional by doing whatever I wanted to do? *No excuses?* And right now, more than anything, I wanted to *talk with Melody!* I joyfully smiled throughout my entire body to know that this *confidence* was going to be at the very heart of the *new me* from now on! My former traits of being *misguided* and *underachieving* were now only distant memories of the past, and I'd make sure they stayed that way! As I neared her house, I saw a wood and stucco building, much like my own place. It was neatly painted in a light tan with dark brown trim. I walked up to the door and knocked. Moments later, Melody opened it, initially shocked, but then smiling at me warmly.

"Hi, Melody," I said calmly, matching her smile. "I was wondering if you might want to walk with me for a while?"

"Sure, Willy," she replied quickly without hesitation. "Aren't you cold in those short shirt sleeves?"

"Nope! I never get cold. I'm part *Viking!*" I laughed as I quickly pulled my right hand into a fist and thrust it into the air to denote my supposed masculinity.

But suddenly looking very concerned as she stared at the inside of my right arm, she asked with concern, "How did you get that long scratch down the inside of your arm?"

I was *shocked* that she could actually see my *etched memory* that the sparrow had given me, and initially, I wasn't at all sure of what to say? Quickly recovering, however, with a smile I said, "Don't worry. It doesn't hurt a bit!"

"But *how* did it happen?" she asked me very curiously.

I decided to be truthful, as I very simply shared, "I was dreaming about a really exciting adventure, and when I woke up, the scratch was *there?*"

She *didn't* even question my response, but smiled and readily accepted it. "That must have been *some dream!*" she chuckled as she added, "Let me just get my coat. Unfortunately, I'm *not* part Viking like you are, and I get *cold* easily!" she smiled as she turned around to grab her coat off a hook on the wall.

A couple of minutes later, the two of us were casually walking the foggy streets of Bree. Since I had put very little thought into this potential *lifechanging* moment beyond simply finding Melody, I struggled a bit deciding how I could best explain my presence here and say what I wanted to say? But as luck would have it, *she* spoke first.

"I hoped with all of my heart that you would find me," she began gently. "But how could you possibly have known where I'd gone?"

I wanted to continue being honest with her, so I handed her the scrap of paper with her name and address written on it that The Dream Master had given me.

"Hey? That's *my* handwriting?" she exclaimed in surprise, after reading it. But then a shocked expression crossed her face. "Wait a minute! A man at my old apartment complex who seemed pretty official, asked me for my forwarding address to send me my mail, so I wrote it down on that paper and gave it to him? But how did *you* ever get hold of it?"

"Was this man tall and thin, and dressed all in white?" I asked mysteriously.

"Yes! That's him!" she confirmed. "Did *he* give this paper to you? Is he a friend of yours?" she asked incredulously.

"Yes and yes," I replied smiling. "I was looking for you and he was able to help me."

"Wow! What were the chances of *that* happening?" she shared, almost in disbelief.

Quickly getting to the point of my visit, I said gently, "Melody, the main reason I wanted to find you was because I thought we had something very special going on between us at Lucinda's Diner before you ran out? And then the next day at the office, when you were gone, before firing me, Mr. Chapman told me that you had quit your job because of my harassing you? Is that true?"

Melody suddenly grabbed me in a tight hug and sobbed. I didn't know exactly *what* was going on in her head at that moment, and although I felt very concerned about her, this was the first time she had hugged me and I very much *liked it*! Pulling back and facing me with tear-stained cheeks, she exclaimed, "*None* of what Mr. Chapman told you is true! Ever since I came to work in that office almost a year ago, he has always had a thing for me. He would follow me around the office and get all touchy-feely trying to get me to reciprocate and be his girlfriend!" she exclaimed. "He *nauseated* me, but he was my boss, so I didn't know what to do? Still, somehow I managed to fight off every one of his awkward romantic attempts!" And then with a frown, she added, "He had an older woman who would actually spy on me too, and report to him every day after work, telling him *where* I had been and *what* I had been up to!"

"That's so *creepy*!" I couldn't help but say. "Who was she?"

"I think it was *his mother*?" she replied hesitantly. "He once bragged to me that she loved him so much, she would do *anything* for him!"

I was shocked, but only nodded.

"Anyway, to make a long story short, the very next time I saw him, he *fired me*!" she said angrily.

"But *why* did you move out of your apartment so fast?" I asked with concern.

Melody hesitated for a moment, took a deep breath and replied, "Well, I honestly didn't want to talk with anyone from the office after he fired me," she began. "But the bigger reason was because Mr. Chapman threatened that if I didn't disappear, he would tell everyone in the office, as well as in corporate, that in addition to having a history of being '*promiscuous*' with a lot of the agents here over the past year, I had also been aggressively trying to get my hooks into *him*!" She took another breath. "I didn't know what I'd do if he spread *that* around? So, I guess I got scared and ran away! I couldn't bear the thought of staying! My reputation would have been in shambles, even though *none* of what he said was true!"

"Of course, it wasn't!" I replied encouragingly. "But you know what? Everything you told me just sounded like *vicious hearsay*," I said with suspicion. "You moved out of your apartment so quickly and didn't tell a soul where you had gone because of *that*? I'm sorry, but I don't buy it. There must have been something more serious than gossip that caused you to do that? Are you *sure* there wasn't something else?"

There was an awkward pause, and then Melody hesitantly agreed with a simple nod. "Alright, there *was* something else. I didn't want to tell you about it because I was afraid it might make you think less of me."

"I don't think there is *anything in this world* you could tell me that could *ever* do that!" I said warmly. "But don't worry. You don't have to tell me if you don't want to."

Melody immediately perked up and said, "No, I *do* want to tell you. I *need* to tell someone!"

I gently squeezed her hand encouragingly as we sat down on a bench at a nearby bus stop, and she began her story.

"Earlier this week, do you remember hearing about how one of our corporate auditors had discovered that over the past year thousands of dollars had *mysteriously disappeared* from our office deposits *before* they reached the bank?" Melody asked.

"Yes," I replied hesitantly. "That was pretty *shocking*! Do you know something about it?" I asked intently.

She nodded uncomfortably. "Two days ago, right after I had seen you at the diner, Mr. Chapman paid me a *surprise visit* at my apartment. At first, he again tried to get physical with me again, but I quickly diffused *that* idea! Then he grew angry and insisted that I stop seeing *you*! He even threatened to *fire you* if I didn't!"

"Mr. Chapman was jealous of *me*?"

"Yes! Ever since he saw the two of us laughing together while I was borrowing stamps from you a couple of days ago," she replied.

I was speechless!

"Anyway, after I refused, he threatened to share that promiscuity story with everyone. When that didn't work, he brought-up the missing company funds. He told me that as office manager, he always kept any money collected by the agents in his office safe until it was time to deposit it in the bank. Then he made a *point* of adding that no one regularly entered his office except for him and *me*. That's when he *accused me* of watching him open the safe soon after becoming his secretary, memorizing the combination and returning to his office sporadically after hours or anytime that he wasn't there during the year to steal a *small* part of the cash, hoping that the loss would *never* be noticed, or attributed to shoddy work by the accounting office."

"Huh?" I exclaimed. "What proof did he have?"

"*None!*" she declared fiercely. "Because I *didn't* do it! But he told me that it would be my word against his, and no matter what happened, people in Bree would *never* look at me the same! So, I might as well get out of town! Then, he threatened that if I ever so much as whispered a word about that conversation to anyone, he'd *destroy* me! The last thing he did was to *fire me*. I didn't know what else to do, so I hid from everyone by packing all night and moving out of my apartment and back in with my folks first thing this morning, as well as changing my phone number!" she explained passionately. "My gut tells me that *Mr. Chapman definitely took the money!* And now that the theft is common knowledge around the office, if he is ever asked about it, by trying to cover-up what he did, I just know he'll pin it *all on me!*" Melody suddenly teared up as she added softly, "But I could never prove any of that, could I?" Then having great trouble holding back stronger tears, she exclaimed, "Willy, ever since I was fired and threatened by him, I've been on pins and needles every second of every day, wondering what lies Mr. Chapman will tell the police and everyone else about me, and what *awful things* will happen to me as a result?"

My *heart broke!* I immediately felt ashamed of myself! I had been so focused on my own unhappy situation over these past few days, I had never dreamed that Melody's would be *far worse?* Coming to an immediate decision, I said gently, "Would you like to walk to my house with me? We need to call the corporate office right away."

"Why?" Melody asked fearfully.

"Relax, Melody. We've got to tell them the *truth* before Chapman begins spreading his lies," I told her. "We've got to report *everything* you've just told me!"

"But what if they don't believe me or choose to do nothing about it?" she asked me in fear.

"That *won't* happen!" I promised confidently. "Because we'll threaten to get a lawyer and *sue* them, as well as reporting every detail of this story to the newspapers and police if nothing is promptly done about this to *your* satisfaction!"

After slowly getting up from the bench and placing my hand in hers, for the first time since seeing her at the diner two nights ago, she attempted to *grin*.

EPILOGUE

Melody, Andy (*not the dog*), Beth (*Andy's girlfriend*) and I were having a great time drinking and chatting at *Benny's*. It had been six months now since Melody and I had pleaded our case to the corporate insurance office, and a lot had happened since then! Beginning that very day, Melody and I had immediately begun *officially* dating and getting to know each other better. Before long, *that* had turned into a romantic relationship and a couple of months later the two of us decided to move into my house together! Just as I'd expected, it was working out *beautifully*! Oh, I almost forgot. We are engaged to be *married* at the end of the year! Mr. Chapman had quite the adventure too. After the results of the insurance company's thorough internal investigation of this matter had found Irving Chapman *guilty* of grand-theft, rather than advertising his crime by involving the police or newspapers and putting the company through a long, expensive and *public* trial, they convinced him to *resign* in exchange for a generous no-fault severance package. The insurance company lost money, of course, and justice was not served, but to them, more importantly they were able to preserve the *professional reputation* of their company's name by sweeping his transgressions under the rug. Following this, both Melody and I were reinstated as employees of the company (*with all owed back pay*) due to being terminated without cause. I was promoted to Mr. Chapman's old job as office manager, and although they offered my former secretary Beverly, the job of secretary in my new position, she politely *declined*, citing this great opportunity for her to at last retire and spend more time with her grandkids. Although I'm sure *that* was true, I also think she wanted to do her part in making

Melody and I happy! I made sure that the company gave her a generous retirement package for her 40 years of service. And then, just as I'd hoped, *Melody* finally became *my* secretary! Incidentally, Mr. Chapman was arrested soon after accepting his severance-package, for *shoplifting* in several downtown stores in Bree. But, I hear that during the arrest he was just as charming as ever. He even smiled for his *mug shots!*

"So, how's the grocery store business?" I asked Andy.

"Couldn't be better!" he grinned. "There's going to be an opening for assistant manager very soon and *I'm* going for it!"

"Good for you!" Melody said encouragingly. "Who decides if you get the position?"

"The store manager," he replied.

"What do you think your chances are?" I asked excitedly.

"I would say *his* chances are very good, considering he's personable, honest, smart, good looking, the hardest worker at the store... and *I'm* the store manager!" Beth laughed.

Everyone else at our table laughed too, and it sure felt great!

As we all sat drinking and laughing, I suddenly noticed a tall, thin man dressed all in white at a table across the room. As our eyes met, he raised his glass in the air as if to toast me? Everyone was having such a grand time together that I had no trouble making my excuses, casually getting up and leaving our table to see what The Dream Master was up to?

"Hello, Willy!" he smiled, as I approached. "I just dropped by to congratulate you on the happy ending to your dream!"

"Well, thank you, Charley! And thank you for all you have done for me!" I replied in complete sincerity as I sat down at his table. "But I've got to ask you, what exactly *was* my specific dream that came true? I'm *not* complaining. My entire life has transformed so beautifully. I just can't seem to figure it out?"

The Dream Master laughed, as he replied, "Well, I'll admit that your dream was really a collection of many smaller ones you had, so it's understandable if it's *initially* more difficult for you to unravel. But, *c'mon*, Willy! Do you mean to tell me that even after all you have been through and all that you have learned as a result, you *still* haven't figured it out?"

Suddenly, my mind was flooded with understanding! Just like the tiny sparrow in the nest, I had eventually learned to face my fears! I knew now why I had taken such an interest in the bird throughout my dreams. The frustrating trials that the bird experienced, indirectly mirrored my own? That is, until we found a *mutual* heartfelt purpose to rise-up and vanquish the monster that was threatening us both, thus restoring the island to perfection! And just like the sparrow, in my own way, I was now confidently flying high and improving every facet of my life!

"Of course!" I said excitedly. "My dream wasn't all that complicated? It was simply to *be happy!*"

"And *are* you?" he sincerely asked me.

I quickly rose from the table and threw my arms around the tall, thin man. "Yes! Much more than I deserve to be!" I laughed. "Thank you!"

As the hug ended, The Dream Master rose from the table to meet me, and said in an especially heartfelt way, which seemed out of character for him, "Have a wonderful life, Willy! You have made your dad very happy!"

Suddenly Willy focused on the letters *DM* that were newly embossed in black on the right side of The Dream Master's previously all white dinner jacket. "The 'DM' on your jacket? It stands for 'Dream Master,' right?"

"It *could*," he smiled.

"I only asked because now that I think about it, those are also the initials of my dad's first and second names, *David Michael*," I shared.

"I know," he admitted impishly, as his face impossibly changed into the smiling face of *my father?*

"*Dad?*" I exclaimed in shock.

"Yes," he said softly as his eyes met mine.

"But, how is this possible?" I asked excitedly.

The Dream Master, my father, gently chuckled with his eyes sparkling, "Like I told you before, Willy. *Anything* is possible in the dream realm." Then he gave me a long and fatherly hug and smiled at me as he said, "I love you, Willy!" before gently turning away and disappearing.

I was *dumfounded*! Had The Dream Master been my father all along? Well, of course, *he had*! And then I laughed. It was just like my dad to die, but refuse to leave until he had *finished* the job he had started, of helping me to get my life on track! I loved him so much, and the biggest smile and greatest feeling I had ever felt in my life suddenly engulfed me as I walked back toward my friends.

"Was that the man who gave you my address?" Melody asked as I sat down at the table.

"It certainly was," I replied happily.

"Was he checking-up on *us*?" she giggled.

"You might say that," I admitted with a smile.

Suddenly, Melody beamed as she handed me a sketchbook. "Hey, Willy! I had a *wonderful* dream about you the other night?" she said cryptically. "I liked it so much that I've drawn my favorite memory of it. Would you like to see it?"

"Of course, I would!" I exclaimed as I excitedly opened the book. When I first gazed at her drawing, I was immediately *stunned*! In addition to obviously being a very skilled artist, she had drawn me on a tropical island that looked *very familiar*. I was stabbing a large monster (*strongly resembling a fire-breathing dragon*) with what appeared to be a spear. Meanwhile, a tiny bird was flying across the island.

"I've got to say," Melody shared with a warm smile. "For some reason, drawing and then looking at this picture makes me feel so happy and full of hope?"

I smiled too, feeling too blessed for words. "It's *perfect*!" I was finally able to utter, as I looked lovingly into her eyes. "Just like *you* are!" And then we gently kissed.

Seven Unforgettable Tales from My Childhood

"*Childhood is where dreams are born, and time is never planned.*"- *Anon.* As you have probably already figured out from the title, these next seven short stories *aren't* fantasy at all, but are in fact autobiographical *non-fiction!* Just the same, I thought they'd fit well in this predominantly fantasy/science-fiction collection, because although these seven tales are mostly true, very honestly, some of them are so wild and crazy that they read as though they were taken *straight out of my imagination!*

Once upon a time, like you, I was a *child*. And *also* like you, when I think about it, I remember lots of amazing, meaningful or embarrassing adventures with my friends or family, and even by myself. Taking from that vast and diverse stockpile of memories, the following seven short stories represent some of my *favorites.* Each one of them took place in the 1960s or *very early* 1970s, in Glendora, California, mostly during those all-important developmental years of elementary school when we each learned and experienced so many important things that often stayed with us throughout our lifetimes.

Looking back on these timeless stories brings to mind all sorts of emotions that I experienced then, ranging anywhere from exuberance to anger, from confidence to depression and everywhere in-between! But most importantly, it reminds me of the indispensable *life lessons* I learned as the result of each of these adventures. It's wonderful how some very simple experiences in our lives, such as these, become so special to us as we grow older *(regardless of how ordinary some of them may appear to others)* that we never forget them because of the incredible significance they hold for us. In fact, we seem to appreciate them more with each passing year. As Brazilian writer Paulo Coelho de Souza, author of '*The Alchemist*' wrote, "*The simple things are also the most extraordinary things... and only the wise can see them.*" Enjoy!

-ONE-
The Incredible Tale of "Tim, Big David and Devil Ringo"

"Logic will get you from A to B. Imagination will take you everywhere."-Albert Einstein. When I was young, probably seven or eight years old, my next-door neighbor and good friend Tim and I used to play a variety of games together outside that were just so much fun! We played mostly on weekends and during the summer. Of these, my favorites were those that enabled us to *'vividly use our imaginations.'* We learned that whenever we used our imaginations *together*, it was crucial for us to always be on the 'same wave-length,' as if we had entered some secret *playtime dimension* designed exclusively for us! When we did this, it enabled us to truly connect and go anywhere our young, creative minds would take us. Which of course, we loved! Although I'm sure I was not aware of it at the time, I believe this may have been the beginning of my great passion for using my imagination to create stories, songs, and games, as well as to participate in creative projects like this one, often with others. In this instance, Tim and I had immense fun playing make-believe, using nothing more than a tree in my front yard and of course, our *imaginations*. At some point during our play, we concocted the character and name, *Devil Ringo*, to always serve as our archnemesis. He was the perfect villain to our perfect heroes because although he was extremely difficult to defeat, in the end of each of our adventures, he *always lost*! The exciting story I am about to share with you is *very loosely* based on distant memories that Tim and I

recently shared together of adventures we had experienced through our imaginations over 60 years ago. I carefully cobbled most of those fractured memories together as best I could, added a generous helping of appropriate enhancement as needed, and *voila*, this story was completed! Tim reminded me that back then, while playing in the tree, although we felt like we were alone in a spaceship, in reality, *we weren't*. He remembers that there were always younger children (*predominantly little Willerts*) running around below the tree, completely unaware of us, playing their own games. This, of course, was true, but as I remember it, that *never* caused us to lose focus from what we were doing. That was because, as you will soon discover, when Tim and I climbed into that tree in my front yard, we were almost always on a very important mission to *save the Earth*! Although this story may not have transpired *exactly* as I tell it now (*due to it including details from many different missions*), in the *spirit* of all the adventures we created in that tree those many, many years ago, it's *100% accurate*!

As a young boy, my day included experiencing unique, magical and mysterious adventures whenever my best friend Tim and I got together. When we did, we would sometimes morph into our superhero alter egos, climb aboard our spaceship and chase the infamous outlaw *Devil Ringo* all over the galaxy! Now, I imagine that some readers are probably rolling their eyes and smiling condescendingly at this point, fully believing that I am talking about nothing more than simple *role playing*, something that young kids are quite famous for doing. But I am most certainly *not*! I swear on the memory of famous Martian pilot *Ybajmknlt*, that the story I am about to share with you is absolutely true! Of course, it's *top secret*, but I know you can be trusted to keep mum, so here goes! The exciting adventure of *Tim, Big David and Devil Ringo*!

It was a cold Saturday morning in January, when I decided to leave the warm confines of my house (*which I shared with my parents, multiple siblings and a big family of cats*) in order to see my best friend Tim, who lived next door. Tim, also shared his house with his parents and a healthy group of siblings. His little brother, like me, was named *David*, so we quickly solved any potential confusion by anointing him '*Little David*,' and me, '*Big David*.' I soon knocked on Tim's front door and his mother answered. She was a very kind woman with a big welcoming smile. She called Tim, and moments later, as usual, we found ourselves walking together outside in the direction of my front yard. We began our conversation simply enough, mostly discussing current TV shows we watched, but very soon, as if on cue, our topic *dramatically* changed!

"So, have you heard from headquarters today?" Tim intently asked me, nonchalantly turning around to make sure that no one was listening-in on our conversation.

I nodded in confirmation. "They told me that Devil Ringo has entered Mars' airspace and may soon be entering Earth's if we don't do something about it, and I mean *fast!*"

Tim acknowledged my strong words with a nod. "Well, I guess we had better get going then!"

"My thoughts exactly!" I agreed.

Moments later, the two of us were standing at the base of our spaceship in my front yard, which had very cleverly been *disguised as a tree* some years earlier by the geniuses who worked at headquarters. It was such a great disguise that to anyone watching, it *always* appeared that we were two young boys happily playing in a tree, even while we were away in space on a secret mission! And although everyone at home who saw us today would think that we were just Tim and Big David up in that tree, in actuality, we were two of headquarters' *top space agents* preparing to travel to Mars in a few moments to meet the inherent dangers that awaited us there! We each climbed up the tree (*something we had a lot of experience doing as space agents*) and immediately it transformed into our spaceship, while Tim and I *morphed* into the most fearless space agents in the galaxy! We even wore cool invisible spacesuits (*once again developed by the geniuses at headquarters*). These spacesuits could never be seen, never ran out of oxygen and included several invisible weapons if (*or more likely when*) we needed them. Tim was the pilot of our ship, as he had seniority. He had graduated from the academy a full year earlier than I had. But as his co-pilot, I was also the gunner. I looked forward to stopping Devil Ringo once and for all by chasing his ship clear out of this solar system! He was like a bad dream to everyone who had the severe misfortune of tangling with him. Something *had* to be done immediately to stop his evilness! As far as I was concerned, Tim and I were more than ready to accept this momentous challenge.

"Ready for blast off?" Tim asked me calmly.

"*Ready!*" I confirmed, giving him a firm thumbs up.

Captain Tim began the countdown. "Ten, nine, eight, seven, six, five, four, three, two, one... *blast off!*"

Within moments, we were catapulted high above the clouds with our ship's mighty engines roaring aggressively. Our ship, The Dominator, was capable of traveling *hundreds of times* the speed of light! Our quest to find and thwart the infamous Devil Ringo and his gang, the Moonbeams, would soon begin! I imagine that space travel could be a very dull and tedious thing if your spacecraft was slow and you were only privy to watching the Earth very gradually growing smaller and smaller through a tiny porthole at the side of your ship? But in this case, our ship was so fast that it seemed like only moments before we had entered Mars' airspace and actually *saw* Devil Ringo's ship in the distance! If you were wondering, the people of Mars, small, greenish folk with great big hearts taking up most of their chests and as you know, with a couple of short antennas growing out of the top of their heads, were currently experiencing a *great recession* due to a lack of interplanetary tourism. The tens of thousands of tourists from other planets who had *planned* on visiting Mars, had suddenly *canceled* their reservations en masse due to their extreme fear of being robbed by the terrifying outlaw Devil Ringo and his notorious gang, the *Moonbeams!* To make matters worse, Mars could no longer afford to protect itself? So, as always, Captain Tim and I were sent to do the job *free of charge*. In describing Devil Ringo's ship, the best word to describe it is **ominous**! It was completely black in color and in the unearthly shape of a devil's skull, complete with frightening horns which were actually two *ferocious gun turrets* that could blast us or anything else clear to kingdom come! No one on Earth had ever seen him in the flesh, but it's widely believed that *Devil Ringo* probably looked a lot like his *namesake* from *down under*! His gang, the *Moonbeams*, each traveled in a small one-man ship that was built for 'swarm fighting,' much like bees, collectively attacking their prey. No one on Earth had ever seen *them* in the flesh either, but our brightest minds speculated that the Moonbeams were probably small Hobbit-like creatures who were *not* too smart, so were easily manipulated by the devious Devil Ringo! There were 25 Moonbeam ships in all, but we weren't afraid of them in the least! We had fought them many times before, and *always* lived to tell the tale because we were the good guys; the mighty *Space Defenders of Earth*, who never accepted defeat!

The Moonbeam ships had already begun speeding toward us in earnest! I manned the gun as Tim expertly flew us nearer to joining the imminent conflict. Soon we were in the thick of a ferocious battle. I placed several direct hits during the fight, which caused enough damage to those enemy ships that they were forced to immediately leave the battle for repairs at the Moonbeam Spaceship Repair Shop (MSRS), which was located in a nearby blackhole. But they had so many ships fighting us, that the temporary loss of a few, honestly didn't make much of a difference. We were hopelessly outnumbered and had given them plenty of time to prepare for us as we'd foolishly opted *not to wait* for the element of surprise! Regardless, we were holding our own and would have gone on fighting... that is, until we saw the infamous horns of Devil Ringo's ship *frighteningly* turning directly toward us! We had heard too many terrifying tales about brave space agents who had chosen to stand their ground against Devil Ringo's incredibly big guns, to their *utter demise*! As if he were reading my mind, Tim abruptly turned our ship around and headed away full speed. The Moonbeams gave chase, but I quickly rolled down my window and threw a giant smoke bomb at them. It exploded, and all of the Moonbeam ships were immediately sent into *disarray*! But we had little time to cheer, as we suddenly noticed that Devil Ringo's ship was also in hot pursuit, and ignoring the fallout from the smoke bomb, he was actually *gaining* on us? Fortunately, we chanced to find a wandering asteroid, which Tim immediately hid our ship behind. We *knew* we would be safe from Devil Ringo there! We stayed there for what seemed like hours before finally sensing that the coast was clear. It was then and only then that we *dared* to leave our hiding place.

About that time, Tim and I were becoming increasingly hungry? You see, we had not eaten since breakfast, and unfortunately we had *not* brought any provisions along on this trip? So, we decided to immediately return to Earth, have lunch, and then continue our exciting adventure afterwards. Tim put our ship into 'hyperspace,' and moments later we arrived on my front lawn and proceeded to climb down from the ship (*or tree, as it appeared to everyone else*). We parted ways; Tim going to his house for a delicious lunch of unknown origin, while I went to mine, where I looked forward to consuming a delicious grilled cheese sandwich accompanied by a tantalizing bowl of bean and bacon soup! This was truly an astronaut's best nourishment after a thrilling space battle. It was even better than *Tang*!

Half an hour later, our stomachs no longer aching for food, Tim and I once again met at the tree (*which immediately morphed into our ship*), climbed aboard and blasted off. We were in Mars' atmosphere within moments, so the next thing we did was to proceed carefully in search of any sign of Devil Ringo and his Moonbeams.

"What do you think?" Tim asked me from his pilot's chair.

"They're out there *somewhere*," I said uneasily. "And if we're not careful, we may find ourselves flying right into a *trap* again!"

"You read my mind," Tim responded slowly, as he was formulating his next thought. "But what if this time it was *us* who laid the trap?"

I laughed in approval as I immediately took his meaning. "I love it! Let's make a plan!"

Tim and I had the uncanny ability of reading each other's thoughts when we set our minds to it. This enabled us to discuss important timely topics like our plans to thwart Devil Ringo, without even the remotest possibility of anyone else secretly listening-in on us. So, for the next fifteen minutes or so, we locked minds and put together what we felt was a foolproof plan! Tim came up with it, and I loved it!

"I'm ready to put our plan into action, Big David. How about you?" Captain Tim announced momentarily.

"Ready, Captain," I replied, like a daring and handsome TV space hero from the early 1960s, who just happened to be eight years old!

And with that, we were off to give Devil Ringo a great big surprise!

At first, everything seemed to be going according to plan. Devil Ringo and his Moonbeams apparently *did not* have a clue that we were returning so quickly, as they were all parked around a local space café, more precisely a *smorgasbord* cryptically named 'AYCEFA,' which stood for '*All You Can Eat for Aliens*.' But then the most embarrassing thing happened? We actually *ran out of space fuel?* Inexplicably, we had *both* forgotten to refuel the ship after returning to Earth for lunch? I mean, with two of the most talented and intelligent space agents on Earth manning this ship, what were the odds?

But, Captain Tim was not the smartest flyer in the galaxy for nothing, as he quickly brought our ship (*which was now running on fumes*) to a gentle stop behind another wandering asteroid, just sitting there in front of us.

"Looks like we definitely need more fuel," Tim smiled wryly, but eloquently, as he sized-up our situation perfectly. "You don't suppose there's an *outer-space gas station* nearby, do you?" he joked.

I laughed. "No, but I just thought of a quick solution to our problem! Why don't I put on my '*jet shoes*' that you gave me for my birthday last year. I've got them right here in my space suit. I can use them to secretly fly over to Devil Ringo's ship? Once I get there, I'll put one end of a hose into his fuel tank while you put the other end of it into ours. Then we'll siphon out *his* space fuel using our handy dandy space vacuum while he and his crew are none the wiser. How does that sound?"

Tim laughed. "Great idea, Big David! Luckily, I brought along a very long hose for just such an emergency!"

"How long is it?" I asked curiously.

"It will *indefinitely* grow to whatever length you need!"

I smiled. Readiness like this was *exactly* why Tim had made captain at such a very young age!

Within a short time, the deed was done, and as Tim and I excitedly prepared to move-in on Devil Ringo and his now *fuel-less* ship, to our immense dismay, we quickly realized that the ship I had taken the fuel from could *not* possibly have been Devil Ringo's! Although it had looked a lot like his ship, *'**Have A Nice Day!**'* was boldly written across the side of it in bright red sequined space paint, with a great big *happy face* drawn beneath it in yellow paint? Although we could certainly make a case for Devil Ringo liking the color *red*, he had *never* been known to wish *anyone* a nice day *or* to draw a big yellow happy face on his evil ship? And the clincher was, he *just hated sequins!* I felt kind of bad now about taking someone else's space fuel, but what's done was done. So, regardless of what happened, I only hoped that whoever they were, the owners of that ship would somehow *find humor* in the fact that they no longer had any space fuel and would laughingly find a way to **have a nice day** anyway! And then suddenly we caught sight of Devil Ringo's *real ship* sneaking in behind us about 100 yards away, preparing to blast *The Dominator* out of existence! Tim was not bothered one bit as he gave me a wink. We were about to put our plan into motion, and although we really didn't know if it would work, we were thrilled to actually see it in action! I mean what's the worst thing that could happen to us if it *didn't* work? *Never mind!* Tim quickly turned our ship around and headed full speed for Devil Ringo, but not in a straight line? As we'd planned, he was carefully moving our ship from left to right and up and down without any pattern, so that Ringo's mighty guns could *not possibly* target us! Meanwhile, not surprisingly, the *Moonbeams* were still nowhere to be seen? That was because, as both Tim and I were very much aware, this was *always* the time of day when in addition to taking their daily lunchbreaks, afterwards the Moonbeams never failed to take their *space naps* right there in the restaurant! Without his gang there to help him, Devil Ringo must have gotten 'cold feet' (*to go along with the long 'yellow streak' screaming down his back*) as he abruptly turned his ship around and putting his pedal to the metal, flew away just as *fast* as he could, surely knowing that he alone was no match for the ingenuity of the Earth's greatest space agents, especially when they were flying the mighty Dominator!

"Great plan, Captain Tim!" I complimented him.

"Thank you, Big David!" Tim replied. "But we never could have done it without your brilliant plan to *get more fuel!*"

I smiled and nodded. Captain Tim was *right!* We had *both* contributed to this success! But I always appreciated the fact that on every mission we flew, he *never* failed to thank me! His humility was yet *another* reason why he made such a *great* captain!

We both cheered as we watched a quickly fading Devil Ringo hightailing it away! You see, our mission had *never* been to catch or destroy the miscreant, only to *scare* him away from Mars, which we had absolutely done! *Mission accomplished!*

What seemed like only moments later (*and probably was*), we flew through space, entered the Earth's atmosphere and successfully landed our spaceship at the *exact* same spot we had taken off from in my front yard. This was no easy task, but with an ace pilot like Tim and a talented navigator like me, we *never* missed our target! After landing, we disembarked to join the people we loved, who had absolutely *no idea* that we had ever left the tree at all? They also had *no idea* what we did for a living? But undoubtedly, our lack of fame was for the best. To everyone around us, we were merely two young kids playing in a tree, *never* to be taken seriously. But to those in the *know*, we had proven once again that we were resilient and brave space agents, who had *saved* the Earth and Mars from that evil scoundrel *Devil Ringo!* Until next time, this is Captain Tim and Big David, signing off!

212

-TWO-
The Surreal Tale of "Mary Poppins and the Record Store"

I believe that sometimes things we experience are so perfect, we simply *cannot forget them*! This story is a prime example of that! The year was 1964, the year of the *British Invasion*, when *The Beatles* were king! The Fact is, they had just released their first movie, *A Hard Day's Night*, to thunderous fanfare in July of that year! But, as much as I loved The Beatles... and *that* movie, I'm afraid that the magical tale you are about to read, featuring my sister Cathi and me, has absolutely *nothing* to do with John, Paul, George or Ringo! You see, there was another spectacular event taking place beginning in August of that year. The extraordinary film (*as well as one of Walt Disney's most enduring masterpieces*) 'Mary Poppins,' was initially released!

Cathi and I were fortunate enough to be inside a theatre watching it during its first weekend and I must say, it was truly *magnificent*! I was blown away watching, feeling and hearing the results of so much hard work, talent and creativity transformed into magic that day on the big screen! In fact, seeing this movie further inspired me to *keep* using my own imagination more in creative projects! Also, seeing this movie confirmed to me that my lifelong love affair with 'everything Walt Disney' (*when he was alive and running things*) was truly a great idea! Here's our story, with the very obvious addition of a little fun imagination in the middle of it to tie

213

the two *historical* sections (*Mary Poppins/The Record Store*) seamlessly together! As a creative writer, in defense of the wild and crazy fiction section I've added to the middle of this non-fiction story? I say, "*Why not?*" As Robin Williams famously said, "*You're only given a little spark of madness. You mustn't lose it!*" So, I wrote and included this fun little fantasy section to make sure that I *didn't!*

There was a time in 1964 when the whole world was anticipating the release of Walt Disney's soon to be *blockbuster* movie, 'Mary Poppins!' I was ten years old at the time, while my sister Cathi, was a couple of years older. As a kid, Walt Disney was already the *closest* thing to a god around our house, what with his entertaining movies, exciting television show and of course, Disneyland. But *Mary Poppins* promised to break new ground in movie musicals through the extensive use of live action *combined* with animation and you guessed it, we could hardly wait!

I recall very fondly that the very first time Cathi and I watched Mary Poppins on the big screen was with our next-door neighbors, the Rattrays, at the Eastland Theatre in West Covina. Their mother kindly drove us there from Glendora and asked us to call her once the movie had ended so that she would know what time to pick us up. Well, we were all so excited! When we got there, the theatre was mostly full of kids (*and parents who were young at heart*) and predictably, once the opening credits of the movie began rolling, every kid in that theatre could be heard screaming their approval! From beginning to end, I was completely enthralled! Julie Andrews sang beautifully, Dick van Dyke was hilarious, and the two children, Jane and Michael... well, let's just say it was easy to imagine them (*a few years earlier*) being Cathi and me! I won't say any more about it except, *IT WAS THE GREATEST MOVIE I HAD EVER SEEN IN MY LIFE!* Cathi loved it too! In fact, she recently shared with me that because of watching that movie, she had developed a *lifelong crush* on Dick Van Dyke! In any case, the movie was so good, that I remember staying at the theatre long after the first showing had ended and watching as much of the *next showing* as possible (*you were allowed to do that in those days*) before calling our ride home.

When we finally left the theatre, the car we drove home in was *massively* overcrowded with kids. Cars weren't required to have seatbelts in those days (*not until 1968*) so you could legally fill-up the backseat with as many kids as you could possibly squeeze into it, even if it meant the smaller kids had to sit on the bigger kids' laps! Anyway, we were all ceaselessly talking (*almost shouting*) over one another about how *wonderful* the movie had been during the entire ride home! Once we arrived at our neighbors' house, Cathi and I fondly said our goodbyes to each of the kids (*who were more like cousins to us than mere neighbors*) and then we began walking the short distance toward the front door of our house next door. Not to change the subject... *exactly*... but have you ever daydreamed so hard that you actually felt it was real? I admit that I did that *all* the time, sometimes to the *frustration* of my teachers and playmates. And I found myself doing that *now*, as watching a masterpiece like *Mary Poppins* in the theatre today had sent my imagination working overtime! Suddenly, everything seemed *very different*! And out of nowhere, Cathi and I looked up to the sky to see a beautiful young woman daintily grasping her umbrella with her right hand while gracefully clutching a good-sized carpetbag in her left as she inexplicably floated down from the sky? Strangely, no one else on our cul-de-sac seemed to notice her?

"Hello, Cathi and David," the woman clearly spoke to us in her refined English accent combined with a confident but muted smile, once she had gently touched ground beside us. I know that I was known for having a 'wild imagination' at times, but *this was real!* As she so elegantly stood there before us on our front lawn, it was all we could do to contain our excitement, which in a special situation like this, seemed indubitably the *proper* thing to do! I really wanted to say something clever... and yet... I found myself *tongue-tied*?

"What's the matter, David? Cat got your tongue?" Mary Poppins asked me with a playful wink.

"Are you really *Mary Poppins*?" my sister brazenly asked her with suspicion.

"Do I look like Mary Poppins?" she asked Cathi with a politely whimsical air.

215

"Yes," Cathi replied confidently.

"Do you *hope* that I'm Mary Poppins?" she added.

"Of course, I do!" Cathi exclaimed.

"Then *that's* who I am!" Mary replied rather matter-of-factly.

"Will you be taking us on an outing?" I asked her excitedly.

Mary Poppins looked at me with the faintest of smiles and replied very reservedly, "Hmm?"

"An outing would be wonderful! *Please*, Mary Poppins? Please?" Cathi exclaimed.

Mary Poppins took a moment to converse with the handle of her umbrella before ultimately saying, "Yes. I agree with you. An outing would be quite nice at this time of day. Are you both ready to go?"

We were shocked and thrilled at the very same time... but mostly *thrilled!* "Of course, we are!" Cathi excitedly replied for both of us.

"But where are we going, Mary Poppins?" I found myself asking, with my eyes wide open and my imagination also in full bloom.

"Well, let me see?" she offered slowly, without expression. "I have not been back to the Egyptian pyramids for quite a while?"

"The *pyramids?*" I exclaimed. "Wow!"

"Close your mouth, David. We are *not* a codfish," Mary Poppins addressed me politely concerning my obviously *fishlike* expression.

"But how shall we get there?" Cathi logically asked with concern. "There are two of us kids, and since you have to hold your umbrella with one hand, that leaves you with only *one hand* to hold *both of us?*"

"Pish-posh!" Mary replied dismissively, as she gently dropped her carpetbag to the ground. "*Teamwork* is the solution, my dear. Take my hand, Cathi, and David will take yours."

I was amazed as I immediately realized that in the amazing movie we had just seen today, *this* was the exact same thing the children had done when *they* went on outings with Mary Poppins! So, equipped with big smiles, we did exactly as Mary Poppins instructed us and true to her word, the umbrella in her right hand effortlessly pulled all three of us high into the sky. It was scary and breathtaking at the very same time as we rapidly flew through the air, inexplicably

216

touching down in *Egypt* just a few moments later? The rest of the story is an exciting blur to me as Cathi, Mary Poppins and I actually *did* visit the pyramids! First, we went inside a glowing golden pyramid where a troupe of *tap-dancing mummies* invited us to lunch. An invitation which Mary Poppins gladly accepted on Cathi's and my behalf, because every child knows how rude it is to disappoint a daddy or a *mummy*! They served us the most delicious meal you could ever imagine (*mostly made of chocolate, caramel and gumdrops*) as they tapped and spun up and down the walls and across the ceiling! Next, we visited an *old pharaoh* who lived on top of the Sphinx, in a hidden room that only Mary Poppins could find! This dusty old pharaoh was especially fond of playing tidily winks, which we played with him for quite some time. In the end, I believe that Mary Poppins *let* him win rather than calling him out for his clumsy efforts at cheating. It actually was not his fault, you see. Being raised as a spoiled prince, he'd never learned how to play '*phar*' (pronounced '*fair*')! Following all of that excitement, we took a friendly ride down the Nile on the backs of three enormous dolphins, which unfortunately resulted in all of us *nearly* being eaten alive by three menacing *purple alligators* named Spit, Spat and Spot! In the end, however, they agreed that it was never polite to *eat* Mary Poppins, her charges *or* innocent dolphins! In a show of remorse for their impertinence, with each of us on one of their backs, the three alligators took us for an *exciting and heart-stopping ride* across the Nile, accompanied by our new friends, the dolphins, who we soon learned were incredible jumpers! After that whirlwind of activity, we flew back home in a matter of a seconds. It was *fantastic*! Finally, waving goodbye, Mary Poppins picked up her carpet bag from where she had left it, raised her umbrella high over her head and effortlessly floated back into the sky to embrace her next adventure. But before completely disappearing from view, I am *almost certain* that I heard her say, "*You both will experience one final outing today to remember me by!*" Outing? But *what* could she have possibly been talking about? I wondered. Suddenly noticing that Cathi wasn't there, I turned toward the front door of our house where she was calling to me?

"Hey, David!" she yelled, in a distinctly pointed tone reserved for big sisters when they are annoyed by their younger brothers. "I've been calling you for five minutes! What have you been doing? *Daydreaming* again?"

I was suddenly crushed as I realized that our wonderful adventure with Mary Poppins had apparently *only* been in my imagination? Still, I thought about Mary Poppins' final proclamation and immediately became *confused* as I disappointedly followed Cathi into the house.

While sitting alone on my bed, thinking about the wonderful movie we had seen today, as well as the exciting adventure with Cathi and Mary Poppins that had followed, I felt a nagging sense of uncertainty? I mean, I still felt *good* about the day overall, but my unshakable suspicion that our incredible trip to Egypt had *never* actually happened, kept my brain from fully appreciating everything else about the day? Sure, our trip to Egypt sounded impossible, but I still had trouble believing that I had only imagined it?

And then mercifully, about ten minutes later, Cathi raced into my room, effectively breaking my stressful focus, with the *most incredible news*! "We have been invited to join Dad at the 'Grand Opening' of his friend's new record store in West Covina! And they promised to play songs from the movie, *Mary Poppins*, the whole time we are there!" she exclaimed excitedly.

Our drive to the record store that night seemed endless! Cathi and I couldn't help but happily sing the songs we remembered from the *Mary Poppins* movie we had seen earlier in the day as we anxiously waited to arrive there! It probably drove our dad bananas, but thankfully for us... it made the drive go that much *faster*! Finally, we entered the brightly lit store, which as promised, was playing the entire soundtrack from *Mary Poppins* over and over again! The place was brightly decorated to the max in a Mary Poppins motif, complete with large posters of the movie hanging on the walls throughout. We were not in the store long, before we were drawn to a colorful rack which featured a stack of albums containing the official soundtrack from 'Mary Poppins,' complete with every song in the movie! And these albums were surrounded by a good number of 45s (*singles*) that boasted some of the *catchier* tunes from the movie, such as '*Jolly Holiday*,' '*Let's Go Fly a Kite*,' '*Supercalifragilisticexpialidocious*,' and '*Step in Time!*' We were in heaven! Next, my dad introduced us to John, the owner of the store, who immediately asked us each to select one record single apiece to take home to remember this wonderful night by! I laughed to myself as I realized that *this* must be what Mary Poppins had meant when she had promised us one *final outing* today! But since her words had come true about this, we *must* have actually traveled to Egypt with her? Right? Suddenly, I felt like I was dreaming again for a brief moment when Cathi's voice whispered into my ear, "It's *all true*, David! I was there *with you*!" Following those magical words from Cathi, *everything* instantly grew louder and brighter! So, it *was* true! We really *had* gone to Egypt and it made me feel so happy! I recall that Cathi and I took our time selecting our singles from the movie because *every song* was terrific and in addition to that, we wanted to stretch this 'Mary Poppins day' as long as possible!

Our visit to the store finally ended and we found ourselves quietly driving home with my dad, both of us deep in thought. To sum this incredible day up for the two of us, the wonderful record store experience, getting to watch 'Mary Poppins' on the big screen *and* traveling to the Pyramids with her afterwards, like Mary Poppins herself, made this day *practically perfect in every way*!

The GO-GO GUYS 1966

-THREE-
The Evolving Adventures of
"The Go-Go Guys... and Beyond!"

"The most effective way to do it, is to do it!"-Amelia Earhart. Have you ever wondered how a trio of starry-eyed adolescent boys who were suddenly inspired by pop music during the mid to late 1960s, with little skill, maturity or experience, could somehow *successfully* form their own pop singing group? Well, I'm sure that answer must vary a lot amongst all of those aspiring young kids who attempted this feat back then, but for my youthful pals and me, I would have to say that we dreamed big, worked hard, and had a *lot* of help! In addition, being so young in the beginning, we obviously had no jobs or other time-consuming obligations to deal with, so, armed only with tremendous passion, we were able to spend lots of time together learning to play the guitar, write songs and rehearse as a group, essentially, *evolving* our talents and skills together over the span of five years, from 1966-71. This is the true story of how Steve Medley, my brother Robert and I gave birth to a pop music trio, which later became a successful duo, completely from scratch!

Although I 'attempted' to play the trombone in the school bands for five years beginning in the fifth grade (*you can read all about that disaster later in this collection of stories*) and took half-hearted piano lessons from my good-hearted mother, I believe the actual beginning of my lifelong passion for creating and performing music coincided with the day Robert and I met *Steve* for the first time. To begin our

221

story, Robert and I, both skinny, shaggy haired blondes, were outside on the street of our cul-de-sac one day after school in 1966 playing 'capture the flag' with a number of other neighborhood kids. Steve, a small, freckle-faced kid with brown hair cut in a mop-top and an impish smile, had just moved into the house at the end of our street a few days earlier. We had seen him outside in his front yard a couple of times, but none of us had actually met him? Right on cue, his older sister Lynn, (who appeared to be a couple of years older than I was) came out of their house with him in tow and asked if he could play with us? I was the oldest kid out there, so I took it upon myself to welcome him to the game. My brother Robert, like him, was in fifth grade at the time, while I was actually a couple of years older than them, in seventh grade, having just started junior high school that year. From that day on, the three of us, Robert, Steve and I, began doing more and more things together after school each day, soon becoming *best friends*.

In 1966, The Monkees, a pop singing phenomenon created for television, starred in their own top-rated TV show of the same name. In addition to being television stars, they were also churning out one hit record after another for several years; while their fan base in America was gigantic, something people had not seen in America since the invasion of The Beatles! The Monkees meteoric rise to fame was *not* lost on me. I was *inspired* by it, in fact! As a result, Steve, Robert and I decided to start our own pop singing group, although we hadn't actually *tried* singing together yet? To be honest, we didn't even know if we could *sing in tune*? Regardless of that 'minor' concern and the fact that none of us really had *any idea* how to get started, the desire to create a pop singing group was still burning bright inside us! To start things off, we knew that the Monkees sang *original songs* and for that reason, we logically believed that *we* should too! But we also understood that at present, we *didn't have any*? And since none of us had ever written any songs before, I took it upon myself as the oldest member of the group to start! I Felt a genuine sense of urgency! I reasoned that regardless of the fact that we were all very young now, as we got older we would undoubtedly be saddled with more and more responsibilities and might *never* find a better time to attempt this exciting musical quest again? In addition, the way I saw it, there was very little stopping us from becoming a popular singing group! I figured that we just needed to write a few catchy songs, practice them, get discovered by a record label and *voila*! I know that sounds a bit 'Pollyanna,' but I wasn't caught-up at all by our obviously *dismal odds* of succeeding, seeing as none of us had *ever* done anything even remotely similar to this before and we *didn't know* anyone who had? The fact is, I was just excited about starting our own singing group, and I believed that worrying about failure was a real buzzkill!

So, I set to work coming up with melodies in my head and matching them with impromptu lyrics (*using current pop songs as my templates*) that were eventually written down on random sheets of paper. Sometimes Robert, Steve and I would even try singing a few of those songs together, but mostly I would just write the lyrics down, remember the melodies in my head and store the song sheets haphazardly in a red folder in my closet. A few of those titles included, '*Right Behind the Sand Dunes*,' '*Lonely Tramp*,' and '*A Girl Named Marylou*.' The lyrics for the latter song began:

There's a girl named Marylou. (La, la, la)
Who is very poor, boohoo. (La, la, la)
She is queer, a freak, a fraud. (La, la, la)
And her clothes aren't very mod. (La, la)
I only know, that she's queer, 'cause she's scared.

FYI: I sang lead in the first four lines while Robert and Steve sang, La, la, la. Then we sang unison on the chorus. I know the word '*queer*' sounds out of place, but at that time it still meant *odd*, with no sexual connotation that I was aware of. This was my attempt at writing a humorous song about a girl in school who didn't fit-in. The second and third verses described her appearance and how sad she was? Thinking about the lyrics today, this song doesn't seem humorous *at all*? In contrast, it seems to be a heartfelt story probably featured on the *Hallmark Channel* about a lonely seventh grade girl struggling to find her way? Well, at least the melody and *la la's* were

223

fun! I'm afraid that my songwriting skills (*especially the lyrics*) were still a work in progress.

None of my early works turned out to be the greatest of titles *or* the greatest of songs, but I had to start somewhere! In any case, I can still remember *most* of the melodies to my early songs and I've kept many of the original lyric sheets to this day. We *never* professionally recorded any of those songs however, because, although I'm embarrassed to admit it, most of the songs were obviously *derivative* of whatever songs I had been listening to on the radio at the time. Apparently I was inadvertently *stealing* melodies and ideas from other songs I liked without even knowing it? For example, I wrote a theme song for our group called '*We're the Go-Go Guys*,' that sounded an awful lot like the theme song from the Monkees' popular television show, '*Hey, Hey, We're the Monkees!*' And then I came up with '*We All Live in a Purple Rocket Ship*,' which had virtually the *same* melody and story as the Beatles' '*Yellow Submarine!*' Obviously, I was very new to songwriting, and had yet to find my own *unique* voice? But *identifying that problem* was truly a godsend that immediately directed me to work harder at writing songs that sounded *more* original and *less influenced* by other ones. Also, putting my derivative songs aside, over time I learned a great deal about songwriting and vocal harmonizing by simply listening to the radio and being inspired by a great number of songs as well as the artists who sang them. I just had to learn *not to copy them!*

Our first impromptu vocal rehearsal took place in October of 1966 at Steve's house when the three of us tried to write a Halloween song together. We called it *Ghosties, Goblins, Witches and Fiends*, which I thought was a great title! I believe that Robert or I came up with it and also the basic melody. We then tried to make-up and sing harmony to it, while Steve *spontaneously* made-up most of the lyrics (*which were never written down*) and sang lead. Sadly, our work on that song never went beyond that one informal session, but at least it *was* a start! Soon after that, we somehow came up with our group's name, *The Go-Go Guys*, and I really think that's when we truly began taking our musical selves more seriously. It wasn't long before we concluded that since we had already written (*what we considered to be*) some catchy songs and were singing them together pretty well, all we *needed* in order to be a complete musical group was someone to accompany us on the guitar, like every other singing group out there had. The only problem was that none of us *played* or *owned* a guitar?

Since I had a little money in my pocket, I promptly went to the local variety store (J.J. Newberry's) and bought a *plastic guitar* in the toy section. It had 6 plastic strings, but could actually be tuned and played like a real guitar. I humorously called it '*the rake*' because my strumming on the plastic strings that covered the thin plastic body of it sounded very much like raking leaves in the yard, with a *faintly audible* guitar chord mixed-in. It may *not* have been the best guitar or even a *real* guitar, but it was perfect for a beginner and a guy with very limited funds (*like me*) to first learn on. I suppose I should have felt embarrassed playing a toy, plastic guitar at age 12, but I was too excited about learning the chords to even think about that! Incidentally the plastic guitar and strings only cost me $1.99, and came complete with exactly what I needed; a *beginning chord book!* Quickly, I started learning to play the chords that I found on the very few pages of that tiny chord book and just as fast, I was writing new songs that I just knew could be *hits!*

In the beginning, I only used the chords G, E minor, C, D and D7, because they were the *first five chords* I had learned, and consequently I was able to change from one to another pretty quickly. Some of the titles of these early 'masterpieces' using *only* those chords included; '*Play Around,*' '*But You're Mine*' and '*Motorcycle Man.*' This led to Steve, Robert and I working together more often on the songs, and learning how to create actual harmonies, accompanied by an instrument for the first time in our group's existence, even if it was only made of *plastic*.

Next, I purchased a more comprehensive book of chords at a local music store. This allowed me to keep faithfully adding to my repertoire of chords as I wrote a couple of songs a week, using the new chords to make sure I didn't forget them. But as a group, we really only worked on a few of those pieces. Our first 'recorded song' was one that I already mentioned called, 'But You're Mine,' lead sung by my brother Robert. A sample of the lyrics (*and chords*) went like this:

G Well, I know you won't come back.

   And I know that guy's a brat.

For D7 taking you away from me, from G me, yes from me.

(But you're mine), you know you are.

(But you're mine), get out of his car.

(But you're D7 mine), you know you are. G Mm.

FYI: In the chorus at the end, Steve and I sang, 'But you're mine' in harmony, while Robert sang the lyrics that followed by himself. I thought as an early effort, it was a pretty fun little song, except that we were 13 and 11 and talking about *girlfriends and cars?* In our defense, lots of the singing groups on the radio were talking about those things! So, regardless of the probability of any of us having either one of those things in our young lives, I think we were just trying to fit-in.

We recorded it on a floppy disk on Steve's mother's Dictaphone machine (*she was a lawyer's secretary*). The recording *did* successfully play on our record player, but it sounded a lot like it had been recorded in the 1920s, due to the irritating *scratchiness* from the machine that accompanied the sound of our voices, while my plastic guitar sounded more like a tiny ukulele? But to tell you the truth, neither of those things bothered us one bit! As far as we were concerned, we had just recorded our *very first record!* Of course, aside from our families, no one else ever heard it. But we still felt gloriously proud of ourselves! Unfortunately, *that* moment appeared to be the climax of The Go-Go Guys existence. Over the next few months, we steadily grew more and more complacent about rehearsing together, with our number of weekly rehearsals dangerously waning to almost zero! Consequently, by the summer of 1967, our group *The Go-Go Guys*, built on the noblest of intentions... was *permanently dissolved.*

However, as fate would have it, by September of 1967, Steve and I spontaneously decided one day to continue singing together as a *duo.* As a result, 'PENGELUM was born!' The name came about because I thought of how the Beatles have *Beat* in their name, while a *pendulum swings*, like I believed we would! We changed the spelling of 'pendulum' to 'Pengelum' because a lot of groups were changing a letter or two from the original spelling of their names like The Beatles (*Beetles*), The Monkees (*Monkeys*), and The Byrds (*Birds*). Thinking about it now, except for The Beatles who validly changed the spelling of their name to include the word *beat* in it, I'm sure that every other group simply liked the *cool effect* the name change gave them visually. Although Robert did not choose to join our new group, he continued to encourage and assist me with my songwriting for as long as Pengelum existed. He was always the first person to hear me play each new song as we sat together in the bedroom we shared, and he would always let me know what he honestly thought about it. Then I'd play that song again with his comments in mind as he timed it for me. His unselfish help and feedback proved invaluable to my growth and confidence as a songwriter. I will always be grateful to him for that!

Steve and I immediately got to work and rehearsed a few songs I had written until it seemed to us that we were ready for the next step. It was then that we jointly decided that what our duo really needed were some opportunities to sing in front of people (*besides my brothers and sisters, who had always been our greatest fans*) and thus effectively introduce ourselves to the world! To begin accomplishing this, we signed-up to compete in a couple of amateur music performance competitions. The first one being a local (*Glendora*) youth talent show, while the second one was a vocal music competition hosted by the music department of Cal State Long Beach. Soon after this, the neck of my plastic guitar snapped off the body and could not be fixed! So, Steve and I rode our bikes to a pawn shop in Azusa, where I was able to purchase a *real wood*, full-sized steel-string acoustic guitar for only ten dollars! It wasn't the greatest guitar in the world, nor did it come with a case, but it was a whole lot better than the plastic one I'd been playing on! With this real guitar, we felt more professional than ever, as we went into both events prepared to impress the judges! But unfortunately, *we didn't.* We failed to win, place or even receive honorable mention at either of those competitions, and it was certainly *not* for lack of trying! To be honest, we felt like we'd been pretty good at both of them? There was obviously something we were missing? Fortunately, it was not long before the answer to what *that was* came to us! We were both so young and naïve that outside of writing songs and singing together, frankly, we *didn't* understand the first thing about the professional music business? What we *needed* was a manager to take care of all that important stuff.

It was then that I realized we *already knew* someone who had intimately worked in the music business. It was *Dale Smallin,* who's cackling falsetto voice can be heard excitedly exclaiming, '*Wipeout,*' at the beginning of the number one hit song from 1965 of the same name! The song was recorded by *The Surfaris (a musical group from my home town of Glendora)* which he had briefly managed, and contributed his 'playful voice' to this once. He currently managed several other musical groups and fortunately for us, he was a friend and former business partner of my dad's. He had actually already heard us sing a year earlier (*while we were still The Go-Go Guys*) and told us that as soon as we had written twelve good songs, he would take us into a professional studio and record us! Remembering this, we instantly grew excited! Steve and I both strongly believed that we already had half that many songs written and learned, so we only had to complete the final six! That job was excitedly accomplished over the next couple of months, and then we contacted him. After hearing us sing, true to his word, in the early months of 1968, while I was in eighth grade and Steve was in sixth, Dale Smallin became our *official manager!*

At this point, Steve and I turned it up a notch and began furiously rehearsing our songs almost daily in preparation for our upcoming *first recording session!* Looking forward to that was *all* the encouragement we really needed! Before recording a note, this upcoming event had already begun to bolster our confidence. We began to believe that because we would soon be professionally recording, with any luck it would not be long before we would be considered an *official* pop singing group! What a great feeling *that* was! When it came time to enter the recording studio for the first time in our lives, we couldn't help it. We were *completely in awe!* But thanks to our hours and hours of practicing these songs together, we felt well-prepared to be there! Like most groups did in the later 1960s, we recorded our music in the studio using four-track reel to reel recording tape. We successfully completed recording all twelve songs, which actually took us two long and grueling afternoons and evenings to complete. I recorded all of the guitar parts on the first day, while we recorded all of the vocals on the second, along with any special additions, which in this case included a track of group handclapping and Dale playing the kazoo. Dale and the engineer then *mixed* the recording tracks together for each individual song to create a good balance among the instruments, special effects and voices.

Although Steve and I were very excited about *all* twelve of our freshly recorded songs, the two that apparently stood out to Dale from that first session as being potential hits, were '*Dreaming*' and '*The Peddler.*' As he explained it to us, this was because both songs had catchy rhythms and melodies, which he believed had a chance to be picked-up by a record label. Due to this belief, we rerecorded both songs at a later date, adding another professional acoustic guitar player (*named Greg*) to strengthen the rhythm guitar parts of both songs and play lead guitar when called for on our new double guitar accompaniment. the lyrics (*and chords*) for, '*Dreaming,*' begin:

G You are sitting *C* in your garden *G* dreaming.
G And you cannot *C* tell your mind is *G* scheming.
G You are a queen *C* in a castle. *G* Lost your king *C* in a hassle.
You're *F* dreaming, oh yes you are *G* dreaming.

FYI: Although these lyrics could be taken more on the serious side, possibly from a dramatic fantasy, nothing could be farther from the truth! In actuality the melody of this song is completely upbeat and catchy!

The lyrics (*and chords*) for, *The Peddler*, begin:
D Every once or twice a year the peddler used to come by here. He'd *G* sell his wares.

D But we people never bought, the items sold were always hot.
He G didn't care.
But he still stayed D poor, selling C all that he could D get.
For his C silly mind was D set.
And he A lived like a bum in the G filthiest slum I D know.

FYI: I know that by themselves, the lyrics of *The Peddler* sound pathetic, almost tragic. But once again, the song is fun to listen to with very catchy rhythms in the melody. This contrast of more serious lyrics combined with a happy, catchy melody seemed to be how I inadvertently wrote a lot of my songs at that time. I really have no idea why?

In addition to paying for *all* of Pengelum's recording expenses, Dale eventually bought me a new and *better* guitar to play for our recording sessions, as well as providing Steve and I with all of our auditioning, performing and recording transportation needs! And not long after completing our first couple of recording sessions, an excited Steve was inspired to *learn* to play the guitar! And before we knew it, he was smoothly changing chords! Following that, for the first time, he began to write his own songs! Soon after that, we discovered that our vocal harmonies were fast growing both tighter and more creative! We were really on a roll!

When school started in September of 1968, Steve and I both found ourselves in junior high. As we continued improving our singing, songwriting and guitar playing, we couldn't help noticing that we were a little older, wiser and had rehearsed together for a couple of years now, so our vocal sound had *noticeably matured?* Dale noticed that too, and he promptly lined-up a series of performances for us including 'The Miss *Azusa Beauty Pageant*,' and a number of appearances for private parties and club events in order to introduce our music to as many people as possible. Arguably the most memorable performance that he secured for us (*at least to me*) was an event held at Disneyland's former Fantasyland Theatre (*where they used to show Mickey Mouse Silly Symphonies all day long*) to audition for a spot as paid musical entertainment in the park! At that time, security at Disneyland was not like it is today (*post 9-11*), and we actually drove *straight into* the backstage of Disneyland one evening with no problem, long after the park had closed for the day. As I recall, we parked in Fantasyland very close to the theatre. We excitedly walked inside and joined a myriad of other acts for an open talent audition. Steve and I were immediately blown away by the number of acts auditioning and how *good* they all were? Our turn eventually arrived and we sang a couple of our songs with every ounce of strength we had! In effect, regardless of all the other people there, we knew that we were actually only performing for a handful of Disneyland *casting agents* sitting in the back of the theatre. Every auditioning act must have known, as we did, that *they* held all of our musical fates in their hands! They were all pros, and consequently very careful about *not revealing* their true reactions to each individual act. So, after we had finished our performance and walked off the stage, we really had *no idea* if they liked us or not? We excitedly waited a couple of days, hoping for the best? But unfortunately, the news that finally arrived was *disappointing*. Dale simply informed us that we had *not* gotten the job. He never mentioned the *reasons* why, but personally I imagine it may have been due to our younger ages and lack of professional performing experience. Regardless, having participated in that audition at 'The Happiest Place on Earth,' was something that two young teenagers like us would *never forget*!

Dale continued providing us with incredible opportunities to record many of our songs in professional recording studios throughout Southern California from 1968 through 1971, and this always pushed us to write better and more original songs with tighter harmonies. To be honest, we *never* stopped relishing the thrill and magic of recording in a professional studio. Every session was so different and exciting! As we recorded more and more, in addition to playing rhythm guitar, we each learned to play simple *lead* guitar, to overdub additional harmonies or just sing over our original vocal recordings in order to make them sound stronger, to occasionally play another instrument like piano or percussion, and Steve's favorite, to use *sound effects* on some songs, especially *reverb*! It was a blast! And I don't think we ever got used to the fact that we were recording at such young ages, and *technically*, now more than ever, we had grounds to actually be considered *recording artists*! The only two things we lacked (*which were both kind of important*) were fans and record sales. We even had studio musicians recording with us a number of times to fill-out our two-guitar instrumental accompaniment. One particular recording session comes to mind. It was a place where many professional world-class singers and pop groups of the past and present recorded their songs, the world-famous *Capital Records Building* in Los Angeles! When Steve and I first arrived there, we were completely mesmerized by all of the building's history! But then we were also star-struck as we learned that *Blood, Sweat and Tears*, a popular group in the 1960s and 70s, was recording at the same time as we were, just *one studio over*! Oh, and the other cool thing was that the completely full classic candy machine outside our studio (*which had probably been there since the building's opening in 1956*), was apparently broken, and gave us as much *free candy* as we wanted! We did tell the engineer about it, but he just laughed. And to top it off, we recorded with a full band that day consisting of double guitar, bass and drums. This was *definitely* a recording highlight for Pengelum!

In all, between 1968 and 1971, we recorded nearly 40 original songs, including part of the soundtrack for a short anti-drug movie that Dale had written and produced for the local schools. To me, many of our later songs, when Steve was in ninth grade and I was a junior in high school, were arguably some of our best, with the growth of our skill and experience clearly shining through. Two examples are Steve's amazing futuristic ballad, *Smile*, which in every way, I have always been in awe of, and then there was my own heartfelt ballad, *To Live My Life*, which I have been told is one of the most thought-provoking songs I have *ever* written. Not to mention a host of other songs we wrote along the way as we honed our craft. We learned to write passionately or just for fun, and sometimes we had *no idea* what style we had written in... we just *liked it*!

We also learned a variety of creative ways to harmonize with each other. Dale had made demos of what he considered to be our best songs and sent them to record companies immediately following *each* of those recording sessions. We *did* get a couple of nibbles, and even met with some record label reps, but I guess fame and fortune were simply not in the cards for us at that time. We amicably broke-up the duo in late 1971, but we both continued to write songs and sing separately from that time on.

We temporarily revisited singing together five years later in May of 1976, with an exciting final performance (*of all new material*) at The Ice House in Pasadena, billing ourselves as 'Stephen and David.' And then in 2011, 35 years after that performance as the piece de resistance, Steve and I jointly released a CD of our favorite Pengelum recordings, that we titled '*Nearly Greatest Hits volume 1*,' and proceeded to lovingly distribute it to our families and friends, as well as selling an *extended* version of it (*which included ten additional songs*), on Amazon for a number of years.

Steve once asked me, years after Pengelum was over, why I thought that although we were so young, we wrote our songs *so old*? Good question. Our song lyrics often did seem to reflect older and more worldly people experiencing older and more worldly situations? I didn't have an answer for him then, but I think I do now. I simply think we wrote *old* because it was a lot more fun and creative writing about things we *hadn't* actually experienced yet than things that we *had*. When we composed songs back then, our imaginations ran wild and it was exciting to consistently imagine ourselves to be adults! In effect, that change of perception always opened an ever-expanding world of new topics for us to write about and in my opinion, that arguably made our song lyrics much more interesting!

From 'The Go-Go Guys' to Pengelum, although we may not have become the pop stars we had aspired toward, we certainly *did have* an exciting time trying! The valuable things we learned through *both* of these experiences we were given, turned out to be simply *unforgettable*! As a result, I have always been *wildly grateful* for that entire improbable journey. All the knowledge, generosity, recording sessions and performances that Dale provided us with, as well as the time I spent singing, writing and playing the guitar as a youngster with Robert and Steve, left me with a lifelong love and appreciation for listening to, creating and performing music.

On a sad note, I remember that the last time I saw Steve was in 2012. He drove down from his home in Missouri and stopped off at my house for a short visit over dinner. It was unreal. We reminisced about all of the friendship and music we'd shared together over the years, but especially in our youth. It was *joyous*. A few months later I received the heartbreaking news that Steve had passed away at the young age of 55. I was truly sad, but to me, through my vast memories of spending so much intense time with him throughout the years and all of the music we had created together, as long as I'm alive, he will *always be here*!

I learned from my experiences with The Go-Go Guys and Pengelum, that music can be one of the most beautiful and meaningful things in our lives! I continue feeling very proud of what the three of us accomplished all those years ago! I am reminded that the most wonderful experiences in life always seem to feel *more* meaningful and satisfying when they're *achieved together*, as this one was. And I learned so vividly that chasing exciting goals at any age, no matter how impossible they may appear, is what living is all about! If there is such a thing as reincarnation, I would not hesitate to join Robert and Steve once again in making beautiful music together from the ground up, regardless of how successful we ultimately became. After all, I believe it's not *what* we achieve that we should consider most important in our lives, but rather for every challenge we undertake, it's how much we *grow* as people and how much we *enjoy* the journey. Needless to say, through this experience the three of us grew a lot, and we enjoyed this unforgettable, once in a lifetime journey... *immensely*!

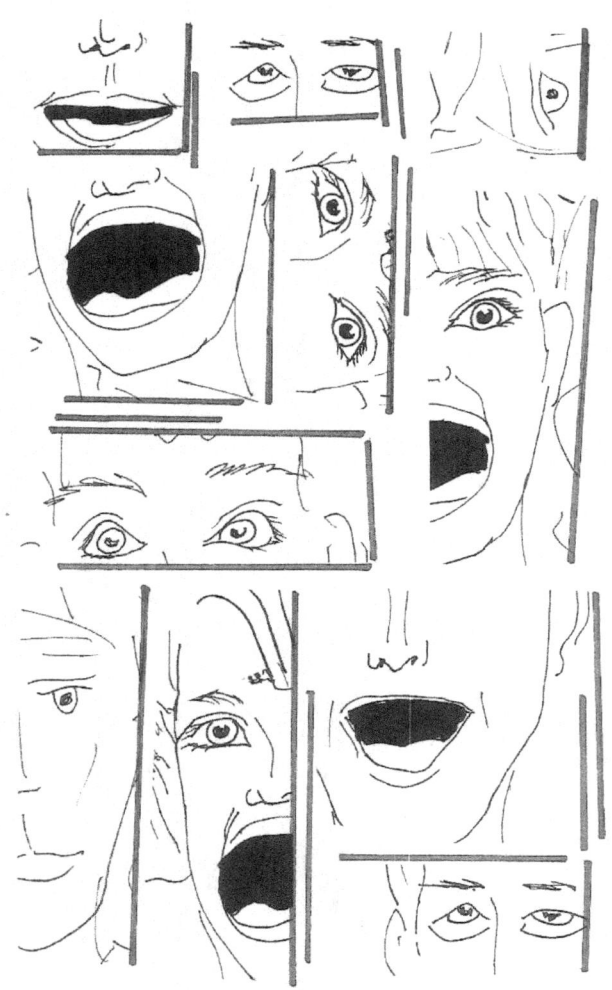

236

-FOUR-
The Spine-Tingling Tale of "The Ghost!"

"I shall not commit the fashionable stupidity of regarding everything I cannot explain as a fraud."-C.G. Jung. Of all the childhood memories I possess, *this* is the only one that I can never seem to fully explain without involving the *supernatural!* I would love to tell you that I have now grown-up and believe that my eyes were simply playing tricks on me back then when I was a young child... but *I simply can't do that!* You see, I saw what I saw and every year as I grow older and supposedly wiser, I continue to believe that very same thing. That I actually *saw a ghost!* My son Alex once told me that he also saw a ghost as a child. Perhaps young children are just more open to accepting a ghost's presence? Could it be? Here's my story.

I'll bet everyone has at least one good *ghost story* to tell. In addition, there have been plenty of great ones throughout the years turned into movies, including both Shakespeare's *Hamlet and MacBeth,* Washington Irving's *The Legend of Sleepy Hollow,* J.R.R. Tolkien's *The Lord of the Rings,* and Charles Dickins' classic tale of *A Christmas Carol.* But I believe mine to be even *more* special than any of those. Why? Because my story *actually happened to me!*

The year was sometime in the early 1960s, and my two younger brothers Robert and Chris shared the back bedroom with me when I was most likely eight or nine years old. Robert, nicknamed '*Beeb*'

237

(*because that is what I had called him after he was born, apparently meaning to say 'baby'*) and I shared a set of bunkbeds. I was the older one, so I chose the top bunk while Robert took the bottom, and the youngest of us, Chris, slept on a single bed at the opposite side of the room. It was a bit crowded in that little room thinking about it now, but we all got along very well and spent many a happy evening playing with our toy soldiers and Lincoln logs.

One night, which was not noticeably different from any other, as I heard *no* sudden rain storm, thunder, lightning or chilling howls of werewolves (*which would generally be reserved for stories of this sort*), my brothers and I were enjoying a nice, pleasant evening of watching television in the living room. I had absolutely *no warning* that this night would be the *most terrifying* of my entire life! At a little past 9:00 PM, we had just finished watching our television shows, so we went to our bedroom, got into our pajamas and quickly climbed into bed. We were breathlessly waiting for the exciting bedtime story my mother would tell us tonight, just as she did every night. Now, I might mention that sleeping on the top bunk, along with having a bit of 'age status,' had one *huge drawback*. Whenever the furnace kicked in, I would immediately be harshly awakened by a loud rush of hot air blowing directly from the vent on the wall (*no more than three feet away*) to my face! I truly *hated* that! Anyway, following my mom's bedtime story, we quickly fell asleep. There was a slight chill in the air that night, so as you have probably already guessed, the furnace kicked-in and the predictable consequence was that I immediately woke-up, feeling incredibly uncomfortable, even *suffocated* by the sudden rush of hot air!

The first thing I did was to irritatingly throw off my covers and sit up in bed as I normally did whenever I found myself in this awful predicament. However, when I turned my head toward the ladder at the end of my bed, I experienced a very sudden and *sharp chill!* Inexplicably, I noticed that Robert (*Beeb*) had apparently gotten out of his bottom bunk, climbed up, and was *right there* on the ladder facing me? To be specific, his head was just above the level of my mattress, and that allowed me to see his face very clearly. Both of his hands were apparently firmly attached to the ladder, because he didn't seem to be moving a muscle? I briefly looked away, hoping that I was somehow hallucinating; you know, seeing *unreal* things that would immediately disappear. But when my eyes returned, he was *still there?* At this point, even though this odd experience was beginning to *unnerve* me, I knew that I had to find out what was going on? So, I intently stared at his face for a long moment, and not only did his eyes seem entirely lifeless, but they in no way showed any recognition of me? That got me to wondering if he was possibly *sleepwalking?* That could explain this phenomenon, right? I had seen a few television programs showing people doing that, and at the moment I could think of no better rationalization for what I was vividly seeing?

The next thing I did was to quietly speak to him. We had been best friends growing up, and I was a little concerned about him falling off the ladder, so I said something like, "Beeb, are you awake?" I patiently waited a few seconds, but there came no reply. I continued looking at him, but still the frozen, lifeless eyes of my brother never acknowledged me? Next, I repeated my words a little louder, but there was *still no response?* By then I was growing a little impatient, what with the heater still blowing on my face and my brother not saying a word? But at the same time, some emerging part of me was becoming increasingly more *suspicious* of this situation and even causing me to grow a little fearful? Still, I somehow gathered the courage I needed and proceeded to reach over to gently tap my brother's head. That was the *only* way I could think of to find out if he was even coherent? At this point in my tale, I beg all of you who are prone to becoming frightened by supernatural happenings to *forget this story* altogether and quickly move on to the next one! You'll *thank me later!* When I finally reached my hand toward Robert, although I could still see him, my hand shockingly went **right through his head** as if there was *nothing there?* I was in *no way* prepared for that? Next, like I imagine most eight or nine-year-old children would probably have reacted given that same situation, being alone in the dark after midnight with a *ghost,* I *screamed* and hurriedly closed my eyes while pulling my covers tightly up over my head! I was *terrified* and my imagination was *running wild!* I remember seriously considering that something terrible may have happened to Robert, resulting in him turning into *a ghost?* Or maybe I was actually looking at his sleeping, *bodiless spirit?* It was sometime later, which although it seemed like an eternity, was probably closer to several minutes, when I 'bravely' peeked out from under my blanket and discovered with relief that my brother was no longer on the ladder. I hurriedly climbed down from my top bunk and confirmed that he was sleeping soundly in his bottom bunk, appearing as if he had *never* left it? Then I slowly climbed back up the ladder to my bed and tried very hard to get back to sleep. But not surprisingly, I had a very *tough time doing it!*

The next morning, I shared this absolutely terrifying story with my mom at breakfast, and although she listened very attentively, her final verdict (*presented to me in a very sweet motherly way*) was that 'I was probably only dreaming.' I also told Robert (*Beeb*) about my experience, but he had *no memory* of having any dreams that matched-up with my story?

Although as an adult, I agree with those people who believe there is some truth to the common notion that sometimes the implausible things young children see and believe can be attributed to their own overactive imaginations, that was *definitely not* the case here! I was not making this story up then, and I'm certainly not making it up now over 60 years later! This bizarre event *actually happened to me*, and whether you believe me or not, with all due respect, that's completely inconsequential to me! What this experience did, besides scaring the *bejeegers* out of me, was give me a firsthand confirmation that there *are* most assuredly things in this life which cannot be adequately explained away during one's childhood, not even by our parents! I also learned a very valuable lesson. This ghost story that I experienced as a child has convinced me, beyond a doubt, that a person *should* continue believing whatever their senses and heart tell them are true regarding *all* things unless that belief has *absolutely been proven false or impossible*, which this one definitely *has not!* And you might be surprised to learn that *my* opinion on this seems to be shared by Sir Arthur

Conan Doyle, creator of the world-famous detective, Sherlock Holmes, who writes, *"When you have eliminated the impossible, whatever remains, however improbable, must be the truth!"*

-FIVE-
The Terrible, Awful Tale of "My Trombone and Me!"

As famous Irish playwright George Bernard Shaw is attributed as saying, "*The trombone is the **worst** brass instrument, please prove me wrong.*" While famous composer Richard Straus is said to have shared, "***Never** look at the trombones, it will only encourage them!*" All humor aside, according to these two quotes, the trombone and trombone player seem to be the most *disrespected* members of the brass section in any band or orchestra? *Why me?*

Over the following *angst-filled* pages, I have briefly chronicled what I felt and experienced over my five long and painful years of 'playing the trombone' in my elementary and junior high school bands from fifth through ninth grades and it *wasn't* pretty! I've focused mainly on how I *felt* during each individual year of this very trying experience in order to make this story more honest and relatable to you, the reader. For better or for worse, I have not seriously altered or edited any portion of this tale. This story happened very close to exactly as I am about to relate it to you. I recently visited Goddard Junior High School, the place where after three torturous years in band, my nightmare finally *mercifully* came to an end *56 years ago*! I relived those three turbulent years in my head while I was there and honestly? I sometimes wonder *how* I ever survived?

To begin my story, when I started fifth grade in 1964, the district band director for the elementary schools, whom I perceived to be a very cool and funny man (*although it probably didn't take a whole lot of wit to get fifth graders to laugh in those days*), stood before the fifth and sixth graders at Williams Elementary School in Glendora at an assembly one day. His purpose was to invite each of us to audition for the Elementary School Band Program! I *was* interested, and I'll tell you why! Ever since I had been very young, I had listened to my dad playing his trumpet every so often when he had gotten the urge. I was always impressed by the bright brassy sound that the instrument produced, as well as the clean and stylish look of it! I also enjoyed listening to his recordings of professional trumpeters Al Hirt and Herb Alpert, and couldn't wait until the day that I could play the trumpet just like *them*! So, I very excitedly decided to audition for band, and *trumpet* was, of course, the instrument I had my heart set on playing. I didn't foresee any problems in achieving that goal, I simply saw this audition as a necessary formality toward quickly seeing my dream come true! So, you can imagine my *shock* and *disappointment* when following my audition to become the second trumpet player in my family, it surprisingly *did not happen?* The band director instead selected me to play that long and bulky brass slide instrument *from Hell* that makes every skinny ten-year-old kid who plays it suddenly appear to be uncoordinated and gawky... THE TROMBONE! I was completely *devastated*!

Although I was a very shy kid, I knew that *right now* would probably be my only chance to hopefully change the director's mind! I somehow found the courage to go up to him and as soon as I had his attention, I strongly objected to my instrument assignment! When I was done passionately (*but politely*) explaining my reasoning to a seemingly attentive and understanding director, he smiled down at me in a parental sort of way. Meeting my eyes, he then calmly explained that I had the wrong *embouchure* for playing the trumpet, but the *perfect* one for playing the trombone. I didn't really understand what the word *embouchure* meant at the time, but from listening to him trying to explain it, I thought he was politely telling me that my *lips were too fat* to play the trumpet? Wow! No lie!

I had *fat-lipped nightmares* for the next week or so following that very disappointing appraisal! Although, I felt shocked and even depressed about this, as well as having some serious doubts about joining band at all, I very *hesitantly* considered joining it anyway. After my dad told me how much my Uncle Bud had enjoyed playing the trombone in his school band, I believe *that* pretty much sealed the deal... although I still *wasn't* very excited about my decision.

Years later, when I actually *became* a public-school music teacher, I quickly learned that every band director has the very thankless job each year of filling every section of the band with the correct number of instruments (*with students attached*) in order to make the group sound balanced. And to be fair, I *can* understand that for the good of the band, the director might sometimes feel *compelled* to audition their students *without* considering their individual preferences, because of this need. I wish I had understood that back in the fifth grade however, because I was ten years old at the time and embouchure or no embouchure, I could *never understand* why that director had not even given me a *chance* to play the trumpet, clearly knowing how important it was to me? Instead, I felt like he was forcing me to play an instrument that I had *absolutely no interest in*, simply because of my *big lips*? I still sometimes wonder how different my band experience might have been if I'd been selected to play the *trumpet*? I'll tell you one thing. It *couldn't* have been any worse!

Well, I committed to playing the trombone in fifth and sixth grades. Each separate family of instruments (*brass, woodwind and percussion*) would meet the band teacher in the school library behind the multipurpose room at our elementary school twice a week for thirty minutes to learn to play our own instruments, as well as playing together as a group of *similar* instruments for the final fifteen minutes. It wasn't very time consuming, and it was a break from our elementary school classes twice a week, so I didn't hate it. In fact, I even participated at the end of both my fifth and sixth grade school years in the District Band's *Spring Concert* with the combined fifth and sixth-grade instrumentalists from all seven elementary schools in Glendora making up one large performing ensemble! Although I

245

still *didn't enjoy* playing the trombone very much, I'll admit that the experience I had putting on concerts with so many other student musicians was surprisingly *kind of fun!* Although I hated practicing and hence was not a very accomplished trombone player at the end of my second year, due to those warm and fuzzy feelings, I decided to stick with band in junior high, which I truly expected to be much more fun than it had been in elementary school!

All too quickly, it was September of 1966 and I was now an excited incoming seventh grade student attending *Goddard Junior High School* for the first time! On that first day of school, I remember wearing my trendy blue jeans and oversized black belt (*influenced by The Monkees TV show*), because I wanted to be sure to look my best for what was undoubtedly going to be the beginning of my most *exciting* schoolyear yet! But unfortunately, the thrill of junior high was severely short lived as I quickly discovered how much I *hated* carrying that bulky trombone two miles to school for the '*before school band rehearsals*' which ran from 7 to 8 AM, and then back home again *every day* at 3:00! That's a total 'carrying my trombone distance' of *four miles a day!* Argh!!! Not to mention that to anyone from school (*especially girls*) watching an embarrassed and skinny kid like me carrying that stupid, gangly trombone case through the streets of Glendora each day, my 'coolness factor' (*which I fear was already suffering*) must have immediately dropped *far below zero!* The daily band rehearsals weren't terrible, but having to be at school every day an hour earlier than the other students on campus was pretty awful! To add to that, I was expected to practice that trombone 45 minutes a day at home? *45 minutes?* Ugh! I tried to do that. I really did! But hearing myself playing that instrument as poorly as I did, and for such a long time each day, I found it to be *beyond depressing!* By this point, I'm sure you realize that with every pore in my body I believed that joining the junior high school band had been a *huge mistake!* I was fast feeling as if that miserable trombone was sucking away a big chunk of my free time and usurping any potential I had to be *happy?* There was little doubt in my mind that I was growing more and more anxious and despondent by the day? So why didn't I just quit, you ask?

Well, the *real* obstacle to my quitting band was my belief that my *staying* in it was truly important to my dad, just as I believed it was for my older sister Cathi to continue playing clarinet in the high school band. She had begun playing her instrument three years before I had, and was currently playing in the Glendora High School marching band. Incidentally, when I recently asked her about whether or not she had enjoyed her tenure in band from fifth grade through her junior year of high school, she surprisingly told me, "No!" She explained that she had originally auditioned to play the flute, but the director had told her that her *embouchure* was all wrong, so he made her play the clarinet! Then she added that she would have quit much sooner, but she had felt very guilty because my parents had *bought* her a clarinet, and it had cost them *a hundred dollars*! Wow! She had stayed in band out of *guilt* too? Oh, how I wish I'd known her true feelings *before* I'd auditioned! Then this miserable tale might be about something much happier? Like *anything*! But I digress. Getting back to my story, although I *knew* what I wanted to do, I quickly realized that my freedom would not be in the cards for quite some time, so I *reluctantly* remained in junior high school band for a second year.

Now, before you get the idea that being in band was a *bad* thing for everyone, let me just correct that wayward thinking. To a kid who enjoyed performing music with other student musicians and had no qualms about practicing their instrument 45 minutes daily or getting to school an hour early, band was *great*! It gave each member an opportunity to learn an instrument, to be exposed to all types of music, to make friends, to be a part of a very organized and musical ensemble, to perform for a variety of audiences, to travel and to have a band room on campus to call their own. This would be plenty to keep most junior high school kids in band happy, but to me, *none of that good stuff* seemed to matter? Looking back at my second year in the Goddard band, I still felt trapped, like I could *never* escape? And another thing! I know it sounds ridiculous now, but back then I seriously considered that two years of carrying that *hideously* heavy instrument four miles every day, to and from Goddard Junior High School, was quite possibly beginning to *irreversibly stretch-out* my left arm, making it noticeably longer than my right and if I didn't quit soon, that terrible condition *might* be for the duration of my life? I was *nearly* convinced of that! On the other hand, I imagined that if I had played the trumpet? Well, then I would have very *proudly* carried that small, classy case to and from school every day, maybe stopping from time to time to play little impromptu concerts for people along the way (*mostly pretty girls*) when they asked me to, resulting in *thunderous applause* at the end!

By my final year at Goddard Junior High and my third unhappy year in band, I was beginning to get into other things like writing for the school newspaper and working on the yearbook, which I enjoyed so much more than playing the trombone in band. In fact, for the first time in my life, I had even tried-out for the boys' basketball team and run for ninth grade class vice-president! Although *neither* of those efforts went very well, I *still* found those two losing experiences to be *much more fun* than band! Although, as a ninth grader I was asked to play in more select musical ensembles, including orchestra and trombone quartet, and I was one of the band's music librarians, those perks could not come close to making up for how much *I truly hated playing the trombone!* As a matter of fact, I could hardly wait until that day finally arrived when my trombone nightmare would *mercifully* come to an end, and *that* time could *not* come soon enough!

Very unexpectedly, one day before band class had started, I discovered that a freaky thing, which I had *never* considered happening, *had happened* to my trombone? And shockingly, it had left it completely unplayable? It seems that the upper tube of my trombone (*one of the two long horizonal metal tubes the slide goes over*) had *cracked* at the part closest to my mouth, where it was attached to the instrument? It was still mostly attached, but I couldn't get my trombone to play in tune because so much air was escaping through the crack, causing my control of the pitch to completely disappear! I really have no idea how it had happened, but I reasoned that *this* might actually be a *godsend*, allowing me to quit band early? Before you ask, *no*, I didn't intentionally break my trombone to get out of playing in band! Although, that *might not* have been such a bad idea?

In any case, I very somberly showed the band director what had happened to my poor trombone and how truly *sad* I was about it. But, moments later, after taking a quick trip to the instrument closet, smiling (*as usual*), that director handed me the 'loaner' trombone. Unfortunately, his timely action *instantly* solved my problem! Curses! *Why me?* I've learned through the years that dedicated and experienced music or other performing arts teachers *always* seem to come up with appropriate solutions to *any* problems their students spontaneously throw at them. *Kudos* to those directors for their ability to effectively think on their feet! But in this case, I really wish he *hadn't!* In the meantime, after a couple of weeks, my unplayable trombone was taken to a local welder, who (*to my chagrin*) repaired the break in my top tube! This of course, allowed me to return the loaner instrument to my teacher and resume playing in band with my *own* trombone. Some guys just *never catch a break!*

Well, at the beginning of the final two months of the schoolyear, something *huge* happened at home? It was incredibly disturbing news regarding my parents, and it took my nine siblings and me completely by surprise? One day, we were all calmly told by my mother, that my father and she had amicably gotten a *divorce.* *WHAT?* My father had *not* been living with us in Glendora for the past two years or so. For some reason, he had been living and teaching in Texas, sending my mom a check every month. Although *that* situation should have raised a red flag a lot earlier, *it hadn't?* Seriously, *none* of us kids had any idea that our parents were dealing with serious marriage problems or even *considering* a divorce until that very moment? All ten of us dealt with this news differently due to our age disparity (*ages 3-18*), but for me being second oldest, I can say that it was *shocking* as I realized that my life and the lives of my brothers and sisters would *never again* be quite the same! But then it dawned on me, like a fluffy white cloud in the middle of a hailstorm. With my parents no longer married and my dad living somewhere else; as tough as that situation might be, the tiny upside was that I *finally* felt secure in making a decision *not* to join band at the high

249

school next year! I was actually going to call it quits after *five thoroughly miserable years*, featuring a spectacularly failed relationship with my gruesome brassy partner! Regardless of the shock I had felt earlier when first hearing about my parents' divorce, right now I felt simply *ecstatic*! However, I still had to get through the final performance event of the year, our annual spring concert!

The night arrived, and I showed up in the gymnasium smartly dressed in my dark J.C. Penney slacks and white dress shirt, giddily prepared to perform in band for the *very last time ever*! When horrifyingly, I suddenly found myself experiencing *déjà vu*, and *not* in a good way! For the second time this year, something *terrible* had happened to my trombone? Completely by surprise and without any warning, the upper metal tube that had recently been welded, had somehow once again gotten a crack in the *exact same place*? What were the odds? I know now that I should have promptly told the director, who very likely would have once again supplied me with that loaner trombone for the concert, but alas, *I didn't*. I reasoned (*incorrectly, of course*) that I only had *one* concert left to go before I was free to quit band forever, so why create a problem for the director now? I was so excited about leaving band, that I apparently threw rational and logical thinking to the wind? As a result, I doubled down on my impatience to quit, ignoring the *real* situation, and came-up with a simply ***dreadful plan***. I can hardly believe that I actually thought it would work? I got a roll of masking tape from the band room and wound it all over the broken tube to (*as I believed*) *temporarily* fix it! After all, it only had to hold together through a short forty-five-minute concert, right? No big deal!

I imagine that you probably expected this severely ill-thought-out, flawed and idiotic plan of mine to have immediately led to disaster! But somehow... *it didn't*? Incredibly, the music gods had apparently felt sorry for me and as a result were smiling down on me, as evidenced by the fact that throughout most of the concert, my trombone playing sounded okay; certainly not much worse than usual. I was able to adjust the pitch a bit by sliding my trombone a little-extra-ways up or down, so as long as the tape held, nothing would sound obviously wrong. I remember actually feeling quite proud of myself for the brilliant way that I had fixed my trombone on the fly! But as we neared the end of the concert and began playing our final piece, unfortunately for me, the music gods had clearly *fallen asleep* as it became dramatically clear to me (*and probably everyone else who could hear my instrument*) that something was *terribly wrong* with the sound I was now making on my trombone? This was because the tape on the metal tube had very gradually lost its adhesiveness from the moisture in the constant air I was blowing through it. Now that the stickiness was *completely gone*, the tape was no longer covering the break and it immediately caused the air to escape freely through the cracked tube on my trombone! To make matters worse, the pitches I was trying to play were now being replaced by a series of *nonmusical blasts*, resembling the moos of *angry cows* who just had their hooves run over by a tractor!

The moment I started making those horrendous sounds, both the director and students closest to me turned sharply to see what was causing that awful noise? I can vividly remember that horrendous moment and how *completely devastated* I felt as the concert killing center of attention! I think I even turned red and began to sweat? The whole thing seemed so incredibly *surreal* to me, like something out of a ghastly nightmare? But unfortunately, I was *completely awake*! I was terrified, humiliated and embarrassed all at the same time? And then, out of nowhere, I suddenly had a very simple epiphany that I *knew* would limit my losses! I immediately stopped blowing, but continued to move the slide of my trombone forward and backward as if I were playing it normally for the remainder of the concert. Thankfully, I am reasonably sure that I fooled most everyone around me and in the audience into thinking that I had merely hit a series of wrong notes (*clinkers, as the director used to call them*) at my hideous 'car crash moment' of the final musical piece of my trombone playing career. Fortunately, this scenario turned out lightyears better than it *could* have, and I am eternally grateful for that! And in answer to your obvious question, "*Yes!*" I agree with you that 'fixing' the break on the upper tube of my trombone with masking tape before the concert was an *exceptionally lame idea*!

Well, I don't believe anyone asked me afterwards about my 'interesting' playing during the concert or my questionable thinking regarding how I had chosen to *fix* my trombone... surprisingly, *not* even the director? And in those days, there were no video cameras or iPhones recording junior high school band concerts as you would see today. So, I guess there is *no evidence* to convict me that this embarrassing event *ever* happened? My little faux pas is now safely *hidden away forever*! But getting back to my ill-fated trombone, it was repaired... *again*. To be honest, I felt a responsibility to have that done, even though I personally vowed to *never* play it again! Truth be told, that good-natured trombone deserved someone who was a much better and more devoted player than I had ever been, and who actually cared about being in band! So, some years later, after college, I ended up giving that trombone away to my brother-in-law, Bill, who happened to be a public-school band director at the time. He assured me that my trombone would be much appreciated by his students.

When I sometimes think about my rough time in junior high school band, I realize that I may have disliked the *idea* of having to play the trombone, but I *never* really hated my trombone itself, or band for that matter. Unfortunately, for so many different reasons, my heart was simply not into either one of them, causing band to just not be a good fit for me. I'm sorry to say that this was especially true because I played the *trombone*. Sadly, that served as a constant reminder to me that I had *not* been chosen to play the *trumpet* as I had always dreamed of doing! I just never got over it? Because of that, I became obsessed with how unhappy my time in band was making me feel! My *fatal* mistake had always been focusing on those *negative feelings* instead of at least *attempting* to accept my situation and adapting to it. Doing *that* could have resulted in my having a better attitude and being a happier person in band, in spite of the fact that I had *never* enjoyed playing the trombone! But unfortunately, in the end, for me, playing the trombone in band had disintegrated into a *very unhappy obligation* that I just couldn't wait to get rid of! That's really all there was to it.

For any reader who was (*by chance*) in band with me at Goddard Junior High School from 1966-1969, I apologize for not being a more conscientious member or a better musician. Through my own bad luck and 'immaturity,' I received a terrible fright at that Spring Concert in 1969, but over the years, the memory of that comical fiasco has now turned into a good laugh. It's wonderful how time and a simple change of perception can somehow make the memory of a very difficult experience in your life *feel better*. And honestly, it's good to finally get that off my chest. This is the very first time I remember sharing my *very unfortunate* experiences at that band concert with anyone since it happened in 1969!

Although being a member of the junior high-school band at that time had always felt to me like a *total bust*, I did learn and experience a number of important things that would go on to help me years later in my forty-year career as a public-school music teacher! These things included a basic education of music theory and notation, learning to focus rehearsals on particular elements of the music including dynamics, blend, balance, intonation and tempo, learning to teach with passion in order to expect passion from your students and especially, being *sensitive* to how truly difficult it is for students who *aren't* enjoying being in your group to become *motivated*. (*I had first-hand experience with that last one!*) For all of these learnings, I am very grateful!

You know? Doesn't it seem likely that enduring such a tough experience as this one, I would find a positive life lesson? Well, *you're right*! There are actually a number of valuable life lessons I learned from my five tumultuous years of unhappily playing the trombone in school band! However, the three that I am about to mention are by far the *most meaningful* to me. The **first** one is very simple and founded in common sense. I learned that the next time I am selected to be a part of a time-consuming obligation that I really, really *don't want to do*? To avoid all of the anxiety and angst I experienced this time around, it's a much better idea to simply say, 'no,' right from the very beginning! The **second** lesson I learned is that if I *don't* say, no, right from the very beginning, consequently getting stuck doing something that I'm really not crazy about but don't hate, I should never give-up hope that times will eventually get better with a good attitude. However, if things *don't* get better, it's *never too early* to begin thinking about and then looking around for things that might *better* suit my talents and desires in the future. Then, when my 'obligation' is finally completed, we have a better place to go! ***Third***, and most important, I call this one the *nuclear option*, not to be taken lightly. If I am ever again part of something that really makes me *miserable* for an extended period of time (*the way my five years in band did*), I *don't* have to continue it. I can always use the *escape hatch*, that's naturally provided for us in every activity we choose to undertake. This option is only to be taken advantage of in *extreme circumstances*, no matter how guilty I may feel about taking it, or how many people may try to talk me out of it by calling me a *quitter*, a *loser* or a *traitor*! I've decided that in the future, whenever I'm in a terrible situation, with absolutely *no hope* of it ever getting better, then *without reservation*, rather than continuing to waste my time and my life (*especially if it involves playing the trombone*), I will henceforth take a deep breath, look forward to better times, smile, and do the thing that I probably *should* have done sometime during my five unhappy years in band... *QUIT!*

-SIX-
The Sweet Tale of
"My First Love!"

"Love is but the discovery of ourselves in others, and the delight in the recognition."-Alexander Smith. I've come to firmly realize that as special as it is, to *first* recognize true love can be a very difficult thing to do at any age, but especially when we're inexperienced at it as an adolescent or a young teen. Red herrings like *'when someone pays a lot of attention to us,'* or someone is just plain *'good looking,'* can make us temporarily *believe* we're in love, only to discover later that it was only a *'crush.'* In the tale I am about to share with you, my first love thankfully *did not* turn-out to be a crush, unlike most of my earlier experiences. Here is the story, the *whole story*, that chronicles how I eventually found her... *my first love!*

Do you remember when you experienced your first love? I'm not talking about *family, friend,* or *pet* love, but *romantic* love? And I don't mean the first time you had a *crush, date,* or *kiss* either. I mean the very first time you felt the *specialness* of being with someone you could actually see yourself spending the rest of your life with? For example, I had a *'crush'* on teen actress *Hayley Mills* that hit me especially hard right after I'd first watched the hit Disney movie, 'The Parent Trap,' in 1962 at the movie theater. She was just so cute and the twin sisters she played in the movie were so much fun to watch! I was completely *taken-in* by her! I might mention that I was only eight years old at the time, and of course, I really had *no* previous experience of this kind to compare it to? And it wasn't long before I sadly figured-out that my feelings would *never* be reciprocated by Hayley Mills, just as soon as it became clear to me that being *eight years* my senior, she was apparently attracted to the *older* boys I saw her with on teen magazine covers at the grocery store! *That* really hurt!

In fourth grade, I also had a 'crush' on a girl in the 'Foothill Elementary School Choir,' who performed with her ensemble at an assembly for all of the upper-grade classes at my school. I thought she was the prettiest girl I had ever seen! She had long brunette hair that framed her face on three sides, making her look even *more beautiful!* When she sang, she looked like an angel! I remember imagining the two of us taking long walks together down the streets of Glendora, smiling at each other and feeling so happy! But I actually never talked to her about that or anything else? Unfortunately, her choir left immediately after their performance, and I doubt that I would have had the courage to talk to her anyway. As it turned out, I never saw her again, and I never even knew her name? So, I guess she *wasn't* my first love either.

In contrast to those two very obvious '*crushes*,' my first feeling that a girl actually *liked* me, occurred on Valentine's Day of my fifth-grade year in 1965. During those fun days of elementary school, it was traditional for everyone in your class to give a valentine to every other student, whether you *liked them* or not! It was an annual event, so no one ever questioned it. In fact, we prepared for it the day before. Every student in my class had made a medium-sized bag out of colored paper and staples, decorated it with hearts and prepared to collect valentines in it the next day. Surely *this alone* proves just how important this annual event really was to us! Like many kids of that age, I was generally... correction, I was *completely shy.* I didn't talk to anyone much in my class before, during or after school, but I *always* looked forward to this yearly ritual. You see, the annual Valentine's Day celebration would always bring along *special perks* to make the event even more fun for the students. For example, we were always served vanilla ice cream from a big tub (*they'd purchased at Thrifty's*) by someone's mom. And if we were lucky, we would also

258

receive small boxes of candy hearts along with some students' valentine, or even from the *teacher*! Hands down, I think these were the *tasty* reasons why every kid in my class always looked forward to Valentine's Day at school!

Once the cards, candy and ice cream had all been distributed, and as each of us carefully perused our stash (*in between bites of slightly melted vanilla ice cream*), I was suddenly moved to *stop*? The reason was due to my feelings of *surprise* mixed with a bit of shock as I read one particular valentine that was not only signed by the person, but actually had a personal message written on it? The valentine read, "*You are the apple of my eye,*" and then this person had written above that, "*This valentine is right!*" I can't explain exactly what I felt at that moment, but it was probably similar to the way a precious stone might feel (*if it had feelings*) once it had been dug out of the ground after millions of years of lying there covered in dirt, alone, unnoticed and unaware that there was anything at all remarkable about it? And then for one reason or another, its finder recognizes something truly special about it? My feelings of insecurity and self-consciousness quickly gave way to something that felt absolutely wonderful! It was the incredible feeling that a girl in my class had actually noticed me? As it turned out, the card in question was signed by a quiet girl named Janice. I couldn't remember ever speaking to her before, but I had seen her in class all year long and I thought she was very pretty, especially with all of those cute freckles! Anyway, I got the courage to walk up to her and it didn't take long before she admitted to me that *she liked me*! I felt a sudden *rush of warmth* running through my entire body! I had *never* felt like this before? I asked myself, "Could this be love?"

Whether or not this actually turned out to be *love*, it was definitely the beginning of a wonderful friendship! Now I had somebody to hang-out with at recess and lunch. As it turned out, she was shy like me, and I think that may have been the catalyst of our initial attraction toward each other? She was easy to talk to and we had some very interesting conversations together about everything in the world of a fifth grader. Unfortunately, our friendship was short-lived as less than a month later, Janice walked up to me at the end of school with a very serious expression on her face? She turned to me and uncomfortably shared that *she was moving.* We were both *instantly* very sad. I felt a terrible pit at the bottom of my stomach as I realized that I was about to lose the person who had quickly become my best 'girl' friend at school! She gave me a small piece of folded white paper with her new address neatly written on it in pencil (*which I promptly placed in my wallet*), and then I promised to write to her just as soon as I could. Unfortunately, the situation grew a little awkward because I don't think either one of us had ever experienced a '*breakup*' before, not even a *friendly* one like this? Well, we looked nervously into each other's eyes for a moment and then hugged *very* politely. Then she walked away and I *never* saw her again. As for writing to her, I wanted to, but my wallet got thrown into the washer with my jeans, and when I retrieved the paper inside with her address written on it, it was in tatters and any semblance of her address was sadly *gone!*

For a while, I would sometimes think about Janice and what could have turned out to be a lifelong friendship and perhaps even a love story? As an adult, I even wrote a song for my high school choirs about that very meaningful experience called, '*My First Love!*' But fifth grade is a *little early* to start considering people you meet as lifelong partners, don't you think? I'm sure now that what we shared wasn't true love at all, but only the beginning of a *mutual* fifth grade friendship. It's just that she was the first girl to ever tell me she liked me, and to me, *that was huge!* It was also the first time I had ever had the opportunity of '*reacting*' to being told that, and experiencing all of the wonderful feelings that went along with it! This was a very special time in my life, as I actually had what I considered to be, such as it was, a *meaningful* relationship with a girl (*who was not related to me*) for the first time in my life! I hope Janice is happy now and give or take a few diversions, that her life has gone *exactly* as she wanted it to. I will never cease being grateful for what we shared for that short time... as simple and innocent as it was. In any case, on February 14th, 1965, the two of us actually experienced first-hand in class what Valentine's Day is truly *all about!* You can't put a price on that!

As I moved on to sixth grade and beyond, I had other (*mostly unrealized*) crushes. Sometimes it seemed like I just couldn't exist without one! In junior high, I even had ten female pen-pals from all over America and Canada, whose names and addresses I had gotten off the back of a DC Superman comic book! We casually wrote to each other bi-monthly for about a year, and I always wondered what it would have been like to meet them? In the world of relationships, I believe that if nothing else, those pen-pals at least gave me more understanding into how young teenage girls think, and how to communicate with them. I really had very little experience with this in real life.

It was not until high school that I had a number of 'live' relationships with girls, some which ended amicably, some that just faded away and a couple that ended badly. Through my junior year, I can only think of one relationship that lasted longer than a few months. However, during my senior year, I finally had a happy, long-term and *meaningful* relationship with a girl! The two of us seemed to click right away and have a lot in common! For the *first* time in my life, I could visualize being with her for as long as I lived! I understood these feelings I had, in large part because of my wonderful Valentine's Day experience all of those years before in fifth grade. This time the special girl's name was *Margaret*, and I have always felt so lucky that in this world full of billions of people, the two of us somehow found each other!

We were married five years later after graduating from college, and of course... we've lived *happily ever after*. It's funny how what we learned as young children *always* seems to come back to help us later in life? For example, although *love* can be defined in a myriad of different ways, I learned through my experiences in this story, that in order for love to be *genuine* and *lasting*, the things defining it must all be felt '*mutually*' between you and the one you love, while your differences should be celebrated as those qualities that make each of you unique. And *that* my friends, is the simple truth!

-SEVEN-
The Enlightening Tale of "My Halloween Party!"

"Not all storms come to disrupt your life. Some come to clear your path."-Anon. I suppose a person's gut reaction to the situation of 'being left out' of an exciting event that everyone else they know was apparently already invited to, can't help but hurt. I can confirm this from the way I felt when discovering one morning at school during my fourth-grade year, that two girls were hosting a Halloween party and as far as I knew (*I waited all day long to be sure*) I was the *only* person in my entire class who had *not* received an *invitation*? To be honest, not that anyone else was probably aware, this situation immediately threw me for a loop, confirming what I already suspected; that kids in my class saw me as a *nothing*! I immediately felt *humiliated*, *worthless* and *invisible*. And then I thought about things very carefully, and determinedly realized that I *could* do something about this if I wanted to? So, I *did*!

As much as I hate to admit it, in fourth grade, I may, just *may* have had an inferiority complex at school *the size of Texas*! Just to bring you up to date, back then I was a severely *shy* kid who seldom spoke to anyone. I'm sure that to those kids in my class who didn't know me, I didn't appear to excel at anything; *not* sports, *not* art, *not* academics and especially *not* when it came to socializing with others. Hence, I was not anywhere near the in-crowd. A kind person at that time might have referred to me as an *upcoming* late-bloomer. But I'm afraid that I wasn't showing signs of *blooming* any time soon! To further paint this picture, I want to make it perfectly clear that I believe there *is* an in-crowd in every group of people at every age. But fourth grade, the first year of being upperclassmen in elementary school, is where I believe the *in-crowd* truly begins in earnest for most of us! In fact, from the start of the year I felt a major difference in that fourth-grade class compared to *every other class* I had ever been a part of? That is to say, in the earlier grades we had weekly class 'monitors' such as line leader, window monitor (*who opened and closed the top windows in the classroom with a long metal pole everyday*) and leader of the flag salute as our *classroom* leaders. They were *all* selected by the teacher at different intervals throughout the year. This system made it possible for *every* student in class to experience being a classroom leader at some point throughout the school year at least once, whether they wanted to or not. But in fourth grade, for the first time, we had official '*class officers*' usurping these duties and more. They were *elected* by our class through a blind show of hands (*heads down on our desks*) and served for the entire year. After their election, it became cool to be friends with them. If you *weren't*, then you were obviously *not* in the in-crowd!

The distribution of invitations to the two girls' party (*incidentally, they both happened to be classroom leaders*) took place in class about two weeks prior to Halloween. I've already expressed my initial hurt at being left off of their list, and although no one else complained about a similar fate, if there were *more* students left off their list, I expect that they more than likely, just like me, had chosen *not* to make waves by saying anything about their bruised feelings to *anyone* in class. Now, I admit that I was definitely *not* social in the least at school, so it probably comes as a complete surprise to you that I was so upset about this apparent snub in the first place? To be honest, I admit that I was a very sensitive kid back then, which made me extremely *thin-skinned*. With that in mind, I think I was especially bothered by the fact that I was apparently viewed by the two girls hosting the party (*as mentioned earlier*) as being *less* than everyone else in class, and *not worthy* of receiving an invitation to their party? Hence, my very painful inferiority complex. In any case, I spent most of that school day feeling very sorry for myself and distracted over this highly upsetting situation. But just because I was shy on the outside, didn't mean that my mind was not moving a mile a minute inside my head, trying like crazy to figure out some way for me to feel better about this? As the day progressed, I began to become tired of feeling like a helpless victim and I started to feel strangely *empowered* instead? As soon as I realized that I was the only person in the world who could truly fix this, I came up with a simple plan and immediately knew *exactly* who I would ask to help me carry it out!

I hurried home after school and asked my mom (*who was always very receptive to my ideas*) what the chances were of my hosting a Halloween party at our house for my class? Initially, she was very surprised and curious *why* I wanted to do that on such short notice (*I planned on hosting it in only a week*), but I think she was also *delighted* that I apparently wanted to be more social! In the end, she assured me that we could certainly do that. The truth of the matter was that our family (*like a lot of large families*) didn't *usually* have a lot of extra money lying around for seemingly *frivolous* things like spontaneously hosting a school party. But my mom always became a *supermom* whenever it came to making things happen for her children, and this was no exception! In the end, she somehow managed to scrape together enough money to make it work! So, that very night, she and I went to the store together, bought invitations, 'scary' Halloween tablecloths, a few prizes for games, and lots of candy (*as well as little bags for each student to carry it home in*). I guessed that would be enough stuff for putting on a party, but having *never* done this sort of thing before, I was a little worried? I really had no idea what activities we should do for this party or how to run it? I just wanted to *have one*! Luckily, my fears were alleviated by the knowledge that if I succeeded in doing this, I *should* feel much better about being left out of the other party. That night, I personally addressed every invitation (*I believe there were about 30 students in my class*). I felt both nervous and excited as I thought about handing out my invitations in the morning, especially since it was only *one day* after my own unhappy *'invitation'* experience. The most important thing to me was that I didn't leave *anyone* out! So, I took my class list and triple checked that I had prepared an invitation for everyone.

The next morning, I arrived at school and quietly delivered the invitations to each and every one of my classmates before the final morning bell had rung. I felt a sensational sense of pride after that! I think it was the initial coming-up with 'my own party' idea, and then finalizing it by handing out the invitations that did it! I was *terrified* of putting the party on, of course, and I tried not to think about that, but I didn't regret anything I was doing in preparation for it! Beginning that morning, kids I had never talked to in class before (*that would include just about everyone*) came up to me during recess and lunch to tell me how excited they were about coming to my party! Well... actually... *not everyone* came up to me. The two girls who were hosting the other Halloween party fell strangely silent that day? But aside from them, I think I talked to *everyone* in my class. That was one very exciting day for me!

That night while lying in bed, my excitement had finally begun to die down and I began to feel *scared*? Irrationally scared that no-one would come to my party (*regardless of the fact that so many people had already told me today how much they looked forward to it*) and scared that after experiencing such an exciting time today, I would go back to school tomorrow once again being invisible? Don't get me wrong. I felt proud of myself too, for what I had already accomplished. But I've got to say, I felt *mostly scared!*

When I arrived at school the *next* morning, I was surprisingly met by the two girls who were putting on the other party? I think they had actually been waiting for me? They were both very friendly as they handed me an *invitation* to their party, apologized for accidentally leaving me off their original list, and thanked me for inviting them to mine. As they walked off, I would have laughed and jumped for joy if I hadn't been so shy! This was the *perfect ending*, which I *hadn't* expected at all? I had just wanted to show everyone in my class that I was capable of hosting my own

Halloween party like the two girls were doing! But, I must admit it felt really nice to be *included* in the other party.

Honestly? All I have is conjecture here. Although the two girls *may* have accidentally left my name off their party list and met me that morning to rectify it, I'm actually more inclined to believe that I was *purposely* left off their list! But I *don't* believe the reason for that omission was mean-spirited in the least. I believe the reason I was left off was because the two girls probably saw me as an immature, nonspeaking, nonentity, who never participated in anything with anyone in class prior to handing-out my own party invitations? And I don't think they thought I would even *want to come?* But when they saw me suddenly inviting people to *my own party*, perhaps then they saw a different side of me? Truth be told, handing out those invitations was the *most* socializing I had done in school all year or in *any other year* for that matter, and it was also the *scariest thing I'd ever done!* If I had been braver, I would have asked the two girls about the reason for my omission from their list back then. But, on the other hand, there really seemed to be no need to do that now, since everything had turned out so well for me in the end.

A meaningful lesson I learned here was *not* the obvious one, that the two girls changed their behavior by inviting me to their party *only* after I invited them to mine? That would have been *manipulation* on my part, which I never even considered. The *real lesson* here was that as difficult as it was, I changed my *own* behavior by forcing myself to deal with my debilitating shyness by being *more* social, through hosting a Halloween party which would include the two girls. This caused a chain reaction of good things to happen, and without really knowing the truth, that's how I *prefer* to remember it.

I was now going to be attending *their* party, causing me great anxiety, and I would also be hosting my own party (*with a whole lot of kids attending*), which was causing me even *greater stress!* But, if I was scared to death of putting on my party (*which I was*), then it was important for me to understand the payoff. Putting on this party was the price I would pay for working toward improving my confidence and self-worth. And the best part was, there was no

267

pressure for me to host the *greatest* Halloween party of all time, because having never attended *any* Halloween parties in the past, I had no idea what making it '*great*' even entailed? So, as I saw it, I just had to relax and host a party.

For me? From a hellish pit of shame and self-doubt following the party snub, deciding to host my own Halloween party was already showing me a way out! That fourth-grade experience actually set me on a course toward *gradually* breaking out of my shell of shyness, as each year after that I faced my fears a little bit more and grew braver about talking with my peers. In addition, I learned that sometimes what we perceive as being a *bad situation* may ultimately turn out to be a *blessing* in disguise, as this experience demonstrated. In this case, not being invited to the party inspired me to take action that ultimately led me to a happier outcome. And it actually began the process that would eventually result in making me a stronger and more confident person!

To sum this all up, I learned that no matter how difficult a goal may appear, if it is of great importance to me and I feel passionately about it, then I believe that I am obligated to tenaciously take *personal responsibility* for getting it done, regardless of any fear or anxiety I might possess. The truth is, *that* simple lesson has worked incredibly well for me at school and in life ever since! In fact, when dealing with especially difficult personal goals, it has very much turned out to be a bonified *game changer!* And to think... it all started with a *Halloween party!*

www.ingramcontent.com/pod-product-compliance
Lightning Source LLC
Chambersburg PA
CBHW060529260626
47161CB00003B/826